**"I KNOW A WOMAN
SHOULD NOT BE SO FORWARD,"
BRIGETTE SAID,
"BUT I WISH WE WERE WED."**

"We are." His voice was a light caress. Then he added, matter-of-factly, "We return to Dunridge in the mornin'."

"No! We cannot go there!"

"We must!"

"Ross." Brigette's voice was a contrite whisper. "I am not a Gypsy—"

Iain's laughter cut off her confession. "I'm aware of the fact ye arena' a Gypsy, Lady Brigette."

"You know who I am? I'm your brother's wife."

"Ye arena' my brother's wife, sweetheart."

"But I am!" she protested. "Iain and I were wed by proxy in England—"

"I am Iain MacArthur, yer husband—Iain Ross Mac-Arthur, heir to the Earl of Dunridge. And yer my bonnie Sassenach bride." His hand reached to caress her cheek.

Understanding lit Brigette's eyes. She slapped his hand away and leaped to her feet, then glared at him in a murderous rage. "You lying . . . scheming . . . vile . . . treacherous—I am returning to England," she added more calmly, her husband's size tempering her wrath. "The marriage will be annulled!"

QUANTITY SALES

HIGHLAND BELLE

Patricia Grasso

A DELL BOOK

Published by
Dell Publishing
a division of
Bantam Doubleday Dell Publishing Group, Inc.
666 Fifth Avenue
New York, New York 10103

ISBN: 0-440-20793-2

Printed in the United States of America

Published simultaneously in Canada

March 1991

10 9 8 7 6 5 4 3 2 1

OPM

This book is dedicated
to five special people:

With deep appreciation to the *real* Marianne
Jacques—lusty secretary "extraordinaire."

And with love to my nieces and nephews (in order
of appearance):

Sean—silent and solemn, prone to falling asleep
in my eighth-grade English class.

Samantha—sweetest of the sweet, wise enough
to stay awake in her dear aunt's class.

Matthew—a gift from God, the love of my life.
You stole my heart and I want it back.

Jessica—enchanting spitfire of the Grasso clan,
demanding that all my books be dedicated to
her.

1

England, May 1564

Drizzle, sheer as a bride's veil, laced the air; summer had arrived in the south of England. Basildon Castle, the ancestral home of the earls of Basildon, rose spectacularly out of the mist like a magnificent beast.

Upon one of the castle's tower walks paced a solitary young woman. Her eyes were anxious as she scanned the surrounding countryside, especially the road leading to the castle.

Brigette Edwina Devereux, second daughter of the late Earl of Basildon, searched the road below and saw what she dreaded. A troop of men were riding through the light mist toward Basildon Castle. Toward her! She shivered with apprehension.

"Lo! The bridegroom cometh!" whispered a voice near Brigette's ear. She whirled around and faced her younger sister, Heather.

"Once I'm wed," Brigette countered, "the queen's eyes will turn on you. Then you, obnoxious brat, will be wearing my slippers."

"As did our sister! When Kathryn was forced to wed the Irishman, you were less than kind." Heather smirked. "Now you'll wed and bed a savage from the north."

"One day Iain MacArthur will be the Earl of Dunridge and I will be his countess," Brigette returned, sounding more confident than she felt. "He's no rebel."

"He's worse than a rebel," Heather spat, then shuddered delicately. "Rebels kill for freedom. Highlanders kill for pleasure!"

"Liar!" Brigette screeched. *"Freckle-face liar!"*

The insult hit its mark. Heather shrieked in rage, but as her hand shot out to slap her sister, she was grabbed from behind.

"Cease!"

"Let me go!" Heather screamed, struggling against her cousin, Spring. "Loose me, you bastard!"

Brigette gasped at her sister's words and Spring's hands dropped away instantly. Surprised, Heather faced her cousin and was ashamed when she saw the hurt in the other girl's eyes.

"Yes, my lady," Spring said coldly. "I'm only your base-born cousin, Lady Brigette's tire-woman."

"I'm sorry. I did not mean . . ."

"The countess sent me to get you," Spring interrupted, looking at Brigette. "Your betrothed has arrived."

The three young women peered curiously over the battlement. Sir Henry Bagenal, Louise Devereux, and the young earl, Richard, stood in the courtyard to greet the Scotsman. Tall and well built, he shook Richard's hand first and nodded deferentially, then greeted Sir Henry. Finally, he bowed low over the dowager countess's hand.

"That must be Iain," Brigette whispered.

"The queen has done well by you, Brie," Spring commented.

"Richard is enjoying himself," Heather remarked. "He'll be furious that Lord MacArthur did not prostrate himself before the renowned Earl of Basildon."

Spring chuckled, but Brigette continued to stare silently at the man who was to be her husband. Heather and Spring looked at her and then each other.

"For once her tongue is still," Heather quipped.

Brigette turned then, a satisfied smile upon her face. "It's time I met my handsome Highlander." She left the tower walk at a dignified pace and then raced down the stairs until she reached ground level. After taking several deep breaths, she stepped outside.

Petite and graceful, Brigette was the picture of fragile femininity as all eyes followed her across the courtyard. Her expression was sweet and her large green eyes, sparkling with excitement, were shyly downcast. A few tendrils of hair, wild wisps of copper silk, had escaped her braids and warred with her image of passive innocence.

Irresistibly drawn, Brigette approached her betrothed without bothering to greet her family or Sir Henry. Her eyes traveled slowly up the Scotsman's body and met his interested stare.

He was tall and slim, but solidly built, his broad shoulders tapering to a narrow waist and hips. His hair was light brown and his eyes were blue, containing a hint of amusement. Silently, Brigette thanked the fates for sending her a young and handsome husband.

Suddenly aware that she was staring, an embarrassed blush stained Brigette's cheeks. She smiled and curtsyed, then extended her hand. "Lord MacArthur, I am Lady Brigette."

"Lady Brigette," the Scotsman said, taking hold of her hand. "This misty courtyard has brightened immeasurably with your arrival."

Sir Henry cleared his throat. "Brie, this is Lord *Percy* MacArthur, your betrothed's brother."

"Oh!" Brigette yanked her hand back. Percy smiled and Brigette, crimson with embarrassment, glanced around the courtyard. "Lord Iain?"

"My brother is still in Scotland." Percy frowned at her bewildered expression. Damn his brother!

"Lord Iain was unable to make the trip," Sir Henry explained, "but sent Lord Percy in his stead."

"I'm to wed Lord Percy?" Brigette asked loudly. Percy chuckled and pockets of laughter erupted from his men-at-arms. The dowager countess shook her head in disapproval, and the young earl, Richard, wore a pained expression.

"To my infinite sorrow yer to wed Iain," Percy said.

"Brie, my dear," Madame Devereux intervened, "Lord Percy will stand as proxy for his brother."

"Proxy?!" Brigette shrieked, shocked and insulted. "No! I'll not wed the heathen by proxy!" Her gleaming green eyes met Percy's, daring him to challenge her words. "There will be no marriage!"

"Brigette!" Madame Devereux cried.

"The queen has commanded that you wed Lord Iain immediately," Sir Henry interjected.

"Let *her* marry him!" Brigette snapped, and Percy burst out laughing.

"Brie!" Richard entered the fray. "I am the Earl of Basildon and your liege lord. You will marry Iain MacArthur and keep your mouth shut!"

"The hell I will!" Turning her back, Brigette stalked away.

"You'll do as I say," Richard shouted, shaking his fist in the air, "or I'll cast you into the meanest dungeon!"

Brigette's pace quickened. Englishmen and Scotsmen alike valiantly smothered their mirth at the sight of the twelve-year-old earl demanding to be obeyed. Watching Brigette retreat, Percy was tickled to think Dunridge's future countess was an English lady with a Highland temper. How surprised Iain would be!

Brigette's expression was sullen as she walked toward the great hall that evening. She had spent the afternoon in her chamber, but not alone. The dowager countess had been Brigette's first visitor and had given her a terrible tongue-lashing. Brigette's behavior was unbecoming a lady and unacceptable from the daughter of an earl. Where were Brigette's pride and honor? Madame Devereux demanded that the Brigette at supper be a completely different young lady from the one who'd made such a spectacle of herself in the courtyard.

Later, Heather and Spring had skulked in and commiserated with her. Spring advised Brigette to speak with Lord Percy and learn what prevented Lord Iain from attending his own wedding. Heather took the practical approach. As she saw it, Brigette had two choices. She could marry Lord Iain or enter a French convent. Neither choice held much appeal.

"Bring no further disgrace upon our family," the dowager countess ordered sternly, intercepting her daughter at the entrance to the great hall.

Brigette nodded.

"Keep a civil tongue in your head, sister," Richard whispered as she passed his seat at the high table.

Brigette ignored him.

Lord Percy rose, smiling, as Brigette moved to her place between Sir Henry and him. Sheepishly, she returned his smile.

"I'm sorry for my earlier behavior." Brigette apologized as supper's first course, leg of mutton stuffed with garlic and shoulder of veal, was served.

"There's nae need," Percy assured her. "Marriage is distressin' and—"

"Distressing?" Brigette's voice rose with anxiety.

"I dinna mean bein' wed, but gettin' wed."

"Oh." Brigette flushed. "I realize you are not your brother's keeper," she said pleasantly, "and so may not be blamed for his ignorance."

Percy nearly choked on his food and wished Iain could hear his betrothed's insults.

"I mean—"

"I ken yer meanin'," Percy interrupted.

"You've a strange accent," Brigette remarked, purposely changing the subject.

"Yer wrong," he teased. "Yer the one wi' the accent."

Brigette smiled and relaxed, pleased with Percy's wit. "Tell me about your home, my lord. I've never been anywhere but Essex."

"It's a land of lonely majesty," Percy began, a faraway look entering his eyes, "wi' white-capped peaks and lush green glens and sparklin' blue lochs." His eyes focused on Brigette's awe-struck expression and he smiled. "That's why a Highlander always goes home, Lady Brigette."

"It sounds lovely, but I would know more."

"Dunridge Castle will be yer home—if ye wed my brother—and is situated on the shore of Loch Awe in the Shire of Argyll," Percy told her. "On the opposite side of the loch is Inverary, which is the seat of the Duke of Argyll, the chief of clan Campbell of which the MacArthurs are part. Now that our bonnie Queen Mary is returned from France, the duke—"

"Have you met the queen?" Brigette asked, her green eyes large with expectation.

"When there's a need, Black Jack or Iain travels to Edinburgh."

"Black Jack?"

"My father. Ye know, this is my verra first journey to England," Percy continued. "I'd love to see yer brother's lands. Would ye care to ride wi' me in the mornin'?"

"Yes, but only if you'll call me Brie—all my friends do."

"Brie?" Percy chuckled. "Like the cheese?"

The Scotsman's wit tickled Brigette and she burst out laughing, a melodious sound that drew the interested gaze of the great hall's occupants. Apparently, Lady Brigette's good humor was restored. The men from the north cast each other knowing glances. If Percy could so easily charm the temperamental lady, then Iain would have no problem taming her.

"Summer is here," Brigette announced as Percy and she rode out of Basildon the following morning.

"How can ye tell?"

"The air is warmer, the mist finer, and the trees are a tad greener than yesterday."

Percy smiled. "If ye like England's climate," he returned, "ye'll love Scotland's. It's colder and wetter and a bit greener in summer."

"I detest the rain and the cold." Brigette was irritated by the reminder of her marriage.

"And green?" he mocked gently.

Brigette's eyes darted to Percy, who was grinning at her, and she was unable to suppress a smile. He had been kind to her. Brigette was sorry she'd snapped at him. "I apologize for—"

"Nae offense taken, Brie. Dealin' wi' great changes in yer life—such as weddin' a foreigner—can be difficult."

"I've no choice in the matter."

"Brie! Brie!" Over a small knoll of green came the young Earl of Basildon, riding hard. "Whatever are you thinking of, Brie, to ride unchaperoned?" Richard turned on his sister when he reached them. "It's not fitting, and Mother is furious!"

"The lass was safe wi' me."

"Oh!" Richard looked stricken. "I—I did not mean . . ."

Percy burst out laughing. "Ye English have a charmin' habit of apologizin' for what ye didna' mean. Let's ride together a bit," he suggested, "before Brie returns to prepare for her nuptials."

Expecting a protest, Richard glanced at his sister, but she said nothing. The three rode in companionable silence for a time and enjoyed the green lushness of the land.

"How long has this land been in the Devereux family?" Percy broke the silence.

"Basildon has been ours since my great-grandfather came from Wales with the Tudor," Richard answered.

"That's the queen's grandfather," Brigette added. "As a reward for his loyalty and service to the Tudor, our great-grandfather was given our great-grandmother, the heiress of all you see."

"We're distant cousins of the queen," Richard interjected proudly.

"But yer mother is French?"

"Yes," Richard answered. "Father was in France on King Henry's business and married Mother—"

"Without the king's permission," Brigette interrupted.

Percy smiled, thinking the children were molded from the father, who had obviously been willful himself.

"But the king was forgiving of his favorite fourth cousin," Richard continued, "and so here we are."

"Three years ago Father was killed by poachers and we became wards of the queen," Brigette said. "I suppose you also have poachers and such in Scotland?"

"In the Highlands," Percy told them, "one clan raids another—for fun and profit, ye might say."

"Fun!" Brigette recalled Heather's dire words and trembled.

"That's why Iain remained in Scotland." Percy glanced at Brigette. "Murdac Menzies has been raidin' MacArthur territory. Black Jack was called to Edinburgh and needed Iain to supervise Dunridge's defenses. Spring, summer, and autumn are our raidin' seasons."

"Then Highlanders do kill for pleasure?" Brigette was unable to bite back the question.

Percy looked at her sharply, but his voice was

gentle when he spoke. "Nae sane mon kills for pleasure, lass, nor does he cause pain where there need be none. I hope ye willna' be holdin' Iain's absence against him."

Brigette squirmed in her saddle, then blurted out, "Why didn't you remain at Dunridge instead of Iain?"

"I think we should return now, or ye'll be late for yer own weddin'," Percy suggested, ignoring her question. Percy was not about to admit to his future sister-in-law that his father and brother considered him a happy-go-lucky blockhead and refused to place Dunridge's defenses in his hands.

Afternoon raced toward dusk, and the shadows in the earl's study lengthened. Sir Henry, Percy, and Father Dowd stood in front of the hearth and chatted while Richard and Heather paced the chamber like caged animals. Occasionally, Sir Henry's eyes drifted to the dowager countess, whose own eyes drifted anxiously to the door. Brigette was late for the ceremony that would bind her to Iain MacArthur.

Humph! Madame Devereux thought. It was not the kind of wedding an earl's daughter should have. Curse Iain MacArthur! And while the Lord was at it, He might as well damn the queen, who'd made the unlikely match in the first place and insisted the marriage take place immediately.

Since the marriage was by proxy, the dowager countess had dispensed with all the fanfare, including the chapel service. Brigette was a faithful Catholic, but she'd already been humiliated by the groom's absence. The countess knew her daughter's pride could bear no more insult.

"Where is she?" Richard snarled, annoyed to be kept waiting.

"It's the bride's prerogative to be late," Percy said, glancing at the pacing boy.

"My God!" Heather cried, with a horrified expression. She stepped away from the door and Brigette entered, making six mouths drop in amazement.

The bride was dressed in black, one of her mother's mourning gowns having been appropriated. Her copper hair was parted in the middle, pulled back severely into a tight knot at the nape of her neck and covered with a black veil. She might be forced to wed the ignorant Scotsman, but all would know she went unwillingly into that blissful state of matrimony.

Brigette paused inside the doorway for effect. Her flashing green eyes were alive with defiance, challenging all to censor her attire.

"Brigette Edwina Devereux!" the countess shrieked, scandalized.

"Shall I appear the radiant bride for an absent groom?"

Richard stepped forward, intending to order his sister back upstairs, but Percy placed a restraining hand on his arm. It was better to let the lass vent her anger before she met her husband. Iain was a good man, but unlikely to be amused by his bride's antics.

Surveying Brigette's attire from head to toe, Percy crossed the chamber. His shoulders trembled with the effort to hold back his laughter. His eyes met hers; she was ready to do battle. Sobering, Percy offered his hand and an encouraging smile. Brigette hesitated, surprised by his lack of anger, and then placed her hand in his. They walked across the chamber to Father Dowd.

The old priest looked Brigette up and down as if she'd suddenly turned purple. He shook his head and silently thanked the Lord for his vow of celibacy. The ceremony began.

When the moment came to speak her vows, Brigette hesitated, unable to find her voice through her constricting throat. She glanced at her mother, whose expression was stern, and then at Sir Henry, who looked away in embarrassment. She cleared her throat. As Brigette whispered the words binding her to Iain MacArthur, a feeling of helplessness descended upon her. Now she was at the heathen's mercy!

The final words were spoken. Sir Henry led Percy and Brigette to the desk across the chamber to sign the necessary documents. In the name of the queen, Sir Henry signed first, then passed the quill to Percy, who signed with a flourish in the name of Iain MacArthur. Brigette stared dumbly at the quill when Percy held it out to her.

The dowager countess opened her mouth to scold, but Percy placed the quill in Brigette's hand and gestured to the marriage documents. Accepting her fate, Brigette signed with a bold flourish. She was Lady MacArthur now, for better or worse.

The dowager countess instantly grabbed her

daughter's arm and steered her toward the door, saying, "I'm certain you'll want to change your lovely gown before supper, my dear."

Reading the warning in her mother's eyes, Brigette nodded and left. As she crossed the foyer, a peal of masculine laughter rang out, Percy's tight control having broken.

2

Almost magically, the mist had disappeared under the cover of darkness. Each person milling around the courtyard noted the change and hoped Basildon Castle would see the sun's rays that day. Since before dawn, the Scots had been preparing for their departure, but now most lounged about, awaiting Lady MacArthur.

Wearing a grim expression, Spring entered and crossed the courtyard. "She's not in her chamber," she told the countess. Percy and Madame Devereux exchanged worried glances.

"If she's run," Richard snarled, "I'll flay her alive."

"Humph!" Heather snorted derisively. "Brie's too much of a coward to . . . Here she is." Dressed for traveling in a dark woolen safeguard and cloak, Brigette entered the courtyard from the castle's chapel and smiled apologetically.

"They thought you'd run!" Heather exclaimed. "I told them—"

"I was bidding farewell to Father."

The countess's expression softened and she opened her arms to her daughter. Like a bereft child, Brigette flung herself into her mother's embrace. She closed her eyes, felt the warmth of her mother's love, and knew nothing would be the same after that day. When Brigette left Basildon, she would be leaving her childhood behind.

"I'm afraid," Brigette whispered.

Her mother tilted her chin up and smiled sadly. "There's nothing to fear, sweet. If Lord Percy is any indication, your husband is a good man. Will you promise me something, Brie?"

Brigette nodded. "Yes . . . anything."

"You are impulsive at times," she said. "Before you do or say anything, remember you are an earl's daughter. Can you do that for me?"

"Yes, I promise."

The countess kissed Brigette, then held her close. "Say good-bye to your brother and sister," she whispered finally.

Brigette turned to Heather. Weeping, the sisters flew into each other's arms.

"I'm sorry I frightened you," Heather sobbed. "I'm certain Lord MacArthur doesn't kill for pleasure."

"And I'm sorry I insulted you," Brigette returned. "I like your freckles. You'll write?" Heather nodded, and they hugged each other a final time.

Brigette looked at her brother. His lips quivered

with the effort not to cry. "Farewell, my Lord Earl," she said and curtsyed.

In a most undignified manner, the young lord threw himself into his sister's arms and nearly toppled her over in his distress. "I'll miss you, Brie."

"Learn your lessons well, Richard," Brigette said, hugging him close, "and you'll grow into as fine a man as Father."

"I will," Richard promised, then glanced sidelong at Percy. "If you need me," he whispered, "send word."

Brigette stood and kissed Sir Henry on each cheek. "I will also miss you, my lord. You've been like a father these past years, and I thank you for caring."

"Be happy, Brie."

Brigette nodded, then turned to Percy. "I'm ready."

Percy helped her mount, then mounted his own stallion. Brigette saw the Scotsman Jamie lift Spring onto her horse and was glad her cousin was traveling with her. At least she would have one friend in her husband's home.

Percy shouted a command. Surrounded by her husband's men-at-arms, Lady MacArthur began her long journey to Scotland. They rode in silence at a leisurely pace, and Brigette studied the countryside, consigning it to her memory. It would be a long, long time before she'd see her homeland again.

The morning progressed and as the sky gradually lightened, so, too, did Brigette's mood. Why must I suffer with an ignorant husband? she

thought. Because the queen commanded it? *Bah!*
If living with the heathen proves intolerable, I'll
run away!

Approving of her newfound confidence, the sun
broke free of its confining cloud cover. Brigette,
feeling the excitement of high adventure, giggled
with youthful joy and spurred her horse forward.
Racing against an invisible opponent, she galloped
ahead of her escort. Cursing, Percy bolted after
her.

Glancing back, Brigette saw Percy gaining on
her. She spurred her horse faster, but his stallion
was too potent for her gelding. Percy shouted for
Brigette to stop, but she ignored him. He reached
over and yanked the reins from her hands, forcing
the gelding to slow and then stop.

"Dinna' be ridin' ahead wi'out givin' fair
warnin'," Percy scolded. "It's dangerous!"

"The sun is shining and it's grand being alive!"
Brigette exclaimed, undaunted by his sternness.
Her joy was contagious, and in spite of himself,
Percy smiled. Glancing back at their approaching
entourage, she added, "I do not approve of the
way your man Jamie has been eyeing Spring."

"I hadna' noticed her complainin'," Percy said.
"I did notice, however, yer changin' the subject."

"How very astute of you!"

"Seriously," he added, "ye canna take off like
that whenever ye wish. It's impossible to protect
ye and there could be highwaymen lurkin' aboot."

"Oh." Brigette nudged her horse closer to his
and looked around, half expecting to be attacked.

"Percy," she asked suddenly, "why did Lord Iain seek an English bride?"

" 'Twas Black Jack's idea. Politics, I'm supposin'."

"Politics?"

"Why did yer queen match ye wi' a Scotsman?"

"Probably so there'd be one less papist in England to worry about," Brigette replied drily.

"As I said, politics."

Each passing mile saw Brigette's mood and derriere chafed by the endless ride. By dusk, her excitement had vanished. They stopped for the night at St. Albans, a town overlooking the Ver River.

They halted in front of the Red Lion Inn where they were expected, one of the MacArthur men having ridden ahead to make arrangements. Too fatigued even to dismount, Brigette swayed precariously in her saddle.

"Puir lassie." Percy clucked. He lifted and carried Brigette into the inn's common room. The innkeeper, a short and stocky man, led him immediately to Brigette's chamber. An equally suffering Spring followed behind.

"No!" Brigette cried, realizing Percy meant to set her down on the bed. "I'll eat standing and sleep on my stomach."

Hiding his amusement, Percy turned to Spring. "Jamie will be back wi' supper. Be ready to leave at dawn."

The door closed, and fully clothed, Brigette lay facedown on the bed. "Forget my supper, cuz. I'm too weary to chew." The last word was barely out of her mouth and Brigette was asleep.

After five days in the saddle, Brigette and Spring were still sore, but suffering less. They'd traveled north, passing through Leicester, Derby, Sheffield, and the medieval town of York.

York was the end of civilization as Brigette knew it. At night, Spring and she slept on uncomfortable cots in a tent raised by the MacArthur men. Unbelievable as it was to the Englishwomen, the hearty Scotsmen wrapped themselves in their black and green plaids and slept comfortably enough on the ground.

Commiserating about their calloused buttocks and debating whether the sun would ever be seen again, Brigette and Spring rode together, surrounded by the MacArthur men. Glancing away from her cousin, Brigette was stunned by the sight just ahead.

"Look!" she cried, pointing a finger.

On the horizon was a carpet of purple heather. Breathtaking mountains, painted a vibrant green by their blanket of trees, rose majestically in the distance.

Alarmed by Brigette's cry, the MacArthur men drew their swords. Realizing there was no danger, Percy ordered the men to sheath their weapons, then reined in beside the two women.

"Your Highlands are beautiful!" Brigette exclaimed.

"Highlands?" Percy was confused.

"Look there, Percy. The Highlands!"

"Och, lass! We've just left England behind."
Percy dissolved into laughter and was joined by his
men. "It's the Cheviot Hills, Brie, no' the Highlands. It's part of the borderlands—Bothwell's
country."

"Bothwell?"

"The Earl of Bothwell," he told her. "Unfortunately, we willna' be enjoyin' Jamie Hepburn's renowned hospitality. He's a guest of yer queen, in
the Tower, but accordin' to rumor, he'll soon be
freed."

"Whatever did he do to be imprisoned in the
Tower?"

"Do?" Percy shrugged his shoulders. "Nothin',
as far as I know."

"Then why—"

"Yer queen doesna' need a reason," Percy interrupted. "It's as I said before—politics."

"Oh."

"I've sent a mon ahead to tell the earl's men that
we'll be passin' through," he added. "I dinna want
them attackin' us."

"*Attack?*" Spring cried, alarmed.

Percy glanced at his sister-in-law's tirewoman.
"The earl's moss troopers are fierce."

"And border raidin' maintains their battle readi-
ness," spoke Jamie, who had reined in beside
Spring. "Dinna worry aboot them, lass. I'll protect
ye wi' my life." Spring smiled radiantly at him, and
over her head, Jamie cast Percy a meaningful look.

"Let's ride ahead," Percy suggested, turning to
Brigette. "If yer interested, I'll tell ye a bit of
Scotland's history."

They galloped ahead a short distance, then slowed their horses to a more leisurely pace, being careful to stay within sight of the MacArthur warriors. Brigette smiled expectantly at Percy.

"The greatest of Scotland's heroes is Robert the Bruce," he began, "who bested yer English forces at Bannockburn."

"I don't believe you!" Brigette cried indignantly. "I've never heard of the Scots beating the English."

"I amna' surprised," Percy returned, "but it's true. Robert the Steward was the Bruce's grandson and James the first was Robert's grandson. All the royal Stewarts, includin' Queen Mary's father, have ended tragically." Percy warmed to his subject. "James the first was assassinated. His son, James the second, was crowned king when he was a six-year-old. Unfortunately, he was accidentally killed by an explodin' cannon, and his son, James the third, came to the throne at nine years of age. Like his grandfather before him, James the third was also assassinated. James the fourth married Margaret Tudor, yer queen's aunt. His fatal error was invadin' England—bein' defeated and killed at Flodden."

"I know of Flodden," Brigette interjected.

Percy smiled wryly. "Again, I amna' surprised."

"I believe 'tis best a country emphasizes its victories and virtues," Brigette said loftily, but a mischievous smile flirted with the corners of her lips. "Do continue."

"James the fifth, Margaret Tudor's son and yer queen's cousin, married Mary of Guise. Queen

Mary is their daughter. Puir James died only a few hours after she was born. Some say he was heart-broken he didna produce a legitimate male heir. A number of his bastards are scattered across the land, some acknowledged and some not."

"How sad!"

"I hope," he added, "whatever curse is upon the Stewart family will be broken wi' our bonnie Queen Mary."

"It would be wise," Brigette commented, "if she refrained from naming any son of hers James."

"I agree wi' ye." Percy chuckled at her reasoning. But then, how could an English lady know the mighty power of the clans? She would never understand the love-hate relationship that generations of self-serving Stewart monarchs had with the Highland chiefs, who were independent monarchs on their own lands. Mostly, the Stewarts' suffering was wholly deserved.

"Well, lass." Percy changed the subject. "Two days and a night of travelin' will see us at Dunridge."

"So soon?" Brigette's voice was unmistakably apprehensive.

"There's nae need to worry, Brie," Percy said. "Iain is a good mon. As a matter of fact, I'll be surprised if we dinna see him before then."

"What do you mean?"

"If Black Jack returns to Dunridge, Iain will surely ride out to greet ye. I'm certain he's anxious to meet his bride."

The next morning Jamie was, as usual, standing beside Spring's horse, awaiting her arrival.

Pleased but shy, Spring approached with a smile on her lips.

"Sweet Spring," Jamie teased. "Ye were aptly named. It's my favorite season of the year."

Spring blushed furiously. "I never knew the Scots were such outrageous flatterers."

"It isna' flattery." With one calloused hand, he cupped her chin. "Be there any more at home as sweet as ye?"

"Three half sisters," she whispered, disconcerted by his touch. "April, May, and June."

"April, M-May, and J-J-June?" Jamie sputtered, bringing a smile to her expression. "I need no' ask when they were born. Only half sisters? Is yer mother dead, then?"

"No." Spring looked away uncomfortably. "We've different fathers."

"I'm sorry ye lost yer own father," he said softly.

"You needn't be," she returned. "I never had one that I knew."

"I'm verra sorry, then." Jamie caressed Spring's cheek, which burned with shame. "I would never cause ye pain."

"Jamie!" Percy shouted. "Cease flirtin' wi' the lady and help her mount."

Now it was Jamie's turn to blush. His face reddened until it almost matched his flame-colored hair, and Spring grinned. Without another word, Jamie hoisted her into the saddle.

Although the day was cloudy and cool, Brigette's disposition was sunny as she rode silently beside Percy. She was nervous about meeting her husband, but glad they would arrive at Dunridge

Castle the following day. Her morning hours were spent in dreamy contemplation, not of her husband, but of the steaming tub she would soak in for hours.

"You do have tubs for bathing in Scotland, do you not?" Brigette asked abruptly.

A smile tugged at the corners of Percy's lips. "Yes, we do."

"Good." Brigette began humming a spritely tune. She could almost feel the water's heat, steaming away her aches and troubles.

Afternoon saw them entering Argyll, the MacArthur's home shire. Aided by low-hanging clouds of dark gray, dusk descended quickly, forcing the MacArthur entourage to make camp earlier than usual. The men divided themselves into two groups. One group went to work raising Brigette's tent while the other lit a cooking fire and began supper's preparation.

When the tent was erected, Spring left the warmth of the fire to make up their cots for the night. Brigette remained by the fire, and soon drowsiness mastered her senses. Her eyelids grew heavy and closed.

Roused by a loud disturbance, Brigette's eyes flew open. Were they being attacked? No sounds of fighting were forthcoming, only the sounds of arriving horses and men's laughter. It must be my husband! she thought. What should I do? If I go to the tent, he'll have the advantage of sending for me; but if I stay where I am, he'll have the advantage of looking down on me. The most dignified action is to meet Iain MacArthur as an equal. Brigette stood and walked toward the laughter.

As she advanced, Brigette recognized the now-familiar green and black of the MacArthur plaid. With his back to her, Percy greeted a red-haired man who resembled Jamie. She started forward but froze as their conversation reached her ears.

"Dugie." Percy shook the other's hand. "Where's Iain?"

"He isna' here," Dugie answered. "We're to escort ye home."

"Black Jack isna' returned from Edinburgh?"

"The laird is returned."

"Well, where's Iain, then?"

"Lady Antonia was havin' some crisis wi' wee Glenda. I dinna know what." Dugie grinned. "Iain was neatly duped like a striplin' lad." Dugie chuckled, then noticed Brigette. "Is that the Sassenach bride?"

Percy whirled around. Brigette's face was pale, and she shook with fury at her husband's devastating insult. With her lips curled in a silent snarl, Brigette stalked off.

Hell hath no fury like a woman scorned, and Brigette Devereux MacArthur was no exception. She stormed into the tent, her sudden intrusion startling Spring.

"What's wrong?" Spring cried, alarmed by her expression.

"He's insulted me again!"

"Who?"

"*My husband!*" Brigette exploded. "He sent his

men as escort, but did not accompany them. Obviously, Iain MacArthur considers me unimportant!"

"Perhaps he was unable—"

"His man gave Percy no good reason for his absence," Brigette snapped. "The man laughed. *At me!*"

"Oh! Perhaps—"

"Do *not* make excuses for a man who does not have one!" Brigette roared. "Whose side are you on anyway?"

"Is this a war?" Spring returned angrily. "Are we to choose sides?"

"This is no war." Brigette's voice was deadly low. "A war must be fought between two, and I'll suffer no more of this."

"What are you . . . ?"

"Brie?" Percy's voice sounded outside the tent.

"Tell Percy that I want to be alone," Brigette ordered.

Spring sighed and stepped outside. "She wishes to be alone, my lord."

"But I must tell her about Antonia."

"Antonia?"

"My brother Malcolm's widow," Percy explained. "She's the reason Iain isna' here."

"Brie is tired," Spring said. "I'm certain she'll be more understanding in the morning."

"Yes," Percy agreed doubtfully, "yer probably correct."

3

"Well?" Spring said, staring at Brigette, who was sitting on one of the cots. At the sound of her cousin's voice, Brigette looked up but made no reply.

"Brie, what are you going to do?"

"Nothing, at the moment," she answered. "I've a need to be alone. Why don't you sup with Jamie?"

Spring studied Brigette a moment longer, then left. Alone again, Brigette's expression froze in a grimace, her thoughts returning to her husband's devastating insults.

Suddenly, Brigette's lips turned up in a winsome smile, the product of an outrageous idea taking root in her mind. Iain MacArthur needs a lesson in humility, she decided. That he needs his legal wife to beget a legitimate heir is a fact he has forgotten, and reminding him will be my pleasure. I am go-

ing home and will not return until that heathen
begs on bended knee for my forgiveness!

Brigette leaped from the cot, rummaged
through Spring's baggage, and pulled out one of
her cousin's older traveling outfits. She couldn't
wear her own clothing on the way home; no one
must guess that she was an earl's daughter.

Brigette hid the garments beneath her cot, then
sat down to plot her escape. Because of the sen-
tries, she could not take her horse. With a sigh,
Brigette resigned herself to a very long walk back
to Basildon Castle. She gave no thought to food or
even where she would sleep, assuming she'd find
accommodations along the way.

Awakening with a start, Brigette realized she'd
fallen asleep and almost lost her one chance to
escape. Her eyes darted to Spring's cot. The other
girl slept.

Rising, Brigette reached under the cot and
pulled out the borrowed clothes. Quickly and quietly, she stripped and donned the threadbare garments.

On tiptoes, Brigette scurried to the tent's flap
and listened. Should she venture out or not? All
was silent, but she knew the MacArthur guards
were lurking somewhere near.

Indecision gripped Brigette. She turned around,
deciding to sneak out the back. Spring moaned in
her sleep, and Brigette froze, only her eyes moving to where the other girl lay.

Several long moments passed. Reaching the
back of the tent, Brigette knelt and lifted the bot-

tom, then peered out at the night. No one was about. On hands and knees, she crawled toward the safety of the forest. When she reached the trees, Brigette stopped and listened for the sounds of alarm. All remained quiet. Slowly, Brigette got to her feet and stepped deeper into the woods.

The sky had cleared, and the moon was brilliantly full, but as the firelight faded, so, too, did Brigette's courage. In her haste to escape, she'd forgotten her fear of the dark and being alone. Now the night's sounds closed in upon her. An owl hooted nearby and Brigette jumped, her heart pounding frantically. She heard a wolf's lonely lament and froze, too frightened to take another step.

With tears streaming down her face, Brigette leaned against a tree. I cannot escape and then return, she moaned. How humiliating that would be! How foolish to place myself in jeopardy because of a man's insults! Brushing her tears away, Brigette sat down and nestled against the tree, then closed her eyes and waited for the dawn.

The night was black when Brigette, having dozed, opened her eyes. The hair on the back of her neck prickled, sending a shiver racing down the length of her spine. Brigette looked around, forcing herself to search for danger, then gasped. A pair of shining eyes watched her. She bit her bottom lip to keep from screaming.

The moon peeked out from behind a passing cloud, and Brigette giggled nervously. The shining eyes belonged to a baby fox. "You're a sly one," she whispered, and held out her hand.

Curious, the fox advanced, then stopped and sniffed the air. Deciding Brigette was no danger, it stepped closer.

"Have you lost your mother?" Brigette murmured, and noticed that its copper hair resembled her own. Feeling not quite so alone, Brigette patted the fox. Responding to the gentle touch, it snuggled against her, and together they settled down for the night.

Dawn was washing the sky a pale shade of gray. All but a few of the MacArthur warriors were still sleeping when a solitary man rode, unchallenged, into their midst. He nodded to the guards and dismounted, then sauntered toward the cooking fire.

Iain MacArthur cut an imposing figure. Six feet tall and muscularly built, there was not an ounce of extra meat upon his frame. He appeared lean, but locked in mortal combat, his enemies soon realized their folly in underestimating his superior strength. His hair and eyes were as black as a moonless midnight. A long, straight nose and full lips blended harmoniously, and his face was made even more handsome by his complexion, tanned and ruddy from exposure to all kinds of weather. Women were fatally attracted to Iain's dark face and form, his image of raw masculinity rending him irresistible.

Iain looked down at Percy, who still slept. Squatting beside his brother, he thought how much

Percy resembled their deceased mother. Leaning close to Percy's ear, he said loudly, "Good mornin' to ye, brother."

Percy bolted up. His face contorted in a grimace, then split into a grin. "Iain!"

"I knew I shouldna' have sent ye to do a mon's job," Iain said. "Yer still a lazy lug-a-bed, like when we were lads."

Percy stood and wrapped himself in his plaid, then turned on Iain. "Congratulations on yer marriage, brother." Percy grinned. "Did ye enjoy the weddin' night?"

"Didna' I instruct ye to do it by proxy?" Iain returned, a smile flirting with the corners of his lips. "It musta' slipped my mind." Percy chortled with laughter. "By the way," he added, "where is the bride I've ridden all night to meet?"

"Sleepin', I suppose," Percy answered, his eyes drifting to the silent tent. "Lady Brigette—Brie, her friends call her—is a bonnie lass."

"Shall we wake her so I can see for myself?"

"I must have a word or two wi' ye first."

"I'm listenin'."

"Patience isna' one of yer finer points, brother," Percy began, "but ye must be patient wi' yer bride. However bonnie she may be, Brie has a fine temper to match yer own."

"However spicy the wench may be," Iain returned, "I'm capable of handlin' her. Let's go."

"No' so fast, brother." Percy placed a hand on Iain's arm. "She's no common wench to be handled, as ye so delicately put it. Weddin' by proxy was an insult to her pride, and the lady is furious. Dinna forget she's an earl's daughter."

"So?"

Percy frowned. "She wore a black gown of mournin' to the ceremony. I'd say she isna' harborin' any fondness for ye. And last night—"

An uproar near the tent silenced Percy and the brothers turned in that direction. Jamie approached with a near-hysterical Spring in tow.

"The Sassenach is gone," Jamie said, and weeping, the tirewoman nodded.

"W-when I w-woke," Spring sobbed, "B-Brie was g-gone!"

"Damn the chit!" Iain swore. "When I find her, I'll beat her black and blue." He raced for his horse.

"He doesna' even know what she looks like," Percy said before following his brother. "Take Spring to Dunridge. We'll meet ye there."

Brigette awakened early and found the fox cuddled upon her lap. She smiled at the sleeping ball of copper fur, then set it aside and rose slowly, each muscle protesting the tense night just passed. When her stomach growled loudly, she realized she was hungry. I must find a stream, she thought. The water will fill me until I find help.

Ignorant of where she was going, Brigette walked. Glancing back, she saw the fox following, and when she turned around, it stopped.

"Come along, if you wish." Brigette held out her arms in invitation, and the fox accepted. "You'll be known as Sly," she added, lifting it. "Understand?"

Percy threw back his head and shouted with laughter.

"I beg a favor, brother," Iain added, and Percy nodded. "Dinna tell Antonia our whereaboots."

Unconscious, Brigette lay in the hunting lodge's only bed. Iain sat beside her and pressed a damp cloth to her forehead.

She's lovely, he thought. I've done well in my bride. Brigette's eyes fluttered open; silently, husband and wife stared at each other. *Green eyes!*

"How are ye feelin'?" Iain broke the silence.

Brigette touched her forehead. "My—my head hurts."

"Ye've a nasty bump," he said. "I'm sorry I frightened ye and caused yer accident. Who are ye?"

"Who are you?" she countered, alert to the danger couched in his question. Whoever he was, the man wore the black and green plaid of the MacArthurs and probably knew her husband.

"Ross MacArthur, bastard son of the Earl of Dunridge, at yer service." Iain smiled. "And ye are?"

"MacArthur?"

"Yes, Ross MacArthur. And ye?"

"I—I cannot recall," Brigette hedged, peeping at him from beneath her long, copper lashes. Would he digest the outrageous lie she was formulating? "A Gypsy! I'm a Gypsy! At least, I think I am."

Swallowing his laughter, Iain's expression remained sympathetic, but his eyes sparkled with suppressed merriment. "It's the rattlin' yer brains took today," he said. "I'm certain ye'll shortly recall who ye are. Take a healthy swig of this medicine."

Iain helped Brigette sit up, and she gulped a large mouthful. Her eyes widened in shock as the whiskey burned a path to her stomach. Brigette choked and then shivered, in the process suddenly noticing her state of undress.

"I'm naked!" she cried, shocked and embarrassed.

"Ye couldna' be put to bed wearin' yer clothes." Iain grinned and patted her arm. "Dinna worry. I've seen many and many naked women before, and make nae mistake aboot it."

Brigette's embarrassment mingled with anger, but Iain pressed her back to the pillow and gently brushed a few strands of copper hair from her forehead. "Close yer eyes and rest. I promise ye'll be feelin' better when ye wake."

When she awakened later, Brigette did feel better, the pounding in her head having subsided to a dull throb. She opened her eyes. Her host was nowhere in sight.

Dizzy but determined to leave, Brigette tried to rise but fell back to the pillow. She closed her eyes and took several deep breaths, then opened them again and looked around.

The lodge was one large chamber. The bed was situated along a side wall. On the back wall was the hearth, where a fire was burning. Something that smelled delicious was simmering in a black pot, and Brigette's mouth watered.

A rug, made from several animal pelts, lay on the middle of the floor. Beyond that was an oak table and two chairs, simple but finely crafted. The door was along the wall that faced the foot of the bed. As Brigette's eyes touched the door, it opened.

"I see ye've awakened." Iain smiled pleasantly. "Feelin' any better?"

"Much better." Brigette smiled faintly in return.

Iain took a bowl from the table and filled it with soup from the black pot, then crossed the chamber and sat on the edge of the bed. "Sit up," he ordered. "Ye must eat some of this."

Brigette obeyed, but Iain neither gave her the bowl nor fed her. He appeared to be in a trance. Brigette followed his mesmerized gaze and gasped. The coverlet had slipped, exposing one plump breast. Blushing to the tips of her toes, she yanked the coverlet up.

"As I said before, I've seen many and many—"

"I heard you the first time!" Brigette snapped irritably. For some unknown reason, the thought of Ross MacArthur viewing parades of beautiful, naked women bothered her.

Iain's dark eyes narrowed at his wife's waspishness, but then he smiled with patience, assuming the cause was the pain in her head. "Have ye recalled yer name yet?" he asked, filling her mouth with soup.

She swallowed, then answered, "Bria, I think."

"Bria?" Iain hid a smile. "It sounds like that French cheese. And what of yer family?"

Brigette hesitated, wondering what she should say. "I remember now! I am a Gypsy!"

"With yer red hair and green eyes," he scoffed, "ye dinna look like a Gypsy to me."

"I resemble my mother," Brigette answered without thinking. "She's French."

"So, yer mother's French?"

"Father met Mother while he was traveling in France, and the rest is history." A lie that contains some truth will be easier to remember, she thought.

As if deep in thought, Iain rubbed the dark shadow of stubble on his chin. "I know of no Gypsies passin' through the area. How came ye to be on these lands?"

"We were on our way to Edinburgh when I became separated and lost."

"Edinburgh, ye say?" Iain choked on a chuckle. "That's the other side of Scotland."

"I just told you that I became lost!"

He made no reply, but stared at Brigette, who had the uncanny feeling he could see into her soul and knew the truth. But how could that be? "If you give me directions to Edinburgh," she said, "I'll be on my way in the morning."

"Ye willna' be goin' anywhere in the mornin'."

"But—"

"I forbid it." Iain's voice rose. "I'd be worried aboot yer welfare forever and a day. Ye'll remain here a few more days, and then I'll see ye safely to yer family."

"But—"

"Nae more talk," he insisted, not unkindly. "Ye

need rest. I'll go huntin' in the mornin' and we'll sup on rabbit stew. Lie back now and close yer bonnie green eyes."

Brigette closed her eyes and promptly fell asleep.

A Gypsy! Iain grinned, thinking her story was most inventive. He rose, dragged a chair over to the hearth, and sat down with his whiskey.

How verra bonnie my wife is, he thought. I've the urge to take her now. One look at that sweet flesh had stiffened his rod to full strength, and remembering it made him tingle. Yes, I've the right to take what I desire, though it's a sorry man who cannot control his urges. But I'll be damned if I sleep in a chair all night!

Iain stood and stripped, then crawled into bed beside Brigette, who slept peacefully, oblivious to her bedmate. He fell asleep but awakened a short time later to the feel of his bride cuddled into him. Her face was buried against the side of his chest, and one of her legs was thrown over his muscular thighs.

To touch yet not touch was the sweetest torture Iain had ever known. He stroked her back lightly, savoring the silken texture of her skin. A sigh escaped her lips, and he smiled in the dark, then closed his eyes and slept.

Brigette awoke the next morning to the smell of something heavenly simmering in the pot. Her nose twitched and she rolled over.

"Good mornin'," Iain greeted, standing in front of the hearth.

"Good morning." Uncomfortable with her nudity, Brigette glanced down. The coverlet was doing its job. "I'd like to get dressed," she said.

With his hands resting on his lean hips, Iain studied her thoughtfully. "Well, ye ought to be spendin' the day where ye are, but if ye promise to rest . . ." With a shrug, he turned away to stir the oatmeal porridge.

"My—my clothing?"

"On the chair over there," he answered, without bothering to look at her.

Brigette's eyes moved from Iain to the chair on the far side of the room, then back to Iain. She stared at him in growing consternation. When there was no movement from the bed, he looked over.

"My lord," she whispered, her face coloring to a vivid scarlet, "I've other n-needs as well."

Iain stared a moment longer and then grinned. "I'll return in a few minutes," he said, then sauntered to the door. "There's a chamber pot in the corner near the foot of the bed."

Brigette thought she would die from the humiliation. How could he be so public about such a private function? Alone, she raced for the chamber pot and relieved herself, then rushed across the room and dressed hurriedly. Dizzy from the activity, Brigette sank into the chair.

The door opened and Iain entered, chuckling. In his arms was a squirming lump of copper fur. "Look what I discovered sniffin' aboot! Have ye ever eaten fox stew, Bria? Would ye like a muff?"

"*Sly!*" Brigette sprang from the chair.

Sly leaped from Iain's arms and ran to Brigette, who knelt upon the floor and gathered him into her arms. "There now," she soothed, cooing to the frightened fox.

"Are ye acquainted wi' this beastie?"

"He's my pet!" Brigette roared, turning flashing green eyes on him. Iain was startled by their murderous glint. Percy had obviously been correct, his wife was no meek lady.

"Sly kept me company when I was lost in the forest," she said more calmly.

Iain grinned. "Does this mean we willna' be enjoyin' fox stew?"

"Would you murder a poor, motherless bairn? Even a Highlander could not be so cruel."

At the insult, Iain's eyes lost their humorous gleam. Frightened, Brigette realized she'd said too much and tried to make amends. "Forgive me," she apologized. "My careless mouth is my worst flaw. Please, may we feed him?"

Iain filled a bowl, then knelt beside Brigette and Sly. "Come on, laddie," he invited, placing the steaming porridge in front of the fox. "Eat yer breakfast."

Over Sly's head, Brigette and Iain looked at each other. Her eyes became trapped by the dark intensity of his. He leaned close; then his lips touched hers. One of his powerful hands traveled to the back of her head, held her immobile. His tongue forced her trembling lips apart, flicked this way and that, exploring and tasting the sweetness of her mouth.

When he finally released her, Brigette's face was

pale, and her expression was dazed from the earth-shattering experience of her first kiss. Iain smiled lazily, seeming to be unaffected.

"A virgin Gypsy?" he mocked gently.

Brigette's complexion took on a rather rosy hue. "How do you know?"

"Och! I've kissed many and many a—"

"Thank you for your hospitality." Brigette cut him off, her voice cold. "Sly and I must be on our way."

"Ye willna' be goin' anywhere 'til yer better."

"It's improper for me to stay."

"Allowin' ye to traipse aboot the Highlands while yer still weak would be even more improper, my lady," Iain countered. "I'll let ye know when yer fit to travel."

"You mean, you'll tell me when I'm feeling better?" Brigette was flabbergasted.

"Correct."

"Why, of all the—"

"Let's eat breakfast," he said in dismissal.

Patting Sly, Brigette watched Iain fill their bowls with the oatmeal porridge. He won't even listen to me! she fumed in growing frustration. How can I win the argument if he refuses to participate?

When she went to bed that night, Brigette wore her chemise. Sleepless, she watched the lodge's other two occupants relax in front of the hearth. Iain sat in his chair, and Sly was curled up on the floor beside him.

When Iain stood and began undressing, Brigette snapped her eyes shut. Never had she seen an unclothed man! Would he sleep naked in the chair? Where *had* he slept last night? The bed creaked as Iain slid in.

"What are you doing?" Brigette shrieked and bolted up.

"Doin'? I'm goin' to sleep."

"Here?" Brigette was shocked.

"Do ye see another bed in the lodge?"

"It's highly improper for you to be in this bed with me," she announced, lifting her upturned nose in the air. "If you won't play the gentleman, I'll sleep elsewhere."

Brigette moved to rise. Iain yanked her back, and she fell against his well-muscled chest. She tried to pull away, but his steely grip kept her from moving.

"Ye must trust in me, Bria. I willna' harm ye but neither will I let ye go."

He kissed the top of her head, then closed his eyes. Gradually, Brigette relaxed. As she drifted off to sleep, she sighed and snuggled against him. In the next instant, her eyes flew open and her body stiffened. What was she doing? Oh, Lord, she was in bed with her husband's half brother!

Brigette squirmed as far away from Iain as she could and turned her back on him. At least, their bodies were no longer touching. Determined to guard her virtue through the night, Brigette stared at the wall.

"Ye'll never get well enough to travel to Edinburgh if ye insist on stayin' awake all night," his voice warned in the darkness. "Dinna worry aboot yer virtue. Yer safe wi' me."

"I'll be the judge of that," Brigette grumbled, but closed her eyes anyway. Too tired to worry about improprieties, she soon succumbed to sleep.

A truce sprang up between dissembling husband and unsuspecting wife. Brigette did not mention leaving again, and Iain's intimacy proceeded no farther than sleeping beside her each night. She had the freedom of the lodge and surrounding area, always supervised, of course, lest she fly. They were pleasant enough with each other, helped along by Sly's unique talent of uniting them in laughter.

And so it went for a week. One morning Iain decided to ride to Dunridge for a few of life's necessities—food, clothing, and whiskey. Uncertain of Brigette's feelings for "Ross," Iain was reluctant to leave her behind, lest she flee while he was gone.

The two of them sat at the table eating their usual morning fare, oatmeal porridge—Sly preferred his in a bowl on the floor. "I'm ridin' to Dunridge today," Iain said casually. "Would ye care to join me?"

"N-no," Brigette sputtered, almost choking on her porridge. "I—I—I think not."

Iain's lips twitched with the urge to smile. "I may be gone several hours."

"I'll be fine," she hastily assured him. "I won't even leave the lodge. And don't forget, I've Sly to protect me."

Iain's gaze drifted to Sly, who appeared to be no

protection at all. "Well, ye might clean up a bit and try yer hand at cookin' supper for once."

"Clean and cook?" Brigette was taken aback by the suggestion.

Iain nodded and smiled.

"But—but I don't know how to cook."

"A Gypsy lass wi' nae idea of cookin'?" His dark eyes gleamed with amusement.

Meeting Iain's questioning stare, Brigette flexed her imagination. "Ross," she explained in a condescending voice, "my father is the king of the Gypsies. I was never required to cook. We'd servants to do that."

Tickled by her glibness, Iain choked back his laughter. His wife was as slick with her tongue as the serpent in Paradise and as sly as the beast she called her pet. "Do ye think ye might try?" he asked.

"Yes, I'd try anything for my rescuer." Brigette smiled brightly, relieved he'd swallowed another of her lies.

Iain arched a brow, certain she'd no understanding of what she offered. He stood to leave, then stooped to kiss her forehead. "I'll be back long before supper."

After he'd gone, Brigette felt lonely and abandoned. She lifted Sly onto her lap and stroked him, more for her own sense of well-being than his pleasure. Ross fills this lodge to capacity, she thought, and without him, it seems empty. Oh, Lord, what a coil! She was beginning to care for her husband's brother. Thinking about *that* would give her a headache. Mindless chores like cooking and cleaning would make her feel better. She hoped.

How does one go about cleaning and cooking? Brigette shrugged her shoulders. If servants could do it, then so could she. Brigette began with the breakfast bowls, and when she'd finished, she felt a real sense of accomplishment. Next Brigette tackled the bed. With that done, she decided to begin supper's preparation. An accomplished cook Brigette was not, but even she knew that stew must simmer. The longer the simmer, the better the stew.

Brigette started a fire in the hearth and gathered the necessary ingredients as she'd seen Ross do. When the pot was filled and simmering, Brigette decided she needed a rest. Cleaning and cooking were wholly rewarding tasks, but terribly tiring, and she'd experienced enough fulfillment for one day. Brigette lay down with Sly upon the bed and fell asleep.

It was late afternoon when Iain returned, pleased with the way his day had gone. When he had arrived at Dunridge Castle, he'd reported first to his father and had assured the earl that Brigette and he would return home soon. He had refrained from mentioning the fact that his bride was still a virgin. That was a thing Black Jack would not understand.

Next Iain had enlisted Percy's aid in gathering food, clothing, and a good supply of whiskey. By the time he'd left Dunridge, Iain had totally managed to avoid Lady Antonia, who had never realized that he'd been there and gone. Escaping Antonia's notice had made the day successful!

Whistling a happy tune, Iain dismounted and entered the lodge. His nose twitched and his stomach growled, calling out to the delicious smell of simmering stew that permeated the chamber. His wife had obviously done well in her culinary efforts.

Iain sat on the edge of the bed and watched Brigette, enchanting in sleep. Her hair was in wild disarray and her cheeks were flushed. Her lips were moist and parted in an irresistible invitation. Iain leaned over and touched his lips to hers. Those incredible eyes of green opened, and she smiled.

"Somethin' smells good," he said. "And I'm so hungry I've a mind to gobble ye up." Brigette giggled, especially when Sly climbed on Iain's lap and demanded his own share of attention.

Iain sat at the table and watched Brigette fill their bowls with stew. "I've brought ye a change of clothin'," he told her.

With a start, Brigette realized he'd probably heard about Iain's runaway bride. "Anything of interest happening at Dunridge?" she asked casually, placing the steaming bowl of stew in front of him. She took her own seat.

"All was as usual." There was a long pause while Iain ate several spoonfuls of stew. "Bria," he said finally, "ye said ye made stew. Is this stew or soup or perhaps spicy water?"

"It's stew," Brigette cried.

"Then where are the meat and vegetables?"

"Damn it! They're in the pot!"

"The pot, ye say? They belong in my bowl."

"I couldn't get them out!"

"What? I dinna ken."

"The meat and vegetables stuck to the bottom of the pot," Brigette answered through clenched teeth, "and I could not get them out."

Iain threw back his head and shouted with laughter. At least she'd been game enough to try. "I amna' laughin' at ye," he lied. "The verra same thin' happened the first time I made stew."

"It did?"

"Even my broth was foul tastin', but yers is excellent."

"Truly?" Brigette's eyes gleamed like emeralds.

"I've tasted many and many a broth," Iain declared, "but I've never tasted a finer broth than this." At that moment, Brigette thought Ross MacArthur was the most wonderful man in Scotland, or England for that matter. Correctly reading her expression, Iain mentally rubbed his hands together.

Several days later, Iain invited Brigette to ride with him. Afraid they would meet her husband along the way, Brigette accepted reluctantly. Since there was only the one horse, Iain pulled her up on the saddle in front of him, and off they went.

On the one hand, Brigette wondered if she should, as planned, return to England; but on the other hand, she was uncertain if she really wanted to leave. The thought of never seeing Ross MacArthur again tugged insistently at her heartstrings. If only she'd not wed Iain MacArthur by proxy!

Enjoying the outing and the man's nearness, Brigette relaxed against Iain. Soon, the warmth of her flesh seeped through her clothing to tease and taunt Iain's desire for her. When she rested her head in the crook of his neck, Iain nearly lost control. The fragrant scent of her hair tormented him, and Iain ached to drag her from the horse and have done with it, but knew he would regret such a hasty action.

They rode into a clearing that became a glen. Brigette stiffened. Dressed in the MacArthur plaid, a group of men were riding toward them.

Panicking, Brigette turned her face into Iain's chest, but kept a watchful eye upon the approaching men. It was finished! She would be taken like a common prisoner to Dunridge Castle! And what would happen to Ross? Would he be punished for harboring her? Percy was among the group and would recognize her. Her red hair alone would attract his attention.

The MacArthur men turned unexpectedly and rode off in a different direction. Relieved, Brigette nearly slipped from the horse, but Iain kept her from falling. Someone above must be watching over me, she decided, and snuggled into Iain's chest. He glanced down at the top of her head, and his lips quirked in a smile.

Stopping at a secluded stream, they walked to the water's edge and then sat beneath a tree. "Ross?" Brigette's curiosity got the upper hand. "Why didn't Percy greet you?"

"Percy?"

"Your brother, Percy."

Aha! Iain thought. At last the truth will out! "How do ye know I've a brother Percy?" he asked, arching a dark brow at her. "And how do ye know he was among those men?"

Brigette froze, realizing her error, and tried to think of a reasonable answer. A sudden idea lit her mind and made her eyes sparkle like jewels. "I— I've the Sight." Her smile dazzled him. "Haven't I mentioned it before?"

"I dinna know ye had such a gift." Lies slip from those rosy lips as if they'd been greased, Iain thought. The viper!

"My sister Kathryn writes that many in Ireland are blessed with it."

"And now we've one in the Highlands," he grumbled.

"You never answered my question," she reminded him.

"What question?"

"Why did Percy not acknowledge your presence in the glen?"

Iain's expression was suitably serious. "I'm a bastard, lass, and—"

"I know you're a bastard," Brigette interrupted, a mischievous smile touching her lips.

Iain grabbed her arm, and Brigette laughed, then appeared properly contrite. "It was a jest."

"As ye grow older," he said, "ye'll learn, I hope, that bastardy is nae matter for jestin'."

"I never realized a bastard's life was so difficult. The earl is a hard man?"

"The earl does what he must to survive and protect his own."

"What of his sons?"

"Sons?" Iain smiled mockingly. "The Sight?"

Brigette grinned puckishly, and Iain was unable to hold back a rumble of laughter. But then he realized how great a fool she believed him to be. Only an idiot would believe her outrageous lies!

"Percy thrives on fightin' and laughin' and lovin'," Iain said, biting back his ire. "The proverbial good-for-naught, ye might say. But what can ye expect from a coddled younger son?"

"And—and the other?"

"Iain? Now, there's a real mon! He and I are closer than brothers, always seemin' to be of the same mind. He's a hard mon, but fair . . . just . . . honorable. . . ."

"A paragon?"

"Aye, that he is." Iain leaned closer until his lips met Brigette's, jolting her with a delightful tingling sensation. The softest of lips yielded to his kiss, and Iain's kiss became demanding. One strong hand held the back of her head, gently but firmly kept her from fleeing. Overwhelmed by his masculine nearness and scent, Brigette surrendered to the more powerful force. Her arms creeped up his chest to entwine his neck.

"Open yer mouth, Bria," he whispered hoarsely. Her lips parted instantly and Iain's tongue slipped in, exploring and tasting the moist sweetness within. Brigette shivered, feeling hot and cold all at the same time.

Leaving her lips, Iain placed feathery-light

kisses on her eyelids, temples, and throat. They fell back to the grass, he lying on top of her. Iain's lips returned to Brigette's, and she felt consumed, as if he would take her very soul.

A gentle breeze tickled her bared breasts, but Brigette was too dazed to care. Iain's dark head dipped lower until his masterful lips reached her breasts. Kissing one of those soft mounds, he worked his way to its center, finally drawing upon its sensitive nipple, which hardened in arousal.

Brigette moaned, and sanity returned in the form of guilt.

"Get off me, you seducing oaf!" Brigette shoved him and pulled away. "Keep your distance, liar."

"Lied about what?" Iain asked, devouring her with his passion-glazed eyes.

"You said I'd be safe with you, but then you tried to seduce me," she accused, covering her bared breasts.

"I dinna try to seduce ye," Iain defended himself. "Ye enticed me."

"I did not!"

Iain muttered several colorful curses and wished he'd done what he'd set out to do in the first place—find his Sassenach bride and drag her back to Dunridge!

"Cursing indicates a lack of vocabulary," Brigette chided.

Iain gave her a scathing look, then said, "Let's go home."

"No," she refused. "I cannot feel safe with you."

Damn! This English bride of his was infuriating. Iain counted to ten, then added another twenty for good measure. "I swear upon my sainted mother's soul to protect yer virtue, even from myself," Iain promised, his voice tinged with sarcasm.

"How can a woman who bore a child out of wedlock be sainted?" Brigette shot back.

"Dinna strain my patience," Iain growled, his expression darkening even more. "I've given my word as a mon of honor, and ye must accept it."

"Very well," Brigette gave in reluctantly. "I warn you that I am quite capable with weapons and will, if provoked, defend myself."

"Please do," Iain said, amused at being threatened by so small a creature as she. "I assure ye, yer virtue and my health are safe." For the moment, he thought to himself, then stood and helped her rise.

Iain went fishing alone the next morning. With his horse grazing a few feet away, he stood at the water's edge and pondered the weighty problem of what to do with his wife. Should he return to the lodge and tell her the truth? No, the seduction must come first.

Hearing a sound behind him, Iain turned to see Percy dismounting. "What's the news from Dunridge?" he asked.

"As usual," Percy answered. "Black Jack wants to know when ye'll be returnin' and Antonia is anxious to meet yer bride." Then he added, "Ye displayed tremendous control yesterday. A feat, ye might say."

"I dinna ken."

Percy grinned wickedly. "Jamie says any earl

who'd hump his countess beneath a tree is a good mon to follow."

"Ye were watchin'?"

"We were guardin' ye, no' watchin'," Percy returned indignantly, but his eyes sparkled with humor. "Is she so hot ye canna wait for the bed?"

Groaning, Iain turned away, but Percy grabbed his brother's arm and studied his pained expression. "She's a virgin still?" Percy roared with laughter. "Good God, mon! Yer losin' yer touch wi' the lassies."

Without warning, Iain struck, his fist connecting with Percy's jaw, sending the younger man sprawling on the ground. "Yer tongue and yer brain are losin' touch wi' each other," he growled. "Open yer mouth aboot this, baby brother, and yer a dead mon."

Iain mounted his horse and left, but the echo of Percy's laughter followed him back to the lodge.

4

"Percy!" Iain exclaimed. "What are ye doin' here?"

"Good mornin' to ye also," Percy said cheerfully as he dismounted in front of the lodge. His eyes quickly scanned the area. "Where is she?"

"Pickin' early berries." Iain frowned, adding, "Ye shouldna' be here."

"Have ye breached her yet?" Percy asked baldly.

"That isna' yer business," Iain snapped, his anger flaring. "I'll thank ye to leave now."

"Black Jack sent me," Percy said, ignoring his brother's invitation to depart. "It's August, ye ken? Our crops and cattle are growin' larger, and Menzies has become more visible."

"Trouble?"

"The northwest sector, nearest the Menzies land. The crops were torched and a substantial number of our cattle were lifted. And that isna' the worst of it. Several of the crofters died protectin' their few possessions. Their women and children were burned in their cottages!''

"Sweet Jesu!" Iain was horrified by the atrocity. Murdac Menzies was worse than an animal. Only an unspeakably evil man could order the burning of helpless women and innocent children.

"Black Jack needs ye," Percy was saying as he took up the reins of his horse and mounted, "and expects ye home."

"We'll return in the mornin'," Iain assured him.

"Iain?" Percy looked down at his brother and smiled. "Have yerself a grand day and an even grander night."

Almost wearily, Iain entered the lodge and sat in the chair in front of the now-darkened hearth. He was glad for the opportunity to sit and think before Brigette returned.

Always, Iain had taken what he desired from women and had given nothing in return. Brigette was different. She was young, very young. She was his wife, but unprepared, he felt, to learn the truth.

Since she'd arrived, his life had been a purgatory of sexual frustration, but Iain was loathe to bed her and chance ruining the easy relationship that had sprung up between them. He wanted Brigette's love and affection and respect, not just her body, much as he wanted that too.

The world outside Dunridge Castle was dangerous and cruel. Iain needed a wife with whom he could live in peace and harmony, a wife to create a haven from warfare and political intrigue. But how could that be if his wife despised him?

I've seen what a bad marriage can do to a man, he mused. When Malcolm passed so untimely on, he was probably glad to escape his wife. Antonia! There's a bitch—as are all women! What a sorry state the world is in; half of humankind are lying, deceitful, and treacherous . . . except Lady Brigette. My Bria is a liar like all the others, but a delightfully charming one. I'm certain she's only been lying to protect herself. And she's beginning to love me. No, he corrected himself, she's beginning to love Ross.

When the door swung open to admit Brigette and Sly, Iain stood and faced her, then grinned. "Put those berries on the table, lassie. We're goin' out ridin'."

"Where?"

"I dinna know, but this day is ours to do wi' as we will."

Brigette grinned.

"Yer lips and teeth are purple," he said, chuckling.

"We've been devouring berries." She giggled. "Sly's tongue is the most vivid purple I've ever seen."

Iain chastely kissed her lips. "Well, ye taste delicious."

"Last evenin' I discovered several pieces of meat floatin' in my bowl," Iain teased as he lifted Brigette onto his horse. "Yer stew is improvin'."

"It was unintentional, I assure you."

They rode together through the glen that led to the stream, a place they frequently visited. It was a secluded spot, a private place where they need not fear discovery by the MacArthur warriors.

Brigette was bewildered by the odd behavior of the MacArthur men-at-arms. Occasionally, she saw them while passing through the glen with Ross, but the men turned away each time without acknowledging their presence. Brigette felt certain the MacArthurs should have recognized her. It was wholly puzzling, but she refused to dwell on it, preferring to enjoy whatever time remained for Ross and herself. Perhaps, she thought more than once, Ross would be willing to leave with me. Brigette knew she was in danger of falling in love with him and was almost certain he had a fondness for her, even when he was gruff, which strangely enough happened each night at bedtime. More than anything else, Brigette yearned to be with Ross MacArthur, but they were doomed. She belonged to that heathen from Dunridge! Unless . . .

A smile flitted across Brigette's face and she relaxed against the object of her thoughts. A marriage is not actually legal, she schemed, until consummated. Iain MacArthur has certainly not consummated his marriage to me—yet! If I gave myself to Ross, would Iain still insist on the marriage? Would he release me from the vows or slay us both? It's worth the risk. . . .

"I suppose, bein' a Gypsy and all, ye've traveled to many places," Iain said, picking up a stone and skimming it across the stream. "Do ye like the Highlands?"

"Yes, I do like the Highlands."

"Do ye think ye could be happy livin' here, I mean, on a permanent basis?"

"I suppose," Brigette answered coyly, "a woman could be happy anywhere, as long as she's married to the right man." He loves me! she decided, but then her face dropped in dismay. With my husband in the vicinity, how could Ross and I live together as man and wife?

Smiling, Iain turned to Brigette, but saw the shadows of sadness clouding her expression. Gently, he forced her to look at him. "What's makin' ye sad, lassie?"

"Nothing."

Her tender feelings for Ross made her sad, Iain decided. When she learned that he was her husband, Brigette would be overjoyed. If only she would confess the truth about who she really was!

"I dinna believe that frown is for nothin'," Iain said. "If ye've a need to share yer troubles, I'm a good listener."

Brigette forced herself to smile brightly. "There, you see, the frown and the thought are gone."

"Would ye like to see me tickle a fish?" he asked, thinking to cheer her up.

Brigette stared blankly at him. Iain removed his boots and hose, then waded into the stream, calling over his shoulder, "Ye must be absolutely quiet and still. Ye ken?"

Brigette nodded her head like a child.

Bending over, Iain slowly, ever so slowly, submerged his hand in the cold water, then stood statue-still. A respectable size fish approached, swimming around and around Iain's legs, investigating. Gingerly, his long finger reached out to stroke its belly, lulling it.

"What are you doing?" Brigette shouted just as he was about to flip the fish to shore. "I can't see!"

The fish darted away. Iain scowled and glared at Brigette, who, being a reasonably intelligent person, read the displeasure stamped across his handsome features.

"Whatever I've done, I'm sorry," she apologized. "May I try?"

"Come on, then."

Brigette removed her shoes and hose, then immodestly hiked her skirt up, affording Iain a superb view of her shapely legs. She waded into the stream, squealing all the while at the water's coldness.

"Bend over," he instructed, "and slowly place yer hand in the water."

"Now what?"

"Ye wait. When a fish swims close, gently tickle his underside with a finger. When he's paralyzed with pleasure, flip him onto the shore."

Brigette waited, and Iain admired most appreciatively the fetching backside she presented to him. A fish approached, drawing closer and closer. She reached out to touch it.

"*Yuck!*" Brigette jumped back, and the fish darted away. Iain reached to catch her as she staggered off-balance. Too late! With a loud splash Brigette sat in the stream and Iain hooted with laughter.

"This is your fault!" she accused. "You made me touch that scaly thing!"

"I didna' do any such thin'. Ye wanted to try."

Brigette smiled sweetly and held out her hand. "Help me up?"

When he grasped her hand, she yanked with all her might, catching him unaware. With an even louder splash, Iain sat in the stream beside her. Brigette laughed uproariously.

"Why, ye wee bitch!" he roared. "I've a mind to set ye over my knee and give ye the skelpin' of yer life."

Giggling, Brigette leaped up and ran, but Iain gave chase. As she reached the shore, a powerful hand caught her arm and spun her around, none too gently. She slammed into his broad chest, and his arms encircled her, keeping her from falling.

All thoughts of punishment fled as Iain became lost in the fathomless pools of Brigette's green eyes. "I've a mind to skelp ye," he whispered huskily, "but I believe I'll kiss ye instead."

When she lifted her face so he could more easily reach her lips, Iain groaned. His lips swooped down and claimed hers in an endless, devouring kiss.

Finally drawing back to look at her, Iain stared at Brigette's dazed expression and knew the time had come to make her his wife in truth. The most tender of smiles touched his lips. "Let's go home, hinny, and get warm."

* * *

Sly gave the shivering couple the warmest of greetings when they arrived at the lodge. Brigette laughed at the fox, delighted by his joyful squeals. Iain smiled at Brigette's happy expression and hoped she'd be equally happy the following morning, after they'd settled what was between them.

"Disrobe and wrap yerself in this," Iain ordered, thrusting a blanket into Brigette's hands, then added, "It will keep ye toasty until a fire's started and the chamber warms."

Brigette stood motionless, waiting for him to leave, but Iain turned away and knelt in front of the hearth. "Will you leave, please, so I may change?"

"No," he answered, his back turned away from her, "but dinna worry. I willna' peek."

Unwilling to start an argument, and feeling very cold, Brigette quickly discarded her wet clothing and wrapped herself in the blanket. Then she sat upon the fur rug and called Sly to her side.

Soon, Iain had a fire burning, then stood and began removing his own clothing. Brigette snapped her eyes shut, but then peeped curiously from beneath her thick, coppery lashes. Her breath caught raggedly in her throat at the sight of his magnificent, well-muscled physique. Leaving his broad, hairy chest bared, Iain wrapped himself in another green and black plaid.

"Drink this," he urged as he sat beside her on the rug and placed a flask of whiskey in her hands. "It will warm ye."

Together, they shared the whiskey and gazed at

the hearth's hypnotic flames. Idly, Brigette
stroked Sly's sleek coat and relaxed. Iain nonchalantly placed his arm around her bare shoulder
and drew her close. She raised her eyes to him so
innocently that he was reluctant to do what he
must. But there were no more tomorrows.

"Did I ever tell ye, Bria," he said, "of the grand
and glorious history of the MacArthur clan?"

Brigette smiled and shook her head.

"In olden times," he began, "the MacArthurs
were Scotland's premier family—second only to
the royal Stewarts—and chiefs of what is now
called clan Campbell. However, through a series
of bitter reversals durin' the past two hundred
years, the MacArthurs are not now clan chiefs, but
we still retain our earldom and the special privileges bestowed upon our family so long ago."

"What privileges?"

"A long, long time ago." Iain warmed to his subject, and the hand resting upon Brigette's shoulder began a slow caress, "King Malcolm conferred
special privileges upon the MacArthur and his pos-
terity. On any occasion when the royal standard is
unfurled, the MacArthurs lead the Scottish army."

"To be first in battle doesn't seem like a privilege to me."

"It isna' if yer a coward," Iain replied, pressing
an affectionate kiss on her forehead, "or a woman,
but the MacArthurs have long been known for
their bravery. There are other privileges, though.
Whenever a king or queen is crowned, the MacArthur, now the Earl of Dunridge, places the crown

upon the anointed head. When Queen Mary was a baby, my father placed the crown upon her head."

"Really?" Brigette was impressed.

"The Earl of Dunridge," he continued, "retains the privilege to sit without permission in the presence of Scottish royalty. Whenever a new monarch is crowned, the earl exercises this privilege, lest the royal Stewarts forget. It's now somethin' of a joke among the noble Scots and Highland chiefs."

"Why?"

"Well, as I said, whenever a new king or queen is crowned, the verra first thin' the MacArthur does is sit in his or her presence; and whenever there is a new Earl of Dunridge, the verra first thin' *he* does is attend the court to sit in the royal presence."

Brigette giggled, then asked, "If the MacArthurs were once clan chiefs, why are they not now?"

"We are the original stock of the mighty clan Campbell," Iain answered. "Ye might say the Duke of Argyll's ancestors were my ancestors' puir relations. John MacArthur, a verra great mon and the leader of a thousand warriors, was the clan chief durin' the reign of James the first. Although John was the king's mon and lived his life accordin' to the MacArthur motto, 'Faithful in Action,' he was much too powerful to suit the jealous King James."

"What happened?"

"The king ordered him beheaded, and the

chieftainship of the clan passed to the Campbell side of the family."

Sitting so close that their bodies touched, Brigette turned her head to look at him. Without forethought, she pressed a light kiss on his cheek.

Iain stared into incredible eyes of green, which glowed with love for him. Through an emotion-constricted throat, he vowed, "I love ye, lass." His lips covered hers, pouring all the love his heart contained into that single, stirring kiss. Like a flower opening to the radiant sun and basking in its warmth, Brigette returned the kiss in kind, and then some.

They fell back to the rug. Iain sprinkled kisses upon Brigette's eyelids, temples, nose, and throat. With his lips hovering above hers, he whispered, "Open yer eyes, sweet." When she obeyed, he asked, "Can ye return my love?"

"I do love you."

Gently, Iain kissed her again, then unwrapped the blanket, baring her flawless body. He smiled with tenderness when she blushed. "Yer verra bonnie, my lady." Iain pulled the plaid from his own body, and his lips swooped down to capture hers.

His hands roamed freely, reveled in the silky texture of his wife's skin. He caressed her breasts, teasing their pink-tipped peaks to aroused hardness. Brigette, feeling a throbbing heat ignite between her thighs, squirmed with desire. When Iain lowered his head to her breasts, licking and nursing upon their sensitive nipples, Brigette's breath caught raggedly in her throat.

Iain's hand slid lower to caress her wildly fluttering stomach, then dipped to the enticing slit between her thighs. Brigette tensed.

"Relax, hinny," he whispered hoarsely, his lips returning to hers. His powerful hand with its gentle touch remained where it was, caressing the soft skin of Brigette's inner thighs. Iain stroked her tiny button, and a bolt of hot sensation burst from that tiny center of her being. Brigette trembled, nearly delirious with the pleasure of it.

"Ye ken what I'm goin' to do?" he asked huskily.

Glazed with desire, Brigette's eyes opened, and Iain was certain that at this precise moment his wife was unable to recall her own name. He kissed her deeply and at the same time positioned himself between her thighs, the scarlet knob of his manhood poised at the opening of her moist, virginal tunnel.

"I love ye." He plunged deeply, breaking the maidenly barrier in one kind but powerful thrust.

Brigette cried out, and tears of surprised pain sprang from her eyes. Iain's mouth covered hers, his tongue thrusting as his manhood pierced. In spite of his desperate need, Iain lay motionless, allowing Brigette a moment to acquaint herself with the feel of him inside her.

My God! he marveled. The ultimate female— soft, hot, and tight! He moved then, in and out, gently and slowly. Brigette's breath came in shallow gasps, the valley between her thighs heating with each sweetly tormenting movement.

"Wrap yer legs around me," he ordered. When

she obeyed, his thrusts came deeper, faster, harder.

Innocence vanished and instinct emerged. Brigette arched her hips to meet each maddeningly wild thrust, building the tension that would surely kill her. She climbed a mountain of ecstacy and then peaked in screaming pleasure, floating gloriously back to earth as if riding a billowy cloud.

Calling her name, Iain tensed and shuddered, his seed flooding her. With their bodies joined as one, Iain rolled to the side and then kissed her, but Brigette was unaware. Her eyes were already closed in sated sleep.

Brigette felt something warm and moist tickling her face. "Ross, don't," she said, giggling, then heard his deep rumble of laughter.

"I amna' the guilty party," he protested, but the tickling continued.

Her eyes flew open, and Iain laughed at her surprised expression. Sly was licking her cheek.

"I'll let him out." Brigette modestly wrapped herself in the blanket, earning a mockingly arched brow from Iain, but he said nothing.

After Sly had answered nature's call, Brigette returned to the fur. Iain, his dark eyes glowing with love, kissed her deeply and thoroughly. Their moment of truth had arrived.

"I know a woman should not be so forward," Brigette said, giving him the perfect opening, "but I wish we were wed."

"We are." His voice was a light caress. Then he added, matter-of-factly, "We return to Dunridge in the mornin'. This raidin' season promises to be especially bloody."

"What?" Brigette stared blankly at him.

"We return to Dunridge, hinny, in the mornin'."

"*No!* We cannot go there!"

"We must."

"Ross." Brigette's voice was a contrite whisper. "Ross, I am not a Gypsy—"

Iain's laughter cut off her confession. "I'm aware of the fact ye arena' a Gypsy, Lady Brigette."

"You know who I am?" She was flabbergasted. "You know I'm your brother's wife?"

"Ye arena' my brother's wife, sweetheart."

"But I am!" she protested and sat up. "Iain and I were wed by proxy in England—"

"Listen to what I'm sayin', hinny," he interrupted, his voice gently insistent. "I am Iain MacArthur, yer husband."

"No, you are Ross MacArthur, the bastard son of the Earl of Dunridge."

"I am Iain *Ross* MacArthur, heir to the Earl of Dunridge," he said, smiling. "And yer my bonnie Sassenach bride, the future Countess of Dunridge." His hand reached to caress her cheek.

Understanding lit Brigette's eyes. She slapped his hand away and leaped to her feet, then glared at him in a murderous rage. "You lying . . . scheming . . . vile . . . underhanded . . . treacherous . . ." she sputtered, searching for a more hideous word to describe him.

Iain stood and towered over her, his size alone threatening. Humor had vanished from his expression; his eyes, so recently filled with love, had hardened coldly against her.

"Ye dare call me schemin' and lyin'?" Iain laughed harshly, then mimicked her lies. "The daughter of the king of the Gypsies, wi' hundreds of servants to do her biddin', no' to mention the cookin'. *The Sight!*" He snorted derisively.

Frightened, Brigette stepped back, but Iain captured her wrist in his steely grip. "We return to Dunridge in the mornin'."

"I won't!" Brigette hurled defiantly, her stubborn streak surfacing at his imperious tone. Absolutely no one, barring the queen, spoke to a Devereux in that overbearing, arrogant tone of voice. "I am returning to England," she added more calmly, her husband's size tempering her wrath. "The marriage will be annulled."

"Ye idiot!" Iain roared. "Our marriage is consummated—there can be nae annulment."

"Knave!" Brigette exploded. "You dirty, stinking, treacherous knave! I hate you!"

What little control Iain had on his temper disappeared with her words. He grabbed her shoulders and shook her roughly, his long fingers digging brutally into her tender flesh. "Ye hate me?" In a dangerously low and deadly voice, he asked, "Do ye know, my wee Sassenach wife, what life is like for the woman whose husband doesna' care for her? *Do ye?*"

Frightened, Brigette shook her head and Iain smiled grimly. He dragged her across the chamber, yanked the blanket from her quaking body, and shoved her onto the bed, then laughed without humor.

"When a mon is tied to a woman who hates him, she becomes a brood mare, a thin' for the breedin' of heirs. Like this . . ." Iain made a move toward her.

"Please, don't hurt me," Brigette whimpered, blinded by a blur of tears.

Iain stopped short, realizing with disgust what he was about to do to the woman he loved.

"Bloody Christ!" he swore, then turned on his heels and left the lodge, slamming the door behind.

Angry and hurt, Brigette lay back in the bed and pulled the blanket up, covering her quivering nakedness. Rolling over to face the wall, Brigette rued the day she'd first heard the name of MacArthur.

"Damn every treacherous one of them to hell," Brigette cursed softly, then surrendered to her sobs. Foolishly, she'd given her heart and body to Ross; but without warning, he'd changed into a monster called Iain. Her sister Heather was correct. Highlanders do kill and maim for pleasure. And torment unsuspecting innocents too!

When Iain returned, he sat at the table and watched her weeping, and became filled with remorse at his cruel treatment of her. In spite of her beguiling beauty, Iain knew his wife was a child, ignorant of men. But he was a full-grown man and should have known better, should have met her misplaced anger with patience. Unfortunately, her professed hatred had rendered him irrational, and he suffered for it.

Absently, Iain reached down to stroke Sly. The fox bared his teeth and growled low in his throat, then joined his mistress on the bed.

With his anger dissipated, Iain longed to offer his wife comfort and love, but his head overruled his heart. Brigette must learn proper obedience and respect, his mind countered unyieldingly. My young wife is obligated to please me, and when she does, I'll reward her with my gentle consideration. If she doesn't? Iain refused to think about that.

For the first time since she'd awakened at the lodge, Iain and Brigette passed the night separately—she sobbing in her sleep on the bed and he, sleepless, rolled in his plaid on the rug.

5

"Get up."

In the swirling mists of her sleep-befuddled brain, Brigette heard the commanding voice and sought to escape it. Rolling over, she drew the coverlet over her head.

"Get up, I said!" Iain yanked the coverlet, and startled, she bolted up.

Except for her puffy, red-rimmed eyes, Brigette looked sensuously bedraggled, as if interrupted in a lover's tryst. Iain's manhood tingled, but he ignored the powerful stirring that urged him to take her. A long day of riding lay before them. There would be many nights in their future when he'd enjoy the leisure to satisfy his urges.

Brigette stared groggily at her husband's forbidding countenance, then blushed, remembering their lovemaking of the previous evening. Almost immediately, fear marred her expression as she recalled what had come after.

"The oatmeal is ready," Iain said and turned away in regret, having recognized where her thoughts had wandered.

Brigette swung her legs over the side of the bed and stood. Retrieving her now-dry chemise, she pulled it over her head, then sat glumly at the table to eat the steaming porridge.

Ross—no, Iain—lied to me, she fumed in silence. He played me for a fool.

You lied too, an inner voice reminded her.

"I've thin's to do outside," Iain said abruptly. "Use this time for yer private needs." He gazed at Brigette for a long moment before leaving, but she refused to look up.

Tears of anger and despair welled up in her eyes, but Brigette fought them back. She forced herself to finish the porridge, then dressed and tidied the chamber in a futile attempt to keep her mind a blank. Brigette didn't want to think of the miserable life stretching endlessly in front of her. At seventeen years of age, she wondered dramatically, how many years of enduring my husband are left before death finally frees me from his clutches? Not only was her future bleak, but she'd lost the man she loved. Ross never existed, she reminded herself. What a fool I've been!

Iain returned and doused the still-smoldering fire in the hearth. With Sly at their heels, they stepped outside.

"Ye'll give me nae problems along the way or I'll tie ye and throw ye across my horse like so much baggage. Ye ken?" Iain threatened. Brigette nodded.

He lifted her onto the saddle and started to mount behind, but Brigette's voice stopped him. "Sly cannot walk so great a distance. Please, pass him to me."

Grim, Iain looked her straight in the eye. "The fox stays here."

"What?"

"Ye heard correctly," he answered coldly. "The beast remains in the wild, where he belongs."

"Sly's my pet!"

"Dinna use that shrewish tone wi' me," Iain warned. "Dunridge is nae place for a fox to abide. Ye had nae business makin' a wild beastie yer pet."

"Please," she pleaded, "Sly won't survive on his own." When he ignored her and mounted, she vowed in a small voice that cracked with loss, "I hate you."

"So ye've said," Iain whispered harshly against her ear, pulling her tightly, painfully against his unyielding body. "Yer repeatin' yerself."

As they rode away from the hunting lodge, tears streaked Brigette's cheeks, and she was unable to control the sobs escaping her throat. Sly tagged along behind them, running excitedly here and there, but always returning to follow the horse.

Brigette saw Sly following them, and eventually her sobbing subsided. Every few minutes, she peeked around her husband to see how her pet was faring. What will happen to Sly when we reach Dunridge? she wondered. Can I save him? If the monster who calls himself my husband causes Sly's death, Brigette vowed, I'll make his remaining years unspeakably miserable.

Each passing mile saw the fox tiring and his mistress worrying more and more. A mournful yelping suddenly rent the air and Brigette stiffened. Iain halted the horse. They looked back to see an exhausted Sly sitting a short distance away.

"He's too tired to go on," Brigette said, "and I'm certain he won't survive on his own."

"Yes," Iain agreed. "Stay here." He dismounted and drew his dagger, making Brigette gasp in horror.

"If you do this," she threatened, a sob catching in her throat, "I swear, at the first opportunity, I'll do the same to you."

"Keep yer mouth shut or ye'll regret it." Purposefully, Iain walked back to the fox. With his wife's muffled sobs at his back, he approached Sly, who wagged his long, bushy tail in greeting. Instinctively submissive to his mistress's mate, the fox rolled onto his back and gazed up with doleful eyes.

Iain glanced at Brigette, whose shoulders shook with grief, and then down at her pet. He sheathed his dagger and lifted Sly into his arms, pausing for the briefest moment to pat the fox. "Percy's likely to roast me for this," he muttered to himself, then walked back to the horse and placed Sly onto Brigette's lap.

Surprised, she looked up, and through tear-blinded eyes, met her husband's gaze. "Thank you," she whispered, and smiled tremulously.

Iain nodded curtly and mounted. Cuddling her beloved pet against her breast, Brigette relaxed and leaned against Iain. He decided, smiling somewhat speculatively at the top of her coppery crown, that subject to ridicule or not, he'd acted wisely.

It was afternoon when they sighted Dunridge Castle. Built in medieval times, the castle appeared bleak and forbidding to Brigette, even though she'd lived her entire life at Basildon, another medieval castle.

Iain halted his horse before they reached the outer gate. "Welcome to yer new home, my lady." His voice sounded almost friendly.

"Where is Loch Awe?"

"On the back side of Dunridge." Iain smiled, pleased that his wife was exhibiting interest in her new home.

"Ye'll act like a lady," he added, inadvertently ruining their truce, "and no' disgrace me before my—" Bristling at his words, Brigette cast him a scathing glance.

Realizing he'd said the wrong thing, Iain broke off and nudged his horse forward. As they passed through the gate and outer courtyard, the guards called a cordial greeting to Iain, then stared at Brigette and the furry creature nestled in her arms. Reaching the inner courtyard, they stopped in front of the main building's entrance.

"Iain! Lady Brigette!" Percy strode toward them. "Welcome!"

Iain dismounted and then helped Brigette, who smiled warmly at his brother. Much too warmly, in Iain's opinion.

"What's this ye've got?" Percy asked.

"My pet—" Before Brigette could finish speaking, one of Dunridge's hounds, having eluded the master-of-the-hounds, bounded up to them, intent on investigating the squirming bundle of copper fur in her arms.

With hackles rising upon his neck and back, the hound growled ominously and then barked. Frightened, Sly leaped from Brigette's arms and ran.

"Sly!" Brigette screamed and gave chase. Iain and Percy dashed after her.

Nipping at the fox's heels, the hound was fast, but Sly was faster. He raced around the side of the keep closest to the garrison house, whose occupants, hearing the uproar, rushed outside. A small fox was being chased by one of the hounds, who was also being chased by a shrieking madwoman who, in turn, was being chased by Iain and Percy! Sly flew into the rear garden, then scooted up the nearest tree. The furious hound leaped at the tree and barked madly, unable to reach his quarry.

Crazed by the thought that her pet might be eaten, Brigette charged into the garden after the hound, but her feet became tangled in her skirt and she fell. Sly's cries of fear and the hound's vicious barking broke the last thin thread of her composure. Downed by her own skirt, Brigette was unable to rise. She pressed her face into the dirt and wept disconsolately.

Rounding the side of the keep, Iain and Percy burst upon this scene. Behind them came a group of astonished men-at-arms. Iain raced for Brigette while Percy ran for the hound.

"Jamie," Percy called, dragging the hound away from the tree, "take him back to the kennel."

Iain lifted his wife from the ground. Nearly hysterical, Brigette wept within the safety of his embrace. She appeared battle weary; her skirt was torn and her face was smudged with dirt and streaked with tears.

"Are ye injured?"

Brigette shook her head and sobbed almost incoherently, "S-S-Sly . . ."

". . . is well," Iain finished.

Percy placed the trembling fox into her arms. Burying her face against her husband's chest, she wept with relief; and caught between the two, Sly fidgeted uncomfortably. Without thinking, Iain kissed the top of his wife's head, then cast his amazed warriors a warning glance. Reluctantly, they dispersed.

"Black Jack wants to see ye immediately," Percy informed them. "Dinna keep him waitin'. He's anxious to meet yer bride."

Iain tilted Brigette's chin up and smiled encouragingly. "Are ye ready, hinny?" In between sniffles, she nodded. He escorted her inside through the garden entrance, and then, certain his father preferred a private meeting, led her into the earl's study instead of the great hall.

The image of Iain as an old man rose from a chair near the hearth. John Andrew "Black Jack" MacArthur was still an impressive-looking man. He was extremely tall, well over six feet, and as sturdily built as an oak tree. His eyes were intensely dark like his son's, his hair liberally salted with silver, and his face was tanned and ruggedly chiseled. There was nothing ancient about this old man.

The earl stared in surprise at the two disheveled travelers and their animal companion. Black Jack saw before him a petite young woman, lovely but incredibly smudged and soiled, commonly dressed like a beggar or worse. Could *this* be the noble bride for whom he'd sent to England?

His eyes narrowed and shifted to his son. "This is yer wife?" he asked in amazed disbelief.

"Father, may I present Lady Brigette." Iain grinned a trifle sheepishly. "Bria, this is my father, the Earl." Humiliatingly aware of how she must appear, Brigette smiled shyly, and then curtsyed awkwardly, due to her grip on Sly.

"What did ye do to her?" Black Jack asked sharply, looking at his son. "And why?"

Iain opened his mouth to explain, but Brigette's tongue was faster. "He did nothing. I fell in the garden," she said. Iain smiled inwardly at his wife's ready defense of him.

"I wasna' speakin' to ye," the earl said. Brigette gaped at his rudeness, and her eyes narrowed into green slits of displeasure.

"It's as she said," Iain confirmed.

"What's that yer carryin'?" the earl asked, his gaze falling on the fox.

Thinking the father was as disagreeable as the son, Brigette looked him straight in the eye and squared her shoulders determinedly, ready to do battle. "This is my pet fox, Sly."

"Get rid of it, Iain."

"The hell he will!" Brigette's anger flared, and Iain fought to hide a smile.

"What did ye say to me?" Black Jack was appalled.

"*I said, the hell he will!*" she roared, then added softly, "Sly is my pet. You have no authority."

"N-nae authority?"

"Ye made the match," Iain interjected, stepping between them. "What would ye have me do?"

"I am returning to England," Brigette announced, stepping from behind her husband, whose eyes lost their humor. "We will annul the marriage. I've no wish to continue with this arrangement, especially after what happened last night."

"Last night?" Black Jack arched a questioning brow.

"Your son almost raped me."

Iain burst out laughing. Black Jack stared openmouthed at her, then asked his son in a loud whisper, "Is she simple?"

"*Simple?* Why, you blustering old man!"

"*Blusterin' old mon?*"

"Enough!" Iain shouted, then turned on his wife. "Dinna talk nonsense, Bria. A mon canna rape his wife."

"But you almost forced me to—"

"It's a mon's right to take his wife as he pleases, whether she be willin' or no'," Iain informed her, then smiled arrogantly. "That's the law."

"The law! You expect me to honor Scotland's law in this? I absolutely—"

"It's God's law, no' Scotland's," Black Jack interrupted. In an amused voice, he asked, "Dinna the English obey God's law?"

Brigette's face mottled with humiliated rage, but Iain deftly brushed over it. "Since the vows have been spoken and the marriage consummated, we'll be hearin' nae more nonsense of annulment. Moireach!" Obviously eavesdropping at the door, a middle-aged woman entered the instant Iain called.

"Bria," he said, giving her no chance for protest, "this is Moireach, the mother of Dugie and Jamie. She'll escort ye and Sly upstairs, then fetch yer tirewoman."

The woman's smile was friendly enough, so Brigette went along with her. "I'll stay for the time being," she said, pausing for a moment at the door to glance back at the earl, "but I must insist your hounds be penned. I won't have Sly terrorized."

"Yer lettin' her keep that beast?" Black Jack asked when she'd gone.

"I dinna have a choice." Iain shrugged his shoulders, then grinned. "The lady threatened to skewer me wi' my own dagger if any harm befell her precious pet."

Black Jack threw back his head and shouted with laughter. "She's verra bonnie and will make ye a fine mate."

"How can ye say that?" Iain countered incredulously. "The twit is a temperamental wildcat."

"That she is," the earl agreed. "But once ye've made her purr, she'll breed us a dozen hellions to

carry on the MacArthur name. And dinna shake
yer head as if I'm droolin' in my dotage."

Well into her middle years, Moireach was still a
handsome woman. Though small of stature and
friendly in demeanor, her crisp blue eyes held an
inner strength that brooked no nonsense from
anyone. Sprinkled with silver, Moireach's carrot-
colored hair spoke of her obstinacy in seeing matters settled to her own satisfaction.

This woman was no mere servant, Brigette decided, but a formidable force within the house-
hold. Only with Moireach's approval and support
could she truly become the lady of Dunridge.

"Yer verra bonnie," the housekeeper complimented as she led Brigette across the foyer to the
stairs. "That young rascal must be glad he bowed
to the earl's wishes and took a Sassenach—I mean
—English wife."

Moireach looked at Brigette, who, ignorant that
"Sassenach" was derogatory, smiled politely but
made no comment. By allowing the accidental insult to pass, Brigette won, however inadvertently,
an important ally.

"Ye were correct to stand up to the earl,"
Moireach's chatter continued. "He's a bit old-fash-
ioned aboot women and such thin's. Iain's like him
in that respect, but I could tell he's taken wi' ye—
no' that I was listenin', mind ye."

Iain's chamber was at the head of the stairs.
Before entering, Moireach paused and pointed to
another door. "That chamber's connected to
Iain's, but I doubt ye'll be callin' it yer own. Yer

randy husband is certain to insist ye share his bed each night. We could make the other a nursery once ye've a babe planted in yer belly."

Horrified, Brigette stared at the housekeeper. She was being suffocated by MacArthurs and their minions. Had it been like this for her mother as a bride? And what of her sister Kathryn, now transplanted in Ireland? I am a Devereux, Brigette told herself. How can I be anything else?

"I'm fairly anticipatin' another wee one to cosset," Moireach said. "He'll be company for wee Glenda."

"Glenda?"

"Iain's niece," the housekeeper answered, then opened the chamber door. "Here we are."

Spring was waiting inside. The two cousins flew into each other's arms, but came up short and giggled. Brigette was still holding Sly.

"Ye've a fine-lookin' pet, Lady Brigette," Moireach said as she left, "but he willna' be welcomed at supper. I'll bring him a bite later."

"Thank you."

After introducing Spring and Sly, Brigette set the fox down and hugged her cousin properly. Here was a familiar Devereux face. "Oh, cuz!" she exclaimed. "I'm so glad to see you."

"It was wrong of you to run," Spring chided. "I was worried."

"I had no choice, but I'm sorry I left you alone to deal with these—these . . ."

"People, Brie. They're very nice people."

"How can you say that?" Brigette cried. "Why, the earl—"

"Is gruff and unpolished," Spring interrupted, "but a kind man, nevertheless. Why did you run away?"

"You know my husband insulted me."

"It was not his fault. If you had only waited—"

"I do not wish to speak of this." Brigette cut her off. "What's done is past."

"Have you forgiven each other?"

"Forgiven each other? For what?"

"Have you forgiven Lord MacArthur for—?"

"I understand your words," Brigette interrupted, "but why should he be forgiving of me? I've done nothing."

Spring was becoming exasperated. "You ran away."

"Is that tub for me?" Brigette asked abruptly. With a disapproving shake of her head, Spring took her cousin's hint.

"Yes, and I can see you're in urgent need of it."

Spring helped her disrobe and climb into the steaming, scented water. Brigette giggled with the simple joy of submerging herself in the hot tub, and began washing. "I owe you an outfit."

"Nonsense! You took only rags."

"I insist. How's Jamie?"

Spring blushed. "I have a certain f-fondness for him."

"And he for you?" Brigette teased, smiling at her cousin's embarrassment.

"Yes." Spring's face was vivid scarlet. "What of Lord MacArthur?"

Evading the question, Brigette dunked her head beneath the water, but her cousin's words had somehow conjured up the man. Spring looked up in surprise when the door opened, and Brigette's gaze followed hers.

"M-m-my lord," she said. "I'm b-bathing."

"So I see." Iain smiled lazily.

"Do you mind?" Brigette asked haughtily, arching a perfectly shaped brow at him.

"I dinna mind at all," he answered pleasantly, as he sat on the edge of the bed and watched, "but if ye must bath first, leave the water warm for me." Stretching his long legs out, Iain relaxed and thoroughly enjoyed the sight of his wife at her toilet.

Tilting her upturned nose in the air, Brigette pointedly refused to acknowledge his infuriating presence, though she was unable to forget he was there. Finishing her bath quickly, she stepped from the tub and Spring toweled her dry. Brigette felt mortified to be naked beneath her cousin's hand and her husband's eye. When Spring reached for a bedrobe, Iain's voice stopped her.

"Dinna bother wi' that, lass." Iain rose and stretched. Looking meaningfully at the tirewoman, he began to undress. With a squeak of dismay, Spring fled the chamber.

Iain glanced at Brigette, nude and frozen where she stood. "Get into the bed," he ordered, not unkindly.

"W-what?"

"Is yer hearin' impaired?" he teased. "I said, get into the bed." For a long moment, dark eyes and green clashed across the short distance separating them.

"The ride from the hunting lodge wearied me,"

Brigette said, turning away to slip into the bed. "I do whatever I choose, not what you command." With that, she yanked the coverlet up to her chin. Sly promptly joined her.

Iain ignored her remark and climbed into the tub, then groaned with pleasure as his body sank into the warm water. "Ye might thank me for savin' yer friend there," he chided gently, casting a mildly reproachful look at Brigette, who was watching him warily.

"Thank you, my lord."

"First thin' tomorrow," he continued, "we'll get some sort of distinguishin' collar for Sly. We dinna want the castle folk reachin' for their weapons when he's aboot."

"Thank you, again, my lord."

Unconcerned with his magnificent nakedness, Iain climbed out of the tub and toweled himself dry. "The earl is quite taken wi' ye," he added casually.

"W-what?" Surprised, Brigette opened the eyes she'd snapped shut against her husband's nudity. She was of the opinion the old man had taken an instant dislike to her.

With his hands resting on his lean hips, Iain stood beside the bed and gazed down at her. "I would clear the air between us, my lady. Will ye answer a question?"

Brigette nodded, afraid to refuse, and her gaze drifted to the flaccid appendage perched at his groin. Even at rest, she thought irrelevantly, it's large.

As Iain noted her expression, his lips twitched

with amusement. "Yesterday ye told Ross ye loved him," he said. "I am Ross, sweetheart, and I havena' changed. Why are ye angry wi' me?"

"You lied to me."

Iain lifted Sly from the bed and set him on the floor. Gently disengaging Brigette's fingers from their tense grip on the coverlet, he slid in beside her. "Ye also lied," he reminded without accusation.

"But you knew!" she blurted.

"Knew what?"

"You knew I was lying."

"So!" Iain chuckled. "Yer angry wi' me cuz I knew ye were lyin', but ye didna' realize I was also lyin'. Correct?"

"I guess," she murmured, her eyes downcast. Put into that context, her anger did seem childish.

Iain gently forced her to look at him, and when she did, he smiled almost tenderly. "May I ask why ye lied in the first place, and why ye ran away?" Embarrassed, Brigette tried to look away, but he prevented her from doing so. "We'll be married a verra long time, my lady, and I would have this behind us."

"I-I was insulted b-because you neither cared to attend our wedding nor rode out with your men to greet me."

"I swear it was circumstances that prevented me, hinny. I did care that I couldna' attend our weddin' and rode all night to reach yer camp by mornin'. Ye'd already flown."

"Oh." Brigette was shamefaced.

Drawing her close, Iain pressed a kiss on her forehead. "Would ye care to ask me somethin'?" When she looked away, he added, "Dinna be shy."

"Why did you lie to me?" she asked, her need to know stronger than her embarrassment.

"Cuz I knew ye didna' like me. I believed it best to become acquainted wi'out our real names gettin' in the way."

"But . . ." Brigette broke off.

"Spit it out," Iain persisted. "If somethin' else is botherin' ye, I want to hear it."

Humiliated, Brigette stared at the mat of dark hair covering his chest. "W-why did you hurt me last night?"

Iain scowled, angry with himself. "I'm sorry for that, hinny. When ye said ye hated me, I nearly lost control."

"But I don't." Brigette looked up and met his dark-eyed gaze. "Hate you, I mean. It was my anger speaking."

Iain grinned. "Ye dinna hate me?"

"No," she whispered, shaking her head in a way that reminded him of a little girl.

"Well, that's a fair beginnin' for us." Without warning, Iain lowered his lips to hers, felt her trembling fear and kissed her gently, so very gently.

Drawing back, he smiled and vowed, "I willna' hurt ye again, my lady, I swear." Again his lips met hers, kissing more deeply this time.

"Brie," she breathed against his lips.

"What?"

"Call me Brie—all my friends do."

"Brie," Iain murmured as his lips covered hers.

Brigette's lips parted in an unmistakable invitation, and Iain's tongue slipped in, caressing the moist velvet within. Intoxicated by her husband's lingering kiss, Brigette's arms creeped up and entwined his neck, her hands moving across his broad, muscular shoulders. Leaving her lips, his tongue teased a path across her silky cheek to her earlobe, then slipped down to her slender throat, sending hot shivers dancing down her spine.

One of his hands wandered to her breasts, then caressed and weighed the small but heavy globes in the palm of his hand. His head dipped lower, and his burning lips blazed a trail to those soft mounds. Drawing back, Iain paused to admire and circled one rose-hued nipple with the tip of his forefinger.

"I love yer titties," he whispered huskily, "so soft and firm. Yer nipples are large, good for arousin' a mon and feedin' a sucklin' bairn."

Brigette quivered at his words, feeling a thousand airy butterflies winging within her stomach. At the same time, a familiar throbbing sensation began pulsing between her thighs.

Iain lowered his head to one tingling breast, and his mouth captured its sensitive nipple, the tip of his tongue taunting the hardened peak. When his lips pulled masterfully on it, Brigette was caught in maddening pleasure. Moaning throatily, she yielded to her husband's powerful force and arched upward, her hands almost desperately pressing his head to her breast.

Iain's hand slid between her thighs, which parted at his light yet commanding touch. One of his skillful fingers traced a path down the wet crevice and then up again. With his wife's own juices, he massaged her female button and groaned to feel it swelling beneath his finger.

With his shaft dripping excitement, Iain knelt between Brigette's thighs, then raised her hips. The knob of his desire touched her moist entry. Its tip teased her nether lips, gently coaxing them open like the petals of a blossoming flower, and then pierced her hot, tight passage. As he moved his hips seductively, Iain watched his fingers taunt his wife's swollen jewel and admired its passionate size.

Wild contractions surged through Brigette's body, and she arched her hips instinctively, urgently. "Fill me, Iain!" she wailed, her brilliant green eyes opening and startling him.

The invitation was irresistible. Iain buried his shaft to the hilt of her female sheath. He pulled back, then thrust fiercely again and again.

Brigette's body rose to meet each mighty thrust of Iain's. She cried out, carried away by wave after wave of blissful sensation. Clasping her tightly, Iain shuddered and flooded her throbbing passage, which squeezed every drop of life he had to give.

After several breathless moments, Iain lowered Brigette to the bed and then kissed her. It was so gentle and tender a kiss that a teardrop slowly coursed down her flushed cheek. Tenderly, he brushed it away and lay down, then drew her close. Both were silent, neither willing to risk losing the love they'd found in their bed, and then they slept.

6

Shifting Sly's weight into the crook of one arm, Iain opened his chamber door and entered silently. He set the fox down, then looked at the bed where Brigette slept.

Man and beast were irresistibly drawn to the sleeping woman. Sly padded across the chamber and leaped onto the bed, then snuggled comfortably against his mistress's back.

Iain followed Sly. Sitting on the edge of the bed, he leisurely surveyed his wife's charms. Her copper hair was in adorable disarray; her creamy skin and rosy lips tantalized his memory of the previous night. Brigette's small, turned-up nose combined with her delicately pointed chin to give proof of her irrepressible nature.

A smile tugged at Iain's lips when he realized he hadn't even begun to inventory what was hidden beneath the coverlet. Brigette's lips were moist and parted in the most compelling manner. Iain leaned over and pressed his lips against them.

"Mmmm." A soft sigh of contentment escaped Brigette's throat.

Iain sat back and grinned as her eyes fluttered open. Warm and lushly green, he thought, eyes the color of a Highland landscape in summer.

"Supper?" she asked groggily.

"Was last night," he answered.

"Oh. Sly?"

"Beside ye."

Brigette reached behind to touch the fox and smiled to feel him snuggled so close.

"We'll breakfast together in the great hall," Iain said. "There are others here ye must meet."

Brigette nodded. Iain caressed her silken cheek, and turning her head, she pressed a kiss on his hand.

"We'll ride to Loch Awe after breakfast," he continued, his voice hoarse at her gesture, "and later we'll visit wi' several of the crofters so they can meet Dunridge's new lady."

"Sly must be in agony," she said abruptly, thinking the fox had been penned in their chamber all night.

"I've just returned from takin' him out," Iain said, then chuckled. "I do believe he's made a conquest of Moireach. There was an empty bowl on the floor this mornin'. Oh, I almost forgot." From the top of his plaid Iain produced a leather dog's collar, dyed a brilliant shade of yellow. "This is for Sly."

"It's certainly bright."

"We dinna want puir Sly mistaken for a wild beastie, do we?"

Smiling, Brigette shook her head and sat up, letting the coverlet dip to reveal the enticing swell of her breasts. At her bidding, Iain fastened the startling yellow collar around the fox's neck.

"Now, dear Sly," she complimented, patting the fox, "you are assuredly the most dashing beast in this realm. Wouldn't you say, Iain?"

"Verra bonnie," he agreed as Sly, frustrated in his attempt to remove the collar, leaped off the bed. "All the Highland vixens will be frantic wi' yearnin' when they see him. Shall I call Spring for ye, hinny?"

A mischievous gleam leaped into green eyes, and Brigette let the coverlet fall to her waist, exposing her perfectly formed breasts. One hand slid up Iain's arm to caress his cheek. "Is it so late?" she murmured. "Must we breakfast now?"

Iain stared at her beckoning, rose-hued nipples. With a growl of pure lust, he pushed her back to the pillows, but her hands reached out to hold him at bay.

"Won't we be missed in the great hall?" she teased with feigned innocence.

"No." His lips covered hers in an endless, devouring kiss.

Morning was a feeble old man by the time Iain and Brigette walked into the great hall, which strangely enough was still crowded. Feeling many curious eyes turn in their direction, Brigette hesitated for a fraction of a second.

"Dinna be nervous," Iain whispered. "Black

Jack is the worst Dunridge can offer, and ye weathered that storm quite nicely."

"I'm not nervous," she returned, lifting her chin a notch, "merely surprised to find so many people congregating here at this hour of the day."

"Is that so?" A dark eyebrow arched at her in mock suspicion. "Was there a hidden motive behind yer seduction of me this mornin'?"

Blood rushed to her face, but before she could reply, Percy was standing in front of them. "Good mornin', brother," he greeted. "Lady Brigette."

"Brie," she corrected, smiling warmly at him. "Call me Brie. Remember?"

"I havena' forgotten." Percy looked at Iain. "As ye can see, those who could lingered aboot to steal a peek at yer wife. Ye disappointed a great many last night by stayin' secluded in yer chamber." Iain frowned at his brother's teasing.

"Where's yer pet?" Percy asked, turning to his sister-in-law.

Recalling the previous day's fiasco in the garden, Brigette blushed and stammered, "Iain—I—we thought it best that Sly remain upstairs."

" 'Tis ill done of ye, Brie. No one has secrets at Dunridge, and many are here to see for themselves this miraculously trained beast of yers."

"Leave off," Iain growled. "Brie and I are verra hungry and want to eat in peace. Ye ken?"

"I ken," Percy teased, "especially considerin' the strenuous exercise to which ye must've subjected yerselves."

Brigette flushed with embarrassment; Iain scowled, thinking the whole castle probably knew the exact number of times he'd had his wife. Without another word to his brother, Iain led his wife toward the high board.

Brigette tensed when she saw a beautiful young woman seated at the place usually reserved for the ranking lady of the castle. As the wife of Dunridge's heir, Brigette was that lady. Unless . . .

"Is your father wed a second time?" she whispered.

"No." Iain's gaze followed hers, and he understood the bent of her thoughts. Damn Antonia! he cursed inwardly.

At the high board, Iain greeted his father. Brigette, uncertain of the earl's reception, smiled but remained silent.

Black Jack nodded at her, then looked at his son. "Well, ye've had yerself a fine rest."

"Yes." Iain grinned at his father's teasing. "And I'm takin' a few hours to show Brie some of the sights. Unless there's somethin' urgent?"

"When ye return will be time enough to begin work." Black Jack's gaze drifted to Brigette. "Ye appear well rested, lassie. Where's yer pet?"

"Safely shut away in our chamber, where he'd better be when we return."

Black Jack burst out laughing. "Dinna worry on that account," he assured her. "Yer husband is yer laird and master. If he's allowin' ye to keep the beastie, I've nae problem wi' it." Black Jack flicked a glance at Iain, then added drily, "I'm only the earl and his father."

Standing nearby, Percy hooted with laughter,

and the earl cast his youngest son a scathing glance. Percy's laughter choked off abruptly to muffled chuckles.

Iain could no longer delay the inevitable. He turned to acknowledge the woman seated beside Black Jack.

Antonia MacKinnon MacArthur was a long-legged, full-bosomed, curvaceously slim beauty. Crowning her goddesslike body was an angel's face. She had eyes of blue, a small, straight nose, and skin of ivory silk. Pale blond hair, thick and luxuriant, was pulled away from her incredible face and plaited into one braid that fell to her waist.

The two women eyed each other stonily, natural enemies at first sight. Brigette was furious that Antonia had usurped her seat as Dunridge's ranking lady; Antonia knew Brigette was the reason her scheme to become Dunridge's next countess had failed.

"Brigette, I present Lady Antonia, my brother Malcolm's widow," Iain said stiffly. "Antonia, this is Lady Brigette."

Determined to make her young adversary feel like an outsider, Antonia looked her over, then smiled coldly. Returning the frigid stare, Brigette merely nodded her head in acknowledgment, her haughty gesture confounding the other woman.

Iain hoped to avoid the brewing storm by leading Brigette to the end of the table. Later, he would order Antonia to give up the position she'd enjoyed until now. Malcolm was dead and she'd not managed to produce an heir. Brigette was

Dunridge's ranking lady and would be treated as such.

"Tsk! Tsk!" Antonia whispered loudly to the earl. "I dinna believe Sassenach women are properly schooled in manners."

Brigette whirled around. "I beg your pardon?"

"And well ye should," Antonia snapped. "Ye failed to curtsy to me."

"Nor shall I," Brigette said in a voice oozing superiority, delighting their audience. "I am Dunridge's ranking lady, and stealing my chair will not change your position."

Black Jack and Percy howled with laughter. Antonia cast them a disgusted glance, then turned beseeching eyes on Iain, appealing for his support.

"Dinna upset yerself, hinny," Iain said to Brigette. Staring coldly at Antonia, he added, "This is the last time she'll be sittin' there."

Iain led Brigette to the far end of the high board, where they would have a small measure of privacy. Once seated, he stared pointedly at the hall's occupants, who were watching in barely contained amusement. It was obvious to all that Iain had been downed by Cupid's arrow. Beneath Iain's dour stare, the MacArthur warriors dispersed to their various duties, but lingering so long had been worth the wait.

"Good mornin'." Moireach appeared from nowhere to greet them, then chuckled. "Or what's left of it."

She set two bowls of steaming oat porridge, accompanied by cream and honey, on the table in front of them. There was freshly baked bread, creamy butter, jam, and cheese. She'd brought a mug of brown ale for Iain and milk for Brigette.

"I'm not overly fond of milk," Brigette said. "I'd prefer ale or wine."

"Now, my lady," the housekeeper insisted gently, "yer ripe to get wi' child. Ye must drink a mug of milk each and every day. Of course, ye'll drink more when I'm certain this rascal's seed has hit its mark. It's best to drink it in the mornin' if ye've nae fondness for it. Then ye willna' be frettin' aboot it the whole livelong day."

"As you wish." Brigette forced herself to smile pleasantly at the well-intentioned woman, then lifted the mug and sipped the milk.

"Ye make such a handsome couple," Moireach gushed. "I canna wait to see yer bairns."

Brigette choked on the milk, and Iain, smothering a chuckle, slapped her back helpfully.

"Well, I've duties need attendin'," Moireach said, turning away. "I'm cookin' Iain's favorite for supper—haggis."

"Haggis?" Brigette asked, turning to Iain. "What is it?"

"A Highland delicacy."

"Consisting of what?"

"The heart, liver, and lungs of a sheep minced wi' suet, onions, oatmeal, and seasonin'." Iain grinned broadly. "Then the whole mixture is boiled in the sheep's stomach."

Brigette gulped, fighting nausea, and pushed her plate away. "I'm not as hungry as I had believed," she whispered.

Iain swallowed his laughter. "Shall we go, then?"

It was an uncommon day in the Highlands, a rarity of cloudless sky and dazzling sunshine and crisp air. The sky was a blanket of blue covering a riot of autumn's vibrant colors—gold, red, and orange mingled with evergreen.

Iain and Brigette gazed silently at the wondrous sight in front of them. Loch Awe shimmered with sunbeams dancing on top of its sparkling blue water. Brigette was overwhelmed by nature's glory and even Iain, accustomed to this sight, was not unaffected.

"Impressive, is it no'?" he commented, catching his wife's expression of wonder.

"Awe-inspiring," she replied. Iain chuckled, pleased by her wit and everything else about his wife.

Leaving the loch behind, they stopped to visit several of the crofters, who greeted them with genuine warmth and offered what little they could in the way of hospitality. Whatever doubts Iain may have had concerning his wife vanished as he watched her charming his crofters and their families.

For her part, Brigette was impressed with the crofters' simple dignity and generosity. She filled with pride at the obvious esteem in which they held Iain and admired him for returning in kind that respect to his people. Most pleasantly surprising of all was their easy acceptance of her as their new lady.

* * *

When they returned to Dunridge, Brigette slipped from her horse. Intending to take Sly for a walk in the gardens, she dashed into the foyer and headed for the stairs, then came face to face with her cousin, who was carrying the fox.

Smiling, Spring shrugged her shoulders. "I couldn't bear the sounds of his lonely whining any longer."

"I'll take him," Brigette said and lifted Sly into her arms. "Order a bath for me. I won't be long."

Brigette stepped outside and looked around cautiously. No hounds were running loose. She set Sly down, then noticed a small girl sitting alone. Thinking the child was Iain's niece, Brigette walked over and sat beside her. They exchanged easy smiles.

Five-year-old Glenda was the picture of Antonia. The only dissimilarity was a smattering of freckles sprinkled across her nose.

"You must be Glenda," Brigette said.

"Yes, ye are Lady Brigette?"

"Yes, but you must call me Brie—all my friends do."

The sparkle that leaped into Glenda's eyes reminded Brigette of Loch Awe. "Are we to be friends, then?"

Seeing the child's hopeful expression, Brigette felt an insistent tugging at her heart. "Of course. Do you want to be my friend?"

"I do."

"Why are you sitting here alone?" Brigette asked.

"It's my play time."

"Well, why are you not playing?"

Glenda's expression drooped. "I've nae friend wi' whom I can play."

"I don't believe that," Brigette scoffed gently. "A sweet girl like you must have many friends."

"I have ye."

"But what of the other children at Dunridge?"

"I amna' allowed to play wi' them. I did once and was punished."

"Who won't let you to play with the others?"

"Mother," Glenda told her. "There's nae use in sneakin', cuz whenever I am doin' somethin' bad, she knows."

"I see." Brigette lapsed into thoughtfulness. What a supercilious bitch Antonia is! As a child, I was allowed to play with the other castle children. Why shouldn't Glenda?

Sly sat down in front of them. Cocking his head to one side, he wagged his long tail.

Brigette chuckled. "I believe Sly has decided to befriend you."

"Sly's yer dog?"

"He's mine," Brigette said with a laugh, "but no dog. Sly is a fox."

"A fox? May I touch him?"

"Yes."

Glenda reached out to pat Sly, who seized the opportunity to lick her hand. When she giggled in surprised delight, he licked her again.

"Sly is a special fox," Brigette exaggerated. "When I was hopelessly lost in the forest, he saved my life."

"Ye were lost in the forest? He saved yer life?"

Brigette nodded solemnly, ready to embellish her tale. "And—"

"How verra impressive," Antonia sneered, towering above them. Brigette leaped to her feet, but Antonia ignored her and vented her wrath upon Glenda. "Yer a naughty chit! I told ye to stay away from the Sassenach. Now go to yer chamber."

"Stay where you are," Brigette ordered, then turned on Antonia. "The child did nothing wrong."

"Mind yer own business," Antonia shrieked.

"What's goin' on here?" Black Jack's voice boomed out as he approached them. "What's all this shoutin' aboot?"

"The Sassenach is interferin' wi' my daughter," Antonia raged. "She hasna' the right!"

"Glenda only spoke with me," Brigette explained. "She's not deserving of punishment."

"I agree wi' ye," Black Jack said.

"But I am Glenda's mother," Antonia insisted.

"That's a fact ye only occasionally remember," Black Jack said, his expression darkening with anger. "Glenda can pass her time wi' whomever she wishes." When Antonia opened her mouth to protest, he added, "As head of this family, I will be obeyed. Ye ken?" Without another word, Antonia stalked off.

"Thank you, my lord," Brigette said.

"Dinna concern yerself wi' her. She's angry cuz Malcolm died and ruined her chance to become a countess." Black Jack looked at Glenda, who was staring up at him with an expression akin to awe. "Do ye like yer new aunt from England, lassie?"

Glenda nodded, too shy to speak to this larger-than-life man who was her grandfather.

"And her wily friend here?"

Again the little girl nodded. Black Jack smiled and decided to give Glenda more of his attention. "Would ye care to walk aboot wi' yer grandfather?"

"I would," she whispered, then shyly placed her hand in his.

"Did I ever tell ye, hinny," Black Jack asked as they strolled away, "who ye were named after . . . ?"

Brigette and Sly walked through the foyer and headed for the stairs. Antonia's voice, raised in anger, drifted out from the great hall. Brigette ignored it and started up the stairs, then halted when she recognized Spring's voice raised in self-defense. How dare Antonia reprimand her cousin! With angry determination stamped across her features, Brigette marched into the great hall.

"I told ye," Antonia was shouting at Spring, "to fetch my sewin', and ye'd better do it."

"And I told you," Spring shouted back, "I must see to Lady Brigette's bath."

Antonia raised her hand to strike, but Brigette grabbed it from behind and whirled her around. "Spring is my tirewoman, not a castle servant. Refrain from ordering her about!"

What little control Antonia had on her temper vanished. With a shriek of frustrated rage, she lashed out, slapping Brigette hard across the face.

Brigette retaliated instantly, slapping the blond beauty just as hard.

"Ladies!" Iain bellowed, striding across the hall. "And I use the term loosely."

Tears welled up in Antonia's eyes as she faced him. "Lady Brigette attacked me for nae good reason," she sobbed.

"Cease orderin' my wife's tirewoman aboot," Iain commanded, unmoved by her delicate weeping. "And dinna strike my wife again. Go to yer chamber and dinna return till supper."

"She struck me," Antonia countered. "What aboot her?"

"I'll deal wi' my wife," he assured her. "She willna' strike ye again."

"Am I to be blamed for this?" Brigette was outraged.

"Antonia," Iain repeated, ignoring his wife's outburst. "I told ye to leave."

"Well?" Brigette challenged after Antonia had gone. "Am I to be sent to my chamber and ordered to keep my hands to myself?"

"I'd never order ye to keep yer hands to yerself," Iain said, then grinned suggestively. "Go to yer chamber—I'll join ye shortly."

7

On a cold and bleak November afternoon, Glenda stood in the winter-barren garden. She threw a ball to Sly, who caught it in his mouth and returned it to her. Laughing, Brigette clapped her hands appreciatively at the fox's newly learned trick.

"My playtime is nearly over," Glenda said glumly.

"I suspect so," Brigette replied. "Would you like to make it last a little longer?"

"Yes, but Mother will be angry wi' me."

Brigette smiled mischievously. "I've devised a system for always doing what I want and never catching trouble."

"What is it?" Glenda's eyes gleamed with excitement.

Before speaking, Brigette glanced around cautiously as if looking for eavesdroppers. "Life has two paths you may follow, the long road and the short road," she told the little girl. "When there's a thing I don't want to do, I always take the long road. That way I delay whatever it is I don't want to do. For example, when playtime is over, the short road is through that garden door. The long road is walking all the way around to the front courtyard."

"What if Mother or Grandfather becomes angry wi' me?"

"You have a course of action available in that event. If it's a man, like your grandfather, you must bat your eyelashes like so." With great exaggeration, Brigette batted her eyelashes, and giggling, Glenda imitated her.

"Excellent!" Brigette exclaimed. "Never forget that a beautiful woman who bats her eyelashes at a man is irresistible." Glenda laughed and Brigette added, "It's silly but true."

"What if my mother is angry?"

"If it's a woman, like your mother," Brigette answered, "then you must do the same thing you do after you've batted your eyelashes at a man."

"Which is?"

"You lie."

"Lyin' is a terrible sin," Glenda cried. "It's naughty!"

"Nonsense! As there are two roads to follow, there are two kinds of lies," Brigette explained. "A bad lie almost always hurts someone. A good lie is an excuse and keeps a loved one from becoming hurt or angry. In other words, a bad lie causes pain, but a good lie prevents it."

"I ken," Glenda said. "When Moireach asks if

I've eaten all of my porridge, I must say yes, even if I've given it to Sly. The real truth would make Moireach angry, and we dinna want that to happen."

"Correct." Brigette hugged her. "The choice is yours. Shall we travel the long road or the short road inside?"

Glenda smiled. "The long road."

Followed by Sly, Brigette and Glenda walked hand in hand around the keep. The earl stood in the front courtyard to greet Iain and Percy, who were dismounting.

"How did it go?" Black Jack asked his eldest. Iain started to reply but caught sight of his wife. Smiling, he watched her advance on them.

"Keep yer mind on business, damn it," Black Jack swore, making his youngest son chuckle. "I asked ye how it went down?"

"Better than we'd hoped," Iain told him. "We lifted aboot thirty head of Menzies' cattle."

"That should be strainin' the mon this winter," Percy said.

"I'm doublin' our own guards 'til the first snow," Iain added.

The earl smiled. "That's good news."

"No, Kevin," sounded Moireach's irritated voice. "Get back to yer duties. Ye willna' be botherin' the laird wi' such a triflin' matter. Get back, I said!"

One of Dunridge's apprentice cooks marched into the courtyard. Moireach followed behind, irately protesting all the way. Approaching the earl, Kevin held a mutilated chicken high in the air for all to see. " 'Tis the third one this week," he announced. "None has been eaten, just killed."

"I'm verra sorry," Moireach apologized, "but he wouldna' listen to me."

"It's all right," Black Jack assured her, then looked at Kevin. "Well, lad, do ye've any idea who did this?"

"I've been keepin' a close watch," the young man answered, "but whoever's doin' it is as sly as a fox."

At Kevin's words, silence enveloped the group. Each glanced nervously at Sly and then his mistress.

"Do ye know anythin' aboot this?" Iain asked his wife.

"Me?" Brigette exclaimed. "Why would I kill a chicken?"

"I dinna mean ye, personally," he returned, his expression grim. "Someone ye know, perhaps?"

Brigette was bewildered for a moment, but then her husband's meaning dawned on her. "How dare you suggest such a vile thing!" she cried. "Sly would not kill for pleasure, and he's certainly not hungry."

"Can ye vouch for his whereaboots every minute of the past week?" Iain countered.

"Yes."

"Brigette."

"All right!" Brigette shouted. "No, but that does not mean—"

"Enough!" he interrupted. "Bringin' him here was against my better judgment. I'll rectify the matter now."

Iain stooped to lift the fox into his arms, but Brigette was faster. She scooped Sly up and ran. Iain reached out and would have caught her, but Glenda kicked his shins viciously, giving the woman and the fox a headstart.

Brigette dashed into the outer courtyard. Iain was close on her heels.

"Run, Sly!" she screamed, and nearing the gate, flung the fox from her arms. Frightened, Sly flew through the gate into the world beyond Dunridge Castle.

Brigette whirled around to face her husband. His expression mirrored his terrible rage, and she trembled, doubting the wisdom of her actions. Iain slapped her hard, leaving a reddened imprint on her cheek, then grabbed her before she fell. He caught her upper arm in a cruel, bruising grip and dragged her back to the inner courtyard. Without a word or glance, Iain forced her past the earl and the others.

"Dinna touch her!" Glenda screeched, charging at Iain. Percy captured the child and swung her up into his arms.

Iain pulled Brigette into the foyer. At the base of the stairs, he gave her a rough shove. "Get upstairs. I'll deal wi' ye later."

With her spine proudly straight, Brigette climbed the stairs to their chamber. Iain watched her, then headed for his father's study. If he went upstairs now, he might strike her again. He needed to calm down, get his anger under control.

Iain poured himself a whiskey and downed it quickly. Then he poured another. How dare she publicly defy me, he raged, then slammed the whiskey down and left the study. As Iain started up the stairs to his chamber, Black Jack and Percy walked into the foyer.

"Iain," Percy called, hoping to speak in his sister-in-law's defense.

"Shut yer mouth," Black Jack growled. "His wife isna' yer business."

Ignoring them, Iain climbed the stairs to his bedchamber. He turned the knob, but the door would not open. His wife had locked herself in, adding fuel to his blazing temper. Iain knocked. Silence was his answer.

"Brigette," he shouted. "Open this door."

"Begone, you heartless bastard!" she shouted back.

Iain banged savagely on the door. "Mark my words, Brigette. If ye force me to break the door, ye'll regret it."

After a silent moment, Iain steeled himself to kick the door in, then heard the sound of the bolt being thrown. The door remained closed.

Iain opened it and walked in, then stopped short in surprised disbelief. A few paces away stood his wife, one of his own gleaming daggers in her hand. He growled menacingly and advanced.

"Whatever you've come to say, have done with it," Brigette ordered, waving the dagger at him. "Keep your distance or I'll tickle your ribs with this steel."

Iain held out his hand. "Give it to me."

"Where would you like it, my lord?"

"I amna' jestin', lassie."

"I amna' jestin' either, laddie," she mimicked his burr. "Speak and leave."

When I get my hands on her, Iain thought, I'll spank her within an inch of her life. "I'd nae other choice out in the courtyard," he explained, inching closer to her. "Sly's guilty. It's what happens, sweetheart, when ye harness a wild thin'."

"Sly is innocent," Brigette countered icily. "Besides, you struck me."

"Ye publicly defied me and were deservin' of a public reprimand." Iain's voice was deceptively low and gentle as he inched closer and closer.

Suddenly, Iain lunged forward and kicked the dagger from her hand. Brigette screamed and scrambled to retrieve it, but he yanked her back, warning, "Dinna point another dagger at me unless ye plan to use it."

Lashing out, Brigette whacked his face with her fist. More annoyed than hurt, Iain shoved her onto the bed and fell on top of her. Frantically, she thrashed and bucked, seeking escape, but he held her easily and waited for her to tire. Then nose to nose, he warned, "Yer duties are to bear my sons and see to my every comfort. If ye dinna ken that, wife, yer life will be less than worthless and death will be a blessin'. Remember, the one wi' the cock gives the orders, and the one wi'out obeys."

Iain stood and stared down at her, then, without another word, turned on his heels and left.

Outside his chamber, Iain paused to calm himself and leaned against the door. The muffled sound of his wife's sobbing assailed him, and guilty remorse coiled itself around his heart and mind, nearly felling him. Sweet Jesu! How could I have struck her? he castigated himself. Though my anger was justified, my actions were not. If only Brie considered the consequences before opening her mouth!

Serving supper at the high table that evening was a thankless chore. Brigette's chair was conspicuously empty and Iain's expression was black. Almost glumly, Black Jack and Percy spoke quietly to each other. Brigette's absence had cast a shadow over the entire hall, even subduing the MacArthur warriors. Only Lady Antonia was in excellent spirits, eating her supper with obvious gusto.

Disgusted by the day's events, Moireach marched into the kitchen. Cruelly, she captured Kevin by his ear and pulled him toward the great hall.

"Ye dolt," Moireach snarled. "Look what mischief ye've wrought. What did the death of a few worthless chickens matter when our lady's happiness was at risk? Ye ken?"

Kevin stared at the high board. His expression became morose when he saw Brigette's empty place and Iain's forbidding countenance.

"I see ye finally do ken." The housekeeper sneered. "Lady Brigette is upstairs sobbin' in her sleep cuz Lord Iain hit her."

"It isna' my fault," Kevin insisted. "I was duped."

"Duped? What're ye sayin', lad?"

"I'd prefer no' to be overheard," Kevin whispered, then glanced around.

With her lips curled in disgust, Moireach led him through the foyer to the courtyard. "Now, pray tell, how were ye duped?"

"Ye willna' breathe a word of this, will ye?"

"Tell me quickly," Moireach threatened, "or I'll sharpen my butcherin' knife on yer hide."

" 'Twas Lady Antonia!" Kevin blurted, then continued in a rush. "She told me to kill the chickens and blame the fox. I didna' want to do it, but she said she'd have me sent away. Please, ye must believe me."

"I believe ye."

"If Lord Iain learns the truth," Kevin moaned, "I'll be sent away. Or worse."

"The truth willna' rectify matters now and will only cause more strife in the family," Moireach said. "Let me think." She paced back and forth in front of Kevin like a general. "I've an idea, but nae faith ye could carry it off. Wait here while I fetch my Jamie."

"Jamie?" Kevin gulped nervously. The man was fierce with a sword.

"My son has a fondness for Lady Brigette's tire-woman and will do my biddin'."

A few minutes later, Moireach returned with Jamie and Spring. "Kevin, lad, tell Jamie yer tale."

"Lady Antonia ordered me to kill the chickens and blame the fox. She threatened to dismiss me if I didna' do it."

"Damn," Jamie cursed.

"Double damn," Spring echoed.

"I've a scheme to help set thin's aright,"

Moireach said. "Will ye help yer sweet mother, laddie?"

Jamie grinned. "Need ye ask such a foolish question?"

Moireach smiled. "Ye must kill a fox, then bring the puir thin' back here. Kevin will take it to Lord Iain and say it's the fox that killed the chickens. Can ye do it?"

"Yes."

"Ye must be verra careful," she cautioned. "Sly's wearin' a yellow collar, so avoidin' him shouldna' be too difficult."

"Killing another fox," Spring commented, "will not return Sly to Brigette."

"Yer correct," Moireach agreed, "but it could begin mendin' thin's between them."

"It won't change the fact that Lord Iain abused her."

" 'Twas his right," Jamie interjected hotly. "She defied her husband and got exactly what she deserved!"

"Oh!" Spring was aghast at his words. Her lips tightened whitely in anger.

"Silence!" Moireach ordered. "Arguin' amongst ourselves willna' help the laird and his lady. What do ye think of the plan, Spring?"

"Well," she relented, "it cannot cause harm, and there is a small chance it could help."

"It's settled, then," Moireach said. "Jamie, get yerself on this in the mornin'."

The next week passed wretchedly for the lord and his lady. The fox conspirators were none too happy either. Apparently, killing a fox was more difficult than they had assumed. The only truly happy person at Dunridge was Lady Antonia. Her mood and temper improved by leaps and bounds each day that Iain and Brigette remained estranged. And estranged they were.

When his anger faded, Iain sought a reconciliation with his wife. Unfortunately, Brigette had other ideas and coldly rebuffed his overtures of renewed friendship. Unused to resisting women, Iain became frustrated, especially disliking this new experience of being rejected. Brigette could not, however, be faulted for disobedience.

No disobedience there, Iain thought more than once. My wife obeys my smallest command and places my merest whim above her own comfort. In fact, she treated him with a frigid politeness that was beginning to grate on his nerves, not to mention his pride. Being near Brigette was like being stranded in the midst of a Highland blizzard.

One morning, Iain happened to pass Brigette in the courtyard and asked her to stop.

"Yes, my lord?"

"Would ye care to ride wi' me today, hinny?" he asked with a hopeful smile.

"No, thank you," she refused, but quickly added, "If you insist, I shall naturally obey."

Iain's expression dropped in obvious disappointment. "It was an invitation."

"In that case, please excuse me." With that, Brigette walked away, leaving him in misery.

* * *

The MacArthur brothers passed through the garden one afternoon during Glenda's playtime. Merry laughter and wild scamperings had vanished from these sessions as assuredly as Sly had vanished from Dunridge. The garden was silent as if deserted, but Iain saw them. Looking like fallen angels cast into a world of woe, Brigette and Glenda sat in the farthest corner of the winter-barren garden. Iain's heart caught in his throat. It was then he decided that desperate times called for desperate measures. Only one thing would bring his wife's smile back. In the meantime . . .

Though Iain had sworn to himself that he'd not force her again, sleeping beside Brigette without touching her was proving the most tormenting of all his trials. Iain's frustration was running high and his patience dangerously low. If his wife was so determined to be obedient, would she grant him his husbandly rights? The time was ripe for seduction, one of his many talents.

Sliding into the bed, Iain decided to test the waters, in a manner of speaking. Brigette was lying on her side with her back to him. He turned slowly in her direction and touched her shoulder. Startled, she turned to look at him. Iain instantly pressed her back to the pillows and covered her lips with his in a desperate, hungry kiss. No response. Kissing his wife felt like kissing a corpse, albeit a warm one. Drawing back, Iain met her icy green eyes.

"Shall I spread my legs now?" she asked coldly. "Won't it be easier that way?"

Iain's desire shriveled. Muttering an oath, he rolled away and turned his back on her.

As she studied her husband's broad shoulders, Brigette's emotional pain was intense, almost physical. She loved him, but could she forgive his abuse of her or his cruelty to Sly?

The fox conspiracy was set, and the action would commence as soon as supper was served. From their various places within the great hall, the conspirators anxiously watched those at the high board. Brigette sat sullenly between her husband and her father-in-law.

"Come the spring," Iain was saying to his father, "I'd like to travel wi' Brie to Edinburgh. If ye can spare me, that is."

Brigette's gaze darted to Iain. Black Jack arched a questioning brow at his son and wondered what the game was. "I dinna see why no'."

"I thought ye might like some new gowns and gewgaws," Iain said to Brigette. "Edinburgh has many fine merchants. Perhaps ye'd like to purchase a few of those imported carpets from the East for our bedchamber?"

A bribe, she thought. Brigette stared expressionlessly at him, not exactly the reaction he'd expected. "As you wish, my lord."

"Damn it," Iain growled, slamming his fist on the table. "What do *ye* wish?"

Unruffled, Brigette answered, "I wish only to serve you, my lord. As you so kindly explained, the one with the cock commands and the one without obeys." She smiled without humor. "The last time I checked, I was still the one without."

Black Jack choked on his wine, Percy guffawed, and Iain's face darkened with rage. "Forget I mentioned it," he hissed and turned away.

"As you wish, my lord."

It was then that Moireach approached. "Lord Iain, young Kevin must speak wi' ye. It's urgent."

Glad to escape his wife, Iain walked to the entrance where Kevin was waiting. Brigette followed his progress and watched as he spoke to the young man. When Kevin lifted the fox high for Iain's inspection, Brigette gasped, horrified, and rose from her seat. Mesmerized by the dead animal, she crossed the chamber to her husband's side.

"This is the fox that killed the chickens," Iain said, glancing at her.

"Sly wears a yellow collar."

With a nod, Iain dismissed Kevin. Brigette stared after him and his gruesome possession.

"Sly isna' guilty. Are ye no' happy?"

"Happy?" Brigette stared incredulously at him, then gestured at the crowded hall. "Sly is not among us, Iain. He is alone in the forest—if he even lives. I will never forgive you."

"Dinna be ridiculous," Iain snapped, catching her arm. "Sly's a beast, no' yer bairn. If ye've the need for motherin', I'll give ye a babe of our own."

Brigette yanked her arm away. "You may command me in anything, but even you cannot com-

mand a woman's love. I want no child of yours."
With that, she fled the hall.

The weeks that followed were even more
wretched than before. The fox conspirators were
disheartened by their failure to ease the strain
between the lord and his lady. Moireach favored
the formulation of another plan, but Jamie op-
posed her. They'd done their best, but it was time
for Iain and Brigette to solve their own marital
problems. Spring sided with Jamie and Moireach
acquiesced reluctantly.

There seemed to be little chance of Iain and
Brigette reconciling. Iain now returned his wife's
coldness with his own. Each morning before she
awakened, Iain rode out of Dunridge and returned at suppertime. He did not seek his own
chamber at night until he was reasonably certain
that Brigette slept.

After several days of being ignored, Brigette's
vanity was ruffled. She was beginning to wonder
where her husband went and whom he saw there,
but refused to grant him the satisfaction of asking.
Iain was leaving her alone, Brigette reasoned, and
that was what she desired. Was it not?

Lady Antonia was beside herself with joy, and
was the sole member of the MacArthur family eagerly anticipating Christmas. Almost nothing irritated her. She stopped scolding the servants and
even smiled occasionally at Brigette, who became
instantly suspicious. Were Antonia's smiles and
Iain's disappearances somehow connected?

Christmas was only a week away. Iain returned
home that evening as supper was being served.

Sitting beside him, Brigette sensed a change in his demeanor. He seemed more relaxed than he'd been in weeks.

Brigette was furious. My husband has taken a lover, she fumed, and pushed her plate away. But vengeance shall be mine, she thought without satisfaction. He cannot get an heir from his mistress.

Finished with his meal, Iain stretched his legs out. He sipped his wine and watched Brigette, who became uncomfortable beneath his scrutiny.

"I'm tired," she announced when she could endure no more. "I believe I'll retire."

"An excellent idea." Iain yawned and stretched with exaggeration. "I'll join ye." He took her arm, then bade good night to Black Jack and Percy, who smothered their merriment at Brigette's dismayed expression.

They climbed the stairs in silence. Iain's casual touch on Brigette's arm sent hot shivers coursing through her body, and her heartbeat quickened. Unwilling to yield to her husband, Brigette desperately missed what he did to her body. Merciful Christ, she cursed inwardly. A virgin's life was so much simpler!

Inside their chamber, Brigette hurried to don her nightshift, but Iain stopped her. "Ye must sleep wi' me as God created ye," his amused voice sounded from behind her.

"But—"

"It's a command, lovey." He grinned wickedly.

"As you wish, my lord."

Brigette scurried into bed. Hugging the farthest edge, she turned her back on her husband. Iain slid in and snuggled close, pressing himself against the silkiness of her back. When he slipped his hand across her body and cupped one of her breasts, Brigette tensed.

"It's my wish we sleep thusly," he whispered.

Moments later, Brigette knew by the sound of his even breathing that he slept. Iain's tantalizing nakedness and possessively cupping hand conspired to make Brigette yearn for what she would not be enjoying that night. It was a long, long time before she was able to sleep.

When Brigette awakened, her limbs were entwined with Iain's. One arm was thrown across his stomach, and one leg was tangled between his muscular thighs. Her face was pressed against the thick mat of black hair covering his chest. Opening his eyes, Brigette found herself staring into her husband's smiling face.

"What are you doing here?" she asked, surprised.

"It's my bed," he returned. "Where else should I be?"

"You've been rising early of late."

"That task is completed." Iain grinned. "I've several days of leisure. It's good news, is it no'?"

"Yes." She almost choked on the words. "It's wonderful news."

Later that morning, Iain happened to meet Brigette in the courtyard and told her to stop for a moment.

"Yes, my lord?"

"Would ye care to ride wi' me?" he asked.

"No, thank you."

"It's a command, hinny, no' an invitation."
When her mouth dropped open in dismay, he
added, "And ye'll ride in front of me on my horse."

Iain lifted Brigette onto the saddle, then
mounted behind and pressed the hardness of his
body against her. By the time they returned, Brigette was certain she was going mad, tormented
by her husband's gentle assault on her senses. Her
body was turning traitor!

Two days before Christmas, winter's first blizzard was upon them. Forgoing the garden, Brigette and Glenda sat in front of the hearth in the
great hall.

Shaking the snow off their plaids, several Mac-
Arthur warriors, including Iain and Percy,
trudged into the hall. Seeing the two downcast
angels in front of the hearth, Iain advanced on
them. "It's an excellent day for playin' Blindman's
Buff," he said. "Would ye care to play?" Glenda
nodded eagerly, but Brigette shook her head.

"It's a command, sweetie." Iain smiled pleasantly at his wife's grimace. "I'll be the Blindman."

When Percy had blinded him with a scarf, Iain
whirled this way and that, trying to catch his wife.
Giggling in spite of herself, Brigette jumped back
out of reach, but someone pushed her into Iain's
outstretched arms. Squirming, she tried to break
free, but was ensnared by her husband's steely
grip.

"Aha!" Iain chuckled. "Whoever can this be?"

One of his hands slid across Brigette's silken
cheek and drifted down the column of her neck to
her shoulders. "Now let me see," Iain thought

aloud. His hand passed over the curve of a shapely
hip, then tweaked a plump breast. "I'd know these
titties anywhere—it's my wife!"

Mortified and scarlet to the tips of her toes, Brigette slapped his hand away and fled the hall.
Howls of raucous laughter chased her all the way
upstairs.

On Christmas Eve, Brigette decided that she
was singularly unhappy. Even Glenda, anticipating the holiday, was less dejected by Sly's abrupt
departure from Dunridge.

"How can ye allow yer men to dice on Christmas Eve?" Antonia complained to Black Jack
when the family had gathered for supper. "It's
blasphemy."

"All should be happy at Christmas," the earl
replied. "If dicin' brings them joy, then so be it."

Antonia cast him an exasperated look, then
turned to Brigette. "Where's Iain?"

"He's fetchin' Brie's present," Percy answered,
"so she doesna' waste a moment of the holiday
feelin' puirly."

Iain walked into the hall at the moment. Cradled in his arms was Sly, bedecked in a bright
yellow ribbon that matched his collar.

Startled mute, Brigette's mouth dropped open.
Iain grinned and placed the fox on her lap. "Merry
Christmas, hinny," he said, leaning down to kiss
her cheek. A lump of emotion formed in Brigette's
throat as she looked from her pet to her husband.

"This is a night to go down in history," Iain
quipped. "For once my wife is speechless."

Brigette buried her face into Sly's neck and

wept. The men exchanged smiles, and Glenda perched beside Brigette to pat the fox. Disgusted, Antonia left the hall.

"Are ye no' happy?" Glenda asked.

"Y-yes," Brigette sobbed, "t-terribly h-happy." Black Jack and Percy burst out laughing.

"Come along wi' me," Iain said and held out his hand. "I want to speak privately wi' ye." He escorted Brigette to Black Jack's study and closed the door.

"I willna' admit to this publicly," he said, "but I was unjust in my judgment and wrong to strike ye in anger. Can ye forgive me?"

"Yes," Brigette answered, "and I admit I was wrong to defy you—publicly. Can you forgive me?"

Iain smiled with tenderness, then lowered his head, his mouth claiming Brigette's in a gentle kiss. Their bodies melted together and the kiss deepened.

"I missed ye," he whispered, his lips hovering above hers.

"As I missed you," she vowed, drawing his lips down to hers again.

8

March in the Highlands was cold, much colder than Brigette remembered the south of England being at this time of year. Pink-cheeked, she and Glenda had passed an hour playing a rousing game of keep-the-ball-away-from-Sly. They were traveling the long road inside, a leisurely stroll through the garden before walking to the front courtyard.

"Buds," Brigette cried, stopping beside a tree.

"What?"

"See." Brigette pointed to a branch. "This tree is birthing buds. Do you know what that means?" Glenda shook her head. "It means winter is leaving and spring will soon arrive."

Glenda giggled. "Here she comes now."

"Brie," Spring called, rushing toward them. "Company has arrived and you're needed in the hall."

"Company?" Brigette echoed, surprised. "Who?"

Spring shrugged. "Someone important. The hall is filled with his men."

Followed by Sly, Brigette entered the great hall and found it was, indeed, filled with strange men-at-arms. She scanned the chamber and saw Antonia curtsying to an older man who was sitting in front of the hearth with Black Jack, Iain, and Percy.

Archibald Campbell, the Duke of Argyll, was of an age with his kinsman Black Jack MacArthur. His features were rugged, and his dark brown hair was tinged with gray at his temples, giving him a decidedly distinguished appearance. The duke's sharp gray eyes missed nothing. Turned with displeasure on a person, those eyes could pierce and wound more painfully than any gleaming sword.

"My lord," Black Jack introduced, "this is Lady Brigette, Iain's bride. Brie, make yer curtsy to the Duke of Argyll, our Campbell clan chief."

"My lord." Brigette smiled and curtsyed.

"Iain, lad," the duke said, returning Brigette's welcoming smile, "ye've got yerself a bonnie lass." His eyes drifted to Sly, sitting beside his mistress. "Am I seein' what I think I'm seein'?"

"If ye think yer seein' a fox," Iain said drily, "then yer seein' what ye think yer seein'. This furry fellow is Sly."

"What in God's holy name," the duke asked, turning to Black Jack, "is a fox doin' in yer home?"

"He lives here," Percy answered, his eyes sparkling with merriment.

"Lives here!" Campbell exclaimed in amazed

disbelief. "Are ye in yer dotage, Black Jack, to allow such a thin'?"

"With all due respect," Brigette spoke up, ignoring her husband's warning look, "Sly is my pet."

"Yer pet!?"

"This is not your home," she snapped, her green eyes flashing with anger, "and I am not your wife. The way we live at Dunridge is no business of yours!"

"Brie!" Black Jack and Iain shouted, appalled.

"It's all right," the duke assured them with a casual wave of his hand. "Dinna scold the wench for her rudeness. What she says is undoubtedly true." He leaned toward Black Jack, saying, "I should've known her temper would match her fiery hair. If ye recall, my late wife was a redhead." Campbell glanced at Iain and smiled sympathetically. "I've much experience dealin' wi' red-haired wenches, laddie, if ever yer in need of counsel."

"I am a lady, my lord, not a wench." Brigette smiled winsomely. "I am also an earl's daughter and have been taught proper respect."

"Taught ye respect, did they?" the duke mocked, his eyes alight with the most enjoyable verbal sparring since his wife had died. "Well, then, what did ye learn?"

Brigette grinned puckishly. "Obviously, not a damned thing."

The duke roared with laughter and wished he could be thirty years younger. Gems like Lady Brigette, he thought, were wasted on young men like Iain or his own son, Magnus. Youth was blinded by a comely face and figure. An experienced man could fully appreciate the lady's intelligence and wit and the innocence that allowed her to speak her mind freely.

"What respect ye get from that one will be hard won and well earned," he said to Iain as he watched Brigette slip away to tend her duties as hostess. "Good luck to ye.

"I envy the grandsons ye'll get from her," the duke said, turning to Black Jack. "My Magnus has been betrothed to Huntly's youngest since the day the chit was born. I'm truly despairin' because he doesna' seem in any hurry to wed and sire me an heir."

"How is cousin Magnus?" Iain asked.

"And how the hell should I know?" the duke barked. "He's forever off aboot the queen's business. Incognito, I might add."

"Ye can be proud," Black Jack said, "ye've instilled in him such loyalty to the queen."

"I'd appreciate a bit of loyalty to me." The duke snorted. "Inverary needs an heir and Huntly's chit is ripe. If it's the last thin' I do, I'll see Magnus wed to her. After she's dropped a few brats, he can disguise himself as the devil and go straight to hell."

Black Jack chuckled. "I must admit Iain knows his duty in that regard. Ye wouldna' believe the long hours he spends lyin' abed wi' Brie." Iain's face reddened with embarrassment, and Percy howled with laughter.

It was the duke's turn to chuckle. "I'd forgotten how it was bein' wed to a comely wench. We must be gettin' old. Speakin' of old, Black Jack, I've sad news concernin' our kinsman, Breadalbane. Colin sickened recently and passed on. Will ye come along wi' me to pay our respects?"

"Yes, and Iain'll also come." Black Jack turned to his youngest son. "Do ye think, Percy, yer capable of takin' charge here for a fortnight? I wouldna' want to return home to nothin'." Now Percy's face reddened with embarrassment, and Iain howled with laughter.

"How long will you be gone?" Brigette asked, reaching for Iain as he slipped into bed with her.

He kissed her lingeringly. "Nae more than a fortnight, sweet."

"I'll miss you."

"Especially in bed?"

"Most especially in bed."

With that, Brigette pushed him onto his back and slithered on top. Sensuously, she rubbed her softness full-length against his hardened warrior's body. Her rosy lips parted and descended to his as she raised her hips and then slowly, tantalizingly, impaled herself on his shaft.

A growl of pleasure escaped Iain's throat as she caressed every part of his body with her own. Holding his own desire in check, Iain watched her eyes fly open in surprised abandon when she dissolved into a quivering mass of hot sensation.

"Yer button was swellin' against me," Iain whispered huskily, then rolled her onto her back and rammed himself into the deepest part of her being. Clinging to him, Brigette wrapped her legs around his waist and arched her hips, meeting his every powerful thrust, her body urging him on.

"Give me a son," Iain panted.

"Yes," Brigette wailed, and they shuddered together.

Lady Antonia awakened early and dressed hurriedly, then rushed downstairs to the great hall. Iain would be leaving at dawn, and she hoped Brigette would sleep through his departure, giving her a few moments alone with him. She must somehow persuade Iain to set Brigette aside before a child was conceived. Loving Iain as she did, Antonia was determined to rekindle the warm feelings he'd once harbored for her, and to become the next Countess of Dunridge. Nothing was going to stop her, even if she had to dispatch the Sassenach with her own lovely hands.

Poised in the entrance to the crowded hall, Lady Antonia was a vision of ethereal perfection. Rising early did not detract from her beauty, her drowsiness giving her eyes a sultry cast.

Iain sat alone at the high table. Antonia smiled and sat down beside him. "Good mornin'," she greeted brightly.

"Mornin'," he returned without looking at her.

"Brie isna' seein' ye off?"

"She'll be down." Iain glanced sidelong at her. "What brings ye here at this hour?"

"I must speak wi' ye." Antonia's eyes beseeched. "It's urgent."

Iain arched a questioning brow. "I'm listenin'."

Antonia hesitated, her eyes sweeping the crowded hall. "I must speak privately."

Iain studied her for a long moment, then rose from his seat. "I'll hear what ye have to say in Black Jack's study."

Antonia led the way. Aware of her deviousness, Iain left the door ajar and stood just inside. When she turned to face him, Antonia saw Sly scurrying past on his way to the garden and knew Brigette would be close behind.

"I love ye," she declared loudly.

Before Iain could utter a word, Antonia threw herself at him and kissed him passionately. Her arms entwined his neck and held him prisoner. Iain was stiff and unresponsive, but Brigette could not see that from where she stood. A thousand daggers pierced Brigette's heart, and she raced after Sly.

Iain shoved Antonia away. "Dinna do that again," he growled.

"There was a time when ye cared for me."

"Yes, but I was young and foolish," Iain returned, his voice filling with contempt, "and ye wanted to be a countess. What I felt for ye once is gone. I love my wife." With that, he turned on his heels and left the study.

Antonia's frown vanished, and the slyest of smiles touched her lips. When the Sassenach is gone, she thought, I'll marry Iain and become the Countess of Dunridge. If this fails, I'll write to my brother. Finlay has always given me wise counsel.

Iain found Brigette in the garden. He walked up behind her and placed his hands on her shoulders, then whispered close to her ear, "I was lookin' for ye. What's this?" he asked, seeing the tears on her cheeks when she turned around.

"Nothing."

"Dinna lie to me."

"I-I'm feeling lonely."

"I'll be returnin' in a fortnight," he said, then patted her stomach and grinned crookedly. "Perhaps yer wi' child and its makin' ye weepy?"

"No."

"We must try harder to make Black Jack happy." Iain lowered his lips and kissed her lingeringly. "I love ye, Brie."

Brigette smiled sadly at her husband's retreating back, then strolled about the garden, hoping the crisp morning air would clear the cobwebs from her troubled mind. I love him, she thought, but refuse to share his affection with another.

Iain was kissing Antonia. The thought pounded in her mind, tormenting her. What am I to do? Brigette wondered distractedly and sat down to ponder her future.

Lady Antonia was pleased with herself when she saw her rival sitting forlornly in the farthest corner of the garden. The Sassenach appears none too happy, she thought with glee. How clever of me to have seized such an unexpected yet timely opportunity! Convincing Iain to set her aside would have been impossible, but now . . .

Antonia strode purposefully toward Brigette, but as she neared her adversary, Sly sensed the woman's enmity and bared his teeth in a snarl.

Antonia quickly stepped back a pace. "He willna' bite me, will he?"

"No, unfortunately."

"That isna' such a nice thin' to say, Brie," Antonia chided.

"Lady Brigette."

"What?"

"Please, call me Lady Brigette. Only my friends call me Brie." She stood, glaring at Antonia.

"Are we no' friends?"

"I loathe the very ground on which you stand," Brigette hissed.

Antonia was taken aback by Brigette's venom. Recovering herself, she said, "I'd like to be yer friend—if ye'd give me a chance."

"You're trying to steal my husband."

"So!" Antonia arched a brow haughtily. "Iain finally told ye?"

"Told me what?"

Antonia appeared nonplussed. "I guess I shouldna' have said anythin'."

"I saw you and Iain in the study."

"Perhaps we havena' been fair to ye," Antonia said, tears of sympathy welling up in her eyes.

"Whatever you've come to say," Brigette ordered, "speak to the point."

"To speak openly would be kinder," Antonia said, controlling the powerful urge to lash out. "Before I wed Malcolm, Iain and I were involved. We'd met in Edinburgh and fell in love, but Black Jack had already contracted wi' my father for me to wed Malcolm. Dutiful daughter that I am, I obeyed my father's wishes. Livin' beneath the same roof was difficult for us, but we always conducted ourselves honorably."

"How exceedingly impressive." Brigette sneered.

"After puir Malcolm died," Antonia continued, ignoring the sarcasm, "Iain, naturally, consoled me in my grief."

"Naturally."

"It was then we realized we still cared for each other, but Black Jack had already contracted for Iain to wed ye. Bein' an honorable mon, Iain wouldna' shame his father by breakin' the contract, but he canna set aside his feelin's for me. Ye ken?"

"I'm getting the general idea," Brigette replied coldly.

"I'm so sorry," Antonia gushed, touching Brigette's arm in sympathy. "Iain willna' set ye aside, but wants ye only to produce an heir for Black Jack. He canna love ye the way he loves me. How wretched to be nothin' but a brood mare!"

Brigette turned her back on the other woman, unable to control the quivering of her lips or the hot stream of tears coursing down her face. Consumed by pain and jealousy, she failed to question the validity of Antonia's words.

Give me a son, Iain had panted in a moment of shuddering ecstasy.

Perhaps yer wi child? he'd asked before leaving with the duke.

Antonia's words rang like a death knell for Brigette's marriage. Taking a deep, ragged breath, Brigette regained her composure, and her pain became boiling rage. Without a thought to my happiness, she seethed, that arrogant bastard married me to honor his father's contract. How dare he profess his love for me one moment and fly to his mistress's arms in the next! All this time the swine and his tart were enjoying a jest at my expense.

Brigette whirled around to confront Antonia, but the blond beauty had vanished. Revenge formed in her mind. We'll see who laughs last in this sordid affair. It's unfortunate but true that a bastard cannot inherit, for that's all the proud MacArthurs will get from Iain and Antonia. I will not be here to whelp a brat each year.

Sly's whining drew Brigette's attention and she knelt to hug the fox. "As much as I love you," she whispered brokenly against his neck, "you may not come along. Basildon Castle is closed to me; either Iain will seek me there or my mother will return me to Dunridge. My destiny lies in London, my precious pet, where you cannot follow. Besides, with me gone, Glenda will need your company."

Dressed in her warmest riding gown and woolen cloak, Brigette paused in the foyer and wondered where Glenda might be. In the library, she remembered, learning her letters with Father Kaplan.

Brigette smiled in spite of her troubles. How strange that the son of a Jewish merchant would be a priest! But that was exactly what Father Kaplan was. The product of a Scottish woman and Jewish merchant, Father Kaplan had been or-phaned at a young age and raised in a Catholic shelter.

The priesthood had beckoned, but once ordained, Father Kaplan had not been taken seriously because of his unusual parentage. So be it, he'd thought, and had begun ministering to the spiritual and earthly needs of the derelicts and outcasts in Edinburgh's poorest section. There, most did not know their own fathers, much less care about his. Father Kaplan had been quite busy; the world was filled with the poor, the homeless, the lost.

Then Black Jack MacArthur had entered his life. A certain lady friend of Black Jack's had done the unthinkable—attempted suicide. Ravaged by guilt, Black Jack was frantic that the dying woman be blessed and honorably buried. Learning the circumstances of the emergency, no priest would come . . . until Black Jack found Father Kaplan. Filled with compassion for the young lord's anguish, the priest had understood that he was ministering more to Black Jack than to the unidentified lady. Without a moment's hesitation, Father Kaplan had accompanied Black Jack to his kinsman's home and administered the last rites of the church to the beautiful, dying noblewoman. Later, he'd blessed her unmarked grave, gaining MacArthur's respect and friendship.

Black Jack had asked Father Kaplan to return to Dunridge Castle with him. When the priest hesitated, Black Jack had vowed there were many poor crofters and drunken men-at-arms in Argyll; all were in need of having their souls saved. So

Father Kaplan had left Edinburgh with Black Jack and remained at Dunridge for the next thirty years.

Glenda brightened when Brigette and Sly walked into the library. "I'm sorry to interrupt," Brigette said to the old priest. "May I speak privately with Glenda?"

"Well, it isna' playtime yet," he replied, "but I suppose we could end our lessons early for once."

"Let me see what you've been doing," Brigette said after the priest had gone.

Glenda grinned and held up her parchment. Written on it in large, childish letters were Brigette's and Sly's names.

"Excellent! And your own name?"

G L E N D A!

Brigette applauded, then squatted beside the child. "As you can tell by my gown, I'm leaving."

"Leavin'?" Glenda cried.

"I'm riding out for a while," Brigette said, patting her arm. "I want you to promise to care for Sly while I'm gone."

Glenda sensed something was terribly wrong. Frowning, she looked from Brigette to Sly, then back again.

"Don't you want to care for Sly?"

"Yes, but I'd rather go wi' ye."

"Not today, sweetheart," Brigette replied. "Sometimes people have a need to be alone and think about their problems."

"I could help ye."

"By caring for Sly, you will be helping me," Brigette said. "Will you do it?"

"Yes."

"You're a good girl and I love you. Give me a hug."

Unaccountably sad, Glenda flew into Brigette's arms, and they clung to each other while Sly scampered around them, whining for attention. Brigette kissed the little girl on each cheek and set her aside, then gave the fox a quick pat and left the library.

"Good mornin'," Percy greeted her in the foyer. "To where are ye off?"

Brigette hesitated. "I—I'm riding out."

"I'll ride wi' ye."

"No!" Brigette refused too quickly, and Percy's brow furrowed into a frown. "I prefer to be alone," she explained.

"What's amiss, Brie?"

"Nothing, but I miss Iain dreadfully."

"Ridin' out alone is dangerous," he said.

"I promise I won't go far."

Uncertain, Percy was silent. If anything happened to Brigette, his life would be less than worthless when Iain found out. The last time he'd been in charge, she'd run away. What a roasting he'd suffered for that folly!

"Please," she pleaded.

Against his better judgment, Percy nodded, but warned, "Be careful and dinna go far. Dinna stay outside the walls longer than an hour."

"Yes, Papa." A smile tugged at the corners of her lips.

Moments later, Brigette waved to the tower guards as she passed through the outer gate. A short distance away, she halted her horse and looked back at Dunridge Castle.

Iain! her heart cried out. *I loved you so!*

With painful regret, Brigette turned and galloped away.

9

With the heaviest of hearts, Brigette wended her lonely way southeast. The day was raw, and by afternoon she was uncomfortably cold and hungry.

What a dolt I am, she berated herself. Though I would have been conspicuous wearing my fur-lined cloak, I also would have been warm. Even worse, I've brought no food.

Worried, Brigette wondered what would happen when night arrived. It was certain she'd be passing the night alone in the woods; there was no inn where she could spend the coins she'd taken. Brigette hoped there'd be no wolves in the area. Bringing a weapon had also slipped her mind.

Rounding a bend in the road, Brigette spied a man walking up ahead. He halted at the sound of her horse and turned around. Cautiously, she advanced.

From a distance, he seemed a strange old man,

his carriage and physique incongruous with the overall impression of advanced age. He wore a long, tattered robe and carried a thick walking staff.

Some sort of holy man, Brigette thought. Coming abreast of him, she realized he was much younger than he appeared, perhaps of an age with Iain.

He was tall and broad shouldered. His long, shaggy hair was a rich chestnut brown. Only his outlandish garb and the stubbles of a beginning beard created the illusion of old age.

As the man eyed her curiously, Brigette halted her horse. Her eyes met his, and she was almost startled by their familiar, piercing grayness. Where had she seen those eyes before?

Without seeming to scrutinize, those sharp gray eyes missed nothing about the green-eyed, copper-haired beauty astride the horse. He noted the quality of her finely made garments, her wedding ring, and the MacArthur horse. When she spoke, he recognized her upper-crust English accent. Very upper-crust English.

"Good day to ye, my lady." The man smiled and nodded his head.

"Good day to you, sir," Brigette returned. "Would this be the road to London?"

As if he could see the road's end, he cast a long glance at the horizon, then looked back at her. "I do believe so."

"Are these MacArthur lands through which I'm passing?" she asked.

The man studied Brigette speculatively, then

decided she was too fine a wench to be a horse
thief. But who was she? A runaway bride? The last
he'd heard, neither of his MacArthur cousins had
married. "We're on Campbell's lands," he answered. "Ye passed the MacArthur land several
miles back, if that's where yer headed."

"I'm for London."

"By all the holy saints!" he exclaimed, a charming grin lighting his face. "I'm also for London. I'll
tell ye a tale for a lift on yer horse."

Instantly suspicious, Brigette glanced sidelong
at him. A frown clouded her features.

"Magnus is my name," he introduced himself,
then swept her a courtly bow. "Gaberlunzie is my
vocation. Can ye no' tell by my garb?"

Brigette stared blankly at him, and Magnus
chuckled. "Do ye know," he asked, "what a gaberlunzie is?"

"No."

"A gaberlunzie travels the roads," he explained,
"and tells his tales for supper. And ye are?"

"Brigette Mac . . . Bria." She gulped nervously. "I hope I'll not be mentioned in any of your
tales."

Magnus grinned, thoroughly and hopelessly enchanted by the mysterious, green-eyed Sassenach.
"Well, Brigette MacBria," he teased, "the price of
my silence is a ride on yer horse."

Wary of traveling with a stranger, Brigette was
uncertain, but her need for companionship over-
rode her caution. "Call me Brie—all my friends
do."

Magnus mounted behind her. Reaching around

her body, he took control of the reins. Brigette was tense, understandably so, since she'd never been alone with a strange man except "Ross" Mac-Arthur. As they rode, their silence was companionable and soothed her rioting nerves. Gradually, she relaxed, almost imperceptibly leaning against the masculine body.

Magnus's unease grew in direct proportion to Brigette's relaxation. He felt the delicate column of her back and marveled at what a fragile creature she was. Her head rested in the crook of his neck, and the fresh scent of her hair besieged his senses. He felt his manhood stirring and stretching beneath his garments.

"So, yer for England," Magnus commented, hoping casual conversation would alleviate his baser urgings.

"Yes."

"Goin' home to yer family?"

"How do you know I'm English?" she asked suspiciously.

"Ye dinna speak like a native Scot."

"Oh."

"Ye've family in London?"

"No."

"Friends, then . . . who?" he asked, and felt her body stiffen. "Perhaps I know them."

"I doubt it," Brigette replied coldly.

She's running away, Magnus decided. "Where is it yer comin' from, lassie?"

"That's none of your business! May I remind you," she haughtily informed him, "you are riding only through my forbearance. If you prove bothersome, my invitation will be rescinded. Do you understand?"

"Quite so," he mimicked her upper-crust accent, then smiled, thinking she had spunk.

They rode along in silence, not quite as companionable as before. Magnus cleared his throat, then ventured slyly, "This steed is MacArthur property." Brigette tensed and he knew he'd struck a nerve.

Instead of responding with anger, Brigette decided two could play his game. "Your hands do not have the look of a working man," she observed.

"A gaberlunzie toils wi' his tongue, lassie."

"Is that so?" She turned one of his hands over. "The calluses on your palms speak of rigorous training with a sword." Magnus was silent. Brigette longed to turn and catch the expression on his face. "In fact," she continued, "although you give the impression of advancing age, I know you are a young man. Why, you must be of an age with—" She caught herself just in time.

"Of an age wi' whom?"

"Nobody. Who are you, really?"

"I'm stronger than ye," he whispered harshly against her ear. "Yer remainin' alive only through my forbearance. If ye prove bothersome . . . Ye ken?"

"I ken," she croaked, trembling with fear. What folly to have given a ride to this murdering rogue! Indeed, what folly to have left the safety of Dunridge's walls!

Magnus halted the horse abruptly, and Brigette held her breath, certain her end was at hand. He dismounted and pulled her, none too gently, from the saddle. As he stared into her green eyes, wide with fright, his forbidding expression softened. "I'm verra sorry for threatenin' ye," he apologized. "A truce is in order, would ye no' agree?"

Brigette nodded quickly and Magnus smiled at her sudden willingness to please him. "We've secrets we dinna want known. Can we no' journey together wi'out pryin'?"

"You pried first."

"I stand corrected."

Caught unexpectedly in the depths of her emerald eyes, Magnus lowered his head to press his lips against hers. When they would have made contact, Brigette's stomach growled loudly, roaring like a wild beast.

Smiling, Magnus drew back. "Are ye hungry?"

"Famished."

"Why did ye no' say so?" he chided.

"Have you food?" Brigette's mouth watered in anticipation.

"No' on my person," Magnus admitted, "but we'll get some."

"How?"

Magnus looked around and then at the sky. "It's nearly dusk," he said. "We'll stop for the night."

"Will you hunt?"

"There's nae need for huntin'. Campbell crofters abound in the area."

"What good does that do us?" Brigette asked irritably.

"It's a custom of the Highlands to offer hospitality to travelers," he explained.

"I prefer my passage south not be marked."

"Dinna worry aboot that, my wee Sassenach," he said, playfully tapping the tip of her upturned nose. "It's also a Highland custom to refrain from askin' a traveler's identity . . ."

Brigette, having declined one of the cottage's two chairs, sat on the floor in front of the small hearth and finished her meal of meatless stew, cheese, and bread. Never had she eaten a more satisfying meal.

Magnus had been correct. Asking no questions, the aging crofter and his wife had invited them to share their meager supper and lodging. However, something in their manner suggested they'd met Magnus previously.

"Ye've a mighty appetite for such a wee lady," Magnus teased, sitting beside her. "The stew was to yer likin', then?"

Brigette blushed. "I was hungry. Besides, better stew than haggis."

Magnus smiled. "It's time for sleep. We leave at dawn."

"Yer welcome to our bed, my lady," the crofter's wife offered.

Looking at the older woman, Brigette decided youth should sleep on the floor. "No, thank you," she refused.

"Wrap yerselves in this," the crofter said, handing Magnus a Campbell plaid. " 'Twill keep ye warm."

Magnus smiled wryly at Brigette. "If we lie together and wrap the plaid around ourselves, we'll be toasty."

"Are there not two we could use?" Her cheeks were scarlet.

"There's only the one." Magnus grinned wickedly.

"Well," she hedged, wondering if the crofter and his wife could be considered suitable chaperones.

"Ye dinna trust me?"

"I—I—I guess I do."

"To a Highlander, Brie, there's nothin' considered more dishonorable than takin' advantage of a person who's placed his trust in ye."

"Are you a native Highlander?"

"I am," Magnus vowed solemnly, but his lips twitched with suppressed merriment.

Green eyes met gray, and Brigette knew he'd spoken truthfully. Shyly, she slid into his embrace. Magnus folded the Campbell plaid around them, sealing out the night's chill, and held her close. Brigette rested her head against his chest, the rhythmic beating of his heart soon lulling her into a deep, dreamless sleep.

Magnus pressed a light kiss on the top of her head and closed his eyes.

Smack! The smarting pain of a lusty whack on her derriere awakened Brigette. *Iain!* she thought in alarm. Iain is here.

"Get up, I say," a stern voice ordered, and Brigette opened her eyes to find Magnus looming above her. "Ye lazy chit. Dawn was an hour past, and the Campbells are hard at work. If ye dinna get up now, I'll leave ye behind." She accepted his extended hand and rose tiredly. "There's porridge for ye on the table."

The porridge was cold. Thinking it might be the only food she'd have that day, Brigette forced herself to eat, then glanced sidelong at her companion.

After neatly folding the Campbell plaid, Magnus packed it in a sackcloth that he swung over his shoulder. He met her questioning gaze. "They've insisted we take the plaid and a few supplies as well."

"To provision passing travelers is also a Highland custom?"

"Nae, lassie, it's the magnanimous generosity of the great clan Campbell."

Afternoon's shadows were fading into dusk when Magnus left the road and entered the forest. They stopped near a stream where they could water the horse and camp for the night.

Magnus dismounted and lifted an exhausted Brigette from the saddle. "Thanks to the Campbells," he told her, "we've nae need to hunt tonight. We willna' build a fire."

"But I'm cold," Brigette whined pitifully. Tears of misery welled up in her eyes.

"I know ye are," he said, caressing her cheek, "but we're nae longer on Campbell lands. Tomorrow will be better, and I'll do my best to keep ye from freezin' tonight. Go on and take care of yer private needs."

Brigette blushed ferociously, then walked into

the trees. When she returned, Magnus had unpacked the sackcloth. In silence, they ate a meager supper of bread and cheese.

"It's time for sleepin'." Magnus held the plaid open in invitation.

"B-but we've no chaperon."

"I dinna think we're likely to find one here. Come to me and I'll keep ye warm."

Brigette moved into his embrace. Magnus wrapped the plaid around them, and as they lay on their earthen bed, his arms encircled her and held her close. Glancing up, she found him watching her.

Captivated by his piercing gray eyes, Brigette was powerless to protest when his lips descended to hers. For the barest fraction of a second, she gave herself over to his kiss, but Iain's image rose in her mind's eye like a spectre, and sanity returned. Her small hands pressed against his chest, attempting to push him away.

"Please," she pleaded as he kissed her eyelids and temples. "I am a married woman."

"Unhappily married," he whispered huskily, without stopping his sensual onslaught.

"Happy or unhappy, it matters naught," Brigette said bitterly. "I have taken a vow before God. Besides, I love my husband."

Magnus sighed in defeat. "And I, unfortunately, am an honorable mon. Yer safe wi' me." Snuggling close, they fell asleep.

They entered London through the Bishopgate nearly two weeks later on a miserable, rainy day.

Wide-eyed with wonder, Brigette was boggled by her first sight of Londontown. Never in her wildest daydreams had she conceived of a place like this, so large and busy.

Crowds of all kinds of people rushed hither and thither, crisscrossing the narrow, muddy streets. The Londoners appeared to be in a race. Perhaps, Brigette speculated, to see who would finish their business first and get out of the rain?

Magnus halted the horse and dismounted, then helped Brigette down. Her feet promptly sank in the mud, and she giggled as droplets of rain dripped from the tip of her nose.

"By God's holy grace, we've finally arrived," Magnus said, staring into bewitching green eyes.

"So we have."

"I've a tale to spin for a fellow. I'll be takin' my leave of ye."

"Oh." A constricting lump of sadness formed in Brigette's throat.

"I could escort ye to yer friend's," Magnus offered.

"No," Brigette quickly declined. "No, thank you."

"It would be nae trouble," he added, reluctant to leave her.

"There's no need," she assured him with a bright smile. "My destination is not far from here. I'll be fine."

"Travelin' wi' ye, Brie, has been a singularly unique experience. Highly memorable."

Brigette grinned. "Is that a compliment or not?"

Magnus chuckled, then drew her into his arms.

His lips swooped down to capture hers in a lingering kiss. "I'll miss ye," he whispered, then walked away.

Feeling bereft, Brigette watched him go and absently stroked the horse. The horse! she remembered suddenly. *"Magnus!"* she shouted and raced after him, pulling the horse along behind. *"Magnus!"*

He whirled around and hurried back. "What is it?"

"The horse." Brigette handed him the reins. "He's a gift from me."

"I dinna ken."

"I've no need for him," she explained. "Ride him back to Scotland when you return."

"Are ye certain?"

"Yes."

"I willna' forget yer kindness." Magnus kissed her cheek, then mounted and rode away. He looked back once and saw Brigette standing like a lost waif where he'd left her, then turned the horse in the direction of the Strand, London's most elite section.

Turning off the Strand, Magnus rode up the narrow coach drive that led to Lennox House, then traveled around to the rear. He dismounted and knocked on the door. When it opened, a sour-faced footman peered out.

"Good afternoon," Magnus greeted the servant.

"What do you want?" the footman questioned imperiously. "You'll find no handouts here."

"I've just arrived from the North," Magnus said,

controlling the urge to lay the man out cold, "and I've an interestin' tale for the earl's ears."

"You wish to speak with the earl?" the footman asked incredulously.

"He's expectin' me."

"Expecting you!" the footman repeated in shocked disbelief.

"If ye value yer position wi' the earl," Magnus threatened, "ye'd best fetch him now!"

"Very well." The door slammed shut.

Several moments later, the door opened again. The Earl of Lennox, middle-aged and expensively dressed, studied the ragged gaberlunzie.

"I've a tale for ye, Lennox, aboot a queen in search of a suitable mate. Would ye care to hear it?"

"Campbell?"

"Aye." Magnus stepped inside.

The Earl of Lennox shook his head, disgusted by the other's tattered robe. "Must you disguise yourself in rags? Why not change for the better?"

Magnus arched a mocking brow. "As whom, do ye think, should I be travelin' the length of Scotland and England? Almighty God? That would be discreet."

As Magnus vanished from sight, Brigette stayed where she was, standing ankle-deep in mud. Wretchedly alone, she looked around and wondered where she could go. Her hastily formulated plan had not included what she would do once she'd actually arrived in London.

I'll follow the crowd, she decided. The busiest

area is probably safest. Ignoring the pelting rain and sucking mud, Brigette began to walk, her thoughts becoming bleaker with each step she took.

Doubts of her continued survival creeped across her mind. What folly to have flown from Dunridge without a proper plan, Brigette berated herself. Each of these passing people has some place to go —a family, a home. Only I have no refuge. If I were not experiencing this, I would never believe a person can be utterly alone in such a crowded, bustling town.

Ignorant of where she walked, Brigette happened upon Cheapside Market, teeming with people. Suddenly, she was jostled from behind by a street urchin, who shouted an apology as he ran past her.

"Be careful," warned a nearby voice, "or you'll find your pockets picked."

Brigette checked her pocket for her coins. Empty! Outraged, Brigette raced frantically after the boy, who she was certain had stolen her money.

As she struggled to run in the mud, her heavily sodden skirt became entangled with her legs and down she went. Tired and hungry and cold, Brigette was defeated by circumstances. There she sat, loudly wailing her misery. That the daughter of a belted earl had sunk so low!

"Yeow!" Someone tripped over her and landed beside her in the mud. Through a hazy blur of tears, Brigette saw a young woman covered with mud.

"What the bloody hell d'ya think ya doin'?" the woman screeched, leaping to her feet. She glared belligerently at Brigette, who cried even harder.

Earthy was the word a casual observer might use to describe the angry woman. Of average height, she was much taller than Brigette and had a well-endowed frame. Curly as a mop, her hair was a light shade of brown, shot through with strands of pale blond. Intelligent hazel eyes topped a nondescript nose that sported a smattering of freckles thrown on for good measure.

The woman looked Brigette over speculatively. *Aha!* she thought when her eyes touched on Brigette's smooth, ivory hands. *An honest day's work is a stranger to those pretty hands. This is no low-class wench, but someone of quality.* "Are ya so addle-brained," she sneered, "ya can't think ta get out of the rain?"

"I—I've n-no place to g-go." Brigette sobbed.

A runaway! Some fine lord will pay a handsome reward for her safe return. The woman extended her hand and said, "Ya have now."

Brigette looked dumbly at the offered hand and then into hazel eyes. "W-what?"

"I said ya got a place ta go," the woman repeated. "Give me ya hand and be quick about it." Brigette accepted the extended hand and stood. "My name is Marianne, but call me Randi—all my friends do."

"My name is Brigette, but call me Brie—all my friends do."

"Ya've got friends?" Marianne asked in mock disbelief. "I'd never have known it by the way ya were wallowin' in the mud like a bloody, squealin' pig."

"Of course I have friends!" Brigette returned indignantly. "Many friends! Quite obviously, they do not reside in Londontown."

"Indubitably so." Marianne mimicked her uppity accent. "I humbly beg your pardon, my lady. How embarrassingly remiss of me not to have realized."

In spite of her woes, Brigette burst out laughing, and Marianne winked at her. "Come along. The Rooster is just around the corner."

"Rooster?"

"The Royal Rooster Tavern," Marianne explained. "Where I live and work."

The two women trudged through the mud. Before reaching the corner, Marianne pulled Brigette into a dingy, foul-smelling alley. "We'll use the back door," she said. "Lookin' like we do, I don't want ta alarm any customers."

Halfway down the alley, Marianne led Brigette into the tavern's kitchen, then shoved her ungently onto a nearby stool. "Stay put, sweetie," she ordered. "I'll get ya somethin' ta revive ya spirits."

Brigette primly folded her hands on her lap and glanced around. Several feet away stood the tavern's cook, staring at her. He was short and grossly stout, bordering on elephantine. His lips were blubbery full, and his dark, beady eyes were snakelike. Brigette had never seen a more repulsive-looking man.

"Drink it all up," Marianne ordered. She passed Brigette a dram of whiskey, then noticed the cook staring at them. "What the bloody hell d'ya think ya watchin', Bertie?"

Bertie opened his mouth to reply, but Marianne's tongue was fast and sharp. "Why don't ya go bugger yaself, pig?" Brigette choked on the whiskey, and Marianne slapped her back, nearly toppling her off the stool.

The door from the common room swung open, and a blond-haired woman walked into the kitchen. She was comely and knew how to flaunt her good looks, as evidenced by her revealing, low-cut blouse.

Spying the two mud-covered apparitions, the newcomer stopped short. "What the bloody hell did ya bring home this time, Randi?" she screeched. "Another stray?"

"Back off, Lil, or ya'll regret it!" Marianne snarled. "And don't never call me Randi—the name's reserved for friends only!"

"What's going on here?" a deep, masculine voice rumbled. The voice belonged to a brawny, roughly handsome man who'd run into the kitchen at the sound of the women's angry voices. "We've customers waitin'. Move ya blasted arses!"

Bertie scurried back to his cooking, and Lil retreated into the common room. The man turned his attention on Marianne. "What the bloody hell happened?" he questioned sharply. "And who's this?"

"I fell over this lady in the street." The sweetest of smiles graced Marianne's face. "Brie, this is Bucko Jacques, the Rooster's owner. Bucko, this young lady is Brigette . . . ?"

"Brigette Devereux MacArthur. It's a pleasure to meet you, Mr. Jacques."

Bucko's dark eyes narrowed and Marianne tugged on his sleeve like a child. "Bucko, love, might we speak privately?"

Bucko nodded and walked to the far side of the kitchen with Marianne. "The wench is not a wench," she whispered, "but a lady in distress. Sooner or later, a rich lord is bound ta come searchin' for her. If we keep her safe here, he'll be ever so grateful and hand us a bag of gold for our trouble."

"I don't know, Randi." Bucko looked doubtful.

"She can work for her keep until he comes. We could use an extra pair of hands."

"Where's she ta sleep?" he protested. "Business is good and we've no empty rooms."

Smiling coyly, Marianne rubbed her lush breasts against his arm. "If she shares the room with Lil, I'll be forced ta share ya bed."

"An excellent idea." Bucko's eyes gleamed with lusty anticipation. "An extra pair of hands, a bag of gold, and you! What more could a man want?"

Bucko returned to the common room, unaware he'd fallen into a tender trap. Marianne smiled with satisfaction at his retreating back, then fetched a pan of hot water and a bar of soap. "Follow me," she ordered Brigette, who fell into step behind her.

They went up the narrow, creaky stairs at the far end of the kitchen. At the top of the stairs, Marianne turned left, and they entered the first chamber. Depressingly small and windowless, it contained two cots, two small chests, and one ancient table, standing almost on its last leg.

"Ya'll share the room with Lil," Marianne said, placing the pan of water on the table. "It's the best I can do." She rummaged through one of the chests and pulled out an old, frayed nightshift, then glanced at Brigette, who'd made no move toward the pan of water. *"Strip!"*

"I—I beg your pardon?"

"Beg it all ya want," Marianne returned, "but drop those clothes and wash, then get into the nightshift."

Brigette removed her muddied cloak and gown but retained her chemise. Then she began washing.

"Ya call that strippin'?" Marianne asked sharply.

"W-what?"

"Strip means ta take everythin' off, sweetie. I want ta see ya bare-arse naked!"

"I beg your pardon?" Brigette's face was a vibrant scarlet.

"Ya really are an innocent babe, ain't ya?" Marianne chuckled. "Listen, angel, ya ain't got nothin' that I ain't got more of. Understand?"

"Your words are quite clear."

"And I ain't bein' naughty," Marianne added. "I want ta wash those clothes."

"Oh." Brigette removed her chemise and stood there, self-conscious in her nudity.

"Hurry up and wash." Ignoring her embarrassment, Marianne grabbed the soiled clothes and headed for the door. "I'll bring ya somethin' ta eat."

Brigette washed quickly and donned the tattered nightshift. Then she sat on the edge of a cot and waited.

Carrying a tray, Marianne returned a few minutes later. "Here we are, baby," she said. "I've brought ya stew, bread, cheese, and mulled wine. Fall to and eat every bite."

Marianne sat on the other cot and watched, keeping up a steady stream of chatter all the while. "I'll be sleepin' at the far end of the hall. Don't let Lil bother ya—she's all titties and no brain." Brigette opened her mouth to speak, but Marianne cut her off. "Eat," she ordered. "I'll do the talkin'. Ya too skinny, and I'm plannin' ta add some flesh ta those bones. In case ya didn't know— flesh attracts men and bones attract dogs."

When Brigette had consumed every morsel of the food, Marianne set the tray aside. "It's time for sleep, sweetie. I'll wake ya early, and ya can come to Cheapside Market with me." In motherly fashion, she tucked the coverlet beneath Brigette's chin.

"You're a great lady," Brigette said softly, unshed tears glistening in her eyes. "You've been exceedingly kind."

"It's noble of ya ta say so." Marianne patted her hand.

"How can I ever repay you?"

"Don't worry about that," Marianne said, then grinned. "I'm certain I'll think of somethin'."

Alone in the darkness, Brigette's thoughts veered to Scotland, traveling those many miles in the blink of an eye. I'll never see Iain again. Has he returned to Dunridge? Does he know I'm not there? Does he even care? Turning her face into the pillow, Brigette cried herself to sleep.

10

"Ye stupid bastard!"

Iain's fist connected with Percy's jaw, sending the younger man crashing to the floor in front of the hearth in Black Jack's study. Percy leaped nimbly to his feet. Poised for battle, the brothers circled each other.

"Brie left while I was in charge, but she wasna' runnin' away from me," Percy jeered. "What did *ye* do to her?"

Enraged, Iain swore loudly and attacked, capturing his brother by the shirt. He raised his fist to strike but was grabbed unexpectedly from behind.

"Dinna be rash," Black Jack said. "Yer brother's a blockhead, but slaughterin' him isna' goin' to bring yer wife home. Ye ken?"

The wisdom of his father's words penetrated Iain's fury. He took several deep breaths to cool his boiling temper, then nodded. Black Jack released him, then cast Percy a scathing glance, more painful than Iain's fist.

"Enter!" Black Jack bellowed, hearing the almost hesitant rap on the door. Moireach and Spring entered at his call. "Ladies," he said, "tell us what ye recall of Brie's departure."

"Nothin'." Moireach shook her head sadly. "I could almost swear she took nae food."

"I ken yer the lady's kin," Black Jack said, his attention turning on Spring, "but tell us what ye know."

"She took no change of clothing, nor did she wear her warmest cloak."

"Yer protectin' her," Iain snarled. "Where is she?"

"I swear I know nothin'."

"Perhaps there's been foul play," Black Jack mused aloud. "Brie couldna' be so lackin' in common sense that she'd flee wi' nothin'."

"Yes, my lord," Spring disagreed, "she could."

"I knew Lady Brie was leavin'," a small voice announced. "She told me." All eyes darted to the door, where Glenda stood.

"Why did ye no' tell Percy two weeks ago?" Iain roared, frightening the child. "Tell us what ye know!"

Glenda's face became deathly pale. Her bottom lip quivered as she struggled to stem a rushing tide of tears.

"Shut yer mouth," Black Jack growled at Iain. He sat down in the chair in front of the hearth, then smiled at Glenda and beckoned her. "Come in, hinny. Dinna be frightened. Uncle Iain's cross because he's worried aboot Lady Brie. Sit yerself right here."

Glenda perched on Black Jack's lap. Enfolding her in his arms, he gave her a hug and a peck on the cheek. "Did ye miss me, hinny?"

"I did."

"I missed ye also. Now, sweetheart, tell me what ye know aboot Lady Brie." Glenda glanced nervously at Iain, who was pacing the chamber like a wild beast.

"Nae need to be frightened," Black Jack assured her.

"I—I was havin' my lessons," Glenda told him. "Lady Brie asked Father Kaplan if she could speak privately wi' me. She asked me to care for Sly while she was gone. I wanted to go, too, but she wanted to be alone to think aboot her problems."

"Did she mention where she was goin'?" Black Jack prodded.

"Ridin'."

"I see." Black Jack smiled at his granddaughter. "And have ye been carin' for Sly?"

Glenda grinned. "Most diligently."

Black Jack hugged the little girl. "She'll be pleased wi' ye when she returns."

"Lady Brie will be comin' home, then?"

"Of course," Black Jack assured her. "Do ye doubt it?"

"I met Brie in the foyer," Percy interjected. "She must've just left Glenda. I offered to ride wi' her, but she refused, sayin' she needed to be alone."

"Ye should have insisted," Iain snapped.

"I amna' the one who caused her unhappiness," Percy defended himself.

"What was her frame of mind," Black Jack asked, "when last *ye* saw her, Iain?"

"She was purrin' contentedly from our lovemakin'."

Black Jack chuckled. "So, ye said yer farewells upstairs?"

"No, Brie was in the garden when I left."

Her spritely step betraying her light heart, Antonia fairly danced into the study. "Oh, Iain," she gushed, pasting an appropriately sympathetic expression onto her face, "I'm so verra sorry Brie has deserted ye. She seemed like such a sweet thin'."

When Iain faced Antonia, he recalled how his sister-in-law had cornered him in that very chamber and thrown herself into his arms. "What did ye do to Brie?" he demanded, grabbing her shoulders and shaking her roughly.

"Nothin'!"

With the vilest of oaths, Iain pushed her away.

"When ye saw Brie in the garden," Black Jack asked again, "what was her frame of mind?"

Iain ignored his father's question. Antonia kissed me, he recalled, and then I found Brigette, strangely disheartened, in the garden. To get to the garden, she had to pass the study door. The *open* study door.

"I believe my wife has returned to England," Iain informed his father. "Hopefully, she's arrived there safely. I'll be leavin' in the mornin' to bring her home."

"I'll come wi' ye," Percy offered.

Iain glared murderously at his brother. "There'll be a Highland blizzard in hell before I have need of yer dubious aid."

Marianne gently nudged Brigette awake. Placing a finger over her lips, she warned her young guest to silence. Lil still slept in the other cot.

"Wash and dress," Marianne whispered, "then come downstairs."

Brigette dressed hurriedly, then went downstairs. Bertie was alone in the kitchen. Swallowing her revulsion, Brigette smiled and asked, "Randi?"

"She'll be along." Bertie was impressed with the change in Brigette's appearance. After studying the beauty of her face, his beady-eyed gaze dropped to peruse Brigette's body as if she were a succulent sweetmeat. Anticipating the taste of her tempting flesh, the cook smacked his blubbery lips together, and a dribble of spittle ran slowly down his chin.

"I'd like ta be ya friend," he murmured, advancing on Brigette, who recognized the lusty glint in his eyes and stepped back.

With a swiftness one would not expect in a man his size, Bertie closed the distance between them and tweaked a plump breast. In the next instant, he shoved Brigette against the wall, but she retaliated by kicking his shins. Bertie's scream of pain rent the tavern.

"What the bloody hell is happenin'?" Bucko shouted as he and Marianne raced into the kitchen from the common room.

"He attacked me!"

"She attacked me!"

"Keep them greasy hands off this lady, ya lecher," Marianne warned in a deadly voice, "or ya'll answer ta Bucko and me." She turned to Brigette. "Let me know if he bothers ya and I'll fix him good. Grab some of that bread and cheese for yaself and we'll be off."

Marianne led Brigette into the common room. It was a surprisingly spacious chamber with two hearths, one at each end. Near one of the hearths was a stairway leading to the second-floor bed-chambers. In one corner stood Bucko's domain—the bar. Small tables and chairs were positioned around the chamber. Even unoccupied, the common room possessed a comfortable atmosphere, exuded relaxation.

They went outside. The previous day's rain had ceased, and Brigette looked curiously at everything around her. The morning was young, but the narrow street was quickly becoming congested with all kinds of people—housewives, merchants, apprentices, vendors.

"This is Friday Street," Marianne told her.

Brigette giggled. "How strange to name a street in honor of a day."

Marianne shrugged. "Perhaps it was built on a Friday."

"Whatever the reason, it's a fair enough day to glimpse Londontown."

"Glimpse Londontown?" Marianne looked at Brigette. "Ain't ya never been ta London?"

"No, I've lived my entire life in the country."

"Whereabouts?"

"I'd rather not say."

Marianne arched a brow. "Don't ya trust me?"

"Of course," Brigette answered, "but I'd still rather not say."

"When we've time to spare," Marianne promised, "I'll take ya ta see some of London's most interestin' sights."

"Where?"

"The Bloody Tower is off ta our left. That's where the queen sends a body when she's unhappy with ya."

"My father was once locked in the Tower," Brigette confided.

"He was?" Marianne was impressed. The Tower was a place of confinement for erring nobility. "Did he get his head chopped off?"

"Nothing so dramatic as that." Brigette chuckled. "Papa was forgiven and released."

"Who's ya father?"

"Nobody—he's been dead for several years."

"Oh." Marianne switched to a more pleasant subject. "Blackfriars is off ta the right. One day we'll cross the Blackfriars Bridge into Southwark, where the bear-baitin' rings are. Want ta see it?"

"I don't think so."

"Why not? It's excitin'!"

"It's cruel to abuse animals for sport."

"Then we'll go for a stroll across London Bridge," Marianne announced. Leaning close, she whispered in Brigette's ear, "Where the tarts are."

"Tarts?"

Marianne laughed. "Not that kind of tart—whores!"

"Whores?" Brigette's face was a brilliant scarlet. "You mean, where a man can—"

"That's correct," Marianne interrupted.

"Brigette MacBria!" a familiar voice shouted.

Brigette scanned the crowded marketplace for the owner of that voice. Suddenly, Magnus materialized from nowhere. Except for the familiar stubbles of a growing beard, a dashingly handsome lord had replaced the gaberlunzie.

"You are beautiful," Brigette cried, flinging herself into his arms.

"I thank ye, fair maiden." His eyes drifted to Marianne, who smiled, thoroughly impressed. "I'm relieved to see ye've found yer friend."

"Randi," Brigette introduced the two, "I would like to present Magnus. Magnus, this is Marianne, also known as Randi."

Smiling, Magnus bowed to Marianne, who was thrilled by his courtly manners. Nobody had ever bowed to her before.

"Where is it yer stayin'?" he asked, turning back to Brigette.

"I've found employment at the Royal Rooster Tavern."

"On Friday Street," Marianne added.

"I must soon return to Scotland," Magnus said. "I'll stop by the Royal Rooster before I leave."

"Do!" Brigette exclaimed. "I would be glad of the chance to see you again."

Magnus grinned and hugged her close, then

kissed her cheek. He turned to Marianne and kissed her hand, then strolled away.

"Sweet Jesu!" Marianne swore. "Nobody ain't never kissed my hand before."

"What of Bucko?"

"Bucko ain't the hand-kissin' type, if ya know what I mean," Marianne said. "But I love him anyway and I'm bound ta catch him in wedlock, even if it's the last thing I ever do. Have ya ever been in love?"

Brigette's eyes misted with anguish. "Once."

From her companion's glum expression, Marianne realized love was a sore subject. "How is it ya know a Scottish lord? Ya sound as English as me."

"My husband is Scottish," Brigette answered in a choked voice.

Marianne placed a comforting arm around her shoulder. "Why don't ya lighten that load? Tell Randi what happened."

Brigette sighed. "I learned my husband is in love with his brother's widow. Involved, in a manner of speaking."

"He admitted he was layin' her?" Marianne's eyes were wide with shock.

Brigette flushed. "Antonia told me."

"Let me get this straight," Marianne said, her eyes gleaming with shrewd intelligence. "This Antonia told ya that she and ya husband are lovers?"

"Correct."

"And ya believed her?"

"Why shouldn't I?"

"What did he say?" Marianne asked.

"Iain was away at the time."

"Ya left without speakin' ta him?" Marianne was incredulous.

"What would you have done?"

"Strangled her and gelded him!"

Supper at the Royal Rooster was a noisy and crowded affair. The tavern was a beehive of activity, filled with men, very few of whom were accompanied by a female.

Marianne and Lil divided the room in half, save for the two tables nearest to the bar, which were assigned to Brigette. Bucko had wisely decided to keep close watch on her.

With a spritely step, Brigette approached her first customers, two successful-looking merchants. One was rotundly piggish. His companion was lanky and sported a hawkish beak that overwhelmed his face. Both were expensively dressed.

"Good evening, sirs," Brigette greeted them. "For what would you care this evening?"

"What've we here?" Sir Pig said contemptuously, arching a brow at her accent. "A tavern wench giving herself airs?"

Brigette's eyes narrowed, a sure sign of danger. "I am a lady, sir, no wench," she returned tartly. "You are no gentleman to speak thusly, no matter the cost of your doublet."

Sir Pig's face mottled with anger at her rudeness, but the hawkish one chuckled. "Very well said, my dear," the Hawk replied. "We'd like a pitcher of ale and a couple of bowls of Bucko's stew."

"Right away, my lord." Brigette scurried to the bar and gave Bucko her order. Beside her, a slightly inebriated patron glanced her way. Pleased by what captured his eye, the man reached out and pinched her derriere.

"*Ow!*" Brigette cried and leaped away.

"What a rump!" The man leered at her. "How about a taste of that after work?"

Brigette's mouth dropped in disgusted disbelief. Before she recovered herself, a pitcher of ale and two mugs were set on her tray.

"Deliver ya order," Bucko said.

Brigette served Sir Pig and Lord Hawk their ale, then raced into the kitchen to get their stew, missing the entrance of the Royal Rooster's newest patron. Magnus took a seat near the door.

"Good evenin', sir," Lil said, admiring his good looks and rich apparel. "What'll it be for ya?" She leaned forward so he could feast his eyes on her ample cleavage.

Magnus perused Lil's tempting mounds of flesh, then raised his eyes to hers and smiled. "I want the copper-haired wench to serve me."

"She's busy," Lil snapped, unaccustomed to having her charms rebuffed. "Ya have ta settle for me."

"A mug of ale and a bowl of stew, then."

Lil raced to the bar, where Marianne stood. "That new wench is bad for business," Lil complained, irritated. "Five of my customers have already asked for her. Is this a tavern or brothel?"

"Oowww!" Bertie's loud wail of pain sounded from the kitchen.

"Keep your bloody hands off me!" Brigette's outraged voice was heard.

Marianne raced for the kitchen, but was met at the door by a red-faced Brigette. "I kneed him in the pins," she said smugly. Marianne threw back her head and roared with appreciative laughter. Those men within hearing distance cringed in sympathetic pain and surreptitiously touched the jewels nestled at their groins.

After delivering the stew, Brigette turned to the men at the next table. She rushed to the bar to get them ale and sidled next to Marianne.

Bucko set the pitcher of ale on the tray, and Brigette, clutching it, swung away from the bar. It was then that Marianne strategically placed a foot in front of her. Brigette stumbled and the tray flew out of her hands, drenching Lil, who stood behind her.

Pandemonium ensued. Screeching, Lil swung at Brigette, who ducked to avoid the blow. Lil's fist connected with Marianne's cheek. Marianne retaliated instantly, and the two adversaries fell to the floor—biting, scratching, and clawing each other. Springing into action, Bucko leaped across the bar and tried to separate the furious women.

Unnoticed at the rear of the tavern, Magnus wiped tears of mirth from his eyes. He stood and dropped a few coins on the table, then slipped out the door. When the queen's business is finished, he decided, I'll return for Brie. Huntly's chit be damned!

* * *

The moon was a sliver of silver, peeking down through swiftly drifting clouds at London's deserted streets. A ragged gaberlunzie passed through the Bishopgate and wended his lonely way north.

Overcast and cool, the day was typical of April. With his memories of a copper-haired woman to keep him warm, a ragged gaberlunzie followed the road north out of York.

After reporting to the queen, Magnus plotted, I'll return to London for Brie. She'll have had her fill of taverns by then, but if she's unwilling, I'll abduct her.

We'll return to Edinburgh and live at the Campbell Mansion. When I discover her husband's identity, I'll arrange a fatal accident for him. Then Brie will become my wife, the future Duchess of Argyll.

Lost in pleasant reverie, Magnus failed to focus on the rapidly approaching danger. Riding hard in his direction was a group of men-at-arms.

"Damn," he cursed, suddenly aware that he must have been seen. "Sweet Jesu!" They wore the MacArthur plaid and were certain to identify his horse as their property.

"Seize him!" Iain shouted.

Kicking his heels into the horse's flanks, Magnus attempted to flee. Dugie gave chase, easily tackling his quarry, and the two men landed in the road. Before Magnus could reach for his weapon, five gleaming swords touched his chest.

"For Christ's sake, MacArthur!" Magnus roared. "Call yer men off."

The MacArthur men remained motionless, their swords poised to skewer. Iain dismounted and stared hard at the gaberlunzie.

"Would ye slaughter yer own cousin?" Magnus asked desperately.

Iain motioned his men to sheath their swords. "Who are ye?"

"Yer cousin," Magnus spat. "If ye murder me before I produce an heir, Argyll will have yer head on a platter."

Chuckling, Iain extended his hand and helped Magnus stand. "Why are ye dressed like that, cuz?"

"I've been travelin' for the queen."

Iain gestured to the horse. "And how did ye come by my property?"

A besotted smile appeared on Magnus's face. "It was a gift from the most magnificent, copper-haired wench."

Without warning, Iain's fist connected with his cousin's jaw, sending him sprawling in the dirt. "That was nae wench," he snarled. "That was my wife."

"Yer wife!"

Iain grimaced, humiliated that his kinsman should learn of his marital troubles, then extended his hand once again. "Ye may as well know," he admitted sourly, helping Magnus rise. "The twit had the temerity to fly home to England."

Magnus shouted with laughter, but then realized his cousin was not amused. Forcing himself to show a more somber expression was difficult.

"When I get my hands on her," Iain ranted, "I'll give her the skelpin' of her life. She willna' be sittin' down for a month."

Unable to control himself, a chuckle bubbled up from Magnus's throat. "Headstrong, is she now?"

"Aye," Iain snapped, "but I'll soon cure her of that. Where is she?"

"I'm verra sorry, cuz, but my benefactress has sworn me to secrecy." Iain growled and reached for Magnus, who threw up an arm to ward off the attack. "However," he added quickly, "I must tell ye that a verra fine quality of Brie is bein' served in London at the Royal Rooster Tavern. On Friday Street, to be exact."

"A tavern?" Iain was surprised.

"Yer countess is employed as a servin' wench," Magnus embellished cheerfully.

"I'll kill her!"

One and all, the MacArthur men-at-arms turned away, biting back their laughter. The Sassenach chit was leading the future Earl of Dunridge on a merry chase, but all roads end somewhere. Lord have mercy on the lady when Iain finally caught her!

"Jamie," Iain ordered. "Escort Lord Campbell to wherever he's goin', then go back to Dunridge and tell the earl we've located my wife."

"I amna' in need of a bodyguard," Magnus protested.

"I insist, cuz. If I sent ye on yer way alone and somethin' happened, Argyll wouldna' forgive me. Remember, cuz, if ye dinna produce an heir, to me and mine reverts the clan's chieftainship."

"Ye canna verra well produce yer own heir," Magnus returned, "if yer wife habitually takes off for parts unknown."

"Dinna forget Percy," Iain countered. "Bein' a blockhead doesna' affect his pecker."

Magnus laughed. "When ye've recovered yer wife," he said, shaking Iain's hand, "come to Edinburgh. The court's aboot to become a most interestin' place."

The MacArthurs mounted and rode south. Watching them, Magnus realized his plan to wed Brigette was finished. No honorable man would dispatch his kinsman and marry the widow. Shrugging his shoulders, Magnus shook off his dream. Perhaps while I'm in Edinburgh, he decided, I'll take a quick peek at Huntly's chit.

Dressed in the English mode, Iain and Dugie entered the bustling common room of the Royal Rooster Tavern. A cacophony of sounds and smells greeted their senses—myriad voices, rumbles of laughter, roasting meat, simmering stew, and heavy drink.

Scanning the chamber, Iain noted two things.

Brigette was nowhere in sight, and the tavern was mostly populated with men. He was not pleased. Wanting to observe without being observed, the two Scotsmen sat at a table against the wall, farthest away from the bar and kitchen.

On their immediate left was a table crowded with young men, apparently sons of well-to-do merchants. A blowsy blonde serving wench was smiling at the men. "What'll it be?" Lil was purring.

"We want the copper-haired wench to serve us," one of them replied.

"She's busy," Lil snapped. "Ya'll have ta settle for me."

Iain's ears prickled. His dark, intense gaze skewered the impudent rascal who'd asked for Brigette's services. Obviously, the lad had more on his mind than supper. Damn her, Iain cursed inwardly. He'd probably end the evening by dueling with every randy scamp in attendance.

Three foppishly dressed men entered the tavern and sat at the table on Iain's immediate right. "I don't see her anywhere," one announced, craning his neck to better view the tavern's occupants.

"Her name is Brie," said another. "One of the other wenches called her that."

"A unique name for—" the third commented.

"For a uniquely prime piece of meat," finished the second. His companions laughed.

"Yes," the first one agreed. "I'd love to taste her tenderloin."

Intending to murder the oblivious three, Iain growled and started to rise, but Dugie placed a restraining hand on his forearm. It was then Iain saw his wife for the first time in nearly a month.

Carrying a tray of food, Brigette walked into the common room from the kitchen. She stopped at a table near the bar and smiled brightly at its occupants. One man resembled a pig and the other had the beak of a hawk. Unmistakably smitten, the pig made a comment, and the three of them laughed in easy camaraderie.

Iain would have confronted his wife then, but Lil was suddenly standing there, smiling coyly and displaying her cleavage. "What'll it be, gents?" she asked.

Iain's eyes flicked disinterestedly over her charms, then rose to meet her gaze. "Two ales and stew," he ordered, pressing a gold coin between her fleshy mounds. "I want the copper-haired wench to serve us."

Fuming, Lil nodded but decided she'd had enough of placing second to the red-haired chit. She hastened to the bar.

"Brie?" Lil sidled up to her beautiful rival and smiled. "Could ya do me the favor of bringin' stew and ale ta the two gents on the far side of the room?"

"Yes." Brigette looked at Lil with some surprise. Usually, the blonde scowled, sneered, or ignored her. This was the first smile she'd received. Brigette got the stew and ale, then hurried across the chamber.

"Brie," Lil called as she served the men next to Iain. "Over here." So intent was Brigette on not spilling the tray's contents, she failed to even glance at the table's occupants. Lil smiled slyly and placed her foot in her rival's path.

"*Yeeooww!*" Brigette tripped, and the tray flew out of her hands.

"Ye clumsy chit!" Iain, dripping stew and ale, leaped out of his chair.

Startled by the familiar voice, Brigette looked from the soiled clothing to the man's angry countenance. Her eyes widened in horrified surprise, and her lips formed a silent, perfect O of dismay. She whirled away, her instinct for survival surfacing quickly.

Iain caught her shoulder and spun her around so violently, she crashed into his unyielding body. Scooping up his wife like a sack of flour, he threw her over his shoulder and headed for the stairs.

"Put me down!" Brigette shrieked, harmlessly pummeling his backside. "You roving bastard!" Her cursing became a cry of outraged pain when he whacked her rump.

Iain stopped at the top of the stairs. "Which is yer chamber?"

"Go bugger yourself!"

Again Iain whacked her upended rear.

"The last door at the end of the corridor."

Inside the dingy chamber, Iain bolted the door and then tossed her onto a cot. Brigette leaped off and backed away, one hand soothing her smarting derriere. Ignoring her, Iain discarded his soiled clothing, and then, magnificently naked, turned to Brigette, who was quaking in fear.

"Ye spoiled, willful brat," he spat, advancing on her.

"Keep your distance, you indiscriminating cock!" she ordered, sounding braver than she actually felt. "You adulterous fornicator!"

That halted Iain in his tracks. "Why did ye leave me?"

"Why?" Brigette echoed incredulously. Her voice rose in righteous anger. "*Why?* I know all about you." She sneered contemptuously. "I saw you kissing Antonia."

"I wasna'—Antonia was kissin' me."

"What the bloody hell is the difference?" Brigette hurled, stamping her foot for emphasis.

Iain lunged forward and, grabbing Brigette's upper arm, shook her roughly. "Who's been teachin' ye such foul words?" He sat on the edge of the cot and dragged her across his lap, then yanked her skirt up, revealing her bare bottom.

"I'll teach ye to respect yer husband," he growled. The flat of his powerful hand came down hard on her exposed buttocks. Shrieking, Brigette tried to escape, but was hopelessly ensnared by her husband's strong arms. Again and again, Iain spanked his wife's creamy, flawless rump until it reddened. Brigette's struggles ceased, and her shrieks became heart-wrenching sobs.

"What the bloody hell is going on in there?" Marianne pounded frantically on the door. "Open up, or I'll call the watch!"

Cursing every last member of the English race, Iain ungently dumped Brigette onto the cot. He crossed the chamber.

When the door jerked open, Marianne was eye level with a hairy, muscular chest. A magnificently masculine chest. Afraid to look down, she gazed into dark, glowering eyes. "Who are ya?" she asked, forcing bravado into her voice.

"Iain MacArthur." He thrust his soiled clothing into her hands and threatened, "See these are cleaned, or I'll take ye over my knee for teachin' my wife obscenities." The door slammed shut on Marianne's stunned expression.

Iain turned back to his weeping wife; his ire faded. Damn, but he loved the impertinent minx. A smile tugged at his lips. Brigette had accomplished an astounding feat by getting herself safely from Dunridge to London. On the other hand, Magnus had undoubtedly assured her success. Iain's smile vanished. What *had* their accommodations been along the way?

Banishing the troubling thought, Iain sat on the cot and drew an unresisting Brigette onto his lap. Gently, he wiped the tears from her face, then gazed into the misty depths of her green eyes. "I've been sick wi' worry," he admitted.

"About me?"

Iain nodded. "I almost slew Percy when I discovered ye'd gone."

"Oh, I'm sorry for that."

"Percy's the one who deserves yer apology," Iain said. Like a scolded child, Brigette lowered her eyes and studied her lap intently. "If only ye'd eavesdropped a few seconds longer."

"I am not an eavesdropper," Brigette said hotly, her eyes flashing with anger.

"I amna' accusin' ye of anythin', but if ye'd

lingered longer near the study, ye would've seen me push Antonia away."

"You pushed her away?"

"I did."

"You don't love her?"

"I love ye, hinny." Iain's voice was a soft caress. "Why else would I have so frantically followed ye?"

"I suffered a month of unspeakable torment for nothing!" Brigette exclaimed.

"Ye would have preferred I no' come for ye?" Iain countered.

"No." Brigette eyed him suspiciously, then asked, "How can I be certain you're to be trusted?"

"My word's nae good?" Iain snapped. When she remained silent, he added, "I'll have Black Jack send Antonia back to the MacKinnons."

"No, I'd miss Glenda. Have you been to Basildon? How did you find me?"

"I met a mutual friend of ours along the road," he answered cryptically.

"Mutual friend?" Brigette was puzzled.

"My cousin, the Duke of Argyll's son."

"I've never met—"

"Magnus Campbell," Iain interrupted.

"Magnus is—?"

"Ye talk too much." Smothering her words, Iain lowered his head and captured her lips in a devouring kiss. His tongue invaded and plundered her mouth, stealing her breath away. She clung to him fiercely. "I'm hungry for ye," he whispered against her lips.

Divesting a beautiful woman of her clothing is the momentary task of an eager man, and so it was with Iain. He pushed Brigette back on the cot and, pausing for the barest fraction of a moment, gazed with anticipation at the rare beauty that belonged only to him.

Iain, too famished to fully admire the sight, craved to feel her. He lay on top of her silken body as if they might melt into one another's being. They kissed endlessly, reveled in the glorious sensation of flesh touching flesh in the most tantalizing way.

Brigette felt his erect manhood pressing against the softness of her stomach. She insinuated her hand between their bodies and touched his pleasure-giving staff. Iain groaned at the intimate contact, then spread her thighs and knelt between them.

"It's like an angry dragon poised to attack the unsuspecting," she whispered.

"No, sweetheart, the monster's but lonely for his home."

"The dragon's lair is here." She guided his ruby knob to her moist entrance.

Iain thrust home and Brigette cried out. Urgently and violently, they mated in the most abandoned, primitive sense of the word. Brigette arched her hips, meeting each of Iain's deep, powerful thrusts. The dragon's lair filled with life as they exploded together.

When their panting eased, Iain rolled to the side and almost fell off the cot. With a horrified giggle,

Brigette caught his arm. "How do ye sleep on this thin' that's posin' as a bed?" he asked.

"I'm not as large as you."

He slid a paw down the length of her spine and cupped a sweetly rounded buttock. "Yer delightful as ye are, lovey."

"I love you too," Brigette said pertly, then kissed the tip of his nose. "To answer your question, I've discovered that the truly weary can find blessed sleep wherever they perch."

"Is that so? I must say, ye make a terrible servin' wench."

"Oh." Brigette feigned dismay, then moved to strike. Iain caught her hand and held her captive against the muscular planes of his warrior's body, then kissed her lingeringly.

"Brie," he murmured, savoring her nearness, "throb of my heart, swear ye'll never leave me again."

"I swear."

Night was never-ending inside the windowless chamber where Iain and Brigette slept. Although the cot was much too small, the reconciled lovers were reluctant to separate. When she fell onto the floor a second time, Brigette cursed and started for the empty cot, but Iain drew her back and pulled her on top of him. Thusly, he satisfied her, then kept her prisoner in that position.

Iain opened his eyes and wondered whether it was day or night. Brigette lay on top of him like a silken coverlet, her kitten's breath tickling his neck. The dragon, harmlessly flaccid, was still inside the heated folds of his lair.

Idly, Iain considered waking Brigette with an intimate jab. That arousing thought startled the dragon from his slumber and with his hands cupping his wife's buttocks, Iain swelled and moved inside her.

"Mmmmm." Brigette moaned in her sleep.

Bang! Bang! Bang! Someone pounded on the door. Muttering his displeasure, Iain slid from beneath his sleeping wife, then smiled at her exposed back and buttocks. Damn! But Brie had the most fetching backside!

Disregarding his nudity, Iain crossed the chamber and yanked the door open. His man stood there, holding a pan of washing water and a package beneath his arm.

"Good mornin'," Dugie greeted. "I've brought fresh clothes."

"Set the pan on that table," Iain instructed, taking the package.

Dugie cast a furtive glance at the cot. Brigette's naked glory was exposed to the world.

"She's sleepin'," Iain whispered, then grinned wickedly. "I willna' mention ye were here."

When the door closed behind his man, Iain washed and dressed, then sat on the edge of the cot. Leaning over, he flicked his tongue across the nape of Brigette's neck. She tensed and rolled over, then smiled drowsily at her husband who was unable to resist nuzzling her breasts and licking their rosy nipples. Brigette's breath caught in a ragged gasp.

"Yer body could incite a monk to lust," Iain said, then chuckled throatily and added, "I'm certain the Pope would follow yer titties through the gates of hell."

"And you?"

"Unfortunately," he answered, his thumb and forefinger tormenting a nipple, "I must ignore them until this evenin'. Dugie's waitin' for us." Iain chortled at her obvious disappointment. "There's clothin' in that bag, and dinna dawdle over it. We've a fair distance to travel today."

Iain paused at the door to study the cot. How he would have enjoyed waking Brigette with an intimate jab! "I believe," he announced, "I'll purchase us a cot for Dunridge."

Lighthearted, Iain fairly danced down the stairs into the common room. At once, he became aware of the chamber's charged atmosphere. Dugie sat at one table while Bucko occupied another, and the two were glaring hostilely at each other.

After casting his man a puzzled look, Iain joined Bucko. "Thank ye for the excellent care ye've given my lassie."

"Humph." Bucko snorted.

"Is there a problem?" Iain asked.

"Problem?" Bucko's fist crashed down on the table. "Ya man got a little too bold with my woman last night!"

Aggravated, Iain glanced at Dugie, then back at Bucko. "Would that be the blonde?"

"No, the other."

"Ye dinna own her," Dugie insisted.

"Dugie made free wi' yer wife?"

"Well . . ." Bucko cleared his throat. "Randi's not actually my wife yet."

"Yer betrothed?"

"Ah, no."

"Och, mon!" Iain exclaimed. "Ye canna claim she's yers unless ye wed her."

"I'm plannin' ta marry her," Bucko declared emphatically, "but the banns must be read."

"Nonsense! If ye want a bride today, ye'll have one. Are ye papist or no'?"

"No."

"Dugie," Iain called. "Find a minister and bribe him to wed this mon to his lady wi'out readin' the banns." Dugie nodded and left smiling.

At Iain's suggestion, Bucko produced a flagon of whiskey. They raised their glasses in salute to their ladies.

"May yer intended give ye a brace of strong sons every couple of years," Iain toasted.

"The same ta ya," Bucko returned the tribute, then gulped his whiskey. "I hate ta see Brie leave," he added. "Her comely face and form helped the Rooster's business."

Iain's expression soured, then he asked, "Was that yer intended bangin' on Brie's door last night? Ye'd do well to wash her mouth wi' strong soap."

"I couldn't stop her."

"Ye couldna' stop her? Do ye intend to let the hen rule the Rooster, then?"

"No," Bucko replied indignantly, but added a trifle sheepishly, "but there are times when Randi cannot be stopped."

Iain patted Bucko's shoulder in masculine camaraderie. "Ye must be firm wi' the lassies, friend, or they'll trample ye beneath their pretty feet. An occasional spankin'—no' too severe, mind ye— does wonders for husbandly discipline."

"Is that so? How is it ya own wife ran away?"

Iain's eyes darkened. "It was a misunderstandin', no' that it's any of yer business. She thought I'd been nestlin' between another's thighs."

As Bucko opened his mouth to comment, the tavern's door opened. Dugie entered with a minister. In the next instant, Brigette and Marianne walked downstairs.

Surprised by the minister's presence, Marianne turned to Bucko. "What the bloody—?"

"Keep ya mouth shut," he ordered gruffly, but in a kinder voice added, "The minister's come ta marry us. Be ya willin' or no?" Marianne's mouth dropped in shock.

"She's willing," Brigette answered for her friend.

Witnessed by the MacArthurs, Bucko and Marianne were united in holy matrimony. His pockets jingling with Iain's coins, the minister left immediately following the ceremony. The two couples, plus Dugie and Bertie, sat down to an impromptu wedding feast.

"Where the hell have ya been all night, Lil?" Bucko said as the blonde flounced into the tavern. "Pull up a chair and join us."

"What're ya celebratin'?" She sneered. "Brie's departure?"

Marianne's smile was triumphant. "Bucko and me was just wed proper by a minister."

"Oh, crap!" Lil halted in her tracks, then turned around and left the tavern.

"I'll roast her good," Marianne said to Brigette. "She'll pay for every insult she gave ya."

"Ya'll do nothin' without my permission," Bucko ordered. Marianne began to wonder into what she'd gotten herself.

"I canna thank ye both enough for guardin' my lassie." Iain broke the ensuing silence.

"It was a difficult task," Marianne remarked, "especially keepin' fat Bertie's hands off her."

Bertie gulped nervously when Iain's formidable gaze rested on him. "I'll be in the kitchen preparin' tonight's stew," he said, making a hasty retreat.

Bucko chuckled. "The Rooster's closin' for today."

"What?" Marianne asked. Bucko ignored her.

"Bucko lad," Iain said, rising from his seat, "we must be on our way." He produced a hefty bag of coins and added, "This is for my wife's upkeep and a weddin' present of sorts."

"I want no reward for guardin' such a sweet angel," the tavernkeeper insisted. "Marryin' Randi is reward enough."

"Silence," Marianne hissed, then looked at Iain and added, "If you please, my lord." She rounded on her husband. "The Rooster's openin' today—think of the money we'll lose!"

"Money's not the most important thin' in life, honey," Bucko chided.

"And what, may I ask, is more important?"

"Creatin' a dozen healthy sons ta help us run the Rooster."

Marianne opened her mouth to protest, but Bucko pulled her into his arms and kissed her until she was limp and dazed. The tavernkeeper glanced at Iain, who nodded supportively.

Brigette eyed her husband, aware that the sudden change in Bucko's temperament coincided with his arrival. As if privy to her thoughts, Iain grinned wickedly. "Say yer farewells, hinny."

"I can't thank you enough," Brigette said, hugging Marianne. "If you're ever in need, come to Dunridge."

"I will." Marianne peeked at Iain. "If he doesn't treat ya like he should, ya've always got a home at the Rooster."

12

"Brie." The husky, masculine voice floated through her mind like a sigh on a gentle breeze. Huddled against her husband's chest, Brigette murmured unintelligibly in her sleep.

"We've arrived," Iain whispered. "Shall I carry ye inside?"

"Arrived?" Brigette's eyes flew open and she sat up.

"I canna believe ye've slept the length of Edinburgh. Campbell Mansion is ahead of us."

Inside the courtyard, Iain dismounted and lifted Brigette from the horse. She yawned and stretched in the most unladylike fashion, then took his arm. They turned toward the mansion.

"Brigette MacBria," a familiar voice called. Wearing his most charming smile, Magnus was hurrying toward them.

"Magnus!" Brigette came to life. Releasing her husband's arm, she ran to Magnus, who laughed and hugged her. When he kissed her full on her lips, Iain frowned and wondered for the hundredth time what their accommodations had been along the road to London.

"I'm glad ye've come to visit," Magnus said, shaking Iain's hand. "Come inside."

He led them into the great hall and the three sat in front of the hearth. A servant brought them wine.

"I didna' think ye'd accept my invitation," Magnus remarked.

"Some time ago I offered Brie a trip to Edinburgh," Iain said. "Yer invitation was propitious."

"Iain promised me a shopping spree," Brigette interjected, her eyes sparkling with mischief. "My husband always keeps his promises—unlike others I know."

"I'm verra sorry I couldna' keep my silence," Magnus apologized, an unrepentant grin appearing on his face. "When yer husband's bein' thwarted, he's prone to violence. Besides, everythin's worked out for the best, did it no'?"

"Yes." A rosy blush stained Brigette's pale cheeks.

"Greetin's to the future Earl and Countess of Dunridge," a voice sounded behind them. Startled, Iain and Brigette whirled around.

"What the hell are ye doin' here?" Iain snapped at his brother.

Percy grinned. "I couldna' let ye have all the fun. I've a yearnin' to attend the court and meet our bonnie queen."

"Ye couldna' properly take charge of Dunridge

for a fortnight," Iain said. "Are ye so intent, then, on bringin' misfortune down on our family?"

"It wasn't his fault I ran away." Brigette smiled sheepishly at her brother-in-law. "Will you forgive me for causing so much trouble?"

"I'll forgive ye if ye swear never to do it again— at least while I'm in charge."

"I swear."

"Damn it, Brigette," Iain snapped. "Ye apologize to Percy but ye havena' apologized to me!"

"I've done nothing to you for which I should apologize."

"Ye've done nothin'?"

Brigette smiled sweetly. "You were the one kissing Antonia, not me."

"I wasna' kissin' Antonia."

"Pardon me," she returned haughtily. "Antonia was kissing you." Percy and Magnus burst out laughing, earning themselves a censorious glare from Iain.

"Menzies is at court," Percy informed his brother. "He's been politickin' the queen against us."

"Yes," Magnus confirmed. "There are many unfamiliar faces gracin' Holyrood Palace these days."

"Such as?" Iain asked.

"The Earl of Lennox and his son Lord Darnley recently arrived from London. Darnley has captured the queen's eye."

"What sort of mon is he?"

"Nae mon at all, I fear," Magnus said, "and I'm regrettin' the part I played in extendin' the invitation. He's fair enough on the outside, almost too fair. Shallow, ye might say. He willna' make the queen a good husband, nor will he be good for Scotland, especially we Highlanders."

"Is she so enchanted wi' him, then?"

"She believes herself in love wi' him." At that, they lapsed into thoughtful silence.

"Women are stubborn creatures," Iain commented finally, "and a woman in love is doubly so. Hopefully, Darnley will ruin himself wi'out our help." He turned to Brigette. "Ye'll need a suitable gown to wear at court."

"I'm to accompany you?" Brigette asked, pleasantly surprised. "And meet the queen?"

"Of course, lovey, what did ye think?"

"When will we attend?"

"As soon as we've purchased the proper attire, sweetie."

"I'm too tired to shop today," Brigette said, yawning. "I'd love a hot tub and soft bed."

"Aggie will see ye to yer chamber," Magnus said. After the housekeeper escorted Brigette out of the hall, he turned to Iain. "Brie doesna' look well. Her skin has lost its healthy bloom."

"She has purple smudges underneath her eyes," Percy added.

"Yes, I've noticed," Iain agreed. "Brie's a fragile thin'. Travelin' and toilin' have weakened her delicate constitution."

"Toilin'?"

"When she left Dunridge, Brie didna' return to Basildon," Iain told his brother.

"She found employment in London," Magnus piped in, "at the Royal Rooster Tavern."

"A tavern!" Percy shouted with laughter and Magnus joined him. Iain scowled blackly. He failed to see the humor in a countess posing as a tavern wench, especially when the countess was his wife.

Iain opened his eyes. With her face pressed into his chest, Brigette was snuggled against him. One of her legs was entwined between his muscular thighs.

His calloused hand slowly slid down the length of her spine, ending in a gentle caress to her buttocks. Brigette stirred but did not awaken. Gingerly, he shifted her onto her back and lowered his dark head to her breast. His tongue teased one of her nipples to aroused attention.

"Mmmmm." A murmur of pleasure escaped Brigette. She reached up to press his head tighter against her breast.

"Take me," she breathed, arching with desire.

Drawing back, Iain's smile was pure love. He spread her thighs, then firmly grasped and lifted her hips. Forcefully, he thrust forward, and Brigette gasped.

"Oh, no!" Dismayed frustration followed burning arousal at the sound of the door opening to admit the Campbell servants.

Iain quickly pulled out, whispering, "Until tonight, lovey."

The bedcurtain was drawn aside by a young maid holding a tray of food. Her face reddened with embarrassment when she realized they were naked. "Excuse m-me, m-my lord," she stammered. "Lord M-Magnus b-bade us see to yer needs. He thought ye'd like to breakfast in bed while yer lady's bath is prepared."

They sat up. Brigette tucked the coverlet beneath her arms, leaving only her smooth shoulders and the top of the tantalizing valley between her breasts exposed. She peered at the tray on her husband's lap.

"I'll have that milk," she said as the maids began preparing the bath in front of the hearth.

Iain cocked a brow at her. "I thought ye didna' care for milk?"

"I don't, but I have a mind to drink it today."

"Here." Iain handed her the mug. "Eat somethin'."

"I think not. My appetite's still sleeping."

"Eat this," he ordered, passing her a piece of buttered bread, "and dinna give me any trouble aboot it. Ye slept through supper last night and yer bones are beginnin' to show. I'm surprised I amna' bruised from them pokin' me while we sleep."

"Very funny." Brigette ate the bread.

When the bath was ready, Brigette rose from the bed. With seductively swaying hips, she sauntered across the chamber, and Iain admired the delicate column of her back, her delectably rounded buttocks calling out to him to be fondled.

Before stepping into the tub, Brigette cast him a blatantly flirtatious look, and Iain roared with laughter. Enthralled by his wife at her toilet, he set the breakfast tray aside and relaxed against the pillows to watch.

While a maid scrubbed her back, Brigette

washed one of her legs, raising its shapely length in the air so her husband could view it. The other was boldly exhibited in the same manner, and Iain felt his desire growing.

Brigette slowly lathered her breasts and massaged them, then rinsed. She glanced sidelong at Iain and smiled inwardly. Her husband was mesmerized by a pair of titties.

In dripping magnificence, Brigette rose from the tub. The maid patted her dry and enfolded her in a fresh towel, then plaited her coppery tresses into one long braid.

"You may leave," Brigette dismissed the maid when Iain started to rise, naked, from the bed. With a horrified squeak, the maid hurried out.

"May I assist you, my lord?" Brigette offered.

Sinking into the tub, Iain grinned wolfishly. "I canna think of anythin' I'd desire more."

First, Brigette lathered and soothingly massaged his back, marveling at its broad expanse and the powerful muscles relaxing beneath her hands. After rinsing it, she moved around to his front, and Iain chuckled at the look of anticipation on his wife's face. Brigette lathered his chest, then glided the tips of her fingers seductively across his nipples, which hardened with her teasing. Her hand slid down his rib cage, past his suddenly quivering stomach, and found the masculine appendage nestled at his groin.

"Ahhh." Iain's breath caught raggedly in his throat when her fingers began taunting his engorged manhood.

"Shopping or bed?" she whispered. "The choice is yours."

"Why no' both?"

"A wise choice." She covered his lips with her own, forced them apart and plundered his mouth with her sweet kitten's tongue.

Iain shuddered. He stood and stepped out of the tub, intending to carry her back to bed.

Bang! The chamber door crashed open.

"What a provocative picture," Magnus remarked at their lack of clothing.

Brigette giggled and blushed with embarrassment. Exasperated, Iain scowled, then asked, "Is there nae privacy in this house?"

"Apparently not. Sorry." Magnus spoiled his apology by grinning. "My coach is at yer disposal —if ye've a mind to leave this chamber today."

Thinking they would be disturbed again if they tarried, Iain and Brigette reluctantly dressed and headed for the courtyard. "To the High Street," Iain instructed the Campbell coachmen.

In the Upper Bow, Brigette purchased several gowns suitable for court. Aware that the men at court dressed as Low-landers, Iain bought a dark blue suit in the English mode. Passing a goldsmith shop, he insisted on splurging and purchased several pieces of jewelry to complement Brigette's new gowns. Except for her wedding band, it was the first costly gift he'd given her, and Brigette was ecstatic.

In the Lawnmarket, Brigette bought various fabrics, which she intended to share with Spring. With very little effort, she persuaded Iain to purchase a doll for Glenda, and at the leather crafts-man's she wheedled him into buying Sly a new yellow collar.

The furniture maker's was their final stop of the morning. Iain ordered a cot, of all things, crafted from the finest oak. Puzzled, Brigette asked him about it, but Iain only smiled and said it was a surprise.

"Where to?" Brigette asked wearily.

"Has yer appetite awakened?"

"I'm famished."

The MacArthurs were soon seated inside Mac-Donald's Tavern on Princes Street. They stuffed themselves with scones dipped in honey, boiled mussels and clams seasoned with herbs, and fruit tarts dressed with nuts and spices. To wash the meal down, there were ale for Iain and cider for Brigette.

"Ye arena' eatin'," he said, chuckling at his wife's miraculously recovered appetite. "Yer feedin'."

"I don't want to injure you while we're sleep-ing," she returned, unamused by his humor.

At meal's end, Iain tossed several coins on the table and stood. Then he helped Brigette rise from her chair.

"Are we bankrupt?" she asked.

"Probably. Keepin' a wife is more expensive than I realized."

"But worth every gold piece?"

"And then some." Iain steered Brigette through the crowded tavern.

As they reached the door, it flew open unexpectedly. Blocking their path were two expensively dressed men. Brigette sensed Iain tense and looked closely at them.

One was of an age with Iain, just as tall but heavier. Marring his face was a long, angular scar running the length of one cheek. His eyes were dark, cold, menacing.

His companion was at least ten years older than Iain. Not powerfully built, he exuded an air of quiet authority.

Iain nodded deferentially to the older man. "Good day, my Lord Stewart."

"MacArthur." Stewart's eyes wandered speculatively to Brigette.

"May I make known to ye my wife, Lady Brigette," Iain introduced them. "Brie, this is the Earl of Moray, the queen's brother."

"My lord." Brigette smiled, then glanced at Moray's companion.

"This is Lord Menzies," Iain said. Brigette nodded, her expression remaining impassive. She recognized the hated Menzies name from bits and pieces of overheard conversations.

"Lady MacArthur." His smile did not quite reach his cold, black eyes. With that, Stewart and Menzies politely stepped aside.

"Moray and Menzies together," Iain mused aloud as he sat down beside Brigette in the coach. "How interestin'."

"Will there be trouble?"

"No." Leaning closer, he brushed her lips with his. "Would ye be interested, lovey, in beddin' a newly paupered mon?"

Brigette's hand dipped to his groin. "With pleasure."

"What could be keepin' her?" Percy asked, pacing the foyer impatiently. The three of them had been waiting thirty minutes for Brigette to emerge from her chamber.

"Relax," Magnus advised. "Women always take longer to dress. It's a universal truth and small revenge against us men for rulin' the world."

"I'll get her." Iain crossed to the bottom of the stairs.

"It willna' do ye any good," his cousin predicted.

"We'll see aboot that." Iain started up the stairs, but halted abruptly when he saw the vision poised at the top. His chest swelled with pride.

Brigette had chosen a gown of forest-green satin. Its neckline was squared and cut low to reveal the swell of her breasts, emphasized by the gold torque with which Iain had gifted her that day. Her shining copper hair had been drawn back and woven into an intricate love-knot at the nape of her neck. Her cheeks were flushed with excitement and her emerald eyes sparkled like jewels. Brigette was a woman any man would be proud to possess.

As women have been known to do, Brigette seized the moment, making a grand entrance for the benefit of her masculine audience. Slowly and gracefully, she glided down the stairs, but nearing the bottom, swayed, a sudden dizziness sweeping over her. Iain's hand was there to steady her.

"Are ye well?"

"Yes," she answered softly, "only giddy with excitement."

"Ye look divine," he whispered.

Magnus rushed over and kissed her hand. "Ye remind me of a fairy princess."

"Yes," Percy agreed. "Well worth the wait."

Brigette positively glowed with happiness. "I believe the great clan Campbell has the handsomest, most gallant men in all of Christendom."

The queen of Scotland was in love, and the court that swirled around her was gay. Dangerous undercurrents and bitter rivalries still abounded, but were not apparent. When the Campbell-MacArthur party entered the noisy chamber, Brigette gazed in wide-eyed wonder at the sea of vibrant colors adorning the many courtiers.

A richly garbed, middle-aged man swooped down on them as soon as they entered. Magnus introduced him as the Earl of Lennox. "You're also a visitor from the English court?" he asked Brigette.

"No, my lord," she answered honestly, making Iain smile. "This is my very first time attending any court."

"I mean, you are a fellow countryman," Lennox explained. "An ally of sorts."

Brigette blushed at her own stupidity. "My brother is the Earl of Basildon."

"And now you're wed to young MacArthur," Lennox continued. "It's an excellent blending, the English and the Scots. Wouldn't you say?"

"A superior blending," Brigette agreed, "but not without its frictions."

Iain chuckled, but the Earl of Lennox lost his smile. He wanted his son to wed the Scots queen and considered such frictions unsuitable for discussion at court.

"Damn," Magnus swore. "Huntly's here and headed this way. I'll avoid him by payin' my respects to the queen."

"I'll join ye," Percy said.

"Lady MacArthur." Lord James Stewart appeared from nowhere. "It's a pleasure to see yer fair face again."

"My Lord Earl." Brigette curtsyed to the queen's half brother.

Stewart shook Iain's hand, then smiled coldly at Lennox. "I believe I'll steal the honor of presentin' Lady MacArthur to the queen." He turned to Brigette. "Would ye care to meet her now?"

"Yes, but I'm quite nervous."

"There's nothing to be nervous aboot." Stewart captured Brigette's arm and led her away from a disgruntled Lennox. "My sister is young and enjoys meetin' potential friends. Presently, she's thoroughly enchanted wi' the English."

Mary Stuart would have been regal, even had she not been born a queen. Tall and gracefully slim, she possessed auburn hair, amber eyes, and pale, flawless skin. Personally charismatic, the queen's radiant smile drew people to her like iron to a magnet.

"Iain MacArthur," the queen greeted them. Smiling, Iain stepped forward and bowed low over her hand. "Yer Majesty, I've brought ye a marvelous surprise." He turned to James Stewart, saying, "I believe *I'll* steal the honor, my lord." Stewart nodded, and Iain drew Brigette forward. "Your Majesty, I present my wife, Lady Brigette." Taking her cue, Brigette curtsyed deeply.

"That's the most graceful curtsy I've ever seen," the queen complimented.

"How kind of your Majesty to say so," Brigette gushed, "especially since I've spent the whole day practicing."

The queen laughed, then flicked a quick glance at the handsome courtier standing beside her chair. "You're English, I'm told."

"Yes, your Majesty." Realizing the courtier was Darnley, Brigette grabbed the chance to strengthen her husband's position with the queen. "I find the blending of the English and the Scots a superior match," she confided, casting blatant cow-eyes at Iain. "Perfectly complementary in every way." The queen's smile grew more radiant.

What a wily witch, Iain thought, staring hard at his wife. Brigette could have been an exceedingly talented stage player; she slips so effortlessly from Gypsy princess to tavern wench to politics-playing countess.

"Come closer and sit by me," the queen was saying.

"I'm honored, your Majesty." Pleased with herself, Brigette stepped forward and perched on a stool.

"Tell me truthfully," the queen bade, "how does my court compare with the heretic's?"

A loyal Englishwoman, Brigette suppressed a frown. "Forgive me, but I am unable to compare the two. I've never attended Queen Elizabeth's court."

"Your father was an earl, was he not?"

"Yes, your Majesty, but he only attended the court on rare occasions."

"Why?"

"Being French and a Catholic," Brigette told her, "my mother was not welcomed there."

"How much alike we are!" the queen exclaimed. "My mother was also French. Did not their different religions create problems for your parents?"

"My parents believed that all problems could be solved with love and compromise."

The queen sent her brother a meaningful look, then smiled at Brigette. "You arrived recently from London?"

"We have, your Majesty." Brigette was amazed by how quickly news traveled. She peered at her husband, who looked decidedly uncomfortable.

Iain's unease was not lost on James Stewart. "What," Stewart asked, "was yer business in London, Lady MacArthur?"

I've talked too much, Brigette realized. "It is of a highly personal nature, my lord." She looked back at the queen, who was obviously unhappy with her reply. Better to be thought a fool, Brigette decided, than something more dangerous. No one had ever been axed for being a blockhead.

"It's extremely embarrassing," Brigette confessed, "and I admit I was at fault. You see, I quarreled with Iain and ran home to England. Naturally, my husband followed me, and as you can see, we're now the happiest of couples."

"You journeyed alone?" The queen was shocked.

"I traveled incognito."

"Incognito?"

"I wore my oldest clothes." Brigette peeked at Iain, who was staring hard at her, unhappy with the conversation. "In London, I secured a position as a serving wench in a tavern."

Usually grim, James Stewart shouted with laughter, drawing the surprised attention of most of the courtiers.

"I applaud your courage." The queen's amber eyes gleamed with good humor. "Lady Brigette is a delightful creature, Iain. You will bring her to court often?"

"As ye wish, your Majesty."

On the far side of the crowded chamber, Magnus had finally been cornered by the powerful, persistent Earl of Huntly. Lord George Gordon was not as easily ignored or outwitted as Magnus had assumed.

"Magnus, lad"—Huntly's voice was friendly enough—"I've been tryin' to speak wi' ye since ye arrived."

Magnus smiled insincerely and lied. "I wasna' aware ye were even in Edinburgh."

"Of course, lad." Huntly's smile was equally insincere. "If ye'd known, ye certainly would've sought me out. We've much to discuss, ye know."

"We do?" Magnus feigned ignorance.

"I'll put it to ye bluntly. Are ye willin' to wed Avril?"

"Avril?" Magnus's bewilderment was genuine.

"My daughter, Avril Gordon," Huntly supplied, cocking a brow at the younger man. "Yer betrothed."

Magnus had the good grace to flush. After so many years of referring to her as "Huntly's chit," he'd forgotten her name. "Well, sir," he hedged, "I —I havena' thought aboot it, bein' busy wi' the queen's errands and all. Is she ripe for marriage? I dinna recall she was the last time I saw her."

"That was ten years ago." Huntly snorted. "She was seven years old."

"Good God! Ten years, ye say?" Magnus looked suitably surprised. "Nae wonder she wasna' ripe!"

"Well, she's ripe now," Huntly replied, "and I need to know yer intentions. Menzies has offered for her, but out of respect for yer father and the long-standin' betrothal, I'm givin' ye first choice. There'll be nae hard feelin's if ye dinna want her."

Magnus frowned. "Menzies?"

"Aye."

The two men stood in silence for a time. Huntly, that expert angler from the North, had dangled his line provocatively. Deeming the information digested, he produced a miniature of his daughter and pressed it into the younger man's hands. "This is Avril." When Magnus looked at the miniature, he was hooked neater than any fish.

Avril Gordon was an uncommon beauty. Her fiery tresses were reminiscent of Brigette's, but her eyes were as crisply blue as a Highland autumn sky. She had a heart-shaped face, stubborn, pointed chin, and small nose.

"How bonnie she's become."

"She's also meek, modest, and biddable."

"I'm nae fool, Huntly," Magnus scoffed. "I willna' believe that angel's face is meek or biddable."

Huntly shrugged. "Life can be verra dull wi'out a bit of spice."

"I agree wi' ye." Magnus extended his hand. "Argyll will adore her."

"Are ye sayin' ye'll wed wi' Avril?"

"Was there ever any doubt?" Magnus grinned. "How aboot after the harvest raidin'? Can Avril be ready by then?"

"She will if I order it."

In another part of the chamber, Percy stood with one of the courtiers. David Rizzio was an Italian court singer whom Queen Mary had favored by appointing as her private secretary, much to the angry consternation of several court factions.

"So," Rizzio was saying, "are you enjoying your first evening at court?"

"How enchantin'!" Percy's voice sounded dreamy. Standing a few paces away was the most beautiful woman he'd ever seen.

She was appealingly petite. Her skin was ivory silk with a hint of roses upon her cheeks, contrasting sharply with her ebony hair and dark eyes. She was an exquisite wood nymph whose very existence was a siren's song to Percy.

"I beg your pardon?" Rizzio was puzzled by the younger man's strange behavior.

"Over there," Percy whispered. "Who is the dark-haired beauty?"

"Which one?"

Percy's eyes darted to Rizzio, who was poking fun at him. The younger MacArthur laughed at himself. "Who is she?"

"Sheena Menzies," Rizzio replied, "and newly arrived at court."

"Menzies?" Percy felt utterly deflated.

"Is there a problem?"

"Yes, the MacArthurs and Menzies are sworn enemies."

"So?"

"So I'm a MacArthur," Percy explained, "and she's a Menzies who willna' even speak wi' me, never mind anythin' else."

"I'll introduce you. If you refrain from exchanging surnames, romance will bloom. Once a woman loves a man, she wouldn't care if he was the son of Satan himself. Any Italian can tell you that." The queen's secretary drew Percy forward. "Lady Sheena?"

"Good evenin', my Lord Rizzio," she greeted the Italian in a soft, melodious voice.

"This is Lord Percy, who's been admiring your beauty."

Sheena blushed. Her eyes drifted to Percy, who became caught in their mysterious, black depths. Recovering himself, Percy bowed, saying, "My lady."

Sheena smiled shyly. Having lived so long with

her brother Murdac's harsh intensity, she was instantly attracted to Percy's devil-may-care stance and easy smile. "My Lord . . . ?"

"Call me Percy," he said as Rizzio slipped away. "All my friends do."

She smiled winsomely. "In that case, call me Sheena."

"All yer friends do?"

"They would if I had any."

"Come now," Percy scoffed gently. "A lady such as yerself must have a mob of friends."

"No," Sheena told him. "I'm newly arrived from my home, Weem Castle. And where is yer home?"

"Would ye care to dance?" Percy asked, ignoring her question.

"Yes." Hand in hand, they joined the dancers.

Lords James Stewart and Murdac Menzies were deep in conversation in a shadowed corner of the chamber. "As usual, ye were wrong." Stewart sneered. "There was nothin' clandestine aboot MacArthur visitin' England."

Angry disappointment whitened the scar on Menzies's face. "What business did he have there?"

"He was chasin' his recalcitrant wife." Stewart snorted derisively. "Her stubbornness willna' be a good example for my sister."

Menzies opened his mouth to reply, but nothing came out; across the chamber Sheena was dancing with the younger MacArthur. Without a word, Menzies started forward, intending to separate the two, who by the look of it had eyes only for each other.

Stewart's hand shot out and stayed him. "Dinna create a scandal in the queen's presence," he warned, then added silkily, "If a MacArthur can partner a Menzies, why no' a Menzies wi' a Mac-Arthur?" Murdac looked blankly at him.

"Claim Lady MacArthur's next dance," Stewart suggested. "There's nothin' her husband can do while his brother partners yer sister."

The cruelest of smiles spread across Murdac Menzies's face, and an unholy light glowed from the depths of his black eyes. He nodded to Stewart, then left to entrap his prey.

As the music ended, Brigette smiled wanly at the Earl of Lennox and scanned the hall for Iain. Her stomach was revolting queasily against the day's excitement, and her aching head felt strangely light. The chamber was much too crowded and noisy, and Brigette was almost desperate for a breath of fresh air, an alarming sensation of suffocating nearly overwhelming her.

"Lady MacArthur?" Menzies touched her arm lightly. "I'd be honored if ye'd dance wi' me."

In spite of her woozily functioning brain, Brigette recognized the scar-faced man from Mac-Donald's Tavern. "I—I," she stammered, uncertain what she should do. "I don't think—"

"Come now," Menzies interrupted. "A dance could go a long way in kindlin' renewed friendship between our clans."

Against her better judgment, Brigette nodded and accepted his hand. However, her wildly churning stomach had a will of its own, and she gulped, fighting the sickness back.

As they danced, Menzies studied her through veiled eyes. Her green eyes, flaming hair, and enticing breasts combined in the most delightful manner. Lady MacArthur is lovely, he concluded, much better than her husband deserves. If only she wasn't so pale.

"I heard ye recently traveled to England," Menzies commented, trying to detect a covert reason for the trip.

"Yes." Brigette's voice was no louder than a whisper.

"A visit to yer family?"

"In a manner of speaking." Purposefully evasive, Brigette was as uncomfortable with his questioning as she was with the airless chamber.

He arched a brow at her. "A cryptic statement if I ever heard one."

In the next instant, the chamber became unbearable. Desperate to escape it, Brigette whirled away from Menzies, who misunderstood her reason for flight. His hand snaked out, grabbed her upper arm and twirled her about, none too gently.

"Oh!" Brigette cried out and collapsed. Well honed for battle, Menzies's reflexes were sharp, and he caught his swooning partner before she hit the floor.

"What did ye do to my wife?" Iain demanded, materializing at the sound of Brigette's cry.

"Nothin'!"

"This is no time for accusations." The queen's voice was heard. "My own physician will attend her."

Iain carried Brigette through the antechamber

into the royal privy chamber. As the queen and several of her ladies looked on, he set her gingerly on the couch.

Lord Ramsey, the queen's personal physician, rushed in. "Ye must wait outside wi' yer kin," he said to Iain, who bristled silently at the order.

"This is all Menzies's doin'," Iain growled as he passed the queen on his way out.

Lord Ramsey wafted a vial beneath Brigette's nose. It twitched at the sharp, reviving smell. Her eyes fluttered open and mirrored her confusion.

"How do ye feel?"

"Ghastly."

"I'm goin' to examine ye," the physician explained, "and ask a few questions." Brigette nodded.

Iain paced back and forth in the antechamber while Magnus, Percy, and James Stewart grew tired watching him. "This is Menzies's doin'," he snarled at the queen's brother.

The words had no sooner slipped from his tongue when the door opened. The queen and Lord Ramsey walked into the antechamber.

"Well?" Iain asked.

"I sincerely hope what ails yer wife isna' Menzies's doin'," the physician remarked.

"Do not tease the man, Ramsey," the queen chided, her amber eyes sparkling with merriment. "Tell him what her malady is." Baffled, Iain looked from one to the other.

"Lady Brigette is pregnant," Ramsey announced baldly.

"Pregnant?" Iain was stunned. He glanced at

the grinning faces of Percy and Magnus, then turned to the queen. "By yer leave, I'd like to take my wife home to Dunridge."

"No, MacArthur," Lord Ramsey cautioned. "Wait until the second trimester. Travelin' willna' be so dangerous for the bairn."

"Come," the queen said, turning to her brother. "Let us assure the court that all is well."

Iain entered the privy chamber. The queen's ladies left, but not without a few arch looks and knowing smirks. He sat on the edge of the couch and smiled at Brigette.

"I've made a spectacle of myself." She moaned.

"That isna' so." Iain reached out and caressed her cheek. "I'm the one who's made a spectacle of himself."

"I don't understand."

Iain grinned. "From the moment ye swooned until just now, I've been rantin' like a madman that this was Menzies's doin'." A horrified giggle bubbled up from Brigette's throat.

Leaning over, Iain pressed a kiss on her forehead. When he would have drawn back, she touched his cheek with the palm of her hand. Anxiously, her eyes searched his. "Are you happy about this, Iain?"

"What kind of a question is that?" he asked. "I want a lassie as bonnie as her mother." Brigette smiled, reassured. Then he added, "Of course, I dinna want the lassie until ye've given me several sons to help control her."

Brigette flew into his arms. "I love you."

"And I love ye," Iain whispered as his lips met hers.

Anticipating the announcement of marriage between Queen Mary and Lord Darnley, the MacArthurs and their Campbell kinsman became regular visitors at the court. Brigette pitied Percy's hopeless attraction for their enemy's sister and made it a point to seek out Sheena Menzies. Opposites in appearance and temperament, the two became fast friends. Sheena replaced Brigette's absent sisters and cousin; Brigette became the sister Sheena had never had.

One rainy afternoon Brigette walked through the Campbell great hall and discovered Percy. He sat alone, staring dejectedly into the fireless hearth. "How now, Percy?" she called. "What are you doing?"

"Nothin'," he answered, without looking up.

Her lips quirked. "Claymore or dirk?"

"What?"

"You appear suicidal. Shall I fetch a claymore or would you prefer a dirk? Poison might be pleasant."

Percy's head snapped up. "Why is life so verra difficult?"

"Life is simple," Brigette disagreed, "until we make it otherwise."

"Breedin' women are always content." He dismissed her with a casual wave of his hand.

"What an outrageous lie!"

"It's easy for ye to speak of life's simplicity."

Percy snorted. "Ye arena' in love wi' Sheena Menzies."

"Iain would be terribly jealous," Brigette quipped, and Percy chuckled in spite of himself. "I wasn't going to tell you this," she added. "I dislike breaking a friend's confidence."

"What is it?"

Brigette hesitated, then took pity on him. "Sheena admitted she has a certain fondness for you."

Percy leaped out of his chair and lifted his startled sister-in-law off the floor, then whirled her around and around. Finally, he set her down and planted a smacking kiss on each cheek. "Ye've renewed my hope. I'll have Sheena, even if I must resort to one of the Highland's most ancient customs."

"Ancient custom?"

"Abduction!" Percy fairly danced out of the hall and, in his glee, almost knocked his brother down.

"What the hell was that aboot?" Iain asked.

Brigette glanced at the empty doorway and then at her husband. "Percy's in love."

Iain rolled his eyes. "Who's the puir lady?"

"Sheena Menzies."

That certainly wiped the smile off his face. Iain's expression was thoughtful, almost calculating.

That look bodes ill, Brigette thought. But ill for whom?

On the twenty-ninth of July, Queen Mary married Lord Darnley in a sunrise ceremony. Follow-

ing the service, the MacArthurs left Edinburgh for
Dunridge Castle. With his brother's blessing,
Percy stayed behind to continue his pursuit of
Sheena Menzies.

13

The garden at Dunridge Castle was lush with summer. Amid the vibrant colors and greenery, two blond heads were close together. Lady Antonia and her brother, Finlay, were speaking in hushed tones.

"So Iain wed the Sassenach," Antonia was complaining. "I tried comin' between them, but it didna' work. When she ran away, he went after her. They're together now in Edinburgh."

"Ill luck, to be sure," her brother sympathized. Finlay MacKinnon was weak, both inside and out. Smaller than his sister, he was almost delicate looking. He had inherited the same blond hair and blue eyes, but his skin was bloodlessly white. Ambitious, sneaky, and cruel, Finlay was devoted to his older sister.

"I was to be the countess," Antonia burst out. "What can we do aboot it?"

"Give me a moment to think."

Out for his daily stroll with Glenda and Sly,
Black Jack walked into the garden. "Finlay Mac-
Kinnon," he called. "It's been a verra long time.
When did ye arrive?"

"This mornin'." Finlay shook Black Jack's hand.
"Yer lookin' hale and hearty, my lord."

"I feel good too," Black Jack replied. "For an old
mon, that is." He looked at Glenda and said,
"Greet yer Uncle Finlay, lass."

Studying her mother's brother, Glenda decided
she didn't like him, and stayed close by her grandfather's side. "Good day to ye, Uncle Finlay."

"Yer as bonnie as yer mother." Finlay smiled at
the image of his beloved sister as a child, then held
out his hand to her. "Would ye care to walk aboot
and become reacquainted?"

Glenda stared at the hand, then up at him.
"No."

Antonia gasped at her daughter's rudeness, and
Finlay lost his smile. Black Jack chuckled, pleased
to be loved above all.

"She's a bit shy," he explained.

"Well, I suppose shyness is appropriate in a female," Finlay remarked. "What's this wild beastie
doin' here?"

"Sly isna' a wild beast," Glenda corrected tartly.

"He's Lady Brigette's pet," Antonia added in a
disapproving voice.

"A messenger arrived earlier," Black Jack told
them. "Iain and Brie will be home before the
week's gone."

"What wonderful news!" Antonia exclaimed.

"That isna' the best part. Lady Brigette is wi'

child." Black Jack turned to Finlay. "How long will ye be stayin'?"

"Only for the night."

"It's grand seein' ye again." With Glenda and Sly in tow, Black Jack walked away.

"Curse and rot her," Antonia spat. "I'll never become the countess now."

"That isna' necessarily true," Finlay disagreed.

"What do ye mean?"

He smiled coldly. "If a terrible fate befell the Sassenach, yer path to Iain would be clear."

"And if she drops a lad," Antonia said, returning her brother's smile, "I willna' be obligated to fatten wi' child. What are ye plannin'?"

"I believe," Finlay replied, "the Sassenach has a fateful appointment wi' the Lady's Rock."

"Lady's Rock?"

"Remember the old tale of what the MacLean did to his Campbell wife when he tired of her?"

"No, I dinna recall the story."

"Located in the Sound of Mull is a large rock that becomes submerged when the tide is high."

"Verra creative and efficient of ye." Antonia grinned. "There willna' be a body to bury."

Finlay preened at his sister's praise. "Of course," he added, his expression clouding, "the Campbell wench had a happy endin'. A couple of passin' fishermen rescued her, and the Campbells revenged themselves by killin' MacLean. Do ye think such fantastic luck could happen twice?"

"Why tempt the fates?" Antonia returned. "Grow a beard and wear the Menzies plaid. If

Brie's somehow saved, the blame will fall on them."

Finlay nodded. "Send word to me after she's whelped the brat. Now, tell me what she looks like."

"Well . . ."

"Speak honestly, sister. I dinna want to snatch the wrong woman."

"Brie's much shorter than I," Antonia told him. "She has red hair and green eyes—"

"Green eyes!" Finlay made the sign of the cross. "It's surely the mark of a witch."

"Dinna be absurd. There's nae such thin' as witches."

"There are," he insisted. "Ye'd have me snatch a witch? What's to prevent her from dispatchin' *me* before I dispatch *her*?"

"Finlay!" Antonia exclaimed, exasperated. Her voice softened. "Do ye actually believe I'd send ye to yer death?"

"No."

"There's nothin' magical aboot the Sassenach," she assured him. "Trust me."

The guards who patrolled Dunridge's walls cheered and waved as the MacArthur entourage approached the castle's outer curtain. The troop passed through the outer gate and proceeded to the inner courtyard. Family and retainers waited there to greet them.

In their enthusiasm, Glenda and Sly rushed forward, heedless of being trampled by the horses.

Black Jack grabbed his squealing granddaughter while Spring restrained the excited fox.

Iain dismounted and turned to assist Brigette, who made his task difficult by waving and calling out to Glenda and Sly. Deeming the courtyard safe, Black Jack and Spring released their struggling captives.

With a whoop of joy, Glenda leaped into Brigette's open arms. All eyes in the courtyard riveted on the heart-tugging picture of the woman and the child clinging to each other while the pampered pet gamboled around and around, whining to be included. Kneeling in the dirt to accommodate her two favorites, Brigette held them close; the girl and the fox nuzzled her neck. Brigette's eyes filled with tears and an unexpected sob caught in her throat.

"Ye left me," Glenda accused, "and I missed ye terribly."

"And I missed you." Brigette gulped back her throbbing emotion. "I've brought you a special gift. Will you forgive me?"

"Do ye promise never to leave me again?"

"I promise."

Glenda's gaze drifted to the fox. "Sly's been feelin' puirly too."

Brigette's lips twitched. "I've also brought Sly a gift. Do you think he'll forgive me?"

"I believe so."

Brigette laughed and gave her a resounding kiss on each cheek. Sly whined for his share of attention. Astonishing everyone but Glenda, Brigette planted a smacking kiss on the wet tip of the fox's muzzle.

Brigette rose finally and greeted Spring, whose face was damp with tears of relief. The cousins hugged and kissed.

"I was beside myself with worry," Spring admitted.

"I'm sorry for that," Brigette apologized, glancing sidelong at Antonia, who was just walking into the courtyard. "It was a horrible misunderstanding. Will you forgive me?"

"I haven't decided," Spring teased. "Did you bring me a bribe?"

"That I have," Brigette said, laughing. "I purchased fabrics in Edinburgh and thought we could share them."

"I forgive you, then."

Turning away, Brigette approached Black Jack, who was speaking with Iain. "I'm sorry," she offered hesitantly, uncertain of her father-in-law's welcome.

"We'll have none of that," Black Jack chided gently, then drew her close and kissed her cheek. "The babe yer carryin' more than adequately makes up for yer foolishness." He patted her hand, then scanned the crowded courtyard. "I dinna see Percy. Where is he?"

"Percy remained in Edinburgh," Iain told his father.

"Why?" Black Jack asked. "My spies tell me Menzies returned to Weem Castle."

"He's in love," Brigette blurted out.

"In love?" Black Jack threw back his head and shouted with laughter. "Who's the puir lady?"

"Sheena Menzies," Iain mumbled, hoping his father wouldn't catch the surname. "She serves the queen."

"Sheena Menzies?" Black Jack echoed.

"She's a sweet girl," Brigette added. "You'll be proud to call her your daughter."

"Charmin' though he may be, Percy's a numbskull who never travels the high road." Black Jack shrugged fatalistically, knowing some things were beyond his control.

"Hinny," Iain said to Brigette, "will ye do me a favor?"

"Anything."

"Wash out yer mouth before I kiss ye. I dinna relish the taste of fox."

"Refreshment is waitin' in the hall," Antonia called cheerfully, determined to behave as if she weren't the reason her sister-in-law had fled Dunridge.

Brigette went into the great hall with the others. Glenda refused to relinquish her hand, and Sly insisted on brushing himself against her legs as a cat would. Brigette could hardly walk, but neither child nor fox was willing to chance losing her again.

Everyone sat at the high table, except Spring, who preferred to sit with Jamie. As soon as Brigette sat down, Glenda scrambled onto her lap.

"Get down," Iain snapped at his niece. Bewildered and hurt, Glenda's bottom lip trembled.

"What's wrong?" Brigette asked Iain, her arm encircling the little girl.

"She'll hurt the babe."

Black Jack, seated beside his daughter-in-law, chuckled at his son's zealous concern. He recalled an earlier time when he had faced impending fatherhood, and knew his son's anxiety would intensify with the advancing months.

"Glenda is fine where she is," Brigette assured her husband. "I'm not as delicate as you believe, and neither is the baby."

"What baby?" Glenda asked.

Brigette guided Glenda's hand to her gently swelling stomach. "I've a baby—your new cousin —growing inside me." The little girl's expression was sheer delight. "Soon he'll be strong enough to live outside my belly, and all of us will play in the garden—you, Sly, the baby, and me. Do you think you'll enjoy that?"

"Yes, but where was he before?"

"With the angels in heaven."

Glenda frowned. "How did he get from heaven into yer belly?" Black Jack and Iain chortled loudly.

"It was Uncle Iain's doing," Brigette answered, blushing. She smiled at him, adding, "Tell her, Uncle Iain, how your son got inside my belly."

Iain frowned. "It happened, Glenda, when I showed her my love."

"I ken," Glenda said. Iain smiled smugly, but nearly toppled off his chair at his niece's next words. "I've got nae babe in my belly," she said loudly. "Dinna ye love me, Uncle Iain?"

Brigette giggled, then explained, "It's a different kind of love, angel, that an uncle has for his niece."

"Oh." That seemed to satisfy Glenda, but then she peered curiously at Brigette. "But how will the baby get out of yer belly?"

"Iain, I think we should present our gifts now," Brigette suggested, ignoring the question.

"I agree wi' ye." Iain bestowed the gifts they'd brought from Edinburgh. Glenda shrieked with joy over her new doll, promptly named Lady Autumn. When questioned about the unusual name, Glenda explained that Brigette had come to Dunridge in the autumn, and she wanted to forever remember that happy day. No one noticed Antonia's lips curl in a silent snarl.

Spring admired the beautiful fabrics. When she left the hall a few minutes later to order Brigette's bath, she carried them away almost reverently.

Iain lifted Sly onto the table and removed the old yellow collar, then fastened the new one around the fox's neck. "There now," he said. "What do ye—?"

Sly's tongue darted out and landed in his open mouth. "*Yuck!*" Iain wiped his mouth on his shirtsleeve and took a swig of ale, then set Sly on the floor.

"Dinna forget to wash out yer mouth, lovey," Brigette mimicked her husband's burr. "I dinna relish the taste of fox."

The family gathering soon dispersed. Glenda went reluctantly to her lessons with Father Kaplan, and Brigette went upstairs to bathe and rest.

When Black Jack retired to his study, Iain took a draft of ale and sat in front of the hearth. Relaxing, he stretched his legs out, then closed his eyes and fantasized about the son that he was certain Brigette carried.

"Yer wife is a whore." A voice sneered.

Iain's eyes flew open and focused on Antonia, who stood before him. "Dinna speak such vile lies to me or anyone else hereaboots," Iain warned. "If ye do, ye'll regret it."

"Regret speakin' the truth?" Antonia countered.

"No, meddlin' in my life," Iain said, his voice deceptively calm. "Ye've caused enough problems between my wife and me. If it happens again, I'll have ye returned to the MacKinnons."

"And lose Malcolm's daughter?"

"Glenda is a MacArthur and remains at Dunridge."

"Ye bastard!"

"I can assure ye, dear sister-in-law," Iain said, "Black Jack and my mother were well and truly married."

"Can ye also vouch for the brat yer wife is carryin'?" Antonia asked, ignoring the murderous expression on his face. "Brie's traveled the road, and I warrant a few men traveled hers."

"Shut yer mouth," Iain snapped. "Brie was well protected by Magnus Campbell."

Antonia arched a brow at him. "Was she now? And who, might I ask, protected her from Magnus Campbell?" With that, she walked away.

Shocked, Iain sagged in his chair. What *had*

Brigette's accommodations been along the road to London? he thought for the thousandth time. Would he ever be certain his firstborn was really his?

After she'd bathed and napped, Brigette dressed for supper. For the first time since leaving Edinburgh, she felt clean and pretty, but her gown was uncomfortably snug across her bosom and waist. None of her garments fit properly, and Brigette made a mental note to start letting out the seams.

Hoping to speak privately with the earl, Brigette went directly to the great hall, but Black Jack was nowhere in sight. Next she tried the study. Relaxing in his chair in front of the hearth, Black Jack seemed to be expecting her.

"I've been daydreamin' of seein' my first grandson," he told her. "How are ye feelin'?"

"Well enough, now the sickness has passed. You won't be upset if I deliver a girl, will you?"

"No, but I dinna think Iain will let ye give birth to a lassie first."

Brigette smiled. "You're probably correct," she agreed, then stammered, "I—I'm sorry for leaving Dunridge. I realize—"

"There's nae need," Black Jack insisted, waving her apology aside. "Will ye tell me why ye ran away? Had ye quarreled wi' Iain?"

"No, I—I . . . Antonia—"

"Dinna go on," Black Jack interrupted. "That one word says it all. Perhaps I should return her to the MacKinnons."

"No!" Brigette cried, surprising the earl, who knew his daughters-in-law could never be friends. "I'd be unhappy without Glenda."

"Glenda's a MacArthur and would remain at Dunridge."

"You cannot separate a mother from her child," Brigette said, her hands wandering instinctively to her stomach.

"Yer more of a mother to Glenda than her own has been."

"Antonia would not see it that way. She'd claim we stole her daughter, and there'd be hostilities between the clans."

Black Jack nodded. "Yer wise for one so young."

"I'm a peahead," Brigette confessed. "Why else would I have run away?"

"If ye recognize yer folly, then yer nae longer a peahead," Black Jack disagreed. "Magnus Campbell escorted ye to London?"

"Yes, he's a good friend and an honorable man."

"The lad takes after his father." The two sat in companionable silence for a time. "I'm an old mon who's seen a lot of things, some good and some bad." Black Jack broke the silence finally. "My advice is to concentrate on deliverin' a healthy heir for Iain. Frettin' aboot what's past willna' help the future. Do ye recall the day ye arrived at Dunridge?" Black Jack chuckled at the memory. "Lookin' worse than a beggar, ye marched into this study and ordered me to keep my nasty hounds penned, lest yer precious pet be terrorized."

Brigette blushed.

"Be patient wi' him," Black Jack counseled. "Like me, Iain isna' easy to live wi', but he'll mellow wi' age. Shall we see aboot supper?"

Brigette smiled. "Yes."

Black Jack escorted Brigette into the great hall and past Antonia, who was seated at the end of the high table. As Dunridge's ranking lady, Brigette's place was between the earl and her husband. Iain was nowhere in sight.

Glenda, invited to eat with the adults for this one night, scampered into the hall. "Sit next to me," Brigette bade her. "Uncle Iain will sit on your other side. Won't that be fun?"

Wearing a dour expression, Iain strode into the hall, and Brigette wondered if there was a problem. Her gaze drifted to Antonia, whose expression was placid. She's angered him, Brigette concluded. The witch is only happy when someone else is suffering.

When Iain sat down and ignored her, Brigette forced a pleasant smile on her face and turned to Glenda. "I don't see Lady Autumn among us," she said. "Where is she?"

"Lady Autumn is suppin' wi' Lord Sly," Glenda told her. "She's taken a fancy to him."

Brigette's smile was genuine. "Is that so?"

"Yes. Dinna tell grandfather this," the little girl added, "but Lord Sly has taken shockin' liberty wi' Lady Autumn."

"The knave," Brigette exclaimed, trying hard not to laugh. "What has that furry scoundrel done?"

"He's been so bold as to hold her hand."

"No! Surely he hasn't held her hand?" Brigette's tone was suitably dismayed, but her lips twitched.

"In his mouth."

Brigette and Black Jack burst out laughing. Even Iain cracked a smile.

"This is a happy group," Moireach commented, arriving with their supper. After serving the family, the housekeeper lingered at the high table to help Glenda. She beamed proudly when Brigette praised her haggis.

"Mmmm . . . delicious," Brigette complimented. "Of what does it consist? I've forgotten."

"Dinna ask, just eat."

Slowly, Brigette chewed another bite, then swallowed. "Well, it tastes good." She patted her stomach and looked at her husband, saying, "Our baby takes after his Scots father."

Iain stared coldly at her, then turned away. Yes, he thought, but which Scotsman is the father?

Is he angry with me? Brigette wondered, bewildered. Have I done something, or not done something I should have?

"Has Spring told ye the good news?" Moireach asked loudly, attempting to smooth things over. "She and my Jamie have handfast."

"Handfast?" Brigette looked over at Spring, who was blushing furiously. Beside her, Jamie was grinning. "Is that like being betrothed?"

"It's a marriage of sorts," Moireach explained.

The fork that was en route to Brigette's mouth halted, and then returned to her plate. "A marriage of sorts?"

"It's perfectly legal, mind ye," the housekeeper

assured her. "They'll live together for a year and then decide whether or no' to wed permanently."

"Your man is dishonoring my cousin!" Outraged, Brigette turned on her husband. "I insist they wed immediately!"

Iain's expression darkened even more. "Jamie isna' forcin' Spring to do anythin'. For once in yer misbegotten life, mind yer own business."

"Misbegotten life?" Brigette would not mind her own business, but she would ignore her husband's insult. He would pay for it later. "This is scandalous," she wailed, appealing to the earl.

Black Jack sat back in his chair. If he didn't settle this now, he was certain to develop indigestion before supper was finished. "Moireach, tell Jamie and Spring to come here." When they stood before him, Black Jack addressed his man. "Would ye be willin' to wed Spring in front of Father Kaplan?"

"Who else would wed us?"

The earl smiled pleasantly. "I mean, immediately followin' supper."

"Ye—ye mean tonight? But—"

"Lady Brigette isna' happy wi' yer arrangement," Black Jack interrupted. "If ye dinna wed Spring proper, she'll be sent home to England."

"Send me home?" cried Spring.

"That bein' the case," Jamie agreed without hesitation, "I'll wed my lassie now."

Supper resumed. Brigette peeked at Iain. His disdainful stare pierced her heart more deeply than any dagger could. If he's angry, she wondered, why doesn't he tell me and have done with it?

"When we spoke earlier," Brigette said to Black Jack, an imp entering her soul, "did you say 'mellow with age' or 'sour'?"

Black Jack laughed, and Brigette joined him. Iain watched them sullenly, positive their jest was at his expense.

"Uncle Iain isna' happy," Glenda piped up, noting his displeasure.

"Yes." Brigette glanced sidelong at him.

"When ye left," the little girl chattered away, "Uncle Iain was verra angry wi' Uncle Percy. It was frightenin' to see."

"What happened?"

"Uncle Iain scolded me harshly," Glenda rambled, "but Grandfather is the laird here and set him straight. Grandfather said Uncle Iain was sick wi' worry aboot ye."

Over Glenda's head, Brigette caught her husband staring at her stomach, and he flushed. "If ye canna behave yerself, Gabby Glenda," Iain growled, "ye willna' be invited to sup wi' us again."

"Do not vent your foul mood on the child," Brigette returned, reaching for Glenda's trembling hand. "It ill becomes you."

Moireach arrived then to clear the table and saved Brigette from a tongue-lashing. The earl called for Father Kaplan, Jamie, and Spring to step forward.

It was a simple exchange of vows, completed in a few short moments. In fact, the bride and groom's passionate kiss lasted longer than the ceremony, or so it seemed to Brigette. A rousing cheer filled the hall as the kiss went on and on. Lest Glenda see or hear what she shouldn't, Moireach led her, protesting, from the chamber.

The earl stood and toasted the bride, then drained his goblet and smashed it against the wall. His warriors drained their mugs but were more careful of their lord's property.

Brigette kissed her cousin and wished her well, then, intending to seek her own chamber, walked the length of the high table.

"Humph!" Antonia sniffed.

Brigette halted and turned around, her green eyes meeting the blonde's disdainful blue. "Was there something you wanted to say?"

"Yer a hypocrite." Antonia sneered.

"Speak to the point."

Aware that all eyes were watching, Antonia rose from her chair, her eyes challenging Brigette's unwavering gaze. "Ye shameless slut, do ye even know whose brat ye carry?"

"You . . . you . . . *wood pussy!*" Brigette lashed out. Turning on her heels, she stalked out of the hall.

"Did ye hear the vulgarity?" Antonia wailed, turning to Black Jack and Iain.

Black Jack laughed, and even Iain was unable to suppress a smile. "I believe," the earl informed his daughter-in-law, "Brie just called ye a skunk."

With her shoulders slumped, Brigette sat on a stool in front of the fireless hearth. The door opened, and at the sound of her husband's entry, Brigette jerked up straight, squared her shoulders, and resumed brushing her hair.

Iain crossed the chamber and sat in the chair beside her stool. Silently, he watched her, but Brigette ignored him.

"Some important questions have arisen," Iain said abruptly. "I need the answers—honest answers." Brigétte continued brushing her hair.

"Damn ye," he snarled. His hand snaked out and halted the vigorous stroking. "Look at me when I'm speakin' to ye!" She turned toward him then, and he saw the tears on her cheeks. Iain hesitated, then asked, "Are . . . are ye carryin' my child?"

Brigette gasped. The hairbrush flew, catching Iain on the side of his face. "It's Murdac Menzies's brat, you idiot!" she shrieked.

Iain grabbed her wrist and yanked her off the stool, forcing her to kneel in front of him. "I amna' jestin'."

"You've been listening to Antonia."

"Dinna blame her for voicin' my thoughts. What were yer accommodations along the road to London?"

Much to Iain's surprise, Brigette burst out laughing. "A-along the road?" Her laughter intensified, rising dangerously close to hysteria. "You—you think M-Magnus and m-me?" Iain gave her a rough shake, then waited while she calmed herself. "You're a fool," she hissed, wiping her tears away. "Magnus Campbell is honorable."

Iain flushed. "I'm relieved to hear it, as I dinna

relish the prospect of dispatchin' my own kin. And when ye stayed in London?" he probed cruelly. "Did anyone get to ye then?"

Her expression of horror answered his question. "Nobody 'got to me,' as you so delicately put it," Brigette snapped. "Do you actually believe Bucko and Marianne would have allowed anyone near me? Ha! I was better protected there than I am here."

"I believe ye."

"How exceedingly kind," she said, then hiccuped.

Feeling guilty now for doubting her fidelity, Iain reached out to touch her shoulder, but Brigette shrugged him off. "You accused me of not trusting you, but you don't trust me," she said, her eyes flashing with anger. "I hope this baby is a boy—for Black Jack's sake."

The unspoken threat of estrangement hung heavily between them. Brigette stood, but Iain pulled her down onto his lap and kissed her deeply. No response.

"Damn it, Brie! I canna help bein' jealous. I love ye."

His admission of love was a mightier weapon than the worst of his angry insults. Brigette crumpled against his chest and wept.

"I'm sorry, hinny," he crooned over and over, his heart wrenching with each teardrop she spilled.

When her sobbing subsided, Iain tilted her chin up and gazed into green eyes shimmering with tears. "Give me a smile, sweetie," he coaxed.

Brigette smiled tremulously, and Iain pressed a kiss on her cheek. "It's been a long, unpleasant day," he whispered. "Let's go to bed."

Once undressed, Iain turned toward the bed, a peculiar sight greeting him. On the other side of the bed sat Brigette, massaging her stomach and breasts with lotion.

"What're ye doin'?" Iain asked, walking around to her side. He admired the way the candlelight and lotion combined to give her skin an appealing sheen.

"Moireach made this for me," Brigette answered, admiring his powerfully built physique in the glow from the candle. "She says it discourages stretching marks."

"May I help ye?"

"Yes."

Iain knelt in front of her, and if his face hadn't been cast into shadow, Brigette would have recognized his grin as waggish. After warming the lotion in his hands, Iain began with her stomach. His strokes were slow and soothing, and Brigette marveled that the touch of his battle-scarred hands could be so gentle. As she watched Iain, so intent upon his task, a tender smile touched her lips.

"It's amazin' to think what lies beneath my hands," he whispered. "In five short months he'll be here."

"Or she."

"Yes, or she."

Iain warmed more lotion in his hands and reached for his two favorite things in the world, his wife's breasts. Brigette closed her eyes. The strokes that had soothed her rounding stomach now tantalized her sensitive breasts.

"Yer nipples are swollen and dusky," he murmured, teasing their tips between his thumb and forefinger. "They remind me of those cherries we ate at court."

Brigette chuckled throatily. A bolt of tingling desire raced from the peaks of her nipples and stabbed the secret spot between her thighs.

Leaning closer, Iain kissed each soft breast. His tongue taunted their hardened centers, and moaning softly, Brigette clasped him tightly. When her hips began to move, he pushed her back on the bed.

Iain's lips slid down the length of one leg. He kissed her foot and licked his way up the inside of her leg, then, pausing to press his lips on her stomach, he murmured, "I love ye." Then his skillful lips lavished the same attention on her other leg.

Returning once more to Brigette's stomach, Iain's head dipped suddenly to her womanly slit. He licked and nipped her female button, and, when she cried out, slipped his tongue inside her. Brigette melted against his face, waves of pleasure sweeping her toward the ultimate paradise.

Iain loomed above her face. "The babe . . . ?"

"Misses you."

Keeping most of his weight off her, Iain slipped into her wet sheath. Slowly, he pierced and withdrew, increasing his tempo with each seductive plunge. Brigette arched, urging him on, and met each exquisite thrust with her own. In the throes of their passion, one maddened, bucking creature was formed.

"Fill me," she wailed. And he obliged by spilling his seed.

When their breathing eased, Iain drew Brigette beneath the coverlet with him, then cradled her in his arms. "Sometimes I'm an ass," he said, then vowed, "May God smite me dead if ever I upset ye again."

Brigette's shoulders shook with silent laughter.

"Well," Iain amended, "if I ever doubt yer love for me. Is that better?"

"Much."

14

"God's earlobe," Brigette grumbled, struggling with her gown. She'd had no heart to summon Spring to her chores the morning after her marriage, but dressing without her cousin's assistance was proving hopelessly impossible.

Brigette was ensnared inside the voluminous folds of her gown, unable to free herself or locate the armholes. Why is a grown woman incapable of dressing herself? she wondered, frustrated. Brigette struggled on valiantly, her determination growing apace with her frustration.

Across the chamber, Iain watched the war being waged between his wife and her gown. The wryest of smiles touched his lips.

Success! Brigette found the sleeves and slipped her arms in. The gown cleared her head and slid into place. Only the buttons remained. Reaching around, Brigette found the button at her waist, and the battle began in earnest. She contorted this way and that, but the sides of the bodice would not meet. Never mind, she told herself. She would begin at the top.

The two top buttons were deceptively easy, and her confidence grew. Brigette could reach the third button but was unable to pull the sides of the bodice together. The fourth button was unreachable, and she was already flushed and damp from her exertions.

Strong hands touched Brigette's shoulders. "Can I help ye?" Iain asked, his breath tickling the back of her neck.

"Yes."

"My fingers are a mite too large for such a delicate task," he said, struggling to pull the sides of the bodice together. "Damn! Suck in yer gut."

"I am."

Heedless of tearing the gown, Iain tugged with all his strength.

"*Stop!*" Brigette cried. "I can't breathe."

"Tsk! Tsk! Tsk!" Iain clucked at her plight. "Yer too fat for yer gown."

"It's one of my favorites," she wailed, a sob catching in her throat.

"I've the perfect solution." Hiding the proof of her widening girth, Iain draped one of Brigette's shawls over her shoulders, then tied it in front. "Given a choice," he said, playfully tapping the tip of her nose, "I prefer battlin' yer buttons to holdin' yer head over the pot."

In the great hall, Black Jack sat alone at the high table. Iain and Brigette joined him there, and as they walked through the chamber, noted many

weary and pained expressions on retainers and
men-at-arms. Apparently, Jamie and Spring's marriage celebration had included a great quantity of
drink.

"Good mornin'," Black Jack greeted, pleased to
see his son's improved expression.

"Good mornin'," they chimed together.

"How are ye feelin' today, Brie?"

"Fat."

Black Jack chuckled. "Ye dinna appear fat to me.
Yer lovely. Isna' that right, son?"

"My wife is perfection," Iain agreed, "but her
gowns are tighter than a virgin's—"

"Iain," Brigette said. "You are incorrigible. Why
do you persistently annoy me?"

"Annoyance makes ye even more adorable than
ye already are."

Black Jack patted Brigette's hand. "Dinna pay
him any mind. A widenin' girth is natural in a
breedin' woman. After all, how could the two of ye
fit into one gown?"

"Two of us?"

"Ye and my grandson," Black Jack replied. "And
I've news that'll make ye feel better."

"What?"

"Antonia willna' be joinin' us for meals 'til her
injured pride recovers from yer name-callin' last
night."

"If ye werena' breedin'," Iain teased, "I'd train
ye to come raidin' wi' me. That waspish tongue of
yers lets blood."

"Speakin' of raidin'," Black Jack said, and Iain
groaned, knowing what his father was about to

say. "It's August, and ye've had a day and a night of rest."

"What's important about August?" Brigette asked.

"Harvest raidin' is the busiest time of the year," Iain told her.

"Unlike last year, when Iain was courtin' ye at the huntin' lodge," Black Jack added, "we spend August honin' our fightin' skills and plannin' strategy. When a clan fails to properly protect itself, a lean winter follows."

Their breakfast of oatmeal porridge, bannocks, ale, and milk arrived then. "Good mornin'," Moireach said, setting a mug in front of Brigette. "Here's yer milk."

"I'm beginning to feel like a cow," Brigette complained.

"And yer beginnin' to resemble one," Iain quipped, then threw his hands up in mock surrender when Brigette, ready to do battle, turned on him. "Around the udders, I mean, the breasts," he amended. Brigette was unamused.

"Come here, sweetie," Black Jack called to Glenda, who walked into the hall. "Come and bid me a good mornin'."

"Good mornin', Grandfather." Glenda climbed onto his lap and batted her eyelashes at him, as Brigette had taught her.

He smiled, then asked, "Did ye sleep well?"

"Yes."

Brigette reached down to pat Sly, who was sitting on the floor between their chairs, then glanced sidelong at the little girl. "I'm wondering," she said, "why my furry friend did not sleep with me last night."

"Lord Sly begged to remain wi' Lady Autumn," Glenda lied.

"Did he now?" Skeptically, Brigette arched a brow at her.

"Yes, but I'll escort him to yer chamber tonight."

Brigette considered the offer, then smiled. "If Lord Sly prefers passing the night in your chamber, it's acceptable to me."

"Do ye mean it?" Glenda's voice rose in excitement.

"To be honest with you," Brigette whispered, leaning close, "Uncle Iain becomes jealous when Sly shares my bed. You'd actually be doing me a tremendous favor by—"

A rousing cheer interrupted her words, and everyone looked up. Jamie and Spring, crimson with embarrassment, entered the hall belatedly.

Iain grinned at their discomfort and called them to the high table. "I hope ye slept well, Jamie," he teased. "The earl has ordered us outside the walls today to begin trainin'." Jamie's mouth dropped in dismay.

"Good mornin', cuz." Brigette smiled knowingly at Spring. "I'll need your help today letting out the seams on my gowns."

Black Jack stood, then resettled Glenda in his chair and kissed the top of her head. "I've plenty of work to keep me busy," he announced. "Ye willna' be seein' me 'til supper." Noting his granddaughter's disappointed expression, he added,

"But I'll be seein' ye at the usual hour in the garden." Glenda grinned.

"I'm going to redecorate the nursery," Brigette informed her husband. "What do you—?"

Ignoring her, Iain stood and quaffed his ale, then pecked her cheek and strode out of the hall. Moaning and groaning, the MacArthur men-at-arms followed him out.

"We've been deserted," Spring observed, taking the chair vacated by Iain.

"Glenda," Moireach called from the entry. "It's time for yer lessons." The little girl feigned deafness. "Come along," the housekeeper ordered, marching to the high table. "Father Kaplan's lookin' for ye. And dinna make me shout."

"Och!" Glenda cried innocently. "I didna' hear ye callin'."

Biting her bottom lip, Brigette swallowed her laughter. Glenda had been practicing her "good" lies. Most diligently, it appeared.

"Come along," Glenda bade the fox. "It's time for our lessons."

"No," Moireach ordered. "Ye know verra well Father Kaplan banished him from yer lessons. He's too disruptive."

When Glenda left, the fox climbed onto his mistress's lap. Absently, Brigette scratched him behind the ears, and Sly sighed contentedly.

"My thanks for insisting Jamie and I wed," Spring said, her cheeks pinkening. "You wouldn't really have sent me home, would you?"

Brigette grinned impishly. "I never said I would."

"What?"

"Apparently, the earl is a master at handling his men." The two cousins dissolved into laughter.

Alone in her chamber, Antonia fumed. The Sassenach will not be so smug when Finlay snatches her, she thought with some satisfaction. I'd love to see the expression on her face when he does. I'd dispatch her myself on this very day, but then I'd be obligated to give Iain an heir.

While Antonia hid in her chamber, the days passed peacefully at Dunridge. Accompanied by her two favorites, Brigette meandered about the garden on the eventful day that Antonia emerged unexpectedly. Glenda, frightened by the determined glint in her mother's eyes, grabbed Brigette's hand.

"I want to spend time wi' my daughter," Antonia announced imperiously. "Ye arena' welcome to join us." She held out her hand to the child. "Come."

Glenda's grip on Brigette's hand tightened. "No."

"You're trying to cause trouble," Brigette accused, positioning herself between them. "You've never shown any interest in Glenda before."

"How dare ye come between my daughter and me!" Antonia's expression was murderous. "Release her."

"No." Brigette's expression was just as murderous. The two beautiful adversaries stood nose to nose, neither willing to retreat.

"What's this aboot?" Black Jack thundered, arriving for his daily stroll with his granddaughter.

"*Sly!*" Glenda cried.

Three sets of eyes darted to the child, then followed her horrified gaze. Sly's hind leg was raised as he urinated on Antonia's skirt.

"Oh!" Antonia leaped back. Enraged, she turned on the fox and tried to kick him. Sly crouched low, bared his fangs, and growled threateningly.

Antonia fled the garden. Black Jack, Brigette, and Glenda burst out laughing. The earl held out his hand in invitation to his granddaughter, then winked at Brigette and said, "I knew the damned beast was good for somethin'."

As harvest neared, Iain's days were spent defending MacArthur territory or invading Menzies's. Although she missed his almost constant presence, Brigette was also busy. She redecorated the nursery beside their chamber and was forever sewing, either baby clothes or the seams on her gowns.

One afternoon in early October, Brigette passed through the great hall. Surprisingly, Iain was there, eating an unusually early supper with a group of his men. Brigette's smile radiated happiness as she rushed to his side.

"What a rare treat to see you so early in the day," she gushed.

Iain patted her swollen stomach. "Seein' yer lovely face is, indeed, the rarest of treats. I do believe yer body's nearin' ponderous, hinny."

"But why are you eating supper now?" For once Brigette ignored her husband's teasing.

"I willna' be eatin' supper later. We're raidin' tonight and willna' return 'til mornin'.'"

Brigette paled.

"It isna' dangerous, sweetie," Iain lied, "only a considerable distance from here."

"You know I don't like being alone in the night," she cried.

"Ye know I'd never willin'ly leave ye alone, dearheart"—he spoke as if to a child—"but I've nae choice in the matter. Why dinna ye invite Glenda and Sly to share the bed?"

"My worrying would keep them awake all night." Brigette burst into tears, and Iain held her close, trying to console her.

There's nothing I can do to prevent his leaving, she realized with a start. If I cry, his mind will be here instead of concentrating on whatever he does while raiding. Brigette forced a watery chuckle, wiped her tears, and lied, "Ignore me, my love, the baby makes me weepy."

Iain smiled, then kissed her lingeringly. Finally, he lifted her off his lap and stood. His men followed him out of the hall.

Alone, Brigette sat in a chair in front of the hearth. Resting her elbows on her thighs, she covered her face with her hands and wept quietly.

Slurp! Something wet tickled her hand. Brigette peeked through parted fingers. *Slurp!* Sly's tongue slipped in between and licked her salty tears. As Brigette stroked him, Sly rested his head on what little lap she still possessed and sighed in beastly contentment.

Sleepless anxiety was Brigette's companion

when she retired that night. After lighting the dozen candles she'd commandeered, Brigette began to pace. What if Iain is injured? Or worse? she wondered, nearly frantic for his safety.

The hour grew late. Brigette knelt beside the bed to pray and promptly fell asleep. Much later, she lifted her head and stood, every muscle in her body stiffly protesting the movement. One by one, she snuffed the candles, leaving only the one on the bedside table.

Brigette crossed the chamber and looked out the window. The night sky had brightened to gray. Placing her hands on her stomach, she felt the baby moving inside and, after making a final appeal to Whomever, lay on the bed and slept.

Iain and his men dismounted in the courtyard and went directly to the great hall, crowded with family and retainers breaking their fast. Brigette's seat was empty.

"All went as planned," Iain told his father. Weary, he rubbed at his red-rimmed eyes. "Where's Brie?"

"She hasna' come down yet," Black Jack answered. "Go on and rest. We'll speak later."

Iain nodded and left the hall. He paused outside his bedchamber, but heard only silence from within, then opened the door quietly and walked in. Brigette was asleep.

Iain's nose twitched; the chamber smelled like one of Father Kaplan's solemn high masses. He looked around and smiled at the sight of all the candles, now extinguished. His fearless wife was afraid of the dark.

Undressing quickly, Iain slipped into bed and was shocked when he glanced at Brigette's face. Purple smudges of fatigue lay beneath her eyes, and even in sleep, her expression was pinched.

An anxious woman births an anxious baby. His pregnant wife had kept a lonely vigil awaiting his safe return, and a lump of constricting emotion rose in Iain's throat. "Brie," he whispered, drawing her into his arms.

Green eyes fluttered open. Smiling tiredly, Brigette reached up to touch his face, and Iain kissed the palm of her hand. Then they snuggled together and slept.

October waned and Brigette waxed. By All Hallow's Eve, she was outrageously large and ached to be harvested like the barley. Two months of waiting stretched endlessly before her.

As she grew in size, Brigette retreated from the petty squabbles and frustrations of the daily life swirling around her. Instead, she wrapped herself in a cocoon of pregnancy; her world revolved around the birth of her child.

Iain became uncharacteristically patient and solicitous of Brigette. Concerned for her health, he steered clear of unpleasant subjects. "Checking the watches" was his euphemism for raiding and defensive skirmishes.

On the morning of All Hallow's Eve, Brigette sat between her husband and father-in-law at the high table. She was tired, depressed, and cranky. A mug of milk and a bowl of porridge were set on the table before her, but she pushed them away.

I want ale, Brigette thought mutinously. Never again will I eat porridge or milk or haggis.

And my gowns! she continued torturing herself. I want to wear my beautiful gowns. Brigette's apparel was now limited to shapeless shifts, albeit of the finest fabric to be had. Necessity had forced her to use the fabrics acquired in Edinburgh, and her heart had nearly broken.

Brigette sighed. It was ill luck to be enormous so soon. Peaceful sleep even eluded her. Each time she lay down to rest, the baby would kick, pummeling her insides as if to punish her laziness. The babe was as infuriating as his sire.

"Raidin' season is almost over," Iain was saying to his father.

"Menzies's winter willna' be lean," Black Jack remarked, "but liftin' his cattle grazin' in the shadow of Weem was a severe blow to the mon's pride."

"We must be alert until the first snow falls."

"Mark my words," Black Jack said, forgetting Brigette's presence. "He'll retaliate wi' somethin' equally devastatin'."

Brigette gasped and paled. Nervously, she looked from one to the other.

"I wasna' speaking of anythin' life-threatenin'." Black Jack patted her hand. "I meant he'll try to wound our pride by hittin' close to Dunridge."

Brigette looked at Iain. He nodded, verifying his father's words, but suspicion nagged at her mind.

"I'll ride out to check the watches along the perimeters," Iain said, rising.

"I'll come wi' ye." Black Jack stood with his son.

"Ye havena' eaten much," Iain chided Brigette, "but if yer finished, I'll help ye up."

"Why should I leave this chair?" she snapped. "I cannot *do* anything."

Iain grinned at her waspishness.

"You dare to laugh at me? This is all your fault!"

"Guilty as charged." His good humor did nothing to restore hers.

"I know your men are betting on the number of babies in my belly," Brigette told him. "If there's more than one, I won't forgive you. Ever."

"Dinna ye want a lad for me and a lassie for yerself?"

"I don't want two," she wailed, her eyes filling with tears. "I don't even want one."

"Ye know ye dinna mean that, hinny," Iain cajoled, fighting to keep a straight face.

"Look at me. I'm grotesque!"

"Ye've never been more bonnie, sweetheart." Iain leaned over to kiss her cheek. "Why dinna I help ye up?"

"I'm not an invalid." Brigette shrugged off his helping hand. "If I can't rise on my own, I'll sit here until I give birth."

"So be it—if ye dinna mind a blistered rump."

After Iain left, Brigette reached for his ale and gulped it down quickly. There was no sense in aggravating Moireach; Brigette offered the mug of milk to Sly, who never refused anything.

With her stomach leading the way, Brigette surveyed the garden. Autumn had already bared the trees and added a crisp bite to the air. The wild shrieks and madcap scamperings of playtime continued in spite of pregnancy, but only Glenda and Sly delighted in running about. Brigette followed at a more sedate pace.

"Fetch it," Glenda ordered, pitching a stick across the garden. With a flash of yellow collar, the fox dashed away. "Father Kaplan says everyone must attend mass in the mornin'," she told Brigette. "It's All Saints' Day."

"That means tonight is All Hallow's Eve," Brigette replied. "It's magical."

"Magical?"

"Tomorrow we celebrate all the saints in heaven," Brigette explained, "but between the hours of dusk and midnight tonight, evil roams the land."

"Evil, ye say?" Glenda shivered. "Spirits?"

"The demons make merry," Brigette embellished, "because at the stroke of midnight, they must return to their place of eternal damnation."

"D-d-demons?"

"Yes."

Sly ran up to them and dropped two sticks in front of Glenda. He sat down, cocked his head to one side, and wagged his tail expectantly. In spite of his great feat, the fox was ignored.

Glenda reached for Brigette's hand. "Dinna ye think we should go inside?"

"Why?"

"The d-demons might c-come early."

"I'm certain that won't happen," Brigette assured her. "Spirits are punctual."

"Oh." Unconvinced, Glenda clung to her hand. "Uncle Iain has great love for ye."

"What?" Brigette was surprised by the abrupt change in topic.

"Yer belly's grown verra large. Ye look like ye swallowed somethin' whole."

"Thank you," Brigette said drily.

"Do ye think Grandfather's angry wi' me?" Glenda asked. "He didna' walk wi' me today."

"Uncle Iain and he rode out earlier. He'll be home shortly." Brigette glanced at Glenda. Teardrops were sliding down the child's face. "Why are you weeping?"

"The d-demons are goin' to hurt Grandfather!"

"No." Sorry she'd frightened Glenda, Brigette tried to console the child, but was incapable of kneeling to gather her close. "Uncle Iain and your grandfather will be home long before dusk . . . Shh!"

Muffled shouts and sounds of alarm from the front courtyard were carried on the wind to Brigette's ears. "Come."

As fast as her bulk would allow, Brigette pulled Glenda through the garden door and raced down the main corridor to the front foyer. Filled with men-at-arms and servants, the foyer was in an uproar.

"Sweet Jesu!" Brigette cried, rushing forward.

With Iain and Jamie holding him up, Black Jack staggered across the foyer. An arrow protruded from his shoulder blade and chest. Seeping blood stained his shirt.

"Grandfather!" Glenda shrieked.

"Get her away," Moireach shouted, racing across the foyer to help the earl.

" 'Twas those evil demons!" Glenda screamed at Brigette, who stared dumbfounded at her. Spring materialized and dragged the hysterical child into the great hall.

Recalling her father's untimely demise, Brigette trembled with fear, but stepped closer to watch Moireach examine Black Jack. Her unborn child kicked hard, seeming to protest the furor, and Brigette gasped, clutching her stomach.

"Dinna consider goin' into early labor," the housekeeper warned, catching the sudden movement from the corner of her eye. She lightly slapped Black Jack's face and asked, "Who are ye?"

"Good God, woman!" he bellowed. "I'm stuck like a pig and ye ask who I am? Have ye taken leave of yer senses?"

"He isna' muddled from the loss of blood," Moireach said to Iain. "Let's take him upstairs to remove the arrow."

With the earl between them, Iain and Jamie started up the stairs. Dazed, Brigette followed them to the earl's chamber.

"Set him here," Moireach ordered. "Jamie, stoke the hearth so I can see what I'm doin'."

"It's my fault." Brigette moaned. "I conjured the evil ones by speaking of them."

Black Jack looked at her and smiled faintly.

"Nae evil spirit did this. I never imagined Menzies would go this far."

"Dinna speak," Iain cautioned. "Ye've lost a lot of blood."

Black Jack caught the housekeeper's eye and glanced at Brigette. She was as white as a person can get and still be breathing.

"Go downstairs, Lady Brigette," Moireach ordered. "Boil water and collect as many candles as ye can." Eager to help, Brigette hurried from the chamber.

"Hold him steady," Moireach said. "Give me yer knife, Iain, and keep the damned arrow from jigglin' aboot."

With a minimum of movement, Moireach cut the head and tail of the arrow and, after a careful inspection, threw them aside. With a steady hand, she pulled out the stem. Black Jack groaned, and blood flowed from both ends of his wound. After cutting his shirt away, Moireach lifted her skirt, tore off a section of her petticoat, and gingerly dabbed at the wounds.

"Jamie, fetch hot water, poultice ingredients, and strips of clean cloth. And dinna let Lady Brie return until ye come back."

"Why?"

"Dinna question me—yer wastin' precious time."

Held steady by Iain, Black Jack sat on the edge of the bed. Moireach knelt in front of him and tried to staunch the bleeding. With his eyes, Black Jack questioned the housekeeper, who answered with an almost imperceptible shake of her head.

"What is it?" Iain asked.

"Tell him before the others return," Black Jack said.

Moireach retrieved the head of the arrow and held it out for Iain's inspection. "See there. It was dipped in poison. Probably neither quick nor terribly painful, it will prove fatal all the same."

"Nae!" Iain railed. "Is there nae cure?"

Moireach shook her head.

"I'll slay the craven bastard wi' my bare hands!"

"I've nae doubt ye'll eventually kill him, son." Black Jack's voice was resigned. "At the moment, however, ye must take charge of Dunridge." He looked at Moireach and asked, "How much time do I have?"

The housekeeper's eyes were blurry with tears. "Long enough to see Iain on the high road."

"Good." Black Jack smiled with grim satisfaction. "Time enough to see my first grandson?"

Unable to meet his searching gaze, Moireach shrugged, saying, "If Lady Brigette's time comes early."

An expression of unutterable sadness crossed the earl's face, but was quickly replaced by solemn resignation. "So be it," Black Jack said, accepting his fate. "When the wounds have been dressed, Iain, bring Father Kaplan. I've the need to confess my sins. Promise what's passed between us here will go nae farther. I dinna want anyone mournin' before I'm gone. Moireach?"

"I swear."

"What aboot Percy?" Iain asked.

"Send for yer brother, but as soon as I'm buried,

he's to return to Edinburgh. Sheena Menzies is too valuable a prize to lose."

Iain gazed at his father's face, which had aged immeasurably in the span of one short day. "I swear."

"Ye've been a good son and will make a fine earl." Iain was not so sure. "If I'm still breathin' in the mornin'," Black Jack added, "bring Glenda to me."

Jamie and Spring raced into the chamber. They were followed a moment later by a slightly breathless Brigette.

"I want ye to stay wi' Glenda," Moireach instructed Jamie and Spring as she began washing the earl's wounds. "The puir thin' must be sick wi' fright, and her mother willna' offer comfort. The earl will be fine and has invited her to visit him in the mornin'. Off wi' ye also, Lady Brigette."

"No! I won't be sent away."

Iain opened his mouth to order her from the chamber, but Black Jack spoke first. "Come here, then, and sit beside me."

Moireach mixed the poultice and applied it, front and back. Then she began binding the wounds.

"Calm yerself, Brie," Black Jack said, aware his daughter-in-law was as terrorized as a fledgling warrior in the midst of his first battle. "I amna' goin' to die. What a stupendous travesty it would be for Him to call His most flamboyant sinner home on All Saints' Day."

"You're not a sinner."

"Done," Moireach said. "Up wi' ye, Lady Bri-

gette. Let's ease him back to the pillow, Iain."
Between the two of them, they gently lowered the
earl. "I'll finish undressin' him. Put yer wife to bed
and then see to the other matter."

Iain led his stunned wife out and escorted her to
their own chamber. He helped her change into a
nightshift and put her to bed. Pausing for a moment, Iain brushed a few strands of hair off her
forehead and planted a light kiss there. When he
tried to draw back, Brigette clutched his hand.

"Oh," she cried in anguish.

"Are ye ill, hinny?"

"I'm sick with dread."

"There's nothin' to fear." Iain struggled to maintain control of his own rioting emotions.
"Moireach said Black Jack would be up and aboot
in nae time at all."

"Are you certain?" Brigette wanted desperately
to believe him. "It's the same as when Papa—" She
broke off, unable to continue.

"Hush." Iain sat on the edge of the bed and
stroked her cheek. "I'm verra sorry. I'd forgotten
aboot yer father. Close yer eyes and try to sleep
while I sit wi' Black Jack." When she obeyed, he
pecked her cheek, then stood and left the chamber.

"He's restin' but awake," Moireach said when
Iain and Father Kaplan entered the earl's chamber. "There's a sleepin' draft mixed wi' wine on
the table. Give it to him when yer finished."

Perching on the edge of the bed, Father Kaplan
took the earl's hands in his. Iain started to slip

away, but Black Jack stopped him. "Dinna leave, son."

Puzzled, Iain turned back. "I'll be out—"

"No!" Black Jack ordered in a surprisingly strong voice. "It's fittin' the next Earl of Dunridge learns how the feud wi' the Menzies clan began."

15

"Do ye hurt?"

"A mite."

"Will ye die?"

"No' today."

"Tomorrow?"

"I dinna ken." Black Jack smiled at Glenda, standing solemnly beside his bed.

"May I go wi' ye?" she asked, a glimmer of hope leaping into her large blue eyes.

"Wi' me?" he echoed. "Dyin' is a thin' each mon must do alone. Ye ken?"

"No." Blue eyes filled with tears.

"Set yerself right here." Black Jack patted the edge of the bed, then winked at her. "I see ye've brought Lady Autumn to visit."

"Yes." Glenda's expression was glum.

"Do ye love me, hinny?"

"Yes."

"And do ye trust me?"

"What's that?" she asked.

"Trust is," Black Jack explained, "when ye believe what a person tells ye."

"I trust ye."

"Good! I've been seriously wounded," he told her, "but I hope to be up and aboot in a few days. But I'm an old mon who's lived his life to the fullest. If I dinna recover and pass over to the other side, I'll wait for ye there. When yer life is over, we'll go walkin' in God's garden forever. Ye ken?"

Glenda nodded. "I'll miss ye if ye go away."

"Ye may be unable to see me, but I'll always be here," Black Jack said, placing his hand over her heart.

The door opened, admitting Brigette, who smiled at them in greeting. "No, Sly!" The fox whizzed past her. He raced to the bed and leaped at Glenda, who leaned over to let him lick her face.

"Dinna bother evictin' him," Black Jack said, then chided his granddaughter. "And dinna let the beastie lick yer face. People kiss people and beasts kiss beasts."

"Lady Brie lets Sly kiss *her* face," Glenda returned.

Ignoring the earl's pointed stare, Brigette settled herself in the chair beside the bed, then asked, "How are you feeling today?"

"Much better," he lied, "especially since my two favorite ladies have come visitin'. And how are ye feelin'?"

"Much better, now that I've come visiting my

favorite father-in-law," she quipped, then grinned puckishly.

Black Jack chuckled. "Ye'd have made a fine diplomat."

"Do you really think so?"

Before the earl could reply in the negative, Glenda's voice rose in anger. "Sly!"

The fox had snatched Lady Autumn and, in a whirl of copper fur, darted from the chamber. Glenda dashed after him, but stopped abruptly at the threshold and ran back to the earl's side. "Sly has a fondness for Autumn," she told him. "I'm glad ye arena' goin' to die today. I'd be lonesome wi'out ye." She kissed his unshaved cheek, then raced after Lady Autumn's abductor.

Black Jack and Brigette looked at each other and laughed. "I'm also glad you're not seriously wounded," she added her sentiments to Glenda's. "I'd miss you too."

The earl's forehead creased in a frown that vanished almost instantly. "I'm plannin' to hold my grandson," he said. "Do ye doubt it?"

"No." Brigette shook her head, then smiled to mask the uneasy feeling that all was not well.

A week passed. The earl was not up and about as he had promised; instead, he seemed to have weakened. Brigette secretly doubted he had the strength to hold a baby, but confused by Iain's optimism, she remained silent on the subject.

Brigette passed long, pleasurable hours in the earl's company. He delighted in seeing the baby's clothing take shape beneath her fingers, even as the babe took shape within her belly. As she sewed, Brigette spoke of inconsequential matters, which seemed to soothe him. Other times, Black Jack reminisced about his younger days with Iain's mother. Whenever Brigette's stomach shifted or she gasped at a sudden kick, the earl's expression became radiant.

"Percy," Brigette cried when the door opened one day to admit Iain and his brother.

"By God, yer bloomin'!" Percy grinned, more than a little surprised by her size. "Wee Glenda was correct. Ye *do* look like ye swallowed somethin' whole."

"Why, thank you, Percy," she returned drily. "I've missed your sweet, flattering ways."

"Would ye leave us, Brie?" Black Jack spoke. "I want to speak privately wi' my sons."

Iain was instantly at her side to help her rise, then escorted her to the door. Pausing outside the chamber, Brigette leaned against the door and frowned.

All is not as it should be, she thought for the hundredth time. Why would Percy leave Edinburgh if Black Jack is in no danger? It's almost as if he'd been called home for . . . *No!* It could not be! Brigette argued with herself. Iain would not hide such a thing from me. But what other reason could Percy have for returning?

Brigette's heart was as heavy as her ungainly body as she walked downstairs to the great hall, where she thought Glenda and Sly would be. The fox was curled up in front of the hearth, but the child was nowhere to be seen.

Thump! Thump! Thump! Sly's tail wagged as

Brigette eased herself into a chair. At his mistress's beckoning gesture, the fox sat beside her, and when she began stroking the silken fur beneath his muzzle, Sly sighed, satisfied with life.

"I see ye've finally emerged from yer chamber." Antonia stood beside her.

"I was with the earl." Brigette glanced at the blonde, adding, "Percy's home."

"I've seen him. I dinna ken why yer wastin' yer time sittin' wi' a dyin' old mon."

"He's not dying," Brigette cried angrily. She tried to leap to her feet to confront her sister-in-law, but was unable to propel her ponderous body up. "And don't call him an old man."

"Ye'll be countess when he's gone," Antonia countered. "Ye should be prayin' for his death."

"I could never wish for anyone's death. Not even yours."

Antonia stalked away in a huff. Tears of frustration and grief threatened to spill from Brigette's eyes. Struggling to control her emotions was a losing battle, and fat teardrops slid down her cheeks.

"What's this?" Iain asked, squatting beside the chair.

"I—I had an argument with Antonia, and when I tried to stand, I couldn't get up. It was humiliating."

Iain chuckled.

"Percy's not home for—for . . ." Brigette searched his eyes for the truth. "Black Jack will recover, won't he?"

"Of course." Iain gently brushed her tears away. "I've said as much. Dinna ye trust me?"

"I do," she replied without hesitation. Knowing he lied, Iain felt his heart sink to his stomach.

Brigette sat between her husband and brother-in-law at the high table and pushed her food around on her plate. Thoughts of Black Jack dying troubled her, especially since Percy's homecoming. In fact, the earl was failing rapidly.

"Ye arena' eatin' much," Iain observed.

"I'm not hungry."

"What's troublin' ye?"

"If you must know"—Brigette turned on him, her expression long-suffering,—"the skin across my belly itches horribly. It's unspeakable torture and I dare not scratch here."

"What misery to be born a woman," Percy quipped, feigning sympathy.

Brigette cast her brother-in-law an unamused look, then turned back to Iain. "I believe I'll retire to scratch in peace. Help me up?"

As she left the hall, Brigette gestured Spring to stay where she was. After all, she thought sourly, I've been unable to squeeze into my beautiful gowns for months. I look more like a scullery maid than a countess. And a *fat* scullery maid at that!

In her chamber, Brigette pulled the brocaded, tentlike shift over her head, then pushed the straps of her chemise down and let the garment fall to the floor.

Vigorously rubbing her distended stomach gave Brigette no relief. She sat down and massaged herself with Moireach's lotion; it soothed her tormenting itch.

Relieved, Brigette pulled a nightshift over her head, then tied the ribbons running from its neckline to navel. After donning her robe, she left her chamber to visit Black Jack.

Moireach was on her way out of the earl's chamber. She carried his untouched supper tray. "He isna' hungry," the housekeeper grumbled.

"That's not a good sign."

"Perhaps," Moireach returned, "he's followin' yer example. Ye didna' eat much tonight either."

Ignoring the admonition, Brigette brushed past her into the earl's chamber. His eyes were closed and he lay motionless. Without a word, Brigette sat in the chair beside his bed.

"Is that ye, Brie?"

"Yes. How are you feeling?" Brigette noted the glaze in his eyes.

"I've seen better days."

Brigette rose slowly from the chair and eased herself onto the edge of the bed. She placed her palm on Black Jack's forehead and decided he felt warm. Gathering his hands in hers, Brigette hesitated and then asked, "You—you're not going to recover, are you?"

Only a dead man would have failed to recognize her anguish. Black Jack was silent for a long moment. "No, lassie," he admitted finally. "I amna' goin' to recover."

Brigette swallowed painfully, fighting back her tears. "Why didn't Iain tell me?" Her voice was a hurt, bewildered whisper.

"It was by my order he held his peace," Black

Jack told her. "I didna' want anyone, especially Glenda and ye, mournin' before I was gone."

"I've come to love you like a father." Her voice cracked with emotion. "Whatever will I do without you?"

"The one who passes on travels the high road," Black Jack said, "but the ones remainin' behind must walk in this vale of tears called life. . . . And I've come to love ye like the daughter I never had. Do ye recall yer first day at Dunridge? I asked Iain if ye were simple."

Brigette smiled wryly. "And I called you 'a blustering old man.'" The dying earl and the future countess chuckled at the memory.

The door opened silently. Iain entered, but stood back in the shadows, reluctant to intrude on their camaraderie.

"My only regret," Black Jack confessed, "isna' bein' here when my grandson arrives."

"But he's already arrived." Brigette shrugged off her robe and untied the nightshift's ribbons from beneath her bosom to below her great mound of a belly. Parting the sides, she revealed her distended stomach.

"Your grandson is here," she said, guiding the earl's hands there.

At first Black Jack felt nothing. Then came a fluttering, a gentle shifting from within. Suddenly, the babe kicked savagely.

"Oh," Brigette gasped.

An expression of sublime happiness appeared on Black Jack's face. "The lad's active." Closing his eyes, he concentrated on the wild thudding inside his daughter-in-law's stomach.

A hand touched Brigette's shoulder. Startled, she looked up into Iain's face.

"I love ye," he whispered.

Black Jack opened his eyes at the sound of his son's voice. "I'm meetin' my grandson," he said, and Iain smiled sadly. "It's definitely a lad. I can tell by his movements. Wi' ye to guide him, he'll grow into a fine mon and warrior."

"My son is *not* going to be a warrior," Brigette insisted. Iain and Black Jack smiled at her.

"Get some rest, Brie," Black Jack suggested. "Tomorrow we'll kill a few hours debatin' that verra point."

Brigette grinned, then drew the sides of her nightshift together and rose from the bed. Iain helped her into her robe. Leaning down, she kissed the earl's forehead and whispered, "Sleep well."

Iain sat on the edge of the bed and studied his father. The earl's face had sagged with Brigette's departure.

"She's a braw lassie," Black Jack remarked, "even if she is a Sassenach."

"I'm grateful ye insisted on the marriage," Iain replied.

"She'll breed up strong sons."

"Yes."

"Heed me, son," Black Jack bade. "The day will come when ye'll send Antonia back to the Mac-Kinnons. Keep Glenda at Dunridge. She's yer brother Malcolm's only child. And dinna fail to send Percy back to Edinburgh. When the time is ripe, he'll get to Sheena Menzies. She's the only chink in the bastard's armor. Be faithful to the queen, but yer first loyalty must be to our clan. The Stewarts arena' always faithful to those who serve them best."

"I hear ye."

"When I was yer age," the earl reminisced, "I didna' believe I'd live to be an old mon and die in bed."

Raw emotion formed a painful lump in Iain's throat. Hopeless, consuming grief coiled around his heart, making it difficult for him to breathe.

"I willna' be wi' ye in the mornin'," Black Jack rasped. "Hold my hand."

Iain's heart broke. He longed to throw himself into his father's arms like a child and wail his misery. Instead, Iain took his father's hand in his, easing his passage from this life to the next. The earl's eyes closed wearily. He slipped away, gone forever.

Iain sighed raggedly, then kissed his father's hand. Resting his cheek against it, he wept bitter tears. Finally, Iain stood, kissed his father's cheek, and whispered brokenly, "Godspeed."

It was well after midnight when Iain walked into his own chamber. The bed was empty. Wrapped in a blanket, Brigette sat, staring vacantly at the hearth's smoldering embers.

"Are ye ill?" he asked anxiously, crossing the chamber in quick strides to kneel in front of her.

"I couldn't sleep. Iain?"

"Yes"—Iain's voice cracked—"he's gone."

Brigette opened her arms and gathered him close. Cradling his dark head against the mound of her stomach, Brigette and Iain shared their tears. It would be one of those rare times in a long, long life together when she would see her husband weep.

The chapel bells tolled for John Andrew Mac-Arthur, the fallen Earl of Dunridge. The earl's body lay in state in the great hall, his plain wooden coffin resting on trestles.

Before the funeral guests arrived, Iain brought Brigette and Glenda to view the earl's body. The great hall was deserted except for Jamie and Dugie, who guarded the coffin.

Iain's gaze met Brigette's. He lifted the coffin's lid, and she stepped forward to bid the earl a final farewell.

Clad in his black and green dress plaid, the earl appeared to be sleeping. Black Jack had peacefully crossed between two worlds, and his expression was placid, unmarked by his fatal injury.

Brigette touched his cheek, then leaned over to kiss it. Straightening, she glanced at her husband, who was struggling to maintain his rigid composure.

Next came Glenda. Iain lifted her into his arms and held her beside the coffin.

"Is he sleepin'?" she whispered loudly.

Iain's lips quirked. "Yes, but he willna' awaken 'til the Judgment Day."

Imitating Brigette, Glenda leaned down and kissed her grandfather's cheek. "Farewell," she said solemnly. "I'll miss ye, then, 'til the Judgment Day. And dinna forget to wait for me so we can go walkin' aboot God's garden."

The four in the hall gulped back stricken tears. Iain set her on the floor, then closed the lid of the coffin. "Take Glenda upstairs," he instructed Brigette. "I want ye to rest before the Campbells arrive."

Brigette nodded and led Glenda away, but the child's words drifted back to the three men. "Brie? When is the Judgment Day? After Christmas . . . ?"

The Duke of Argyll and his entourage, including Magnus and his bride, Avril, arrived at Dunridge as afternoon's shadows were lengthening toward dusk. Iain, Percy, and Antonia stood in the courtyard to greet them.

The duke dismounted and shook Iain's hand, then Percy's. He'd been badly shaken by the untimely death of his most steadfast friend, whom he'd relied upon hundreds of times throughout the years. The duke felt somewhat responsible for Black Jack's death. After all, he thought guiltily, the feud with Menzies would never have begun if . . . Bah! That particular folly of his had occurred so long ago.

"This is a sorry business that brings us together," the duke remarked. "Who would've thought? So many of my dearest cronies are passin' on. It's surely a harbinger of my own fate." Old, painful memories rose up to torment the duke. "Before passin' over, did yer father speak of—?"

"Yes," Iain cut him off, "but it's the recent past I'm concerned wi'. Takin' my father's life will cost Menzies his own."

"Iain. Percy." Magnus shook their hands, then gently drew his bride forward. "This is my wife, Avril, Huntly's chit—I mean, daughter."

Avril curtsyed. "My lords. Countess."

"My lady," Antonia corrected, smiling, pleased with the mistaken title. "The countess will be wi' us shortly."

"This is Lady Antonia," Iain introduced the two women, "my brother Malcolm's widow."

He led the group into the great hall, where the funeral supper would be served. Several moments later, Brigette appeared in the entrance, and beneath the amused eyes of all, Iain rushed to her side and escorted her to the high table.

In friendly exuberance, Magnus hugged her. "Ye've grown since the last I saw ye."

"Yes." Brigette's face reddened. "Forgive me for failing to curtsy," she said, turning to greet the duke. "As you can see, I'm incapable of such movements."

"Ye look bonnie," the duke complimented, long years of experience having taught him that breeding women required the gentlest of handling. "There's nae finer sight to a mon than a woman heavy wi' child." He glanced at Iain. "Especially when the woman is the mon's wife. I'm hopin'," he added, "it willna' be too long before our Avril looks exactly like ye."

Avril gulped nervously. Her blue eyes were

large with horrified fascination as she stared at Brigette's enormous stomach.

"Brie," Magnus introduced, "this is my wife, Avril."

"My best wishes on your marriage," Brigette said, smiling. "I'm sorry we were unable to attend the ceremony, but my size does not allow travel." Avril nodded and returned the smile, but her eyes never left Brigette's stomach.

"Dear Brie has grown so outrageously large," Antonia piped in, her voice dripping sugar. "One wonders if she might have miscalculated the time of conception." The significance of the remark went unnoted by all but Iain and Brigette, who chose to ignore it.

For obvious reasons, supper was a subdued affair. Salmon, mutton, sweetmeats, and bread were served.

"What are ye plannin' for yer revenge?" the duke asked.

Iain opened his mouth to reply, but felt Brigette's hand on his arm. Dark eyes met green, and he was unable to resist her silent plea. "It's formin' in my mind," he answered the duke. "I'd like yer advice on it after the funeral."

The duke nodded, his gaze drifting to Brigette. "Does that beastie of yers still abide hereaboots?"

"Yes." Brigette relaxed, thankful she need not listen to her husband's plans for war and death.

"Beastie?" Avril asked, puzzled.

"Sly is my pet fox," Brigette told her. "He adopted me in the forest when I ran away from Iain."

"Ye ran away?" Avril's eyes sparkled, and she glanced sidelong at her own husband. "There's a solution I never considered."

"Ye've never needed solutions, hinny," Magnus scoffed, "because ye never had any problems. Huntly spoiled ye rotten."

Anger flared in Avril's eyes, but Magnus only chuckled and kissed her cheek. "Dinna whip yer temper into a frenzy," he admonished, close to her ear. "Remember why we're here and behave yerself."

Avril kept her mouth shut, and Magnus turned to Percy. "Will ye return to Edinburgh, cuz?"

"I'll be leavin' in a few days."

"Yer welcome to stay at Campbell Mansion," the duke interjected.

"And I'll be there sometime after Hogmanay," Magnus added.

Glancing at Avril, Brigette smothered a chuckle. High rage reddened the young woman's cheeks. Obviously, Lady Avril would be remaining at Inverary while her husband danced to the queen's tune.

"Just be certain Avril has a bairn in her belly before ye get yerself killed on the queen's behalf," the duke warned.

"I canna promise anythin'," Magnus returned pleasantly, "but I'll give it my best effort."

After supper, the pipers played a mourning lament. The MacArthur warriors, paying homage to their fallen leader, swirled around the hall in the traditional funeral dance. At its end, they drifted away, but the family remained for the death watch, guarding the earl's corpse until interment the following morning.

"Why dinna ye take Avril to her chamber and then go to bed," Iain said to Brigette. "It's unnecessary for ye to keep the watch."

"I'm staying."

"I'll show Lady Avril to her chamber," Antonia offered, unwilling to lose sleep for a dead man and eager to befriend the future Duchess of Argyll.

The family sat on a hard, wooden bench that had been placed beside the bier. An hour passed in silence. During the second hour, Brigette fidgeted uncomfortably. The baby was active, shifting her belly from side to side.

"Yer uncomfortable," Iain whispered. "Go to bed."

"I'm staying," she insisted. "The baby will keep me awake upstairs too."

Iain shook his head, then stood and left the hall. He returned a few minutes later and handed her a dram of whiskey. "This will calm the babe's restlessness."

Brigette pinched her nostrils together and gulped the whiskey, then grimaced and shuddered delicately. A short time later the baby quieted, and Brigette also drooped. Her eyes closed drowsily.

"I'm takin' ye upstairs," Iain whispered, putting his arm around her, "and dinna argue wi' me." Brigette was too weary to protest. Her eyes opened at the sound of his voice, then closed again. He lifted her into his arms and carried her out of the hall.

At dawn the great hall filled to capacity for the funeral procession. Eight MacArthur warriors, including Dugie and Jamie, served as the earl's pallbearers and led the way. Behind them was Father Kaplan, followed by the earl's family and invited guests. The pipers, clansmen, and retainers were followed by the crofters who'd come to pay their respects to their laird, a man who'd treated them fairly.

The somber procession wended its way to the chapel, where Father Kaplan celebrated the solemn high mass of the dead. When the pallbearers lifted the earl's coffin to slide it into its vault, Brigette clasped both Iain's and Percy's hands. Entwining her fingers with theirs, she shared what meager strength she possessed.

Instead of feeling relieved that the ceremonies were over, Brigette was restless. Leaving the others in the great hall, she headed for the garden, where Sly was wandering about.

Sly rushed to her side with an offering. Brigette patted his head and accepted the stick, then threw it across the garden. Sly raced off to retrieve it.

Life at Dunridge without Black Jack will be strange, she thought. His death has left a vacuum to which each must adjust.

"Is that the fox?" Lady Avril's voice sounded behind her.

"Yes." Wearing a smile of greeting, Brigette turned toward the voice. Her smile froze and then vanished when she saw harsh condemnation stamped across the other woman's face.

"I'll speak to the point," Avril announced curtly. "Are ye carryin' my husband's bastard?"

Brigette was flabbergasted.

"I said, are ye—?"

"You stupid chit," Brigette snapped, her eyes green slits of displeasure.

"Stupid!"

"You've been listening to Antonia's spiteful tales," Brigette accused.

"She's been honorable enough to mention the possibility," Avril admitted.

"If you heed her wild tales," Brigette warned, "Antonia will ruin your marriage, as she's tried to ruin mine."

"Why would she cause trouble for me?" Avril scoffed. "Besides, ye havena' answered my question."

"Antonia is causing *me* trouble, not you. The Countess of Dunridge is a title to which she aspired. She cares nothing for your marriage."

Avril was silent for several moments, digesting that bit of information. "I'll believe ye," she said finally, "if ye swear that isna' my husband's bastard."

Before Brigette could open her mouth, a hand grabbed Avril's shoulder and whirled her around. With the flat of his hand, Magnus slapped her hard. "How dare ye! How dare ye accuse Brie of such a thin', and she eight months gone wi' Dunridge's heir!"

"B-b-but—"

"Shut yer mouth," Magnus roared. "Do ye actually believe I would've dishonored Iain's wife? Besides, ye could've questioned me. Yer behavior is unbecomin' a Duchess of Argyll. Apologize at once."

Avril's face was crimson. "I'm verra sorry for upsettin' ye. Sincerely sorry."

"Antonia's poison can be very convincing," Brigette replied. "I've also fallen prey to it several times."

"Accept my apology also," Magnus added. "I wouldna' have Iain or ye upset for anythin'."

A Highland blizzard, the first of the season, swept through Dunridge the following week, forcing Brigette and Glenda to pass their leisure time sitting in front of the hearth in the great hall. Afternoon playtime was very much different than it had been previously. The shrieks of blindman's buff and other wild games no longer echoed in the chamber.

Dunridge was a ghost keep. Black Jack's presence was sorely missed. Returning to Edinburgh, Percy perched at court like a bird of prey, ready to swoop down at a moment's notice upon Sheena Menzies. Iain was especially busy with his new duties as the Earl of Dunridge and head of the MacArthur family.

As Christmas approached, Brigette's burden dropped, making her even more ungainly. Her waddle was slower than a snail's pace.

Brigette tried to make the holiday cheerful, but failed dismally. She did manage, however, to elicit hearty laughter from Glenda and Iain when she presented Sly his gift. The fox became the not-so-

proud owner of a doublet, fashioned from a Mac-
Arthur plaid.

Supper on the eve of Hogmanay passed quietly,
although the MacArthur warriors drank heavily
and began dicing as soon as the trestles were
pushed aside. Lady Antonia was noticeably absent,
preferring to greet the new year alone in her
chamber. When Moireach called Glenda to bed,
Iain and Brigette sat alone at the high table.

Glancing sidelong at him, Brigette thought how
tired he looked. "I'm going to bed," she announced, drawing his attention. "I've a raging
headache and my back hurts. Stay and share a few
cups with your men."

Iain helped her stand, but when he would have
escorted her upstairs, she refused, saying, "Spring
shall see to my needs."

"I willna' be late," he assured her, then kissed
her cheek.

Clad in a heavy robe, Brigette sat in front of the
blazing hearth. After helping her change, Spring
had left, but returned a few minutes later with a
cup of warmed wine. Moireach had ordered it to
ease Brigette's lower backache. Not only did it
ease her discomfort, but her eyes closed drowsily
in sleep.

Iain, feeling more relaxed than he'd been in
over a month, climbed the stairs to his chamber.
My father has been taken from us, he thought, but
my son will soon fill that void. Or daughter, he
reminded himself, entering his bedchamber.

"Ohhh . . ." A low moan sounded near the
hearth.

Iain crossed the chamber quickly and knelt in front of Brigette, then nudged her awake. A sharp cramp gripped her lower abdomen and doubled her over, leaving her breathless.

"I'm wet!" Fear and confusion leaped from her eyes.

"It's the baby. I'll fetch Moireach." Iain stood, but was rooted to the spot.

"Don't just stand there." Brigette's voice rose in panic.

"Will ye be all right alone?" he asked nervously.

"Get Moireach or you'll be playing the midwife. Ohhh!"

Iain sprang to life and flew out of the chamber.

A few minutes later, Iain returned with Moireach and Spring. "Firstborns are notoriously slow," the housekeeper said. "This will be a long night."

"I've wet myself," Brigette told her.

"Fetch a clean nightshift," Moireach instructed Spring. "Then wake Kevin and tell him to keep water boilin'."

"Ohhh!" Another spasm gripped Brigette. She moaned like a wounded animal and clutched at her husband's hand.

Moireach chuckled, noting Iain's pallid complexion. The fiercest of warriors was quaking, helpless in the face of his young wife's labor. "Perhaps it willna' take so long as I thought," she remarked, helping Brigette into the clean nightshift. "Iain, help her up. I want ye to walk aboot wi' her."

"I cannot walk," Brigette cried. "I'm in heavy labor."

"Heavy labor?" Moireach grinned. "Dinna be a ninny. Walkin' aboot will make yer delivery easier. When the pain grabs ye, hang onto Iain and pant. Ye'll ken when yer labor gets heavy."

"Worse than this?"

"Dinna be frightened." Moireach patted her shoulder. "Yer in capable hands."

Time passed slowly. Within the protective circle of Iain's embrace, Brigette paced the chamber. Each time a contraction trapped her in its agonizing grip, Brigette groaned and leaned heavily against his solid frame.

"I hear bells," she said at one point.

"Ye know," he replied, "Father Kaplan welcomes the new year wi' the tollin' of the bells."

"A new year and a new life," she murmured. An excruciating pain, worse than any other, stabbed Brigette. She cried out and nearly fell to her knees.

"Put her to bed," Moireach said. Iain lifted and carried Brigette across the chamber to the bed. Without a thought to modesty, the housekeeper pushed up Brigette's nightshift, exposing her distended stomach and swollen breasts, then gently examined her. "Go downstairs, Iain, and send Spring wi' the water."

Iain nodded. "I willna' be long," he assured Brigette.

"Ye must remain in the hall wi' yer men," Moireach insisted.

"But—"

"Yer wife willna' thank ye in the mornin' for watchin' her laborin'."

"Don't leave me," Brigette wailed as another contraction knifed through her lower regions.

"I willna' leave ye, hinny."

"Humph!" Moireach snorted in disgust. The wife was falling to pieces beneath the husband's kind encouragement. At this rate, the baby would take days to be born. "Lady Brigette," she chided, "yer behavior is unseemly. A Highland woman bears her burdens bravely."

"I'm not a Highlander, you old crone! *I'm English!* Tell her, Iain. Tell her I'm English." The absurdity of her statement split Iain's face into a broad grin.

"You bastard," Brigette screamed. "You dare laugh at your dying wife? You did this to me. Ohhh!" Another contraction ripped through her.

"Pant," Moireach ordered. "Pant against it." Through her pain, Brigette heard the voice of authority and obeyed.

"Relax," Moireach crooned, massaging Brigette's stomach. "I'm sendin' Iain for the water." Brigette nodded, too weary to protest.

"Dinna return until I send for ye," the housekeeper whispered out of the side of her mouth. "Ye ken?" He nodded and left.

Battle-fatigued, Iain found Spring and then retired to the great hall. Several groups of men still drank and diced in the far corners of the chamber. Iain beckoned Dugie and Jamie, then sat at the high table and called for ale.

"How fares Lady Brigette?" Dugie asked.

"Sufferin' horribly."

"It's expected in a laborin' woman."

"She's in capable hands, though," Jamie interjected.

"Women die in childbirth," Iain said miserably.

"Yes, but many dinna," Jamie countered.

"Our mother safely birthed two," Dugie offered, "and she's alive and breathin', helpin' Lady Brie."

Iain's expression cleared somewhat. "My own mother safely birthed three."

"Lady Antonia safely birthed wee Glenda," Jamie added.

"Mary of Guise safely birthed our bonnie Queen Mary." Dugie upped his brother.

"And the Pope's mistress safely birthed—"

Iain burst out laughing, then suggested they sit in front of the hearth. This time he called for whiskey.

Hours passed. Instead of emptying, the hall filled as news of the impending birth passed through Dunridge.

Just before dawn, Iain left the hall with Sly. He paused in the foyer and looked anxiously toward the stairs, then headed for the snow-carpeted garden.

Sly darted here and there while Iain, sick with dread, paced furiously. Bloody battles were nothing when compared to his wife's torment. *Not knowing what's happening is the worst part of it,* he told himself repeatedly. *Given a choice, I'd prefer being the one in labor.* He smiled inwardly, thinking his wife would certainly disagree.

Tentacles of light crept into the eastern sky. Iain called Sly, and the two returned to the great hall, now filled to capacity with MacArthur warriors and retainers.

"My lord!" Iain whirled around at the sound of Spring's cry. "It's a boy!"

A deafening cheer shook the rafters. Iain's mouth dropped in shock, but his feet moved. He dashed out of the hall into the foyer, then took the stairs two at a time. As his hand touched the door-knob, Iain heard the lusty wail of a baby. My son! he thought, filled with wonder, then walked in.

"Congratulations." Moireach smiled. "Black Jack would've been proud of ye." Then she was gone.

Brigette was sitting up in bed. Her breasts were bared, and attached to one was a tiny dark head, leisurely working a nipple.

"Meet our son," she said, a tired yet triumphant smile on her face. She detached the baby from her nipple and turned him around to face his father. "Isn't he perfect? He resembles you."

Perching on the edge of the bed, Iain scruti-nized his son. The baby was large for a newborn, dark-haired and ruddy, and wrinkled like a wiz-ened old man.

"Well," Iain hedged, "he does have my colorin', but I was never that ugly."

"Iain!"

"Dinna worry, hinny. His skin will smooth out in time—I hope."

"Iain!"

The baby wailed, as if protesting his father's insult, and cooing, Brigette offered him her nipple. The baby quieted instantly, making his father smile.

"What he lacks in appearance, he possesses in brains," Iain quipped, his dark eyes glowing with love. "What intelligent mon wouldna' crave a taste of yer sweetness?" He caressed her cheek, then leaned close and kissed her tenderly. "Thank ye for my son, lovey."

"Want to hold him?"

"Yes." Iain reached for his son and cuddled him awkwardly against his chest. "His name will be John Andrew, for my father."

"Agreed. Who will stand as his godparents?"

"Magnus and Avril Campbell," Iain answered. "The duke or his heir always stands as godfather to Dunridge's heir. It's a tradition. Perhaps we'll betroth him to their firstborn lassie."

Brigette arched a brow. "Another tradition?"

Iain grinned. "No, good politics."

The baby whimpered, and Brigette held out her arms to take him. "Scheme away, if you must," she returned, "but I have what John Andrew desires most in this world." With that, Brigette offered the baby her nipple. As she watched her son, joyous contentment filled Brigette's heart to overflowing. With her husband by her side and her son in her arms, Brigette knew a peace she'd never imagined possible. Nothing bad could ever break through their circle of love to harm them. Nothing.

16

The tip of Brigette's nose tickled and twitched. Opening her eyes, she found herself staring into the thick mat of black hair covering Iain's chest. They lay on their sides, their naked limbs entwined intimately.

Peering up at his face, Brigette saw that he slept. A lusty gleam, boding ill for her husband's peace, shone from her eyes. Ever so lightly, her hand glided down the side of his body and fluttered across his stomach to caress the masculine appendage nestled at his groin. Her fingertips swirled around and around the knob of his shaft until it grew and pulsed, almost angrily.

"Lassies who play wi' fire get burned." Iain's husky warning sounded above her head.

Surprised, Brigette looked up into his dark, smoldering eyes, but her fingers never faltered in their tantalizing motion. "You'd best be careful yourself," she challenged softly.

Iain chuckled throatily and moved to capture her, but Brigette was faster. She pushed him onto his back and straddled his hips, then smiled lazily down at him.

"I give up," Iain surrendered. "Do wi' me as ye will."

"You're very easy," Brigette murmured, and lowering her hips, impaled herself on his erect shaft. Both gasped at the incredible pleasure of female softness meeting male hardness as she began to move up and down, tauntingly.

When Iain flicked his thumbs across the dusky buds of her breasts, a jolt of scorching desire ran from the sensitive tips of her nipples to the core of her womanhood. Brigette burned and throbbed. The first wave of pulsating pleasure washed over her, carrying her away in its relentless surge.

Iain yanked her down. Savagely, he suckled upon a milk-laden breast.

"Iain!" Brigette exploded and clung to him.

With a quick twist, Iain flipped her onto her back. He drew her legs over his shoulders and rammed his raging dragon into her hot, throbbing lair.

"Brie!" he cried, shuddering his own completion.

Panting, they lay motionless. When his breathing eased, Iain kissed her lips and the tip of her nose, then gazed into her eyes and smiled. "Whatever happened to my virgin Gypsy?" he asked.

"You seduced her."

Bang! The chamber door crashed open, and

Moireach entered with their squalling son in her arms.

"Oh," Brigette cried, embarrassed. Iain chuckled and withdrew from her body, then pulled the coverlet up to his waist and leaned back against the headboard.

"Dinna tell me ye were sleepin'," Moireach warned. "I heard yer matin' howls belowstairs. Wee Black Jack's hungry and verra angry wi' his mother."

"I told you," Brigette corrected, reaching for her son, "John Andrew's nickname is Dubh. 'Black Jack' is no proper name for a three-month-old baby."

"Ouch!" Dubh ferociously attacked his mother's nipple, teaching her the folly in keeping him waiting for breakfast.

"There's nothin' improper aboot callin' him 'Black Jack,' " the housekeeper argued. "Dubh is the Gaelic for 'dark' and 'Black Jack' means . . . 'Black Jack.' Wherein lies the difference?"

"It's what Iain and I prefer," Brigette insisted. "We are his parents, are we not?"

"Dinna use that uppity tone wi' me, Countess," Moireach chided, pausing at the door. "I'm the one who caught him when he slipped from yer body." Her eyes settled on Iain. "Percy's messenger is in the hall."

Iain offered his son a finger and smiled when the baby's tiny hand closed around it. Dubh's eyes were large as he stared up at his father, but his mouth never stopped working his mother's nipple.

"I canna believe the strength of Dubh's grip," Iain marveled.

Brigette rolled her eyes, certain all fathers were similarly impressed with their sons, especially the first. Iain winked at her and rose from the bed, then washed and dressed.

"I get less respect as a countess than I did as the second daughter of a belted earl," Brigette complained, shifting Dubh to her other breast.

After pulling on his boots, Iain crossed the chamber and tilted her chin up. "Ye mean, lovey, the exceedin'ly pampered second daughter of a belted earl."

Brigette's eyes narrowed, but she said nothing, refusing to become ruffled by his teasing.

"I'll see ye downstairs," he said, walking toward the door. "And I must commend yer self-control, hinny. A year ago ye would have risen to the bait."

"I am not a bear to be baited," she returned, the hint of a smile flirting with her lips, "merely your long-suffering wife."

"Each puir soul has a cross to bear," Iain countered, "and yer mine." He ducked out of the chamber before she could throw something.

After feeding Dubh and returning him to the nursery, Brigette washed and dressed hurriedly, then went to the great hall. She sat down beside Iain at the high table and was served a bowl of oatmeal porridge.

"There's an emergency," he told her. "I'll be leavin' wi'in the hour."

A spoonful of porridge halted en route to Brigette's mouth, then returned to the bowl. "Emergency?"

"A group of the queen's loyal nobles have assassinated her secretary. Ye remember Rizzio, the Italian." Iain relaxed back in his chair, his hand reaching out to touch her shoulder. "The queen's six months gone wi' child and bein' held prisoner."

Brigette was shocked. "The queen is being deposed?"

"The traitors wouldna' dare"—Iain snorted—"at least 'til she's birthed an heir. Contrary to the queen's commands, they dragged puir Rizzio from her verra presence and stabbed him to death. The worst of it is that Darnley was part of the plot." Iain chuckled without humor. "The queen's consort doesna' ken his usefulness will be ended if she delivers a boy, and his own royal life may be short-lived. I see Jamie Stewart's fine hand etched in this."

"Buy why must you go?" Brigette protested. "Surely Magnus—"

"Magnus isna' in Edinburgh," Iain interrupted. "He's off aboot the queen's business, and Argyll's at Inverary. Besides, the duke's an old mon. The bastards were clever enough to wait 'til Edinburgh cleared of Campbells."

"What can Percy and you accomplish, besides getting yourselves killed?" Brigette's voice rose in distress.

"Dinna panic, sweetie," Iain teased. "Yer milk will curdle. I amna' plannin' on bein' killed. Loyal forces are plottin' the queen's escape. If Mary springs the trap while I'm en route, she'll still need every mon she can get to ride wi' her and crush the bastards. I'm leavin' Jamie in command, and dinna give him a difficult time."

"Me?" Brigette grinned puckishly. "Create trouble for others?"

Iain leaned close, one of his powerful hands capturing the back of her head. His lips hovered above her. "Ye've a penchant for trouble, and make nae mistake aboot it."

A week later, Brigette sat alone in her chamber. Dubh was suckling on her teat and kneading the soft flesh of her breast. She smiled at him and caressed his downy cheek. Still no word from Iain, she thought for the hundredth time. He must have reached Edinburgh by now. Please, Brigette sent up a silent prayer, don't make me a widow.

"Need help?" Slipping into the chamber, Spring interrupted her cousin's reverie.

"Can you spare a nipple for a hungry boy?"

"Dubh would starve." Spring sat on the stool beside Brigette's chair. "Thanks for steering clear of trouble while my husband is in charge."

"What do you mean?"

"Iain almost dispatched Percy for losing you," Spring answered. "He'd suffer no qualms about slaughtering Jamie. I wouldn't care to be made a widow."

"I was just thinking the same thing," Brigette commented wryly.

"What?"

"I dislike the thought of becoming a widow, and there's been no word from Iain."

"I'm positive all is well," Spring said encouragingly. "When Dubh goes down to nap, why not ride out with Glenda to the loch?"

"Jamie might forbid it."

"It's not so far and the land is well guarded." Spring cocked a brow at her. "You are the Countess of Dunridge, are you not?"

"That I am, cuz." Brigette grinned. "Who would dare refuse the countess in her own home?"

After persuading Dubh to sleep, Brigette changed into an old skirt and blouse, then grabbed her shabbiest riding cloak. As she walked down the stairs to the foyer, she heard Moireach's voice, raised in anger, even before the housekeeper came into view with Glenda and Sly in tow.

"I told ye before," Moireach was scolding the little girl, "ye'd better come when I call ye. Father Kaplan's waitin' in the library."

"I didna' hear ye callin'," Glenda hotly defended herself.

"Dinna be lyin' to me, ye naughty chit. It's a terribly bad sin."

"I amna' lyin'," Glenda shot back. "Canna Sly have his lessons too?"

"No!" Moireach was adamant. "He attacks the quills and eats the parchment."

Brigette stepped into the foyer, and Glenda appealed to her. "Canna Sly come to lessons wi' me? He has need of it."

Brigette looked from Glenda to Moireach, but the housekeeper's frown discouraged the laughter bubbling up in her throat. "Moireach said 'no.' "

"Yer the countess," Glenda argued, "and she's yer servant. It's yer privilege to order her aboot."

Moireach's eyes narrowed in angry consternation. Brigette shifted uncomfortably beneath the
woman's unwavering gaze and wisely chose to
evade the issue. "I am the countess," she said dip-
lomatically, "but the earl is not in residence at the
moment."

"If Uncle Iain isna' here," Glenda reasoned,
"then yer in command."

"Uncle Iain left Jamie in charge," Brigette countered.

"Tell Jamie to tell Moireach that Sly may come
to my lessons," Glenda demanded, exasperated.

"It would do no good."

"Why?"

"Because blood is thicker than water."

"I dinna ken."

Brigette knelt in front of Glenda, her eyes level
with the child's. "Moireach is Jamie's mother and
he's duty-bound to obey her."

"Is Moireach in charge of Dunridge, then?"
Glenda cried. Brigette burst out laughing.

"I'd love to know what ye've been teachin' this
once-biddable child," the housekeeper speculated.

"Perhaps Lady Autumn would care to join you
for your lessons," Brigette said to Glenda. "I'm
riding out—"

"No!" Glenda threw herself into Brigette's arms
and pleaded, "Dinna leave me behind again. I
promise I'll listen to Moireach . . . and obey her
too. . . . Please, dinna leave me!"

Holding the child close, Brigette spoke soothingly to her. "I'm only riding to the loch, and I'll

even take Sly along for company. How's that?"
Glenda remained silent, her face buried into
Brigette's neck. "It's a fair day, sweetie, and guess
what?"

"What?"

"Dubh has never seen the garden."

"Never?" Glenda was amazed.

"Not once. When I return, shall we show Dubh
the trees birthing their buds?"

"I'd like that."

"Humph." Moireach snorted. "I'm hopin' my
Jamie knows what yer aboot."

"I'll ask his permission first," Brigette said, rising. "Come along, Sly."

Entering the courtyard, Brigette saw Jamie
speaking with several MacArthur warriors. A few
paces away from the men, she hesitated, uncertain
how to handle her cousin's husband. One of the
men nudged Jamie and gestured toward her.

Jamie turned around. "Good mornin' to ye," he
greeted.

"Good morning. May I speak with you?"

"Certainly." Jamie wondered if his good luck
had just run out.

"I'm riding to the loch." Brigette smiled pleasantly. "I'll return in an hour or so."

Jamie raised his brows. "Are ye askin' permission or tellin' me?"

"Asking permission. Iain did leave you in command, did he not?"

"He did," Jamie replied evenly, "and I dinna
think it's wise for ye to be ridin' out alone, especially when yer husband isna' here."

"I won't be alone," Brigette returned brightly. "Sly will accompany me."

Jamie's eyes fell to the small fox, sitting obediently beside his mistress. "That wee beastie isna' proof against foul play or anythin' else."

"The land is well guarded, is it not?"

"Aye."

"Then foul play is unlikely," she concluded. "What else could happen?"

"Are ye certain ye arena' runnin' away, perhaps to England?" Jamie blurted out.

"And leave my son?"

"I suppose no'," he conceded, then asked suspiciously, "Ye wouldna' be traipsin' after Iain to make certain he isna' in any danger?"

"I'm not that brave."

"No, but ye are that foolish."

Brigette's expression turned to stone, and Jamie cursed his tactless tongue. "Have yer way aboot it, then," he relented. "But if anythin' happens and Iain sharpens his sword on my flesh, I swear I'm comin' back to haunt ye."

"Don't worry," Brigette called over her shoulder as she headed for the stables. "I'll be fine."

"She'll be fine," Jamie grumbled to himself. "That's what she said to Percy."

As she passed through the gate, Brigette waved jauntily to the tower guards. She felt freer, released from the prison Dunridge had become without Iain's presence.

"Here, Sly," she called to the fox, who dashed aimlessly about, almost as excited by the freedom as his mistress.

The day was a Highland rarity of blue skies and dazzling sunshine. Birds were chirping loudly and busily building their nests upon the limbs of trees that were giving birth to buds. Sly was scurrying hither and dither, sniffing and snorting and sneezing at everything in sight.

Delighted by all she surveyed, Brigette turned her mount toward Loch Awe and started down the travel-worn path through the woods. The entire world and its wondrous creatures are being reborn, she thought in a rare philosophical moment, then giggled with simple joy. No longer did she feel the weighty responsibility of being a wife, a mother, and a countess; for several refreshing moments, Brigette reveled in being young and riding out on a glorious day.

And then the idyllic mood shattered. She suffered the uncanny feeling of being watched. The fine hairs on her neck prickled; a sudden chill caressed her spine. Brigette's senses froze in near panic but her horse kept moving.

My husband's lands are well guarded, she told herself. I forgot my fear of being alone, and my wild imagination is making me skittish. With a sigh of relief, Brigette left the woods and rode onto the loch's sun-drenched shore.

Sly raced past her. The hackles on his neck were raised against the unseen presence.

Danger! Brigette kicked the flanks of her mount and galloped down the beach.

Whoosh! Something whizzed past her. A heart-wrenching yelp of pain rent the air. Sly went down, an arrow protruding from his right haunch.

"Holy Mother of God!" Brigette shrieked. She tugged savagely on the reins and stopped short, nearly toppling headfirst from the saddle, and ran toward her pet, which was howling in pain.

"Sly." Brigette knelt beside him and reached out with a trembling hand, but a shadow fell across the injured, dying fox. She whirled around to face their assailant.

A black and white plaid—Menzies! Brigette raised her eyes, but saw only pale blond hair framing a face cast in shadow by the glaring sun at his back.

Sly whimpered, and Brigette's rage erupted with volcanic force. "You bloody bastard!" Snarling with fury, she leaped to her feet like a kitten challenging a lion. It was then the stranger's fist connected with her jaw.

"Ooph." Brigette collapsed in his arms.

Ignoring the injured fox's whimperings, the man produced a cord and tightly bound Brigette's hands together, then lifted and slung her across his horse. Seemingly unconcerned with the danger in lingering there, he rested his head against his saddle. He'd waited so long to catch the Sassenach alone, he thought, feeling faint. He couldn't falter now. Antonia was depending on him!

"Damn," Finlay MacKinnon swore softly. His whole body was damp with nervous sweat, and his hands were shaking badly. The Sassenach is definitely a she-devil, he thought with growing trepidation. The green of her eyes and the fierceness of her spirit do betray her witch's heart.

Finlay made a protective sign of the cross, then

mounted behind his unconscious captive and nudged his horse into the cover of the woods. Sly's pain-wracked whining dogged his every step.

Brigette slowly regained consciousness. At first she thought she was dreaming; then she thought Iain was hogging the bed, forcing her to hang over the edge. Every muscle in her body protested her uncomfortable position and the motion of the horse.

"Please." She moaned.

At the sound of her voice, Finlay halted the horse and dismounted, then pulled her off. Brigette promptly collapsed, her legs having fallen asleep. She bowed her head in utter misery and wept quietly.

Finlay studied the petite beauty lying at his feet. She's bonnie, he thought, crouching down beside her, even if she is a Sassenach witch. "If ye swear to cause nae trouble," he whispered close to her ear, "I'll cut yer bindin'."

Brigette's head snapped up and she looked into his face for the first time. He was slim and almost delicate-looking, with pale skin, blond hair, and blue eyes. Though Brigette was certain they'd never met, there was something vaguely familiar about his face, especially his eyes.

Staring into her compelling green eyes, Finlay struggled against the urge to make the sign of the cross. He realized it would be foolish to let the witch know he was nervous in her presence. Only the devil's spawn, Iain MacArthur, had the courage to wed a she-devil.

Brigette nodded her obedience. Finlay drew his dagger and cut the cord binding her wrists.

"My husband will kill you for this," she hissed.

The horrifying image of Iain MacArthur with sword in hand formed in Finlay's mind, and a ripple of fear danced down his spine. "Shut up," he snapped, then forced Brigette onto the horse and mounted behind her.

They rode on, seemingly endlessly. For obvious reasons, Brigette no longer took pleasure in the glory of the day. Awakening from their slumber, her legs prickled painfully. Brigette gingerly worked her throbbing jaw, attempting to discover the extent of its damage. It certainly felt broken. Most annoying of all were her breasts, achingly laden with mother's milk.

How will Dubh eat? Brigette wondered, a barrage of troubling thoughts piercing her mind. What will Menzies do to me when we arrive at Weem Castle? And Sly! My precious pet lies wounded, probably dead.

Silent tears streamed down Brigette's face. Through blurry eyes, she saw Finlay reaching up to caress her breasts.

"Keep your bloody hands off me," she snarled, "or you'll be sorry."

Finlay's hand dropped instantly. Surprised but relieved, Brigette wondered why he, after abducting and beating her, would heed her threats.

"You killed my pet," she accused.

"Ye mean yer familiar." He sneered.

"My what?"

"Ye canna fool me." Finlay snorted. "Yer a witch and that beastie was yer familiar."

Brigette made no reply. Witch? Familiar? The man was insane! She would be lucky to arrive at Weem Castle.

Afternoon lengthened toward dusk. A pungent saltiness tickled Brigette's nose, and her nostrils flared as she tried to discern its source. The smell grew stronger with each forward step.

"It is the sea," Brigette murmured as they left the woods and entered a tiny cove.

"The Sound of Mull," Finlay said, dismounting and pulling her off the saddle. "Sit down."

With a loud groan, Brigette eased herself onto the nearest boulder. Finlay knelt in front of her and tied her ankles and wrists with a cord.

"What are you doing?" she protested.

"We canna leave 'til the tide turns, and I willna' have ye flittin' away in the night." Finlay pulled a flask from his sackcloth. "Drink this."

Parched from the long road, Brigette swallowed a gigantic gulp. Her eyes widened in shock; she choked and wheezed as the potent whiskey blazed a trail of fire to her stomach.

Finlay laughed and slapped her back roughly, then went about starting a fire. After the fire was lit, he retrieved his sackcloth and produced a handful of oatcakes, then offered a few to Brigette, who gobbled them hungrily.

"What's your name?" Brigette asked. No reply. "What shall I call you?"

"Naught."

Brigette's eyes narrowed dangerously. "I demand you release me at once! It would be fatal folly to do otherwise, Sir Naught."

Finlay studied her suspiciously. Was the danger from Iain MacArthur or her magical powers?

"Well?"

"Shut yer mouth," he barked, "or I'll shut it for ye."

Brigette wisely remained silent. Huddled miserably on her boulder, she pondered her situation. *Jamie was correct—I should not have ridden unescorted. Oh, why did Iain have to be in Edinburgh? He would have saved me by now. My poor son must be wailing in hunger. And Sly!* Brigette buried her face in her hands and wept.

"What's the matter now?" Finlay asked, irritated. How he despised mewling women!

"If you must know"—her voice was muffled— "my breasts ache to feed my son."

"Touch me," Finlay whispered huskily. "I'll suckle yer titties to ease their pain."

Brigette's head snapped up. Finlay, his flaccid member exposed, stood beside her. Unholy hatred leaped from her green eyes, and her lips curled in a snarl.

Without thinking, Finlay stepped back and crossed himself, then hurled, "Witch!"

"Thimble prick!"

The insult hung in the air for the briefest moment, then Finlay slapped Brigette hard across the face. She toppled off the rock, and there she remained, down but not defeated.

"Do that again," Brigette threatened, "and I'll change you into the toad you really are."

Backing away, Finlay found protection—and courage—on the opposite side of the fire. "Ye willna' be talkin' so bravely in the mornin'."

Brigette rolled over, turning her back on him. She closed her eyes and prayed for the MacArthur warriors to arrive before morning. Her prayers went unanswered. A boot nudging her backside rudely awakened her the next morning. She rolled onto her back and opened her eyes.

"It's time," Finlay said, looming above. Without another word, he walked away, and pulled a decrepit-looking dinghy from behind a boulder, then dragged it to the water's edge.

"I'm not climbing into that," Brigette insisted. "I absolutely refuse! I can't swim."

Finlay smiled harshly. "Ye willna' be needin' these, then." He squatted in front of her and cut the ankle and wrist cords, then wafted his dagger beneath her nose. "Get up slowly and walk to the dinghy."

Reluctantly, Brigette obeyed. With his dagger clenched between his teeth, Finlay pushed the boat out, then jumped in. Grabbing the oars, he began rowing into the sound, toward a cluster of rocks bared by low tide.

"Where are you taking me?" Brigette demanded.

"Where Iain MacArthur will never find ye."

Brigette gulped nervously. There was no avenue of escape.

Approaching the largest rock in the cluster, Finlay grabbed its edge with one hand while waving the dagger at Brigette with the other. "Climb up there."

"No!" she cried. "You can't leave me here!"

"I can and I am. Climb!"

Cursing her captor with her eyes, Brigette stood and reached for the rock. "Woe be to you and yours—forever and a day."

Irrational fear filled Finlay's eyes. "Take it back!" he shouted, and lunged for her.

Clinging to the side of the rock, Brigette kicked out savagely, catching her captor's groin. Caught off balance, Finlay toppled back, and the dinghy flipped over with him. "I canna swim! Save me!"

Brigette scrambled to the top of the rock and looked down. Finlay was gone. "Holy Mother of God!" she wailed, watching the dinghy drift away. "I'm alone in the middle of the sea. . . . *Help! Help!*"

Only the squawking seagulls heard her desperate cries.

17

"Help!" Brigette croaked, her abused throat succumbing to long hours of useless screaming. Trembling from the cold, she glanced down at the taunting sea, rapidly rising to the top of the rock.

I'm too young to die, she thought hysterically. Please, Lord, I swear I'll be the perfect wife, obedient in every way. Don't let me die alone here!

Through tear-blurred vision, Brigette scanned the horizon and saw a dark speck in the distance. It grew larger with each passing moment. Unwilling to believe her eyes, she blinked and shook her head.

A boat! How could she get its attention? Then it came to her. Brigette pulled her blouse off and waved it wildly above her head.

Young Danny MacDonald, sitting in the lookout perch on board the pirate vessel *The Jaded Lady,* was bored. Something in the distance caught his eye, and Danny stared hard, unwilling to believe what he was seeing. Waving frantically, a half-naked woman stood on top of the infamous Lady's Rock.

"Yo! Uncle!" Danny called to Alasdair, pirate chief of the MacDonalds of Oban. "Lady's Rock!" The boy pointed in that direction.

On the deck below, Alasdair MacDonald lifted his tubular magnifier toward the Lady's Rock.

"What is it?" his companion asked. Wordlessly, the MacDonald passed the magnifier to the queen's emissary, Magnus Campbell. "A stranded woman. We'll rescue her?"

From his great height, Alasdair MacDonald gazed solemnly down at the queen's man and asked, "For what?"

"She'll drown."

The pirate chief shrugged nonchalantly. "If a mon wishes to be rid of his wife, why should I thwart him?"

"Ye canna leave her there to die! It's inhuman!"

"If the husband doesna' want the lass," Alasdair argued, "then I'll be stuck wi' her."

"I'll accept responsibility," Magnus assured him.

"So be it," the pirate chief acquiesced, certain the young lord was making a grave mistake. "Rob! Ye and Colin set the dinghy in the water." He turned back to Magnus. "Ye may as well go along and collect yer booty."

Half naked and screaming almost noiselessly, Brigette seemed like a madwoman to the three men in the boat. The brisk wind whipped her waist-length hair, hiding her face, and as they neared, Brigette fell to her knees and wept with hysterical relief.

"Swim to the dinghy!" Rob shouted, unwilling to chance being smashed against the rock. Wildly, Brigette shook her head.

"Shit!" Rob pulled off his boots and jacket, then dove into the cold water. Breaking the surface near the rock, he easily swam the remaining distance, then climbed to the top and helped Brigette stand.

"Th-thank y-you," she sobbed, clutching him tightly.

A giant of a man like his father Alasdair, Rob peered down at the petite woman whose head came only to his chest. "Yer safe wi' me, lassie," he assured her. "We'll swim together to the dinghy."

"Bring the dinghy here!" Brigette cried. "I can't swim!"

"I canna do that. Hang onto me and I'll carry ye over. Ye'll float, so dinna panic. Take off yer boots. Now the skirt."

"My skirt?"

"The fabric's too heavy," he explained. "It will drag us down."

Brigette removed the skirt. Except for her lacy chemise, she was naked.

Rob paused for a moment to admire the exquisite woman's flesh, then instructed, "I'll go down first and then ye. Ken?"

Brigette nodded and glanced apprehensively at the rising sea. When she looked back at him, Rob read the terror couched in her eyes. He raised his fist to strike, but Brigette saved him the trouble by fainting.

After hoisting her over his shoulder, Rob slowly climbed down and lowered himself into the frigid water. He turned Brigette around in his arms and cupped her chin in one hand, then swam back to the dinghy.

The two in the boat lifted her over the side. Magnus removed his cloak and wrapped it around the unconscious woman, in the process seeing her face for the first time. "Sweet Jesu! Brie!"

"Yer acquainted wi' her?" Rob asked, settling himself in the dinghy.

"She's my cousin's wife."

Rob chuckled. "Will he be forgivin' ye, then, for thwartin' his plans to be rid of her?"

"I'm certain Iain had nothin' to do wi' her bein' here," Magnus said.

Rob gazed down at Brigette's pale face. "I dinna ken why a mon would rid himself of an angel."

Arriving in Oban, Magnus carried Brigette to the cottage the MacDonald had put at his disposal and gingerly set her on the cot. After stripping her, he wrapped her in several blankets, then lit a fire and returned to sit on the edge beside her.

"How's the lass farin'?" Alasdair's voice sounded from the doorway.

"A fever's beginnin'."

"I'll have someone bring food," the pirate offered, crossing the chamber. "Anythin' else I can do for ye?"

"Send a messenger to Dunridge Castle,"
Magnus said. "Inform the earl his wife is here."

"Countess?" Surprised, Alasdair peered curiously at Brigette. She looked more like an or-
phaned waif than a noblewoman.

"Have ye a midwife aboot," Magnus asked, "wi'
the knowledge to dry a mother's milk?"

"Mother's milk?" Alasdair echoed, puzzled.

"The countess gave birth recently," Magnus explained. "I noticed she's in desperate need of . . .
of . . ."

"Dryin'." Alasdair turned to leave, saying, "I'll
send my wife."

While Brigette's feverish delirium lasted,
Magnus rarely left her side. When she trembled
with chills, he built up the fire and bundled her
tightly in woolen blankets. When that didn't help,
he crawled beneath the blankets with her and
shared his own body's heat. When Brigette grew
hot and kicked off the blankets, he bathed her
with cool water and bundled her up again.

At regular intervals, Magnus force-fed her water and cooled herb-laced broth. Leaning her head
against his chest, he forced the liquid into her
mouth and gently stroked her throat to assist her
in swallowing.

When the MacDonald's wife, Ina, visited the
cottage, she chased Magnus outside, insisting that
she would take care of the soiled linens and the
unpleasant chore of keeping Brigette clean.
Magnus, Ina said, was in no way to undermine the
countess's dignity, even though she was sick and
not in her right mind. Magnus ignored the Mac-

Donald's wife and returned to the cottage to nurse his kinsman's wife. And so it went.

Magnus passed the long hours contemplating his own life. In Black Jack MacArthur's untimely death, he saw the demise of his own father. Before he passed on, the duke deserved to meet several grandsons. Fate is a woman of whimsy, he concluded, and I'd be wise to tempt her no more. His decision was made; after reporting to the queen, he would hasten to Inverary and Avril. With his feet propped up on the edge of the cot, Magnus dozed in one of the cottage's two chairs.

"Magnus," Brigette whispered weakly.

At the sound, his eyes opened, and Magnus found himself staring into green eyes, sunken and shadowed with illness. For a moment, he wondered if she was still delirious, but then her face split into a poor imitation of a smile.

Magnus sat on the edge of the cot and placed his palm against her forehead. It was cool. "How do ye feel?"

"Terrible."

"And well ye should," he said. "Ye gave me quite a scare."

"Water."

Magnus brought a cup of water and, lifting her head, held it to her parched lips. Nothing had ever tasted better to Brigette than that first, refreshing sip.

"How did you find me?" she asked, assuming he'd been part of a search.

"By chance, but we willna' speak of it now. I'll

fetch Ina and bring ye some broth. Close yer eyes and rest while I'm gone."

The MacDonald's wife ordered Magnus to stay away from the cottage for an hour. By the time he returned, Brigette had fallen asleep again.

"Hello," Magnus greeted her cheerfully the moment she opened her eyes. He sat on the edge of the cot, then ordered, "Sit up and I'll feed ye some oatmeal porridge."

Naked beneath the blanket, Brigette sat up and primly tucked it beneath her arms. When she looked back at Magnus, he was staring at her display of cleavage.

Brigette blushed furiously, and Magnus flushed to see her blushing. She chuckled and he joined her, their laughter sweeping away the awkward moment.

"Ye've lost some flesh," he commented, offering her a spoonful of porridge, "and I want ye to eat every bite in this bowl."

"How did you find me?"

"Open yer mouth. That's a good girl. I was negotiatin' wi' the MacDonald on the queen's behalf when we happened upon ye. How did ye get there?"

Brigette opened her mouth to reply, but Magnus filled it with porridge. She chewed and swallowed, then leaned back, saying, "I can eat no more. A Menzies warrior abducted me and left me there to wash out with the tide."

"Are ye certain he was a Menzies?"

"He wore the black and white plaid."

"I see." Magnus held up a spoonful of porridge. "Ye must eat a little more."

"I cannot," she insisted.

Ignoring her words, Magnus aimed the spoon at her mouth. She turned her face away, but the spoon gave chase.

"No!" Brigette laughed, and the spoon slipped into her mouth.

The door swung open unexpectedly, and a grim-faced Iain filled the doorway. He was unpleasantly surprised by the sight of his wife, obviously naked beneath the blanket, laughing and enjoying herself with his cousin. She did not, at first glance, appear to have suffered at all.

"Iain," Brigette cried, so relieved that she failed to recognize the forbidding glint in his dark eyes. She held out her arms, then remembered her state of undress and pulled up the blanket.

"By all that's holy!" Iain roared. "What the hell are ye doin' wi' my wife?"

Magnus stood and faced him. "What do ye mean, cuz?"

"What are ye doin'," Iain growled, "sittin' wi' Brie on that poor excuse for a bed, and she bare-arse as the day she was born? And why are *ye* always the one who rescues her?"

"Brie's been out of her mind wi' fever," Magnus ground out. "And I rescued her by chance—or would ye have preferred her washed out to sea?"

"Washed out to sea?"

"Aye." Magnus snorted. "She'd been left on a rock in the middle of the sound."

"I've been sick wi' worry," Iain said, holding up his hand in a gesture of apology.

Brushing past his cousin, Iain sat on the edge of the cot and gathered Brigette into the circle of his arms. Her face was pale and haggard, he noted, and her eyes, usually sparkling emerald-green, were dull and sunken in her small face. Iain tilted Brigette's face up and kissed her tenderly.

"Are ye feelin' better?" he asked, holding her tightly.

Feeling secure in her husband's embrace, Brigette nodded and relaxed against him.

Iain kissed the top of her head and confessed, "I came so close to losin' ye, hinny. I dinna know what I'd do wi'out ye. Yer my life, my reason for livin'."

Brigette sighed. "Your words make almost being killed *almost* worthwhile."

Iain chuckled. "I'm glad ye havena' lost yer sense of humor." He glanced at Magnus, saying, "Sit down, cuz, and tell me what ye were doin' wi' the MacDonalds."

"The queen granted them amnesty, providin' they willna' pirate our Scots vessels."

"Ye missed the excitement," Iain told him. "Rizzio was assassinated and the queen held prisoner."

"What!" Magnus leaped to his feet. "We must do somethin'!"

"It's been done, ye dolt."

Magnus sat down again. "What happened?"

"The queen persuaded that mewling husband of hers that the conspirators would dispatch him next. Darnley helped her escape, and they joined wi' Bothwell and others still loyal. The conspirators should be put to the horn, but Jamie Stewart is spoutin' forgiveness and mercy."

"Forgiveness is folly," Magnus remarked, shaking his head.

"I agree wi' ye, but Jamie has his sister's ear. She canna see the danger in trustin' her power-hungry brother."

"What about me?" Brigette piped in.

"If ye dinna mind," Iain said to Magnus, smiling, "I'd like some privacy wi' my puir, neglected wife."

"Tell me what happened," Iain said when Magnus had gone.

"I rode to the loch," Brigette began, then shivered recalling that frightening day. "A Menzies warrior ambushed me and left me to die on that rock in the sound. The tide kept rising and I kept screaming for help, but no one came. I was nearly submerged when the MacDonalds found me."

"Yer certain the mon was a Menzies?"

"He wore the black and white plaid."

"I'll kill the bastard wi' my bare hands!"

"Don't bother," Brigette announced matter-of-factly. "I've dispatched him already."

"Ye what!" Iain was stunned.

"While he was attempting to drown me," she proudly informed her husband, "I drowned him."

"Ye bloodthirsty wench," Iain chuckled and caressed her cheek. "He didna' touch ye? I mean—"

"No, I frightened him."

"I canna credit that, hinny." Iain's voice mirrored his disbelief.

"But it's true," Brigette vowed. "He thought I was a witch. . . . The MacDonald's wife fed me herbs to dry my milk. How will I feed Dubh?"

"Dinna worry about that. Moireach willna' let the lad starve."

"And Sly!" A sob caught in Brigette's throat. "My precious Sly is dead!"

"Sly isna' dead." Iain laughed, thinking of the fox. "He's alive, albeit a mite bandaged. When I left Dunridge, Glenda was tormentin' him; she and Lady Autumn are in charge of his convalescence."

Early the next morning, Brigette sat alone in the cottage. Dressed in a borrowed skirt and blouse that had seen better days, she'd plaited her hair into one thick braid and then tidied the chamber. There had been nothing left to do except await her husband's return.

"Are ye ready, hinny?" Iain asked, walking through the door.

"Yes."

Pulling her into his embrace, Iain lowered his lips to hers in a passionate, earth-shattering kiss. "I swear to guard yer safety with my life," he vowed. "Ye'll never be frightened again, I promise ye."

"Please, don't feel guilty," Brigette begged, her heart wrenching at the desperate anguish in his voice. "The folly was mine. I'm sorry my careless behavior has caused you worry."

"Thank ye for that, hinny," Iain said. He kissed her again, then grabbed the borrowed woolen cloak off the cot and wrapped it tightly around her. "Keep that close aboot ye. I dinna want ye catchin' another chill."

Outside, Magnus and ten MacArthur warriors, including Brie's cousin's husband, Jamie, were mounted and waiting. Alasdair, his wife, and several of the MacDonalds stood in their midst. Taking Ina MacDonald's hands in hers, Brigette kissed the older woman's cheeks, then thanked Alasdair and his son, Rob, who'd swum to the rock and saved her life.

Iain lifted Brigette onto his horse, then turned back to the pirate chieftain. He produced a hefty pouch from his plaid and handed it to Alasdair, then offered his hand, saying, "I pledge ye my friendship for all time."

"Yer a rare one, MacArthur," Alasdair commented wryly. "Many a mon would've become my sworn enemy for savin' his wife. The countess must be very special."

"No," Iain disagreed, mounting behind his wife. "When it's healthy, her tongue never rests." Everyone but Brigette laughed. Turning their horses east, the MacArthurs began their journey to Dunridge.

Leaning against her husband, Brigette relaxed and enjoyed the feel of his strength at her back. She peeked at Jamie, riding on their right, and wondered if he or Spring would ever speak to her again. "Jamie," she apologized, "I'm sorry for the trouble I caused you."

Jamie glanced sidelong at her and nodded. What else could he do? A mere warrior, angry though he was, could not throttle his laird's count-ess, foolish though *she* was.

"And," Brigette continued expansively, "I'm glad my husband refrained from sharpening his sword on your flesh."

"I'm too even-tempered to act so rashly," Iain insisted. Riding on their left, Magnus chortled, earning an admonishing glare from his "even-tem-pered" cousin.

Several miles passed in silence. The steady mo-tion of the horse lulled Brigette, and she closed her eyes. Sleep did not come, but rather the trancelike daze that bridges consciousness and sleep.

"What did you give Alasdair?" Brigette asked drowsily.

"Gold."

"Gold?" She perked up at the word.

"The rascal demanded a ransom for savin' ye," Iain told her.

Brigette giggled at the man's audacity, then fell silent for a long, pensive moment. "Well?" she asked finally.

"Well what?"

"What is my worth in gold?"

Iain smiled down at the top of her coppery crown. Accustomed to his wife's maneuverings, he knew her casual tone belied a burning curiosity. "The question's unfair, sweetie," he replied eva-sively. "It was an uneven exchange."

"Some of the best things in life are expensive," she said. "Exactly how much did I cost you?"

"Trust me, lovey. Yer nae bargain."

Brigette frowned, uncertain if she'd been complimented or insulted. My price must have been great, she decided, a delighted smile gracing her lips. "I'm certain," she said modestly, "your high opinion of me is based on love, not necessarily worth."

Chuckling, Iain nuzzled the side of her neck. "I love ye," he growled against her ear, "but I'd love ye better if ye cost less."

"Oww! You're impossible."

"But ye love me?"

"As if you didn't know it."

Their entourage arrived at Dunridge at dusk. Weakened by her illness, Brigette slept with her head nestled in the crook of Iain's neck.

As they passed through the outer gate, the guards shouted a greeting. Brigette stirred, but did not awaken, and Iain nudged her gently when they halted inside the courtyard.

"Shall I carry ye inside?" he asked.

"No." She yawned and stretched.

Iain dismounted and reached to lift Brigette, whose eyes were sultry with sleep. Merciful Christ! he thought, feeling his manhood stir. I can hardly wait until supper's done and we're alone in our chamber.

With her husband on one side and Magnus on the other, Brigette walked into the crowded great hall. Shrieking with joy, Glenda threw herself into Brigette's open arms.

"I'm sorry I went away," Brigette said, holding the little girl close. "I did not intend—"

"That bad mon snatched ye!"

"Yes, you must thank Cousin Magnus, for he saved me from drowning."

"What aboot Uncle Iain?" Glenda asked loudly. Uncle Iain frowned at the reminder that his cousin had a talent for rescuing his wife.

"Uncle Iain brought me home," Brigette added hastily.

"Thanks for savin' Lady Brie," Glenda said to Magnus, then looked at Iain. "And thank ye, Uncle, for bringin' her home." She tugged at Brigette's sleeve, saying, "Come on. Sly's waitin' for ye."

Smiling at her husband, Brigette shrugged her shoulders and was led away.

Thump! Thump! Thump! Sly's bushy tail whacked the floor in greeting when Brigette knelt beside him. She reached out to pat him, but the fox's tongue was quick, licking her hand.

"My poor, poor Sly," Brigette crooned, inspecting his bandage. The fox whined pitifully, gaining even more sympathy.

Brigette stood to greet Moireach and Spring. "I'm sorry for causing trouble," she apologized, hugging her cousin and then the housekeeper.

"It wasna' yer fault," Moireach said.

Spring nodded. "You don't look well, Brie."

"I've been ill, but I'm much better now," she told them. "In fact, I'm famished."

"Sit down," the housekeeper said, "and I'll bring supper."

"Fetch Dubh, please," Brigette said to Spring, then held out her hand to Glenda. "Sit with me while I eat." Sly hobbled after them.

Brigette sat between Iain and Magnus at the high table. Glenda was glued to her side until Iain lifted her onto his lap and ordered her to stay. Sly's whines for attention bothered Brigette. She lifted him onto her lap, and he licked her chin, making the others laugh. Magnus took the fox when Dubh arrived.

"My son," Brigette cried, reaching for him. Dubh's tiny arms and legs flailed about, making it difficult for her to snuggle him close. "He remembers me."

Iain laughed. "Did ye think he'd forget his own mother?"

Brigette kissed Dubh's cheeks. "I missed you, my son."

"What aboot me?" Glenda asked pettishly.

"I missed you terribly," Brigette answered. Sly whined. "And I also missed you, my pet."

"What aboot me?" Iain mimicked Glenda.

Brigette cocked a brow at her husband. "Especially you, my love. Tonight, you'll know exactly how much." She turned to Moireach, and asked, "Did you hire a wet nurse for Dubh?"

The housekeeper grinned and shook her head. "He's been drinkin' warmed goat's milk from a wineskin."

Lady Antonia arrived then and cast a blatantly insincere smile at Brigette. "Yer back—how wonderful!"

Refusing to let her homecoming be spoiled, Brigette ignored her.

"Cousin Magnus," Antonia said, "it's grand

seein' ye again. Ye've a talent for rescuin' my dear sister-in-law."

Magnus grinned. "It's grand seein' ye also, Lady Antonia. Yer always of such good cheer. As for the other . . ." He shrugged. "Let's say it was fate."

"Tell us what happened," Antonia urged.

"Let me say first," Brigette began, "what happened was my own fault, not Jamie's. I was foolish to ride unescorted. Anyway, when I rode to the loch, a Menzies warrior shot Sly and knocked me unconscious. He left me to die on a rock in the Sound of Mull. Fortunately, the MacDonalds happened by and rescued me."

"Were ye frightened?" Glenda asked, wide-eyed.

"Would you have been frightened?" Brigette countered, and the little girl nodded. "So was I."

"Do ye intend to let Menzies get away wi' this?" Antonia asked Iain.

"Ye know better than that."

"What of the warrior, Brie?" Antonia asked, her tone casual. "Can ye describe him?"

"There's nae need for descriptions," Iain said loudly. "My fearless wife dispatched the bastard." Thunderous cheering shook the rafters.

Antonia paled. Finlay! The Sassenach murdered my brother! Nobody noticed when she slipped away.

The conversation at the high table turned to other, more pleasant subjects. Dubh was passed from mother to father to godfather and then back to his mother.

"It's bedtime," Brigette announced, "for wee

children and convalescing beasts." With Glenda glued to her side, Brigette carried Dubh out of the hall. Sly limped after them.

"Dugie! Jamie!" Iain called, and when the brothers stood before him, ordered, "First thin' in the mornin', prepare the men for war."

"Aye." Dugie grinned.

"Wi' pleasure," Jamie added, then walked away with his brother.

"Ye've a happy family," Magnus commented, stretching his legs out. "It makes me yearn for Inverary."

"Who would've guessed a Sassenach twit could make me happy? How's Avril?"

"I havena' seen her these past two months," Magnus replied, "but after I report to the queen, I'm for Inverary. It's past time I settled down and gave Argyll a few grandsons to coo over."

Iain laughed. "I canna imagine Argyll cooin'. Would ye care to troth yer firstborn lassie to my Dubh? Eventually, she'd become a countess."

"It's a deal." Magnus smiled and shook his cousin's hand, then changed the subject. "How will ye flush Menzies out of Weem Castle?"

Iain grinned broadly. "Percy's the one who'll do the flushin'."

"Percy?" Magnus echoed doubtfully. "That blockhead?"

"When ye see him in Edinburgh, give the lad a message from me."

"Which is?"

"Swoop."

18

Edinburgh Castle

"Ye dinna mind takin' my duty wi' the queen?"

"I'll say yer unwell today."

The queen's youngest ladies-in-waiting were like a mixed-matched pair of dolls, opposites yet complementary. Both were petite, but Sheena Menzies's dark hair and eyes contrasted sharply with Dorothea Drummond's flaxen locks and pale blue eyes. They were like magnificent jewels, beautiful when solitary but startlingly exquisite when placed in the perfect setting of the other's company.

"It's sooo romantic," Dorothea gushed, her youthful imagination taking flight. "Lord Mac-Arthur and ye sharin' a forbidden love . . . a secret rendezvous. . . . Ohhh! I wish it were I!"

"We're only sharin' a picnic lunch." Sheena laughed. "Ye make it sound illicit."

"Stolen moments of forbidden ecstasy." Dorothea sighed.

"Yer correct aboot that," Sheena agreed. "If Murdac were at court, we wouldna' be boldly paradin' around Edinburgh."

"Highlanders are wild—nae offense meant to ye, Sheena. Perhaps Lord MacArthur will carry ye off to his castle."

"Nae offense taken, Dorothea." Sheena's dark eyes shone with mirth. "Percy doesna' have a castle. His brother is the Earl and master of Dunridge."

"But what would ye do," Dorothea asked, "if he spirited ye away to his brother's castle?"

"Why, I'd call for a priest," Sheena quipped, making her friend laugh. "I'll return before supper and take yer duty tonight."

Leaving her chamber, Sheena walked down the long corridor to the stairs. Outside, she hurried to the stables where, having sent word earlier, her horse was saddled and waiting. She gifted the freckle-faced stableboy with a smile and pressed a coin into his hand.

Percy waited in the castle esplanade. As usual, Sheena thrilled to the sight of him. His laughing blue eyes and easy smile were vastly different from her brother's grim intensity.

"Where are ye leadin' me?" Sheena asked, shyly peeking at him from beneath dark lashes.

"It's a fair enough day," Percy commented as they rode up High Street. "I thought we'd ride outside the town. Are ye game, lass?"

"Only if ye remembered to bring the food."

"How could ye think," he asked, feigning dismay, "I'd forget anythin' as important as the food?"

Although the sun was not shining, the cloud cover was a pale shade of gray, and the day was unseasonably mild. Edinburgh was soon left behind.

"It's grand ridin' out and no' carin' who sees us," Sheena said, enjoying the unexpected pleasure of being alone with the man she loved. "If only Murdac would remain at Weem permanently, every day could be like this for us."

"Life is filled wi' if onlys," Percy remarked. "People who succeed dinna rely on fate; they make their own luck."

Leaving the road, they cut through the woods and stopped beside a stream. Percy dismounted and then assisted Sheena. After the horses had drunk from the stream, Percy tethered them and placed feed bags around their necks.

"I see ye've thought of everythin'," Sheena said, grinning.

"Of course." He winked at her, saying, "And now for our lunch."

Percy produced a blanket from one of his saddlebags and tossed it to Sheena. While she spread it beneath a tree, he brought their lunch of bread, cheese, sweet ham, and wine.

After they'd eaten, Percy lay back on the blanket while Sheena packed up the remains of their meal. He reached out to touch her back, and smiling, Sheena turned around.

Percy pulled her down onto his chest and kissed

her lingeringly. She sighed and he groaned, then gently rolled her onto her back. His mouth covered hers, branding her with his searing, earth-shattering kiss.

Drawing back, Percy gazed longingly into Sheena's shining, dark eyes. "I love ye," he whispered.

"And I love ye. If only—"

"Damn 'if only'!" he swore. "Will ye marry me, Sheena?"

"Yes," she answered without hesitation, and he smiled. "But how will we ever convince Murdac to give his permission? Perhaps the queen . . ."

"Damn our brothers and the queen," Percy growled, his smile vanishing. "I can wait nae longer."

"W-what do ye mean?" Sheena asked, suddenly apprehensive. Risking her brother's anger was madness, not to mention suicidal.

"I mean, we arena' returnin' to Edinburgh. We'll be married at Dunridge."

"No!"

Grim-faced, Percy stood without a word and walked toward his horse. Puzzled, Sheena sat up and watched.

Percy pulled a cord of rope and a length of cloth from his saddlebag, then strode purposefully back to her. "Do ye come willin'ly," he asked, "or do I carry ye off?"

Shocked, Sheena recalled for one insane moment her conversation with Dorothea. But where had Percy's good humor flown? Where was the easy smile that had captured her heart? Coming to life, Sheena leaped to her feet.

She would have run, but Percy grabbed her arm and whirled her about. When Sheena raised her hand to strike, he caught it in a brutal grip and forced her to the ground, then bound her wrists together and yanked her to her feet.

Sheena opened her mouth to scream, but Percy gagged her with the length of cloth. Venomous fury leaped at him from her dark eyes.

"I'm sorry for treatin' ye this way," Percy apologized, dragging her toward the horses, "but there's nae other way." He lifted her onto his horse, then untied both horses and mounted behind her. Leading Sheena's horse, Percy rode west toward Dunridge Castle.

Two days later, they entered Argyllshire, the home of Campbells and MacArthurs. Percy saw a lone rider approaching in the distance. Argyllshire was not danger-free; should he stay on the road or take cover in the woods? By all that's holy! Percy decided. I will not hide on my own territory!

As the rider came closer, Percy's face split into a grin. Cousin Magnus!

Coming abreast of them, Magnus halted and looked from a red-faced Percy to a bedraggled Sheena, then back at his cousin. His mirth won out and Magnus shouted with laughter. "Greetin's, cuz," he finally greeted them. "Mistress Menzies."

A muffled sound came from behind Sheena's gag.

"Good day to ye," Percy said, thinking perhaps

abduction had not been a wise idea. "Do ye ride from Dunridge?"

"Aye. And might I say, cuz, I believe ye possess the Sight."

"The Sight?"

"Iain bade me tell ye to swoop." Magnus flicked an amused glance at Sheena. "But I can see ye've already swooped."

"I'm beginnin' to wish I hadna'."

"Why is that?" Magnus grinned broadly, adding, "And why is Mistress Menzies bound and gagged?"

"Because she willna' keep her mouth shut," Percy snapped, then added in a long-suffering voice, "I can tell ye, takin' a captive bride isna' so easy as a mon's led to believe."

"Takin' any bride," Magnus returned drily, "isna' so easy as a mon's led to believe. Lady Brigette recently sent Iain racin' across the breadth of Scotland to Oban."

"Brie?"

"Menzies had her snatched and tried to kill her." Acknowledging the muffled shrieks of protest, Magnus nodded at Sheena. "Nae offense, Mistress Menzies."

"Brie is unharmed?" Percy asked.

Magnus nodded. "She was lucky. Much as I'd love to see the endin' of yer romantic adventure, I canna linger." He reached out to shake Percy's hand, then smiled mockingly at Sheena. "Best wishes on yer forthcomin' nuptials, Mistress Menzies. May yer hearth be blessed wi' harmony and a dozen fine sons."

Outraged squawks issued from behind the gag. Laughing, Magnus rode away.

It was suppertime at Dunridge, and the great hall was a beehive of activity. Brigette entered on the run and hurried to the high table.

"Yer late," Iain observed.

"I was feeding Dubh," Brigette replied, reaching for the bread. "I can't believe how well he drinks from the wineskin." As an afterthought, she added, "I pray Dubh doesn't grow to be a drunkard."

"Drinkin' goat's milk from a wineskin willna' lead him into drunkenness."

"Are you certain?"

Iain rolled his eyes. "Ye dinna plan to pass the next eighteen years worryin' aboot it, do ye?"

When Brigette did not answer, Iain glanced at her. Her face had drained of blood. "Hinny?" Whirling about, he looked in the direction she was staring.

Standing in the hall's entrance were Percy with Sheena Menzies, bound and gagged and filthy. The hall grew silent as warriors and retainers noticed the unlikely couple. Then Percy moved, dragging his captive across the watching chamber to the high table.

"Percy!" Brigette cried, horrified. "How could you do such a vile thing?"

"How did ye get my message so quickly?" Iain asked, baffled. "Magnus didna' leave 'til—"

"Where's Father Kaplan?" Percy interrupted.

"Release Sheena at once," Brigette demanded.

Percy was about to refuse, but Iain caught his eye. "If I was ye, baby brother," he advised, "I wouldna' cross swords wi' my wife. Brie's already dispatched one mon, and she's dangerous when provoked."

Percy looked from Iain to Brigette. Reluctantly, he removed Sheena's gag and untied her hands.

"Are you well?" Brigette asked. Sheena nodded, bleakly.

"Get the priest now," Percy ordered.

"Ye bastard!" Sheena shrieked, turning on him, astonishing everyone in the hall. "I wouldna' wed wi' ye even if ye were the last mon in Scotland!"

"Ye'll marry me," Percy said grimly, "or I'll beat ye black and blue."

"I willna'!" Sheena stamped her foot for emphasis.

"Silence!" Brigette cried, leaping from her chair. "There will be no wedding until Lady Sheena has bathed and eaten."

Percy hesitated, then agreed sullenly, "Verra well."

Brigette walked around the table, took Sheena's hands in hers, and led her out of the hall, crooning, "You poor thing. Come with me."

Iain grinned at Percy, who'd sat down beside him. "I didna' think ye had it in ye, baby brother." Percy scowled, encouraging his brother's sarcasm. "The lass may wed ye," Iain continued, "but I doubt she'll bed ye unless ye also bathe." With an uncharacteristic growl, Percy stood and left the hall.

Brigette and Sheena sat together in one of the

bedchambers upstairs. An untouched plate of food lay on Sheena's lap.

"I amna' hungry," she said coldly.

"Suit yourself," Brigette replied, then asked, "Truly, you don't want to marry Percy?"

"I've said as much, haven't I?"

"I'm certain Iain won't force a marriage. You don't love Percy, then?"

Sheena was silent.

Merciful Christ, Brigette thought. She reminds me of myself. And I feel like my mother! "Sheena, do you love Percy or not?"

Dark eyes met green. "I love him," Sheena admitted.

"Then what is the problem?" Brigette's irritated tone revealed her frustration.

"He's a beast," Sheena cried. "I've never been so mistreated in my life."

"Cruelty is contrary to Percy's nature," Brigette remarked. "He must love you greatly to behave in this barbaric manner."

"Do ye really think so?" Sheena asked uncertainly. She hadn't thought of it that way.

Brigette nodded. "The decision is yours, Sheena. Marry Percy tonight or live without him for all time." Beneath the grime, Sheena paled, and Brigette gently pressed her advantage. "Which will it be?"

"I—I'll marry him."

Brigette sighed with relief. My mother must have felt like this, she thought, after I'd signed the marriage documents.

When the bath was ready and the last servant

had gone, Sheena disrobed and climbed into the tub. She sighed, sinking into the steaming, scented water. "Is it true what Lord Campbell told us?" she asked Brigette. "Did Murdac have ye snatched?"

"Yes."

"I'm sorry. How can ye be so kind to me?"

"What a goose! You're not responsible for his actions." Brigette handed Sheena a towel. "Wrap yourself in this. I'll return in a minute."

Sheena rose from the tub, then dried and wrapped herself in the towel. Brigette returned, carrying the most breathtaking gown she'd ever seen. It was an exquisite satin and lace creation, adorned with hundreds of seed pearls.

"Behold," Brigette announced. "Your wedding gown."

"How beautiful! Was it yours?"

"It was supposed to be." Brigette gazed wistfully at the gown. "I actually wore a black mourning gown."

"You what!"

"I was insulted because Iain sent Percy to stand as his proxy. To demonstrate my displeasure, I wore one of my mother's mourning gowns." Brigette grinned puckishly, adding, "A rather effective way of punishing my husband, wouldn't you say?"

Sheena burst out laughing and hugged Brigette. "I'm glad we'll be sisters."

Word spread quickly, and the great hall was filled to capacity. Those MacArthur retainers

who'd been absent earlier were now in attendance.

Father Kaplan and the MacArthur brothers
waited in front of the hearth for the bride to arrive. When Brigette and Sheena appeared in the
entrance, the hall grew silent. Percy turned and
saw his bride, and his mouth dropped at the vision
she had become.

Smiling shyly, Sheena walked slowly toward
him. When she finally stood before him and looked
up, Percy lowered his lips to hers and kissed her
passionately.

Wild cheers and whistles erupted throughout
the chamber. Father Kaplan cleared his throat,
but was ignored. "Percy?" The old priest placed
his hand on the younger man's shoulder, saying,
"It's best to save that for after the vows, my son."

Breaking the kiss, Percy smiled sheepishly and
apologized. "Sorry." Sheena turned to face the
priest.

"We are gathered here," Father Kaplan began,
"to join this mon and this woman in the holy state
of matrimony . . ."

Iain sidled up to his wife. "Perhaps," he whispered close to her ear, "Percy's nae blockhead
after all."

Brigette glanced sidelong at him, and her words
wiped the smile from his face. "He's a barbarian—
like you."

"Fetch it!" Glenda tossed a stick, and Sly hobbled after it as fast as his injury would allow. The
morning was young, and the child and the fox

were alone in the garden. Instead of returning the stick, Sly scurried past Glenda, who whirled around and saw Brigette.

"Good mornin'," Glenda called, rushing to Brigette's side. "Yer early today."

"I'm keeping out of Uncle Iain's path."

"Why?"

"Because I called him a barbarian," Brigette answered without thinking.

"What's that?"

"Another word for a Highlander," Brigette lied, then quickly changed the subject. "Sly is walking much better."

"Yes, but he limps."

Brigette made a show of scanning the garden. "I don't see Lady Autumn anywhere."

"She was verra tired this mornin'," Glenda whispered loudly out of the side of her mouth. "Lord Sly kept her awake all night."

Brigette looked at Glenda in surprise. The child could not be referring to *that*, could she? "Why did Sly keep Autumn awake through the night?"

"He was chewin' on her hand."

"The rogue!" Brigette burst out laughing. "Did you know this is a special morning, Glenda?"

"Special?"

"You have a new aunt this morning."

"I do?" Glenda was impressed but puzzled. "Who?"

"Lady Sheena is your new aunt because she married Uncle Percy. Shall we breakfast?"

Hand in hand, they entered the great hall, already filled with men-at-arms and retainers breaking their fast. Iain and Antonia sat at the high table.

Brigette told Glenda to sit between Iain and her. Sly sat between their chairs; he knew anything the little girl dropped was his.

Feeling important to be sitting in the countess's seat, Glenda looked at Iain and gestured to the MacArthur warriors, saying, "Look, Uncle. The hall is filled wi' barbarians."

Iain's spoon halted in midair. He looked at Brigette, who was biting her bottom lip to keep from laughing, then cast a quick glance at Antonia, whose hand had flown to her mouth to hold back the laughter bubbling up.

Iain grinned, and Brigette could no longer contain her laughter. Confused, Glenda looked from one to the other.

"And here's the littlest barbarian of all," Brigette quipped, taking Dubh and his wineskin from Spring.

A rousing cheer went up when a grinning Percy and a blushing Sheena paused in the entrance to the great hall. The younger MacArthur led his bride to the high table and introduced her first to Antonia and then to Glenda.

"Yer my new aunt," Glenda announced.

"Yes, I suppose I am."

As she sat down beside Brigette, Sheena felt happily overwhelmed. Marrying Percy had given Sheena something she'd yearned for all her life, a family. Until now, Murdac had been her only living relative, and he could hardly be called affectionate.

"This wee piglet is my son Dubh." Brigette turned the baby around to face her.

Sheena held out a finger, but Dubh would have none of it. Screeching his displeasure, he received his heart's desire, the wineskin.

"He's a handsome lad," Sheena complimented, making Iain a friend for life, "and I believe he resembles the earl."

"Especially when he opens his mouth," Brigette added, casting her husband an I-got-you-last look.

Smiling, Moireach served the newlyweds their breakfast. "Here's yer ale, Percy," she said, setting two mugs on the table. "And for ye, my lady, fresh milk."

"Milk?"

"Now that yer likely to get wi' child, ye must drink a mug of milk each day."

Brigette laughed at Sheena's stricken expression and whispered, "She told me the same thing on my first morning at Dunridge."

It was then Sheena spied Sly, who, begging for food, had placed his paw on Glenda's arm. "What's that wild beastie doin' here?"

"Sly isna' a wild beastie," Glenda cried indignantly.

"Sly is my pet," Brigette explained. "I found him in the woods when he was just a baby and had somehow lost his mother."

"When I was a little girl," Sheena said, "I wished for a kitten."

"And did yer wish come true, hinny?" Percy asked.

Sheena shook her head. "Of course, there were

many mousers runnin' aboot Weem, but I yearned for my own special pet to keep me company at night." She held out her hand, and Sly circled around Brigette's chair to sniff and then lick it.

"Sly likes ye," Glenda said.

"But why didna' ye get a kitten?" Percy asked.

"Murdac wouldna' allow it. He'd purchased imported carpets for my chamber and believed the kitten would ruin them."

"What a nasty mon," Glenda declared.

"That isna' a nice thin' to say about Lady Sheena's brother," Iain reprimanded the little girl. Even if it is true, he thought to himself.

Blushing, Glenda looked down the table. "I'm verra sorry, Lady Sheena."

Percy excused himself from the table just as a courier entered the hall and strode toward the high table. The man wore the Devereux livery.

"Someone is dead," Brigette whispered, paling.

Halting in front of Iain, the courier bowed, saying, "Greetings from the Earl and Dowager Countess of Basildon. I carry a letter for the Countess of Dunridge." At Iain's nod, the man handed it to her. Brigette tore it open and quickly scanned the contents, then laughed. "Bucko and Marianne are the proud parents of a daughter, Theresa. And Lil married Fat Bertie!"

Chuckling, Iain turned to the courier. "Find yerself a perch and eat. The countess will want to send a message back wi' ye."

Percy returned, carrying a squirming ball of fluffy white fur. "Yer wish is my command, madame," he said, placing a kitten on his wife's lap.

"Oh!" Happy tears welled up in Sheena's eyes. "Where did ye get it?"

Percy shrugged. "There's always a litter of somethin' bein' born around here."

"She's precious. Or is it a he?"

"I amna' certain," Percy said, grinning, "but it looks like a she."

"I'll call her 'Bana,' " Sheena announced, cuddling the kitten.

"Bana?" Brigette asked.

"It's the Gaelic for 'fair.' "

Resting his head on Sheena's lap, Sly sniffed at the frightened, mewling ball of fur. Slurp! The fox's tongue slipped out and licked the kitten.

Brigette glanced sidelong at her niece, saying, "It appears Lord Sly fancies Lady Bana."

"Good," Glenda replied. "Perhaps now Lady Autumn will be granted some peace."

Duncan the crofter felt the first stirrings of fear when he entered the foyer. Never had he been inside the walls of Weem Castle, though many times as a boy he'd wished he could see it. Now Duncan was sorry that he'd gotten what he'd wished for, but there was no escape.

Murdac Menzies, the Earl of Meinnich, was a hard man, and the message Duncan carried was not good news. Would the earl vent his anger on the bearer of bad tidings? the crofter worried. Was the gold piece the stranger gave him worth more than his own life?

Flanked by two of the earl's warriors, Duncan entered the great hall and shivered involuntarily.

He gazed the length of the enormous chamber to the high table where the earl sat.

Powerfully built, Murdac Menzies was as cruel as he appeared. What could have been a passably handsome face was marred by an angular scar running down the length of one cheek, but what truly frightened people were the earl's eyes. His were the cold, black eyes of a serpent, betraying his lack of compassion.

How will my wife and children survive without me? Duncan worried as the warriors ushered him across the hall. He was not a cowardly man, but his legs trembled as he walked toward the high table.

"My lord." One of the warriors spoke as the crofter bowed to the earl. "This mon insists he has a message for ye."

Menzies looked at Duncan, who, he noted with satisfaction, shifted nervously beneath his scrutiny. "What have ye to say?"

"M-me n-name is D-Duncan, laird," he stammered, fumbling in his pocket for the gold coin. "A stranger give me this and a message for ye." Duncan paused; his mouth had gone dry, the words unable to come.

"Spill it," Menzies snapped, scowling.

"MacArthur snatched Lady Sheena," the crofter blurted out. "She's bein' held at Dunridge Castle."

"Ye lie!" Menzies leaped up, his face mottling with rage. Frightened, Duncan stepped back. Not immune to the danger, the Menzies warriors also stepped back.

A disturbance at the hall's entrance saved the

three from the earl's wrath. Accompanied by another of the earl's men, a courier strode briskly toward the high table. The man wore the livery of the Earl of Moray, the queen's half brother.

"My Lord Menzies?" At Murdac's nod, the courier handed him the missive.

Menzies quickly read the message and looked up. Deadly fury shone from the depths of black serpentine eyes, and he vowed in a chilling voice, "I will turn Dunridge—nay, the whole of Argyll— into a wasteland!"

19

Spring became summer, and the sun rode high in the sky. A message from Edinburgh arrived in June; Queen Mary had delivered a son, James, but there was no time for rejoicing at Dunridge.

War, especially bitter, raged between Iain MacArthur and Murdac Menzies. One casualty was the women's activities. They were no longer allowed beyond the castle's walls, much to the frustration of Brigette, who felt the garden closing in on her.

One morning in early July, Sheena spied Brigette marching purposefully toward the stables. "Brie," she called, running to catch up. "Where are ye goin'?"

"I'm riding to the loch," Brigette answered. "Care to join me?"

"The loch?"

"That's what I said."

"But the earl's forbidden us to—"

"The earl is a jackass," Brigette snapped. "I refuse to be a prisoner in my own home. Are you coming?"

Brigette turned away, and Sheena followed her to the deserted stables. They saddled their own horses, then mounted and rode toward the outer gate.

Unexpectedly, their path to freedom was blocked. Iain, Percy, and a troop of MacArthur warriors filled the portal. They'd been out surveying the damage done by Menzies the previous night.

"Where do ye think yer goin'?" Iain growled, grabbing Brigette's reins.

"Your request to remain inside the walls is unreasonable," she told him.

"It was an order, no' a request."

"I'm not your prisoner."

"Yer my wife and will obey me."

Challenging him, Brigette tugged at her reins, but Iain held them firmly in his iron grip. Angry dark eyes warred silently with determined green ones. "Dismount," he ordered, "and walk back." Casting him a scathing look, Brigette dismounted and stalked off.

Iain's eyes drifted to his sister-in-law. "Ye also, Lady Sheena."

Sheena glanced at Percy, who, wearing the most aggravating smirk, looked away as if she were a stranger. Humiliated, Sheena dismounted and followed Brigette.

"The ladies aren' permitted outside," Iain shouted to the guards. "Do whatever ye must to stop them."

"Insufferable . . . pigheaded," Brigette was mumbling when Sheena caught up with her.

"And my husband didna' even defend me," Sheena complained.

"I'm breaking out of this decrepit pile of rock," Brigette vowed, "even if I must scale the walls."

"And we dinna need their horses," Sheena added. "We can walk out instead of ride."

"Ha! If I know Iain, he's already instructed the guards to stop us from leaving."

"We could sneak out the postern gate," Sheena suggested.

Brigette flashed her a brilliant smile. "Why, you're more devious than I am."

Sheena grinned. "Thank ye."

"When Glenda takes her lessons with Father Kaplan," Brigette said, "I'll meet you outside the gate. We'll be back before anyone realizes we've gone."

When Antonia left the great hall that afternoon, she noticed Brigette skulking around the end of the corridor and stepped back to watch. Brigette scanned the garden and then darted out the door. Perplexed, Antonia followed.

Outside, Brigette scurried behind a section of shrubbery, then dashed to the back of the garden and hid behind a tree. A moment later, she fled her hiding place and flew through the garden's rear door.

Antonia reached the back of the garden in time to see Brigette disappear through the postern gate. What in God's Holy Name was the Sassenach doing?

Curiosity got the better of Antonia, and she opened the postern gate. A hand shot out and yanked her through.

"What the bloody hell are you doing?" Brigette demanded angrily.

"I could ask ye the same thing," Antonia returned, lifting her nose in the air. She looked from Brigette to Sheena and then disdainfully at Sly. "I'm tellin' Iain."

Pulling a dagger from the waistband of her skirt, Brigette waved it beneath the blonde's nose. "You're coming with us."

"That's right," Sheena added. "Ye willna' ruin our chance for a few moments of pleasure."

"Where are ye goin'?" Antonia asked.

"To the loch and back," Sheena answered.

"Verra well, I'll come."

"And keep your mouth shut," Brigette warned, "or we'll be caught."

Silently, they walked through the woods and reached the shore of Loch Awe without being detected. The three women and the fox strolled along at a leisurely pace, enjoying the summer's day.

Sensing rather than hearing the thundering of hooves, Sheena turned and saw Sly, with hackles raised, whine and dash into the woods. *"Run!"* Sheena screamed, then darted into the woods after the fox.

Brigette whirled around and saw the men riding hard toward them. Black and white Menzies plaid! She started after Sheena, but noticed Antonia running in a panic down the shoreline.

"No!" Brigette shrieked, racing after her. *"Run into the woods!"*

An arm hooked Brigette's waist and yanked her up.

"Release me, you bastard," she screamed, struggling against him. His fist connected with the side of her face, and Brigette's struggles ceased.

Dusk had snuffed the last mauve ray of light from the western sky when the Menzies warriors and their hostages arrived at Weem Castle. Sitting in front of her captor on his horse, Brigette felt trapped in the midst of a recurring nightmare. A throbbing jaw was her sole link with reality. Rousing herself, she glanced at Antonia as they halted inside Weem's inner curtain. The blonde was visibly shaking with fear.

The war party dismounted. Brigette's captor yanked her roughly off the horse, and in the process she nearly toppled to the ground. Baring her teeth, Brigette growled menacingly, but the man merely laughed at her bravado. It was like being threatened by a flea.

Grabbing her upper arm, the man dragged her inside, and Brigette knew she'd wear those bruises for many weeks. Antonia and her captor walked behind, followed by the other Menzies warriors.

Weem's great hall was crowded for supper. Brigette was led across the chamber to the high table and recognized Murdac Menzies at once.

"Good evenin', ladies," Murdac greeted them, then smiled coldly. "Welcome to my home."

Shaken by their predicament, Antonia re-

mained uncharacteristically silent, but Brigette
was defiant to the last. After all, she'd escaped his
clutches in the Sound of Mull. Why not at Weem?
Brigette gazed disdainfully about the hall.

"So, this is the hornet's nest," she said contemptuously, her flashing green eyes challenging him.

Menzies threw back his head and shouted with
laughter, but no humor shone from his black,
serpentine eyes. He stood and walked around the
table to tower over them, his very size threatening
their existence.

"It's a pleasure to see ye again, Countess." One
of his calloused paws touched Brigette's bruised
jaw. "I apologize for any inconvenience my men
may have caused," Murdac said pleasantly, then
asked as his gaze drifted to Antonia, "And who
have ye brought along?"

"Lady Antonia," Brigette replied, "my wid-
owed sister-in-law."

Taking Antonia's hand in his, Murdac raised it to
his lips in courtly fashion, then complimented, "If
I had known someone as beautiful as ye lived at
Dunridge, I would have abducted ye long ago."
Dumbfounded, Antonia stared at him.

"Indeed," he continued, "I'm an uncommonly
lucky mon to have two rare beauties come to
visit."

"You'd have even more," Brigette returned,
heedless of the danger, "if only you had enough
men to scour the countryside and snatch them."

"I see the journey's made ye irritable," Murdac
remarked. "Perhaps ye'd like to rest before supper?"

"Actually, I'd like to be returned to Dunridge."

"That's impossible at the moment. Ye willna' be leavin' Weem 'til my sister is returned to me."

"Tsk! Tsk!" Brigette chided. "Would you put asunder what God has joined together?"

"What do ye mean?"

"Sheena married Percy MacArthur," she informed him. "Willingly, I might add. If you don't believe me, ask your men. They'll tell you, Sheena ran away when she recognized them."

Murdac's eyes darted to his man, who nodded and looked away.

"Even as we speak," Brigette continued boldly, "my husband and his men are riding for Weem. You'll fail, as you did the last time."

"The last time?" Murdac echoed, puzzled.

"Don't play the innocent with me," Brigette snapped. "By your order, I was left to die on that rock in the Sound of Mull. Unfortunately for you, I escaped."

"Yer husband must have many enemies." Murdac snorted. "I amna' the one who masterminded that." He looked Brigette up and down, perusing her charms, then smiled suggestively and said, "I know of better thin's to do wi' a beautiful woman. Take them away."

Upstairs, Brigette and Antonia were locked in one of the bedchambers. While Antonia perched on the edge of the bed and stared vacantly into space, Brigette paced back and forth in high agitation.

She crossed the chamber, then turned around

and retraced her steps. How can we escape? Brigette wondered, her mind as restless as her body. I've got it! I'll stand behind the door and overpower the next person who walks through. No, that wouldn't work. We'd still have to fight our way out of here.

Brigette's eyes fell on Antonia. No help there. If only Cousin Magnus were hereabouts, on one of his missions.

A key turned in the lock, and a moment later, the door opened. A middle-aged servant woman entered, carrying a bucket of steaming water. A couple of towels were slung over her arm.

The woman set the bucket and towels on the table, then turned to look at them. "The earl thought ye'd like to wash before supper," she explained.

Brigette stared coldly at her. Frightened by the hate-filled green eyes, the woman crossed herself and hastily retreated, locking the door behind her.

Realizing escape was impossible, Brigette sighed and surrendered to her fatigue. She sat on the bed and closed her eyes, but thoughts of escape persisted.

Antonia stood abruptly, marched across the chamber to the table, and washed her face. Finished with her toilet, she began pacing the chamber instead of returning to her perch.

Retracing her steps, Antonia's eyes fell on Brigette, and a sudden, calculating thought popped into her mind. Menzies is an unmarried man, and I am not without certain attractions. I could persuade him to dispose of the Sassenach. If Iain loses,

I'll wed Murdac and become the Countess of Meinnich; but if Iain wins, he'll be free to make me his countess. Either way, I cannot lose.

Antonia halted beside the bed. "What have ye to say for yerself, ye stupid Sassenach slut?"

One green eye opened a slit. "I see you've recovered," Brigette commented drily.

"This is yer fault."

"My fault?" Two green eyes opened wide.

"If ye hadna' disobeyed Iain, we wouldna' be here."

"Do not blame me." Brigette stood and confronted Antonia. "If you hadn't followed, you wouldn't be here; and if you hadn't run down the beach like a madwoman, *I* wouldn't be here. You nosy, stupid bitch!"

Whack! The force of Antonia's slap snapped Brigette's head back.

Whack! Brigette returned the favor.

"Ladies!" Murdac Menzies lounged against the doorjamb. "Violence detracts from yer femininity. I've come to escort ye to supper," he added pleasantly, sauntering into the chamber. "Yer lookin' much better, Lady Antonia."

"Thank ye, my lord," she said, smiling.

He turned to Brigette, saying, "Ye should have been washed before now, Countess."

"I've decided to wait and sup with my husband," she returned. "He should be here momentarily."

Murdac laughed harshly, then warned, "Ye'll starve before the Earl of Dunridge sets a foot in Weem Castle."

"In that case," Brigette hissed like an angry kitten, "I shall break bread with you in hell."

Murdac's good humor vanished, the scar on his cheek whitening with anger. Fighting the urge to slap her into submission, he stared grimly at Brigette. "Suit yerself," Murdac said coldly, then turned to Antonia and smiled, offering his arm. "Surely ye'll sup wi' me?"

Returning his smile, Antonia placed her hand on his arm. Together, they left the chamber.

"Antonia!" Brigette screamed, banging on the door. "You traitor!"

Hungry lips descended to Brigette's, covering her mouth with a savage intensity. "Iain . . ." she breathed against the lips. A dream, Brigette thought, awakening slowly, yet the fleshy pressure against her mouth remained. Her eyes flew open and filled with obvious revulsion. Murdac Menzies was kissing her!

Smiling lazily at her horrified expression, Murdac lightly ran a finger down her cheek. When that same finger traced her kiss-bruised lips, Brigette bit it.

"Ye little bitch!" he roared, flinching away from her. Brigette scrambled off the other side of the bed and backed away. The table prevented any further movement.

Grim-faced, Murdac stood and faced her. Sunbeams danced through the chamber's window behind him, and Brigette realized that morning had come.

Adding insult to injury, Brigette wiped her

mouth on the sleeve of her blouse, then brushed off the contaminated sleeve. Growling low in his throat, Murdac stepped menacingly closer.

"Keep your distance," she warned, "or I'll kill myself. Then you'll have no hostage."

"Have ye forgotten Lady Antonia?"

"My husband won't care if you keep Antonia; in fact, you'll be doing him a favor."

"How exceedin'ly odd," Murdac remarked. "Antonia was bent on persuadin' me to dispose of ye."

"Where is she?" Brigette demanded. "What have you done with her?"

"We passed a delightful but tirin' night in my chamber. The lady is still abed." Murdac laughed at Brigette's expression. "Dinna look so shocked, my dear. She was willin' enough to spread her legs, and I didna' kill her afterward, as yer late father-in-law did my aunt."

"What!"

"Surely ye know how the feud began? Black Jack abducted, ravished, and murdered my aunt."

"You're a bloody liar!"

"Believe what ye want," Murdac said with a shrug of his shoulders. "What will ye do to keep breathin'?"

Brigette's stomach knotted in fear, but her voice remained strong and steady. "Touch me and I'll kill you," she threatened.

"I'm shakin'," he mocked. Smiling at her bravado, he stepped forward.

Keeping her eyes on him, Brigette reached behind, blindly searching the table for a weapon. In a flash of movement, she grabbed the bucket of now-cold water and hurled it at him.

"Lucky for ye," Murdac said, safely sidestepping, "I adore spirited women. Their ultimate surrender is that much sweeter." Sauntering to the door, he added, "I'll leave ye in peace—for the moment."

Grumbling to himself about the impulsiveness of women, Murdac strode across the great hall to the high table, then sat down and inspected his injured finger. A group of his men, sitting near the table, were deep in a conversation about hunting.

A doe hunt, Murdac thought, a cunning smile lighting his face. He ordered two serving women to bring his guests to the hall.

Several moments later, Brigette was escorted into the chamber and led to the high table. "Traitor," she hissed when Antonia stood beside her.

"Give me yer attention," Murdac called to his men, then stood and walked around the table to tower over his captives. Smiling wickedly, he inclined his head. "Good mornin', ladies."

Antonia returned his smile. Brigette's stare was colder than a Highland blizzard.

"I'm sponsorin' a doe hunt for the pleasure and entertainment of my men and, of course, myself," Murdac announced. "We'll be the hunters and ye, my ladies, will be the doe."

"B-but—" Antonia began to protest.

Murdac's hand shot out and struck her. Antonia fell against Brigette, who steadied her.

"And if we refuse?" Brigette challenged.

"Dinna ask that question," he returned, "unless yer prepared to hear the answer."

"As I said, and if we refuse?"

"Dinna dwell upon the negative. Consider the hunt yer chance to escape."

"Are we to be murdered?" Brigette asked.

"Oh, lassie! How black ye must believe my soul is!" Murdac exclaimed, feigning dismay. He looked her up and down insolently, saying, "Woman was created for mon's pleasure, no' to be harmed."

Brigette cocked a brow at him. "So, we're to be raped?"

Murdac's lazy smile was her answer.

"Iain will tear you apart"—she sneered—"piece by loathsome piece."

"Enough!" he snapped. "Remove yer gowns."

"Please—" Antonia pleaded, tears streaming down her face.

Murdac drew his dagger and pointed it at her, its sharp tip touching her throat. "Keep yer mouth shut," he ordered, "and disrobe."

With shaking hands, Antonia unfastened her skirt and let it drop to the floor, then pulled her blouse over her head and stood in her chemise. The men went wild, cheering and whistling and banging their hands on the tables.

"Now yer shoes and stockings," Murdac ordered. When she obeyed, he threw her lace garters at the mob of men, who scrambled frantically over each other to catch them.

Murdac laughed crudely. His eyes darted to Brigette. "Yer turn, Countess."

"Go bugger yourself!"

With all his strength, Murdac backhanded Brigette, sending her sprawling on the floor. Blood trickled from the corner of her mouth. "It's beyond my ken how MacArthur abides wi' ye and yer mouth," he spat, "but I amna' as soft-hearted." He gestured to the two serving women.

Brigette's head spun dizzily. She forced herself to rise, and in a moment, the women had divested her of skirt, blouse, shoes, and stockings. Brigette stood there, clad in her chemise.

Murdac devoured her with his eyes and, unable to resist, tweaked one of her breasts. "Ye've thirty minutes to get away," he said, gesturing to the hall's entrance, "and then we're comin' after ye."

"Let's go," Brigette said, but intense fear kept Antonia rooted to the floor. Taking her sister-in-law's hand in hers, Brigette led her out of the hall.

"Do what ye want wi' the blonde," Murdac told his men, "but the copper-haired wench is mine. He who forgets is a dead mon."

Goosebumps erupted on Brigette's arms when they stepped into the courtyard. Damn, she cursed inwardly. It was summer by the calendar, but too cold to run half naked through the woods.

Brigette cast Antonia a measuring look and knew her pampered sister-in-law would slow her down. They would be lucky even to leave the immediate vicinity of the keep before thirty minutes was up, she realized in dismay.

Drawing Antonia along in her wake, Brigette walked briskly into the outer courtyard and headed straight for the gate. Alerted by the earl,

the guards allowed the women to pass un-
molested.

"I dinna know aboot anyone else," one of the
warriors said, licking his lips with anticipation,
"but after the earl passes by, I'm joinin' the hunt."

"But what aboot Weem's defense?" a second
asked. "If Dunridge attacks while—"

"The devil take Weem's defense," the first man
spat. "If the earl was worried aboot MacArthur, he
wouldna' be offerin' us the wenches."

"I agree wi' ye," a third warrior piped in. "Why
should we miss the fun?"

"I never futtered a high-born lady," the second
warrior said, persuaded by the others' comments.
"I've a mind to know what it feels like."

"The earl willna' kill all of us for leavin' our
post," the first man reasoned.

"It's settled, then," the third concluded. "We'll
go."

Terrified, Antonia halted just beyond the gate
and refused to budge. Turning back, Brigette
urged her onward.

"I canna," Antonia cried.

Grabbing her sister-in-law's shoulders, Brigette
gave her a rough shake, then slapped her tear-
streaked cheek. "Listen to me," she snarled. "Do
you want those vile men touching you?"

Antonia's eyes widened. She shook her blond
head vigorously.

"We'll go into the woods that way," Brigette told
her. "Once out of their sight, we'll double back
and hide on the other side of the loch."

"Loch?"

Brigette nodded. "There's a loch behind Weem. I saw it from the window. When it's dark, they'll give up the hunt, and then we'll start for Dunridge."

"But we'll freeze to death," Antonia whined.

"You blockhead," Brigette snapped. "Don't you think Iain is already on his way to Weem? We'll meet him long before we've frozen. Let's go."

With Brigette in the lead, the two dashed into the woods south of Weem. Once out of the guards' sight, they left the path and plunged into the dense woods surrounding them. Periodically, Brigette glanced behind to check on Antonia. Unused to physical activity, the Highland beauty was tiring quickly and soon developed a painful stitch in her side.

"Brie," Antonia cried as she tripped and fell.

Swearing, Brigette trodded back to her. What else could she do? Leave Antonia behind? "Are you hurt?" she asked.

Tears brimmed over Antonia's eyes. "I've twisted my ankle and my side hurts terribly."

Brigette helped her stand. "Put your arm around my shoulder."

"I canna make it," Antonia wailed. "Why dinna ye save yerself?"

Tempted to do just that, Brigette hesitated, her eyes meeting Antonia's. Her sister-in-law had no scruples and so believed no one else did. No doubt Antonia would be long gone if their roles were reversed.

"Well?"

"Shut up," Brigette hissed.

"Why dinna ye leave me?" Antonia repeated.

"And have your ghost return to haunt me for the rest of my days? I think not."

A wild, lusty shout sounded in the distance. Both women stiffened, gut-wrenching fear sweeping through them.

"The hounds of hell have caught our scent," Brigette observed wryly. "Thirty minutes cannot have passed. The bastard's cheating!"

"The gate's open, and I dinna see any guards," Percy said. "Do ye think it's a trap?"

Grim-faced, Iain shrugged his shoulders. "Trap or no', I'm ridin' in."

The MacArthurs had arrived at Weem Castle and, hidden by the dense woods, separated into two groups. Iain and Percy led the main troop in the woods facing Weem's gate. Dugie and Jamie led a smaller group that had circled around the keep to locate the postern gate.

"Dugie must be in position by now," Percy said.

Iain nodded. "There'll be nae escape for Menzies this time. My only regret is I canna kill him twice."

Drawing his sword, Iain raised it in the air to signal his men, then nudged his horse forward. With swords drawn, the MacArthur warriors followed. Leaving the protective shelter of the woods, they became vulnerable to assault by arrow, but no defender appeared on the walls of Weem Castle.

The MacArthurs rode closer and closer to the keep, yet all remained strangely, eerily silent. Not a soul appeared to challenge them. Weem Castle was a ghost keep.

"I dinna like this," Percy whispered nervously as they reached the gate. "Somethin's amiss. Let the men go through first."

"Brie's *my* wife."

With his brother at his side, Iain rode into the keep. Nothing happened. As they moved through the outer courtyard, a sudden movement flashed between their horses.

"Sly!" Percy exclaimed in a loud whisper.

Iain's lips twitched. "The rascal must've followed us."

Halting his horse, Iain scanned the inner courtyard. Where was Menzies? And where were Brigette and Antonia?

Iain dismounted. The MacArthur warriors also dismounted, albeit reluctantly, certain they were about to be slaughtered. The muffled sounds of stealth alerted them to imminent danger, but it was only Dugie's men circling around from the postern gate.

"I canna credit what I'm seein'," Dugie said to Iain.

"Ye mean, what we arena' seein'," Jamie corrected. "This place is givin' me the creeps." At his words, more than one MacArthur warrior crossed himself for safety's sake.

With Iain leading the way, they entered Weem's main foyer. Sly, having caught the faintest trace of a familiar scent, scurried past them and disappeared through a door. He knew Brigette was here, somewhere.

"A wild beastie," shrieked a feminine voice.

The MacArthurs followed Sly and found themselves in the great hall. It was deserted except for two serving women and the castle's steward, who exclaimed, "A MacArthur!"

"*The* MacArthur," Iain growled, pointing his sword at him. "Where's yer master?"

"W-w-we're only s-servants here," the man stammered. "The earl is huntin'."

"Huntin'?" Iain echoed incredulously. "Ye expect me to believe he went huntin' and left Weem unprotected?"

" 'Tis true, I swear."

"Give us his hostages," Iain ordered.

"I—I—I canna do that."

Iain's eyes narrowed dangerously. He flicked a glance at Dugie and Jamie, who grabbed the man's arms. "Cut off the head of his shaft," Iain ordered savagely.

"Look," Percy called, squatting beside Sly. A woman's garment hung from the fox's mouth.

Inspecting it, Iain was relieved to find no bloodstains. "Brie was wearin' this blouse," he said, his expression more forbidding than Menzies at his worst. Stepping closer to the steward, Iain snarled, "I'll cut the mon's pecker off myself."

"Wait!" the steward screamed, tears of fear for his manhood sliding down his face. "The ladies arena' here."

"Where, then?"

"I dinna ken exactly. The earl made them strip and leave the keep. He's huntin' them for sport."

"Aye, my lord," one of the women verified.

"The earl said the men could have the ladies—if ye ken my meanin'. The guards must've wanted a taste and joined the hunt."

With an oath, Iain raced out of the hall with Sly at his heels. The MacArthur warriors followed behind.

"Jamie," Iain ordered, halting in the courtyard, "ye and yer group stay here in case they return." Iain lifted Sly and, nuzzling the fox, commanded, "Find Brie, Sly. Find Brie." The fox sprang from his arms and dashed for the outer courtyard. The MacArthurs leaped on their horses and followed.

Frenzied shouts of unbridled masculine lust rent the air frighteningly near them, and hearing it, Antonia whimpered like a wounded animal. So much for strategy, Brigette thought, staggering with fatigue from bearing Antonia's weight. A few paces more, she told herself, little realizing they would be more vulnerable in the open.

"The loch," Brigette said, stepping from the edge of the woods. They trudged agonizingly slowly down the shoreline in search of a suitable hiding place.

"Help!" Strong hands wrenched Antonia from Brigette's side.

"You bloody bugger!" Brigette screeched, berserk as a madwoman. Grabbing Antonia's arm, she tugged with all her might and, when that failed, attacked the man ferociously—kicking, scratching, biting.

As if Brigette were an annoying mosquito, he shoved her away and she landed facedown on the grass. Determined to save Antonia, Brigette started to rise but stopped short, her eyes locking on a pair of shining black boots standing beside her head.

"Allow me, Countess." Murdac's voice oozed sarcastic contempt. He leaned over to capture his prize.

In one swift motion, Brigette poked her fingers in his eyes and rolled away. She leaped to her feet and ran.

Recovering himself, Murdac gave chase. With her flaming hair swirling wildly around her, Brigette looked like a frightened wood nymph as she raced down the loch's shoreline. Two steps behind, Murdac reached out, grabbed her fiery mane, and yanked savagely. Brigette cried out in excruciating pain and toppled back.

"Bitch," Murdac snarled, whirling her around and viciously slapping her, sending her sprawling on the ground. He loosened his codpiece.

"Iain!" Brigette screamed in desperation. Her world went black, and she missed the deadly barrage of MacArthur arrows that flew through the air from the woods.

"Brie." Someone whispered her name. Brigette opened her eyes and gazed at her husband's worried expression.

Iain smiled with relief and held her protectively close. "Do ye hurt?" he asked, when she began to weep.

Clinging to him, Brigette shook her head, then pressed it against his chest and closed her eyes.

Slurp! Something wet licked the salty tears from her cheek.

"Sly!" Brigette exclaimed, opening her eyes.

"In case ye hadna' noticed, brother"—Percy's voice sounded beside them—"yer wife is almost bare-arse naked." Grinning, he handed Iain a blanket, then walked away.

"Antonia?" Brigette asked, her face scarlet with embarrassment.

Iain shook his head. "She took an arrow, but didna' suffer."

"Menzies?"

"Willna' be botherin' us again."

Iain wrapped her in the blanket and lifted her into his arms. His dark eyes held hers captive, and cocking a brow at her, he asked, "See what happens when ye dinna obey me?"

"I'll never disobey you again," Brigette vowed, wrapping her arms around his neck.

Iain's lips twitched. "Ye know as well as I, lovey, lyin's as great a sin as disobedience."

Epilogue

Edinburgh Castle, December 1566

"Make haste, will ye?"

Hearing the impatience in her husband's voice, Brigette cast him a sidelong glance. Dashingly handsome, Iain wore the black and green Mac-Arthur dress plaid, topped with a white silk shirt and black velvet doublet. Frowning, he stood in front of the chamber's hearth and watched her.

Brigette smiled placidly, then teased, "Has anyone ever told you what well-shaped legs you have? The sight of your calves makes me quiver all over."

"Dinna vex me, Brie," Iain snapped. "Can ye no' hurry?"

"Fetch my gown, please." In an instant, he was at her side with her new court gown of forest-green velvet. "Put it over my head," Brigette in-

structed, "but don't disturb my hair or I'll have to
start over."

"Why am *I*, the Earl of Dunridge, reduced to
playin' yer tirewoman?" he asked, irritated. "Why
didna' ye bring Spring along?" Brigette's answer
was muffled beneath the folds of her gown.
"What?" he asked.

"I said," Brigette repeated, coming up for air,
"Spring is in the earliest stage of pregnancy."

"So?"

"So, she's prone to vomiting. Anywhere, at any
time."

"Oh."

"Spring and Sheena and Avril, all with child,"
Brigette said. "This is certainly a year for babies."

"Dinna forget yerself." Iain grinned and patted
her swollen stomach. "Five months gone, and
aboot ready to burst. It must be another lad."

"Four of us pregnant at the same time. I wonder, do you think something was carried on the
Highland wind?"

Iain burst out laughing, then scoffed, "Dinna be
silly. I made ye swell, no' the wind. Turn around
and I'll battle yer buttons."

"One thing is for certain," Brigette told him,
turning her back. "I'm burning that damn cot."

Iain smiled at her back. "The cot didna' make ye
pregnant either."

"It helped."

Finishing his task, Iain gently twirled her
around to face him and kissed the tip of her upturned nose. "Ye never looked lovelier, sweetie."

"The cot still goes." Brigette turned away to

study herself in the pier glass. I'll do, she decided, then frowned, seeing the profile of her bulging stomach.

"If we dinna leave now," Iain said, biting back his laughter, "we'll be late for Percy's investiture."

"Just imagine," Brigette said, "Percy will bear Murdac's title and live at Weem. I wonder what Black Jack would think. I still don't understand how this can be."

"By the courtesy of Scotland's law and the queen," he explained, "when a mon marries an heiress, he may receive her family's title and estates. After today, Percy will be the Earl of Meinnich and Weem Castle will be his home."

"We English don't do things like that."

Iain tilted her chin up and gazed deeply, lovingly into her emerald eyes. "Ye English are barbarians."

Unamused, Brigette let the insult pass. "How exactly did the feud with Menzies begin?" she asked. "Did Black Jack abduct his aunt?"

"No, though Murdac may have believed so."

"Well, then?"

"Black Jack dinna abduct or murder Menzies's aunt. I canna tell ye any more, lovey, 'til the Duke of Argyll passes away," he replied, escorting her to the door. "Will ye trust me 'til then?"

"Yes."

Iain opened the door, and both started through at the same time but couldn't fit. They stepped back and faced each other.

Brigette giggled and gestured to the doorway.

"There's an old English proverb that covers this exact situation."

"Which is?"

Brigette scurried across the threshold, then turned around. Rubbing the mound of her stomach, she said, "The one with the belly leads the way and the one without follows behind. What say you to that, my illustrious earl?"

Smiling, Iain followed Brigette across the threshold and closed the door, then drew her into the circle of his arms and kissed her thoroughly, stealing her breath away. "I love ye, hinny," he whispered, then nibbled on her irresistible bottom lip and added, "but I could love ye so much better if ye werena' so damn *fat.*"

"Ohhhh!"

Experience the Passion and the Ecstasy

Heather Graham

☐ 20235-3 Sweet Savage Eden $3.95

☐ 11740-2 Devil's Mistress $3.95

Megan McKinney

☐ 16412-5 No Choice But
            Surrender $3.95

☐ 20301-5 My Wicked
            Enchantress $3.95

☐ 20521-2 When Angels Fall $3.95

 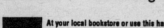